CW00361271

About the A

Meg Maxwell lives on the coast of Maine with her teenage son, their beagle and their black-and-white cat. When she's not writing, Meg is either reading, at the movies or thinking up new story ideas on her favourite little beach (even in winter) just minutes from her house. Interesting fact: Meg Maxwell is a pseudonym for author Melissa Senate, whose women's fiction titles have been published in over twenty-five countries.

Kimberley Troutte is a *RITA*® Award–nominated, *New York Times, USA Today* and Amazon top 100 bestselling author. She lives in Southern California with her husband, two sons, a wild cat, an old snake, a beautiful red iguana and various creatures hubby and the boys rescue. To learn more about her books and sign up for her newsletter, go to kimberleytroutte.com

Margot Radcliffe lives in Columbus, Ohio, right now, but surrenders to wanderlust every couple of years, so it's hard to say where she'll end up next. Regardless of location, her apricot dog will be by her side while she writes fun romances that hopefully will make readers laugh and space out for a bit, with heroines who aren't afraid to take what they want and confident heroes who are up to a challenge. She loves creating complicated, modern love stories. She can be found @margotradcliffe on X and @margot_radcliffe on Instagram.

Sugar & Spice

Sugar & Spice:
Love and War

MEG MAXWELL

KIMBERLEY TROUTTE

MARGOT RADCLIFFE

MILLS & BOON

First Published in Great Britain 2024
by Mills & Boon, an imprint of HarperCollins*Publishers* Ltd,
1 London Bridge Street, London, SE1 9GF

www.harpercollins.co.uk

HarperCollins*Publishers*
Macken House, 39/40 Mayor Street Upper,
Dublin 1, D01 C9W8, Ireland

ISBN: 978-0-263-32046-6

THE COOK'S SECRET INGREDIENT

MEG MAXWELL

In dear memory of Gregory Pope.

Chapter One

Olivia Mack added a generous sprinkle of powdered sugar to the chocolate-dipped cannoli and then handed it through Hurley's Homestyle Kitchen's food-truck window to the waiting customer. Would the confection work its magic? Of course it would. Olivia's food—from blueberry pancakes to fried chicken to lemon chiffon pie—had been lifting spirits for as long as Olivia had been cooking, which was since girlhood. According to her mother, Olivia had a gift. Supposedly her food changed moods, healed hearts, restored hope.

Come on. Olivia hardly believed that. Comfort food comforted; it was right there in the name. If you were feeling down, a plate of macaroni and cheese did its job. And a chocolate-dipped cannoli with a sprinkling of powdered sugar? How could it not bring about a smile? Nothing magic about that.

Sorry if you don't like it, but you have a gift, same as I do, same as all the women on my side of the family, her mother had always said. Miranda Mack passed away just over a month ago, and Olivia still couldn't believe her larger-than-life mother was gone.

"Did you add chocolate chips to one end and crushed pistachios to the other like I asked?" Penny Jergen snapped from the other side of the food-truck window as she inspected the cannoli, her expression holding warring emotions. Olivia could see anger, pain, humiliation and plenty of heartbreak in Penny's green eyes.

Which had Olivia refraining from rolling her own eyes at Penny's usual rudeness. "Sure did." *As you can clearly see.*

Barely mustering a thank-you, Penny carried the cannoli in its serving wedge over to the wrought iron tables and chairs dotting the town green just steps from the food truck. Olivia watched Penny stare down the young couple at the next table who were darting glances at her, then sit, her shoulders slumping. Olivia felt for Penny. The snooty twenty-six-year-old local beauty pageant champ wasn't exactly the nicest person in Blue Gulch, but Olivia knew what heartbreak felt like.

Everyone in town had heard through the grapevine that Penny had caught her brand-new fiancé of just one week in bed with her frenemy, who'd apparently wanted to prove she could tempt the guy away from Miss Blue Gulch County. Ever since, Penny had walked around town on the verge of tears, head cast down. A barista at the coffee shop, Penny had handed Olivia her iced mocha that morning with red-rimmed eyes, her usually meticulously made-up face bare and crumpling. Olivia had been hoping Penny would stop by the food truck so Olivia could help a little. This afternoon she had.

As Olivia worked on a pulled-pork po'boy with barbecue sauce for her next customer, a young man with a nervous energy, as though he was waiting for news of some kind, she eyed Penny through the truck's front window. Penny bit into the cannoli, a satisfied *ah* emanating from her. She took another bite. As expected, Penny sat up straighter. She took another bite and her teary eyes brightened. Color came back to her cheeks. She slowly ate the rest of the cannoli, sipped from a bottle of water, then stood up, head held high, chin up in the air.

"You know what?" Penny announced to no one in particular, flipping her long blond beachy waves behind her shoulders. "Screw him! I'm Penny Jergen. I mean, look at me." She ran her hand down her tall, willowy, big-chested frame. "That's it. Penny Jergen is done moping around over some cheating jerk who didn't deserve her." With that she left her balled-up, chocolate-dotted napkin on the table and marched off in her high-heeled sandals.

Olivia smiled. Penny Jergen, like her or not, was back to her old self. Presto-chango—whether Olivia liked her ability or not. The moment Penny had ordered the cannoli, chocolate chips on one end, crushed pistachios on the other, Olivia had instinctively known the extra ingredient the dessert had needed: a dash of "I'm Gonna Wash That Man Right Outa My Hair." A person couldn't get over heartbreak so fast—Olivia knew that from personal experience. But Olivia's customers' moods and facial expressions and stories told her what they needed and that telling infused the ingredients of their orders with…not magic, exactly, but something Olivia couldn't explain.

Her mother used to argue with her over the word *magic* all the time, going on and on about how there *was* magic in the world, miracles that couldn't be explained away, and Olivia would be stumped. All she knew for sure was that she believed in paying attention: watching faces, reading moods, giving a hoot. If you really looked at someone, you could tell so much about them and what they needed. And so Olivia put all her hopes for the person in her food and the power of positive thinking did its thing.

This was how Olivia tried to rationalize it, anyway. Special abilities, gifts, whatever you wanted to call it—she just wasn't sure she believed in that. Even if sometimes she stayed up late at night, trying to explain to herself her mother's obvious ability to predict the future. Olivia's obvious ability to restore through her food. It was one thing for Olivia to fill a chocolate cannoli shell with cream and sprinkle it with powdered sugar while thinking positively about female empowerment and getting over a rotten fiancé. It was another for those thoughts to actually have such a specific effect on the person eating that cannoli.

You have a gift, Olivia's mother had repeated the day she passed away. *My hope is that one day you'll accept it. Don't deny who you are. Denial is why—*

Her mom had stopped talking then, turning away with a sigh. Olivia knew she'd been thinking about her sister, Olivia's aunt, who'd estranged herself from Miranda and Olivia five years earlier. If her aunt had a gift, Olivia had never heard mention of it.

She forced thoughts of her family from her mind; she couldn't risk infusing her current customer's order with her own worries. She had to focus on him. She turned around and glanced at the guy, early twenties, biting his lower lip. He was waiting for a job offer, Olivia thought. Her fingers filling with good-luck vibes, she added the delicious-smelling barbecue sauce to his pulled-pork po'boy, wrapped it up and handed it to him through the window. She loved knowing that in about fifteen minutes, he'd have a little boost of confidence—whether or not he got the job.

And she wasn't in denial of who she was. Gift or no gift, Olivia knew exactly who she was: twenty-six, single and struggling to find her place now that her world had shifted. Until a week ago she'd been a caterer and personal chef, making Weight Watchers points-friendly meals for a few clients, gluten-free dishes for two other clients, and creating replicas of favorites that Mr. Crenshaw's late wife used to cook for him. She would never quit on her clients; she knew the effect her food had on them, but spending so much time alone in the kitchen of her tiny house, after having her heart broken and losing her mother, she'd needed *something*, something new, something that would get her outside and interacting with people instead of just with her stove.

And then Essie Hurley, who owned the popular restaurant Hurley's Homestyle Kitchen, had called, asking if Olivia, who she often hired to help out in the kitchen for big events, had any interest in running Hurley's Homestyle Kitchen's new business venture—the food truck. Olivia hadn't hesitated. Two other cooks at Hurley's would split the shifts, so Olivia was on three days a week from 11:30 a.m. to 3:30 p.m., and two days from

3:30 p.m. to 7:30 p.m. That left lots of time for her to cook at home for her clients and make her deliveries. The Hurley's Homestyle Kitchen food truck was parked several blocks down from the restaurant and business was bustling, the residents of Blue Gulch coming back time and again. Because—if she said so herself—she was a good cook. She really would like to think that was all there was to it. Good food, comforting food, delicious food, made people happy. End of story.

Olivia glanced out the window, grateful there was no one waiting and that she could take a break and have a po'boy herself. She was deciding between roast beef and grilled chicken when she realized that the stranger who'd been standing across the sidewalk in front of the coffee shop was still there, still watching her. At first she'd thought he was reading the chalkboard of menu items hanging from the outside of the food truck. But for twenty minutes?

And he didn't look particularly happy. Every time she caught his eye, which was every time she looked at him, he seemed to be glaring at her. But why? Who was he? Blue Gulch was a small town and if a six-two, very attractive man had moved in, Olivia would have heard about it from the grapevine. People chatted at the food-truck window as they passed the time until their orders were ready. Sometimes they talked out loud to her, sometimes she just heard snippets of conversation.

Olivia couldn't remember ever seeing the guy before. He stood to the side of the door of Blue Gulch Coffee in his dark brown leather jacket and jeans and cowboy boots, his thick brown hair lit by the sun, a large cup of coffee in his hand.

Just as she decided on grilled chicken with pesto-dill sauce, he walked up to the food truck. Whoa, he was good-looking. All that wavy chestnut-brown hair, green-hazel eyes, a strong nose and jawline and one dimple in his left cheek that softened up his serious expression a bit. Late twenties, she thought, unable to stop staring.

"May I help you?" Olivia asked, her Spidey senses going on red alert. This guy was seriously pissed off at something—and that something was her. Could you be angry at someone you'd never met? She tried to read him, to feel something, but her usual ability failed her.

He glared at her. "I'll have a sautéed-shrimp po'boy. Please."

She could tell that he'd struggled to add the *please*. "Coming right up."

He waited a beat, his eyes narrowed, then he glanced inside the truck, clearly trying to look around. For what?

She got to work, adding the shrimp, coated with her homemade Cajun seasoning, into the frying pan, and realized she was getting absolutely nothing from him. No vibe, other than his anger. But suddenly, a feeling came over Olivia, a feeling she usually didn't have to think so hard about. He was worried about someone, she realized. She had no idea who or why or what. She only knew the anger was masking worry.

She dared a peek at him. He stood to the side of the window, staring at her, his expression unchanged. *Is he worried about a relative?* The thought flitted out of her head as quickly as it had come in. She wasn't psychic. She couldn't read minds. But sometimes a thought would drift inside her like smoke, sometimes so fleetingly she couldn't grasp it.

She slathered each side of the French roll with the rémoulade of mustard and mayonnaise and horseradish sauce, then layered the sautéed shrimp and added tomato slices and onion. She could feel "it'll be okay" sparking from her fingers, infusing the po'boy.

She handed him the yellow cardboard tray holding his sandwich. He nodded and thanked her, then moved a few feet over to a pub table that lined the edge of the grass.

He shot another glare her way, then glanced left and right, up and down Blue Gulch Street. Was he waiting for someone? Watching for something? He'd been eyeing the truck for at least twenty minutes. He took a bite of the po'boy and she could tell, at least, that he liked the sandwich. He took another bite. No change in his expression. Then another. Still no change.

He appeared at the window. Same expression. Same glare.

The sautéed-shrimp po'boy hadn't worked on him. According to the man's face, it most certainly was not going to be okay.

Huh. That was weird. And a first, really.

"Are you the daughter of Miranda Mack?" he asked.

She stiffened. "Yes," she said, wondering what this was about.

He looked around the inside of the narrow truck before his hazel eyes settled back on her. "So you just serve po'boys and cannoli out of the truck? Not fortunes, too?"

Did he want his fortune told? Olivia didn't get that sense from him at all. "I'm not a fortune-teller. Just a cook."

He stared at her. "Look, I'd appreciate it if you could settle a family problem your mother caused."

Uh-oh. She'd been here a time or two or three or four over the years. Sometimes her mother's predictions upset her clients or their families, and when pleading with Miranda hadn't helped, they'd come to Olivia, asking her to intervene, hoping she could convince her mother to change the fortune or "see" something else.

He stepped closer. "Your mother told my father a bunch of nonsense about the second great love of his life, and now he's traveling all over Texas to find this woman. I'd appreciate it if you could put an end to this…ridiculousness."

Oh, boy.

"Mr.…" she began, stalling.

"My name is Carson Ford."

Olivia knew that name. Well, not Carson, but Ford. Her mother had mentioned a Ford. Edward or something like that.

"My father is Edmund Ford," he said, lowering his voice. "Suffice it to say he's a bigwig at Texas Trust here in Blue Gulch. He's also a vulnerable widower. Your mother told him that his second great love is a hairstylist named Sarah with green eyes. He's now racing around to every hair salon in the county asking for Sarahs with green eyes. People are going to think he's nuts. He's had seven haircuts in the past two weeks."

Oliva froze. Hair salon. Sarah. Green eyes. That could only be one person.

He narrowed his eyes at her. "She filled you in on this scam?"

Olivia bit her lip. Her aunt, her mother's sister who'd

gotten into a terrible argument with Miranda five years ago and hadn't been seen or heard from since, was named Sarah. And a hairstylist. With green eyes.

What the heck was this? *Oh, Mom, what did you do?*

He waited for her to respond, but when she didn't, he said, "Look, will you please talk some sense into my father? Explain that your mother ran a good game, a scam, fed people what they wanted to hear for lots of money. My father can go back to his normal life and I can focus on my own. This is interfering with my job and people are counting on me."

She felt herself bristle at the word *scam*, but she ignored it. For now. "What is your job?" She hadn't meant to ask that, but it came tumbling out of her mouth.

"I'm a private investigator. I specialize in finding people who don't want to be found—mostly of the criminal and/or fraudulent variety," he added with emphasis.

She stepped back, not expecting that. She didn't know what she'd expected him to say he did for a living, but private investigator wasn't it. Actually, she'd been thinking lawyer. Shark, at that.

She herself had thought about hiring a private investigator to find her aunt when her own online searches had led nowhere. Suffice it to say, to use his own phrase, that Carson Ford would not be interested in helping to locate this particular Sarah. "My mother is not a criminal or a fraud." *And she's gone*, she thought, her heart pinching.

He didn't respond. He just continued to stare at her as if waiting for her to give something away with her expression, catch her in a lie. This man clearly also paid attention to people; it was his job to do so. She would have to be careful around him.

Wait a minute. No, she did not. Her mother's business was her mother's business. Olivia had no secrets, nothing to hide about Miranda Mack.

Her mother's face, her dark hair wound into an elegant topknot affixed with two rhinestone-dotted sticks, her fair complexion, her long, elegant nose, her penchant for iridescent silver jewelry and long filmy scarves all came to mind. Olivia ached for the sight of Miranda. What she would give for one more day with her mother, another hug.

Despite their differences, Olivia missed her mother so much that tears crept up on her constantly. In the middle of the night. When she was brushing her teeth. While she was making her mother's favorite meal, pasta carbonara with its cream and pancetta, the only thing that could comfort Olivia lately when grief seized her. And guilt. For how Olivia had always dismissed her mother's surety that Olivia had a gift. Or that Miranda, the most sought-after fortune-teller in town—in the county—had had a gift, either. A crystal ball and some floaty scarves and deep red lipstick and suddenly her mother turned into Madam Miranda behind garnet velvet curtains. People liked the shtick, her mother had insisted. Olivia would say that three quarters of the town's residents believed that Miranda had been the real deal. A quarter had rolled their eyes. Olivia was mostly in the latter camp with a pinkie toe in the former. How to make sense of all her mother's predictions coming true?

Like the one about Olivia's own broken heart. A proposal that would never come from her long-term boyfriend. *He's not the one*, Miranda had insisted time and again, shaking her head.

"My mother passed away six weeks ago," Olivia said, her own blindness, her losses and this man's criticism all ganging up on her. "I won't stand for you to disparage her."

His expression softened. "I did hear about her death. I am very sorry for your loss."

She could tell that part was sincere, at least.

And she'd been right, she thought as she glanced at him. He was worried about a relative. His father.

He cleared his throat. "My father is expecting me for dinner tonight at his house. If you could come and talk some sense into him, I'd appreciate it."

What? No. No. No. He was inviting her to dinner at his father's house? To talk the man out of looking for this second great love? Who, according to Miranda, was very likely Olivia's aunt.

A woman her mother had been estranged from for five years. Had her mother "known" that this prediction would lead the man's son, a private investigator, to get huffy and intervene? That it would bring Sarah Mack home? *If* it brought Aunt Sarah home.

Olivia had never known her mother to do anything for her own gain. Never. If Miranda had told Edmund Ford that his second true love was a hairstylist named Sarah with green eyes, then her mother absolutely believed that to be true. Aunt Sarah or no Aunt Sarah.

"I—I…" She had no idea how to get out of this, or what she could possibly say anything to his father about his fortune. "My mother believed in her gift. Her fortunes came true eighty-five percent of the time."

He rolled his eyes. "Yes, I know all about the power of suggestion."

So did Olivia. And she also knew how badly her mother wanted Olivia to find Aunt Sarah. On the day of her death, Miranda had told Olivia she'd written a letter to her sister and that it was her dying wish that Olivia give it to Sarah along with a family heirloom, a bracelet passed down from their mother. Over the past six weeks, Olivia had tried to find Sarah by doing internet searches, but all her leads were for the wrong Sarah Mack. She'd even searched for Sarah Macks in hair salons in the surrounding counties and had come up empty, too. No wonder Edmund Ford hadn't been able to find her. No one could.

Maybe she should tell Carson Ford he didn't have to worry, that it was doubtful his father would ever find his "second great love."

"I'm surprised your father hasn't asked you to find her," Olivia said, wiping down the window counter. "I mean, there must be hundreds of green-eyed hairstylists named Sarah in the state of Texas. No last name, nothing else to go on?" she asked, fishing. It was possible that Edmund Ford's second great love wasn't Sarah Mack. There likely *were* hundreds of green-eyed hairstylists named Sarah in Texas.

He stepped closer to the window, bracing his hands on the sides of the wooden counter. "First of all, my father did ask me to help. But come on. How would trying to find this woman actually *help* my father? It's a wild-goose chase and nonsense. Second of all—" He stopped, as if realizing he was about to disclose personal family business to a stranger. He cleared his throat again. "There was one more thing," he added.

"My father asked your mother how he'd know for sure which green-eyed hairstylist named Sarah was his predicted love. Your mother said he would know her instantly, but that she would have a small tattoo of a hairbrush and blow-dryer on her ankle."

So much for the possibility that Miranda hadn't been talking about Sarah Mack. Olivia was twelve when her aunt had gotten that tattoo. The brush was silver and the blow-dryer hot pink, Aunt Sarah's favorite color.

"I'm not sure what I could possibly do or say to help you, Carson. I'm not a fortune-teller. I don't know how my mother's ability worked. If she said that his great love was this green-eyed tattooed hairstylist named Sarah, then she truly believed it. And like I said, her predictions were right most of the time."

He grimaced. "Oh, please. I don't believe that. I don't believe any of it."

Olivia didn't want to, either. But evidence was walking around all over town in the form of couples her mother had brought together or people who'd changed their lives because of what Miranda had predicted. "She was responsible for over three hundred marriages. She directed people to their passions, stopped them from making mistakes. Sometimes they listened, sometimes the heart wants what it wants even when a fortune-teller says it won't happen."

He scowled, then pulled out a checkbook from an inside pocket. "I'll pay you for your time. One hour, two tops, for you to talk some sense into my father. Five thousand ought to do it."

Five thousand dollars. Man, she could use that money. And she felt for Carson, she really did. "It's not about the money, Carson. It wasn't for my mother, either. I know that's hard for you to believe, but it's true."

He put away the checkbook. He tilted his head back, frustration and worry etched on his handsome face. She could feel it all over him, swirling in the air between them. "Please," he said. "My father hasn't been the same since my mother died five years ago. He's so... vulnerable. I know he's terribly lonely. I don't know what made him seek out your mother—*if* he sought out your mother—"

"My mom didn't lure clients to her," Olivia said gently. "She didn't need to. She had an excellent reputation. People came to her."

He scowled. "Edmund Ford would not go walking into some fortune-teller's little velvet-curtained room. He must have been led by something or fed some lies. Your mother ensnared him and then filled his head with nonsense. I can only imagine how much he paid her. My father, as I'm sure you know, is a very wealthy man. Making fraudulent claims, taking money from vulnerable people—that is against the law."

Anger boiled in Olivia's belly. "My mother was not a criminal! How dare you imply—"

"Dada!"

Olivia stuck her head farther out the window at the sound of the little voice. She watched a toddler, no older than two, run to Carson, who kneeled down, his arms wide, a big smile suddenly on the man's face. All traces of his anger were gone.

He wrapped the child in his arms and scooped him up. The little boy pointed at a picture on the food truck's menu, probably one of the cannoli.

"I have cookies for you at home," Carson said, giving him a kiss on his cheek.

A woman in her fifties, who Olivia recognized from around town, approached wheeling a stroller, and Carson smiled at her. "I'll take him from here," he told her. "Thanks for taking such good care of him, as always."

"My pleasure, Carson," she said. "I'm happy to babysit for as long as you're in town. See you tomorrow, sweetie," she added to the little boy, ruffling his hair before turning to walk away.

"Bye!" the boy called and waved.

"Your son?" Olivia asked, noting that Carson wasn't wearing a wedding ring. She smiled at the adorable child. "He looks just like you."

He nodded. "He's eighteen months old. Daniel is his name. Danny for short."

She wondered where Danny's mother was. Was Carson divorced? Widowed? Never married the little one's mother? It was possible. Olivia's mother hadn't married Olivia's father or anyone else. Her aunt Sarah had never married. Now Olivia was following in the family tradition.

Danny tilted his head, his big hazel eyes on his father. "Chih-chih tates?"

Carson smiled and pulled an insulated snack bag from the stroller basket. He unzipped it and handed the boy a cheddar cheese stick. "How about some cheese for now and then yes, in just a couple of hours we'll be going to Granddaddy's house for your favorite—roast chicken and potatoes with gravy." He glanced at Olivia. "*Chih-chih tates* is toddler speak for *chicken and potatoes*."

Danny grinned and munched his cheese stick. The

boy was so cute that Olivia wanted to sweetly pinch his big cheeks.

Carson put the snack bag away and shifted the toddler in his arm. "One hundred Thornton Lane," he said to Olivia. "Six thirty. Please come. Please," he added, his eyes a combination of intensity, pleading, worry and hope.

Yes, please come and talk my father out of finding the woman he's meant to be with, the very woman Olivia had been searching for six weeks so she could fulfill her promise to her mother.

Oh, heck, she thought. What was she supposed to do? She wasn't about to tell the Fords that the woman in question was her aunt. But how could she not? And she certainly did understand Carson's concern for his dad. But what if her mother was right about Edmund and Sarah?

What if, what if, what if. The story of Olivia's life.

Not that Carson was waiting for an answer. He was already heading down the street, holding the toddler in one arm, pushing the stroller with the other. The boy's own little arms were wrapped around Carson's neck. His son sure loved him. That feeling swirled inside Olivia so strongly it obliterated all other thought.

Six thirty. One hundred Thornton Lane. She knew the house. A mansion on a hill you could see from anywhere on Blue Gulch Street. At night the majestic house was lit up and occasionally you could catch the thoroughbreds galloping or grazing in their acres of pasture. Sometimes over the past few weeks, when Olivia felt at her lowest, missing her mother so much her heart clenched, she'd look up at the lights of One Hundred Thornton and feel comforted somehow, as though it was a beacon, the permanence of the grand house high on the hill soothing her.

She didn't know what she could possibly say to Edmund Ford that his tightly wound, handsome son would approve of. But at least Olivia knew what she was doing for dinner tonight.

Chapter Two

Carson stood by the open window in his father's family room, watching his dad and Danny in the backyard. Fifty-four-year-old Edmund Ford held the toddler in his arms and was pointing out two squirrels chasing each other up and down the huge oak. Carson smiled at the sight of his son laughing so hard.

"Let's pretend we're squirrels and chase each other around the yard," Edmund said, setting Danny down. "You can't catch me!" he added, running ahead at a toddler's pace, which couldn't be easy for the six-two man.

"Catch!" Danny yelled, giggling.

Edmund let his back leg linger for a moment until Danny latched on. "You got me! You're the fastest squirrel in his yard."

"Me!" Danny shouted, racing around with his hands up.

Edmund scooped him up and put him on his shoulders, and they headed over to the oak again. Danny pointed at the squirrels sitting on a branch and nibbling acorns. Carson could hear his dad telling Danny that the squirrels were a grandpa and grandson, just like them.

Who was this man and what had he done with Carson's father? Carson's earliest memories involved watching his father leave the house, his father's empty chair and place setting at the dinner table, his father not making it to birthday parties or graduations or special events. He'd been a workaholic banker and nothing had been more important than "the office." Not Carson, not his mother, not even his mother's terminal diagnosis of cancer five years ago, leaving them just four months with her. But then came the moment she'd drawn her last breath, and Edmund Ford had been shaken.

I didn't tell her I loved her this morning, his father had said that day they'd lost her, his face contorted with grief and regret. *I always thought there was later, another day. I didn't tell her I loved her today.*

Tears had stung Carson's eyes and he gripped his father in a hug. *She knew anyway, Dad*, he'd said. *She always knew.*

Which was true. Every time Edmund Ford disappointed them, his mother would say, *Your father loves us very much. We're his world. Never doubt that, no matter what.*

Carson had grown up doubting that. But since his mother died, his father had changed into someone Carson barely recognized. Edmund Ford had started calling to check in a few times a week. He'd drop by Carson's office for an impromptu lunch. He'd get tickets to the Rangers or the rodeo. But instead of Carson's old longing for his dad to be present in his life, Carson had felt…uncomfortable. He barely knew his father, and this new guy was someone Carson didn't know at all. Suddenly it was Carson putting up the wall, putting up the boundaries.

Then Danny was born, and Edmund had become grandfather of the year. The man insisted on weekly family dinners with Carson and Danny, making a fuss over every baby tooth that sprouted up, new words, a quarter inch of height marked on the wall. And yes, Carson was glad his son had a loving grandfather in his life. But Carson couldn't seem to reconcile it with the man he'd known his entire life.

The first week of Danny's life, when his now ex-wife, Jodie, had still been around, they'd both been shocked when Edmund Ford had come to the hospital's neonatal intensive care unit every single day, to sit beside his bassinet and read Dr. Seuss to him, sing an old ranch tune, demand information from the doctors in his imperious tone.

"Grandparenting is different from being a parent," Jodie would say with a shrug when Carson expressed his shock over his dad's suddenly interest in family.

She must have been right because by the end of Danny's first week, she was gone, with apologies and "you knew I was like this when you married me," and his father was there. And everything that seemed normal about the world had shifted.

His father's housekeeper and cook, Leanna, came into the room and smiled at Carson, then walked over to the screen door to the yard. "Danny, want to help me make dessert?"

"Ooh!" Danny said. His grandfather set him down and he came running in.

The sixtysomething woman, with her signature braided bun, scooped up Danny and gave him a kiss on the cheek. Carson loved how much sweet attention his son got at his grandfather's house. "Twenty minutes 'til dinner," Leanna called out before heading through the French doors with Danny.

Carson glanced out the floor-to-ceiling windows on the opposite side of the room. If he craned his neck he could just make out the circular driveway in front of the mansion. No car, other than his own. He wondered if Olivia Mack would show up or not. Probably not.

"I could cancel my health club membership with all the exercise I get from playing with Danny," Edmund said as he came inside. He took a long sip from his water bottle, then sat down in a club chair and pulled a small notebook from the inside pocket of his jacket. "Oh, Carson, I won't be around tomorrow afternoon. I'll be on the road, checking out four potential hair salons for my Sarah."

Enough was enough. "Dad—"

Edmund held up a palm. "Well, it's what I have to do since my own son, a private investigator, won't do his job and help me find the person I'm looking for."

Carson crossed his arms over his chest. And sighed. "The person you're looking for doesn't exist, Dad."

Edmund shook his head. "We've been over this. I'm done arguing with you. I'm just telling you I won't be around tomorrow in case Danny wanted to see the more fun Ford man in his life."

His father *was* the fun one. Unbelievable. He shook his head, staring at his dad as though the concentration would help him come up with a way to reach the man, get to him to see how foolish and fruitless this quest was. And how potentially damaging. Edmund Ford was a handsome man, tall and fit, with thick salt-and-pepper hair adding to his distinguished appearance. And he was very, very wealthy. This Sarah, if he found someone who fit the bill, would latch on to him fast enough to get her hands on his bank account, then take off. She'd probably get herself pregnant, too, to keep the gravy train going for quite some time. Yes, Carson was that cynical.

The doorbell rang and Carson perked up. He glanced at the grandfather clock across the room. Not quite six thirty. Could it be the fortune-teller's daughter? Had she come?

Lars, Leanna's husband of thirty-two years and his father's butler for the past five years, appeared in the doorway. "A Ms. Olivia Mack is here." A short, portly man in his sixties, Lars always stood very straight in his formal uniform.

"Olivia Mack?" Edmund repeated. "Do I know an Olivia Mack? Is she selling something? I wouldn't mind a couple boxes of those mint Girl Scout cookies."

"I invited her," Carson said. "Show her in, will you, Lars?"

Edmund stood and wiggled his eyebrows at Carson. "*You* invited her? Finally dating? You definitely need a woman in your life."

"Not dating," Carson said. "I'm busy with raising my son and working."

Edmund rolled his eyes. "Your son is asleep fourteen hours a day. And you don't work twenty-four hours. You have time for romance, Carson."

Carson wasn't having this discussion. Luckily, the French doors opened and Lars presented Olivia Mack.

Carson had only had a head-and-shoulders view of Olivia inside the food truck. He'd had no idea she was so tall and curvy. She wore a weird felt skirt with appliqués of flowers, a light blue sweater and yellow-brown cowboy boots. Her hair, which had been up in the food truck, now tumbled loosely down her shoulders in light brown waves. A ring, bearing a turquoise heart on her thumb, seemed to be her only jewelry. Did people wear rings on their thumbs? Fortune-tellers probably did.

Olivia glanced back as Lars shut the doors behind her. She turned to Carson and offered an uncomfortable smile.

"Dad," Carson said, dragging his gaze off Olivia. "This is Olivia Mack, Miranda Mack's daughter."

Edmund Ford stepped toward Olivia. "Miranda Mack, Miranda Mack," he repeated. "Is she a loyal customer at Texas Trust? I'm sorry but the name isn't ringing a bell."

"Her mother was *Madam* Miranda," Carson said. He couldn't help but notice Olivia's eyes cloud over. She was obviously still grieving over the loss of her mother. Six weeks was nothing. It had taken Carson a good year before he got used to the fact that his mother was gone, that he would never see her again.

"Oh, of course!" Edmund said, hurrying over to Olivia and wrapping her in a hug. "I'm so sorry about your loss, dear. Your mother changed a lot of lives for the better. I understand that I was her very last client before…" He cleared his throat. "She told me the second great love of my life is out there waiting for me to find her. I intend to do just that."

"Actually, that's exactly why Olivia is here," Carson said. "To tell you you're wasting your time and energy."

Edmund frowned and turned to Olivia. "Is that right? Is that why you're here?"

Olivia bit her lip and looked from Edmund to Carson and back to Edmund. "Mr. Ford—"

"Please call me Edmund."

"Edmund," she began, "my mother's gift worked in mysterious ways. That's all I know," she added, glancing at Carson.

He grimaced at his son. "Carson begged you to come and tell me I'm wasting my time and energy on a wild-goose chase? Offered you a pile of money to make me see reason?"

"Well, he did, but I didn't accept," Olivia said. "He did also express how worried he is that you might be chasing after a fantasy that doesn't exist. I can understand that. I suppose that's why I'm here. To tell both of you that I don't understand how my mother's abilities worked. I do know that she brought together hundreds of couples. I also know there were times her predictions did not work out."

"Well," Edmund said, "I believed in her."

Carson caught Olivia's expression soften at that.

"Carson mentioned that you've been looking for the woman she told you about," Olivia prompted.

"No luck so far," Edmund said. "I've called around to a bunch of hair salons in the area, but most folks who answered the phone thought I was some nut and hung up on me. I visited several over the past two weeks, asking for a 'Sarah who I heard was a great hairstylist,' but most of the time, no Sarahs. The four times there was a Sarah, she didn't have green eyes." He let out a breath. "I guess this does sound kind of silly."

"Romantic, though," Olivia said on practically a whisper.

Carson frowned at her.

"I think so, too, young lady," Edmund said, the gray cloud gone from his expression. "And I may be fifty-four, but that doesn't mean I'm not a whiz with technology." He pulled out his smartphone. "I've got a map of every hair salon in the county with digital pushpins of ones I've visited." He held it up. "If there's no green-eyed Sarah, I've marked it red. I've got nineteen salons to visit tomorrow in two counties."

Carson rolled his eyes and shook his head. "What about the fund-raiser you're supposed to speak at to-morrow? What about the board meeting to prepare for?"

"Carson, I'm your father. Not the other way around."

"Dad, I—"

"Dinner is served," Leanna sang from the doorway with Danny in her arms. "Danny helped make dessert."

"Ert!" Danny called out.

"Dessert monster!" Edmund said, rushing over and tickling him and carrying him over his shoulder. Danny squealed with laughter.

This ridiculous quest to find this nonexistent green-eyed hairstylist was just another example of how much his father had changed, especially since Danny was born. For Danny's sake, Carson liked the devoted, fun grandpa his formerly workaholic, bank-before-family father had become. But this silly search to find a gold digger masquerading as a predicted great love? No. Not on Carson's watch.

He had about forty-five minutes to shift this conversation back his way. And Olivia Mack was his only hope of stopping his father from ruining his life.

In the biggest dining room that Olivia had ever been in, she sat across the huge cherrywood table from Carson. At the head sat Edmund Ford with little Danny in a high chair beside him. Watching grandfather and grandson did a lot to ease the tension that had settled in Olivia's shoulders ever since she'd arrived. Edmund clearly adored the toddler, and baby talk—*Who ate all his chi-chi? My widdle cuddlebomb did, that's who! C'mre for your cuddlebomb!*—was not beneath the revered banker. Olivia hadn't known what to expect from Edmund Ford, but this warm, welcoming man was not it.

The three generations of Fords looked quite alike with their dark thick hair, though Edmund's was shot through with a distinguished silver. The three shared the same intense hazel-green eyes.

"Edmund, how did you happen to become a client of my mother's?" Olivia asked. She smiled up at Leanna, who walked around with a serving platter of roasted potatoes. As the woman put a helping on Olivia's plate, she wondered what it would be like to live like this every day. Maids and butlers and a family room the size of the entire first floor of Olivia's house.

"When I moved to Blue Gulch four years ago, a year after my wife passed," Edmund said, "I would hear this and that about a Madam Miranda and didn't give it a thought. To me, fortune-tellers were about crystal balls and telling people, for a fee, what they wanted to hear."

"And you were right," Carson said, fork midway to his mouth.

Edmund ignored that. "But then I overheard a few conversations that stayed with me," he continued, taking a sip of his white wine. "A very intelligent young equity analyst at the bank was telling another employee that she went to see Madam Miranda about her previous job and whether she should dare quit without having another lined up first. Madam Miranda advised her to quit immediately because an old college friend who worked at Texas Trust would call about an opening there and she would apply, interview and be offered the job with a significant increase in pay. Oh, and she'd love working there. The analyst risked quite a bit by taking that advice. Three days later, an old college friend called. And the rest is history."

Carson was doing that thing again where he rolled his eyes *and* shook his head. The double dismissive whammy.

"I would catch some stories like that," Edmund said, "and I just sort of tucked them away, not having any interest in paying Madam Miranda a visit."

"What changed your mind?" Olivia asked, taking a bite of the rosemary chicken. Mmm, that was good. So well seasoned. Olivia hadn't had a meal she hadn't cooked herself in a very long time.

"About two months ago, I overheard two young women talking in the coffee shop," Edmund said. "I was waiting for my triple espresso, and I heard a woman say that Madam Miranda's prediction for her had come true, that if she'd find the courage to break up with her no-good, no-account boyfriend, she'd find real love with a handsome architect whose first name started with the letter *A*."

"Oh, come on," Carson said, shaking his head.

Edmund kept his attention on Olivia. "The young woman went on to say she'd been dating the terrible boyfriend for two years but Madam Miranda's prediction gave her something to hope for, even if it was silly and couldn't possibly come true, despite being so specific. She dumped the guy, and three months later, she struck up a flirtation with a young man doing some work in the new wing of the hospital where she worked as a nurse. An architect named Andrew."

Carson put down his wineglass. "Madam Miranda probably heard his firm would be working on the new hospital wing. She put the idea in the nurse's head that she and this guy belonged together and voilà, instant interest when she might have otherwise ignored him."

"Talk about far-fetched," Edmund said to his son.

"I have a million of those stories," Olivia said. "I've seen much of it firsthand. And my mother may have been a lot of things, but a liar or a cheat wasn't among them."

Carson put down his fork. "Right. So my father's second great love is a stranger named Sarah standing in a hair salon giving some guy a buzz cut. Come on."

"Why not?" Olivia asked. "Why isn't that possible?"

Carson sighed. "Because it's hocus-pocus. It's nonsense. It's make-believe. It gets people to pony up a pile of money for malarkey—and just like that nurse said, it gives hope where there's none. It doesn't mean a damned thing."

"Watch your language," Edmund said, covering Danny's ears. The boy giggled.

"Larkey!" Danny shouted gleefully.

"How much did you pay the madam for this fantasy?" Carson asked his father. "Hundreds, no doubt, once she knew who you were."

"I've told you at least three times that she refused to accept money from me," Edmund said, taking a bite of his chicken. "She told me she thought my bittersweet story was deeply touching and that was payment enough."

Olivia knew her mother often didn't charge those who clearly couldn't afford her services. But Edmund Ford was a zillionaire. His story really *must* have touched Miranda—or had her mother known that he was destined to become part of the family because of Aunt Sarah? Hmm.

"But," Edmund continued, "considering that her fortune-telling parlor was inside her home, which was on the small side, a postage stamp, really, I left her a thousand dollars in cash anonymously. She deserved it."

The head shaking was back. "Right, Dad. I'm sure that's how she hooked, lined and sunk her wealthy clients, pretending to care, finding their pasts just so touching, and fully knowing they'd load up her mailbox with cash and gifts. Payment enough—ha."

"Could you *be* more cynical?" Edmund said, once again covering little Danny's ears and making the boy giggle.

"I'm not cynical, Dad. I'm realistic."

"Who's ready for desserty-werty?" Edmund said to Danny, kissing his soft little cheek. "I know I am!"

"Me!" Danny shouted.

Olivia glanced at Carson, who was brooding in his

seat. She'd say for this round, each man had scored a point each. They both made sense.

Carson let out a breath and shook his head, crossing his arms over his chest.

Edmund stood and lifted Danny out of his high chair and set him down. "Sweets, why don't you go play with your toys for a few minutes until Mrs. Hilliard brings out dessert."

The boy went running for his toy chest, surrounded by brightly colored bean bags and low bookshelves.

"Right after I overheard that young lady telling her friend about finding true love," Edmund said, "I started having all these strange feelings." He glanced at Carson. "About wanting that for myself. I loved your mother, Carson. Very much. The last eighteen months especially, I've found myself changing, becoming very family-oriented when I wasn't before."

Carson glanced out the window, but Olivia could tell he was listening.

"After five years as a widow," Carson continued, "with a new appreciation for loved ones, I found myself longing to find love again. And so I made an appointment with Madam Miranda to see what she might say about my chances."

Carson let out a deep breath. "It's not that I don't want you to find love again, Dad. I just don't want you to go on some crazy wild-goose chase and end up getting hurt by a gold digger."

"I know you care, Carson," Edmund said, his tone reverent. "And I appreciate that you do. But I believed Madam Miranda. I consider myself a pretty good judge of character and that woman looked me in the eye with truth."

It was like a hug. After Carson's criticism of her mother, after her own years and years of trying to find some rational explanation for her mother's abilities, to hear her last client say this with conviction in his voice was like the warm hug that Olivia had needed for six weeks. Her only other family member—Aunt Sarah, very likely Edmund Ford's second great love—was somewhere out there, long out of hugging distance.

"Will you stay for dessert?" Edmund asked her.

She took another glance at Carson. The man was scowling. His plan to have her derail his father's belief in her mother's fortune hadn't exactly worked.

"I'd better get going. Thank you for dinner," she said. "I'm so glad we got to meet."

"Well, rest assured that I will make good on your mother's prediction for me," Edmund said. "I will find my green-eyed, hair-cutting Sarah." Olivia smiled and he took both her hands in his. "I'm very sorry for your loss, Olivia. I know how it feels to lose someone you love so deeply."

What a dear man he was. "Thank you."

"I'll see you out," Carson said between gritted teeth.

"Bye, Danny," Olivia said, smiling at the toddler.

"Bye!" Danny said with a smile and a wave and his grandfather joined him in his toy area.

As she and Carson walked through the marble foyer and out the front door, Olivia could tell Carson was waiting until they were outside to let her have it for not backing him up. She could feel the tension in him.

But all he said, while looking around the circular drive, was "Where is your car?"

"I walked, actually. My car is almost fifteen years old and might not have made it up the hill to the drive."

He seemed surprised. "I'll walk you home. Let me just tell my dad and Danny I'll be gone for a while."

"Oh, you don't have to—"

"I insist," he said.

Now he'd have a half hour to give her an earful about how she'd messed up the one thing he wanted.

"I suppose you feel like I got to eat that amazing rosemary chicken and roasted potatoes and perfectly timed asparagus for nothing," Olivia said as they headed down the hill toward town.

Carson raised an eyebrow and glanced at her, struck again by how lovely she was. She had a delicate, fine-boned face and her long light brown hair framed it in waves. The cool breeze blew her sweater against her full breasts and he found himself sucking in a breath at how sexy she was. Flower-appliqué felt skirt and yellow cowboy boots and all. He realized he was staring at her and glanced ahead at the twinkling lights in the distance, where the shops and restaurants of Blue Gulch Street were just winding down. How could he be attracted to her?

"Meaning, I don't think your dad will give up on the quest to find this woman," Olivia said.

"Well, I appreciated that you came and were fair," Carson said. "It's not like you were necessarily on either our sides." He felt her looking at him. "And I don't think he'll give up, either. I've tried for two weeks now, ever since he first mentioned it to me. You were my last hope."

"Two weeks? My mom's been gone for six, and I know their appointment was just days before she passed away."

"He said he tucked the fortune away, let himself really think about it, and then decided he was ready to see if it was possible, if there really could be a second great love out there."

"Carson?" she said, darting a glance at him. "Is the reason you're so against his trying to find the woman because of your mother?"

"My mother died five years ago. I don't begrudge my father love or companionship. It's the fortune-telling aspect that I have problems with."

"My mom tried to keep a list of all the marriages she was responsible for. Her last count was three hundred twelve."

Please. "I don't believe that."

"You don't believe much," she said.

That wasn't true. He believed in a lot. In his love for his son. In doing his job and helping bring criminals to justice by tracking them down for the police. In the way Olivia Mack's big brown eyes drew him, making him unable to look away from her face.

Olivia looked past him toward the beautiful horse pasture. The thoroughbreds weren't out tonight. "Did you grow up in that house?" she asked.

"No, I grew up in Oak Creek." A town over, Oak Creek was the fancy cousin of Blue Gulch, filled with estate ranches and mansions. "My father sold the family house a year after my mother died. He said the memories were killing him and he needed a fresh start and had always liked Blue Gulch with its quaint mile-long downtown."

"Ah," she said. "That's why I haven't seen you around. I think just about everyone in town has been to the food truck in the two weeks it's been open."

"I meant to tell you—the shrimp po'boy was pretty darn good. I have no doubt that word of mouth will bring in business from the surrounding towns."

She smiled. "Thanks. My mother's business worked that way, too. Word of mouth brought in client after client, just as it did with your dad. Relative and friends came in from neighboring states, too, for a chance to meet with Madam Miranda."

"So tell me how this supposedly works. Your mother had this magic ability to predict the future but it wasn't passed down to you?"

"According to my mother, all the women on her side of the family have a gift," she practically mumbled.

"What number am I thinking of?" he asked.

She smiled. "I have no idea."

"So what is your gift?" he asked.

"That's a lovely tree," she said, eyeing the weeping willow at the edge of the Ford property. She clearly didn't want to talk about this.

He leaned toward her. "You can read minds. You can move objects with your eyes. You can make yourself invisible."

She laughed. "None of the above. I'm not sure I want to talk to about it, Carson. I've struggled with believing it myself, but based on what I've seen with my own eyes, I seem to be able to affect people with my cooking."

What? "Your cooking?"

She nodded. "Aside from running the Hurley's Homestyle Kitchen food truck during the week, I'm a personal chef. I seem to be able to change moods and lift hearts with my food."

She glanced at him, and he tried to make his expression more neutral but the disappointment punching him in the stomach made that impossible.

"Not what you want to hear, I know," she said. "But this is my family. This is me. I'm not saying I understand it or even want it, but I seem to have this…gift."

He resumed walking, shoving his hands in the pockets of his leather jacket. "You made me a shrimp po'boy. What effect did that have on me?"

"I don't think any. Which is unusual."

He *was* disappointed. For a moment there, despite everything, he'd felt drawn to this woman. But here she was, spouting the same nonsense her mother had. He wanted to walk away, but he wasn't going to just abandon her in the evening on the sidewalk, even in very safe Blue Gulch. He'd been raised to be a gentleman.

So he'd play along. Maybe he'd trip her up, get her to admit how ridiculous the idea was. Lifting hearts with her food? Lord. "So how do you set this up? You offer customers a chance to turn their frown upside down for an extra five bucks?"

She shot him a glare. "Did I say one word to you when you ordered? No. I don't charge extra. I just get a sense of what someone needs and I infuse the food naturally. Maybe an insecure person will get a boost of confidence. A hurting person will feel a bit stronger."

"And a pissed-off man like me, worried about my father wasting his time and energy on some crazy fortune? Why didn't the po'boy change my mood?"

She bit her lip and looked down at the ground. "I really don't know."

"Shocker."

"You don't have to be rude," she said, crossing her arms over her chest.

Right then, under the darkening sky, the combination of her hurt expression and how alone she seemed made him feel like a heel. "Sorry. I'm just…my father is new to me, Olivia. My whole life, until my mother died, my father was a stranger I barely saw. Work was the most important thing in his life. Now, he's a different person. Kinder, interested in family, in people, in the community and world around him. I once thought he had no heart, and now he has too much heart. You see how he is with Danny."

She tilted her head. "Can a person have too much heart? He's wonderful with Danny. A dream grandpa."

"All that extra heart means a lot more room to be hurt and easily swindled." He stopped walking for a moment, struck by what he'd just said. He hadn't realized how worried he was that his father would be hurt—not just swindled. The man who made Danny laugh and shout "yay!" whenever Carson mentioned they were going to see grandpa was not going to get that heart stepped on by a con artist.

"I think my mother meant every word of that fortune, Carson."

Why was she so frustrating? Who cared if Madam Miranda believed in her phony "gift"? There was no such thing as predicting the future. There was probability and possibility and plain old-fashioned guesses. But there was no crystal ball. "Right, Olivia. So somewhere out there is a green-eyed woman named Sarah in a hair salon with some ridiculous blow-dryer tattoo. And she's my supposedly my father's second great love."

Olivia nodded. She seemed about to say something, then looked away.

"Well, I'm not going to let my father go on some

wild-goose chase and let some swindler snow my dad for his money. I finally have my dad. I'm not going to let him get hurt."

"Or you could have a little faith, Carson Ford."

He rolled his eyes. "I'd laugh but I don't want to be rude again."

She lifted her chin. "I live just down this street," she said, pointing to Golden Way. "Please thank your father for his hospitality." Then she stalked off.

He watched her walk to the second house on the left, a tiny yellow cottage with a white picket fence and a bunch of wind chimes. A black-and-white cat was sitting on the porch and wrapped around her legs, the yellow-brown cowboy boots. Olivia bent down and scratched the cat behind the ears, then picked it up and gave it a nuzzle before carrying it inside.

When the door closed, he felt strangely bereft, the lack of her so startling that he wanted to knock on the door and argue with her a little more just to be near her.

He had to clamp down on that feeling. He'd been through the wringer with his ex-wife and had no interest in feeling anything for a woman. Everything he had, all the mush and gush he had left, went to his son. Olivia Mack was likely in on her mother's scam, though she did strike him as honest, and Carson considered himself a pretty good judge of character, of sizing someone up.

She wasn't going to help dissuade his father from heartbreak and a big time-waster. Which meant he had to forget Olivia Mack and the way she got under his skin.

Chapter Three

By twelve thirty in the afternoon the next day, Olivia had sold thirty-seven po'boys and thirty-two cannoli. Not bad for an hour's work. Being so busy in the food truck had taken her mind off a certain tall, sexy PI. She'd barely slept last night, tossing and turning as she thought about all Carson had said, all his father had said, her mother's prediction, her aunt Sarah, who she missed terribly. Carson was a complicated man. The situation was complicated. But cooking wasn't complicated at all. You followed a recipe and there you had it. Simple.

She stood at the cannoli station, which was a two-foot-long section of stainless-steel counter, and added a dusting of powdered sugar to a mini strawberry cannoli.

"Here you go," she said to Clementine Hurley Grainger,

who sat at the swivel stool at the tiny desk near the cab of the truck.

Twenty-five-year-old Clementine's dark eyes lit up and she put down the stack of receipts she'd been going through. "Ooh, that looks amazing—thank you." She took a bite. "Absolutely delicious!"

Among Olivia's favorite words.

Clementine took another bite, then put down the cannoli. "I'm amazed by these receipts!" she said, picking up a few. "One order alone was for seven cannoli—and not even the lower-priced minis!"

Olivia smiled at her friend and one-quarter boss. Clementine's grandmother, Essie Hurley, owned Hurley's Homestyle Kitchen, where Clementine was a waitress. Clementine had had the brilliant idea for the food truck while on a family honeymoon with her new husband, Logan Grainger, his twin three-year-olds and the foster daughter they were in the process of trying to adopt. On a road trip across Texas, everywhere they stopped there were brightly colored, inviting food trucks with long lines of customers. One family meeting later, some numbers crunched with Georgia Hurley—Clementine's sister, who baked for the restaurant and handled the books—and creating the menu with Annabel Hurley—their other sister and the lead chef for the restaurant—and the food truck came into existence. Working with the three Hurley sisters and Essie to get the truck ready for business had given Olivia such purpose the past weeks.

"Mandy from the real estate office bought those," Olivia said as she sautéed onions, celery and garlic for the next batch of pulled-pork po'boys. "She says they tend to put clients in signing mode." And for the past week, one o'clock meant she'd have a line of hungry customers from Texas Trust, the employees at the coffee shop, plus the construction crew working on a house just around the corner that always ordered three po'boys per guy.

"We get compliments on your po'boys and cannoli all the time at the restaurant," Clementine said. "I can't tell you how many times I've heard people say, 'I could be in the worst mood, have one of Olivia's cannoli and suddenly have a skip in my step.' Whatever you're doing, keep doing it. Gram is thrilled with the success you've made of the truck."

"I'm so happy to hear that," Olivia said. "I don't know what I would have done without this new venture to focus on and throw myself into. I owe you and your sisters and grandmother everything."

"We're even, then," Clementine said, taking another bite of her cannoli. "Ooh, hot construction workers coming your way," she said, upping her chin at the group of six men walking toward the truck. Olivia laughed. "Well, I'd better get to work myself. See you later."

By two o'clock, Olivia had made over a hundred po'boys and seventy-five cannoli, which was up since she'd started offering the mini cannoli.

"Excuse me, but I was here first!" a grumpy female voice snapped.

"Actually I was, but please, go ahead," responded a familiar deep voice.

Olivia peered out the window, setting aside the head of lettuce she was about to rip apart. A thirtysomething woman was elbowing Carson out of her way, jockeying for position in front of him at the food-truck window. Carson moved behind the sourpuss, who was busily texting so fast, with such fury on her face, that Olivia was surprised the phone didn't explode from the sparks.

"May I help you?" Olivia asked the woman. She glanced past the woman at Carson. He wore cop-like sunglasses and his leather jacket.

No response.

Olivia cleared her throat. "Next!" she called out, which always woke people up.

"Meatball-parm po'boy with extra parm," the woman grunted without looking up from her phone. "And two mini cannoli, one chocolate with chocolate chips on the ends and one peanut butter."

There was anxiety under the woman's anger, Olivia knew suddenly. Someone close to her—a boss? A teenager?—was driving her insane.

"Do you want me to take the test for him?" the woman screeched at the phone, shaking her head. She seemed to be yelling at a text she'd received. "Never get married," she said to Olivia, fury on her face. "Then you'll never have to deal with an idiot ex-husband who blames you for your fifteen-year-old's F in chemistry and D in Algebra Two."

Olivia tried for a commiserating smile. "Your order is coming right up," she said, heating the meatballs in the sauté pan. She scooped them out onto the baguette and layered the sauce—her aunt Sarah's old recipe—and then added the Parmesan cheese, then another layer, per the request. She could feel a shift in the air around the po'boy and knew her abilities were at work. Exactly how the woman would be affected was a mystery.

Olivia handed over the order in a serving wedge and the woman stalked over to the pub table a few feet away.

"She practically ran me over since her face was glued to her phone," Carson said, stepping up to the window. "She even stepped on my feet with those clod-hopper cowboy boots."

Olivia smiled. "How are your toes?" She bit her lip. Was she flirting? She didn't want to flirt with Carson Ford.

He smiled back. "They'll survive."

"Oh, God," the grumpy woman said from her table. She held up the po'boy and examined it, taking another bite, letting the Parmesan cheese stretch high in the air before gobbling it up. "Oh, my God, this is good." She inhaled the rest of her po'boy, then sipped her water and took a very deep breath, exhaling as though she was meditating. She held up one of the cannoli. "This almost looks too pretty to eat, doesn't it?" she said cheerfully to Carson.

"It looks very edible, actually," he said.

The woman laughed as though that was hilarious. She took a giant bite of the chocolate cannoli. Then a bite of the peanut-butter one. "Scrumptious. Absolutely scrumptious!" She grabbed her phone and pressed in numbers. "Donald Peachley, please. I don't care that he's in a meeting. Tell him it's an emergency." Olivia eyed Carson. "Donald, your ex-wife here. I have an idea. Let's get DJ a tutor and we'll split the cost. Since I make twenty percent more than you, I'm even willing to pay twenty percent more…Great…Bye now." She then popped the rest of the chocolate cannoli in her mouth, quickly followed by the peanut-butter one.

Olivia smiled at Carson. An innocent smile. An I-told-you smile.

"Excuse me," Carson said to the woman. "But I'm curious about something. You seemed very upset five minutes ago. But you came up with a good solution to your problem and handled it very well," he said in a fishing tone.

"Well, I know what a cheapskate tab-keeper my ex is, so I figured if I offered to pay a little more for the tutor he'd go for it. It's funny, though—before lunch I never would have been so...reasonable or generous. I've been accused of being my own worst enemy. Can you believe that?"

Carson didn't answer that. "So you probably had low blood sugar, had some food and felt better, which got you thinking clearly."

"Low blood sugar? I had two slices of pizza at Pizzateria ten minutes before I came over here. When I'm furious, I eat."

Carson scowled.

"Something about these cannoli always peps me up," she said. She glanced at her phone. "Back to the grind. See y'all."

Carson crossed his arms over his chest. "People like cannoli," he said to Olivia. "It's a pick-me-up. That's all there is to it."

"I agree," Olivia said. "That's how I look at it most of the time. Until I start thinking about how my food seems to have such specific effect on people. Then I start to doubt myself as a doubter."

And the more Carson insisted her gift was malarkey, the more she was forced to acknowledge that it wasn't. Deep down she'd always known and didn't want to acknowledge it. But she did have some kind of gift to restore through food.

Except maybe when it came to this man.

"What can I get you?" she asked. "Special today is pulled pork. I have six kinds of sauces. And the cannoli of the day is the peanut-butter cream."

"I actually came to tell you that I made a decision about my father and the prediction. My dad has business he can't just blow off this week. Which is crazy because when I was growing up, I would have loved for him to put his personal life before work. Now here I am, insisting he honor his commitments. I'm going to track down his Sarah for him."

Olivia froze. "You are? I thought the last thing you wanted was for him to find this mystery woman."

"I'm going to find her for him because I can do it quickly—it's my job to find people. And when I do find her and he feels absolutely nothing for her, I can prove once and for all that the fortune is a bunch of hooey. We can both get on with our lives."

Well, that sounded cynical, but everything inside her lit up at the idea of reuniting with her aunt. "So you've started the search?" she asked.

"No. I'll do some research tonight and hit the road tomorrow. I need to make this quick. I have a pending case and people counting on me."

"I'll help," she said. "And come with you to find her."

"What? Why would you want to do that?"

Olivia took a deep breath. She had to tell him. "Because this green-eyed hairstylist named Sarah with the brush-and-blow-dryer tattoo sounds exactly like my estranged aunt."

The hazel-green eyes narrowed.

* * *

Disappointment conked him over the head, then fury punched him in the stomach so hard he almost staggered backward.

He stared at Olivia and then turned and stalked away.

"Carson, wait!" she called.

He kept walking, wanting to put as much distance between himself and the lying, swindling Mack women as possible. A daughter, a mother, an aunt. All in cahoots.

"Carson!" she called and he could hear her chasing after him. "Please hear me out!"

He noticed some people stopping on the sidewalks, pausing in their window shopping. Busybodies.

He kept walking. He would not hear her out. There was nothing to hear. Of course she'd said she'd help him find "Sarah." He had no doubt Olivia Mack knew exactly where her aunt was. This was all probably one great big ruse to make this air of mystery around Sarah's whereabouts so that his father was pulled in even more. No one wanted what came easily. Damn, they were good at being lying swindlers. They reeled in Edmund Ford and now were playing the game, putting the aunt out of his reach just until the fantasy would take over any issues with reality. At this point, his father was in love with the fantasy. She was his predicted second great love, and that's all he'd need to know.

"Carson, please!" she called.

He kept walking, the cool February air refreshing against the hot anger spiraling inside him. He'd parked his car on a side street, and when he reached it, he got in and sped off toward Oak Creek.

When he opened the front door of his house, he

could smell apple pie in the air. Danny's sitter had made two pies with her little helper, and he was now napping. He let the sitter know he would be doing some research, then tiptoed into Danny's room. He watched his son's chest rise and fall, his own tense shoulders relaxing. Watching his son sleep never failed to relax him.

In his office, he sat down on the brown leather couch and pulled out his cell phone to call his dad and tell him this Sarah person was just Olivia's aunt and the fortune-teller's sister. And what a nice parting gift to hook up the family with a wealthy widower.

Cheap shot, Ford, he chastised himself.

He punched in his dad's cell number.

"Edmund Ford speaking."

"Dad, I just found out this supposed second great love of yours is the fortune-teller's sister. Clearly, you've been set up."

"Her sister?" Edmund said.

"Olivia told me the person Madam Miranda described sounds a lot like her estranged aunt. Down to the name, the job, the eye color and the tattoo."

Silence. His father was a smart man. Clearly he now knew this was a ruse and he probably felt exactly like Carson had on the street—sucker punched upside the head and in the gut.

"That's great!" Edmund said. "That means we have a last name! Maybe even a Social Security number to help track her down. And a physical description beyond eye color. This is great news."

Was Carson the crazy one? "Dad, are you telling me you don't think the fortune-teller made up this crazy prediction to land her sister a wealthy widower?"

"I did this to you, didn't I?" Edmund said.

"Did what?"

"Made you so cynical."

"Do you mean realistic?" Carson asked. "And yes, you probably did. But being realistic is a good thing, Dad. Being grounded in reality is a good thing."

"I'm going to find my Sarah with or without your help."

Click.

Without or without your help.

He'd heard those same words from Tug Haverhill, his neighbor at their old house in Oak Creek. Tug had two sons around the same age as Carson but he'd always invited Carson to throw a football or to come fishing. When Tug's younger son had turned eighteen, he'd run off to—according to a note he'd left—"see the world my way." Apparently, Tug Haverhill had been around a little too much for Brandon Haverhill, insisting Brandon follow the path he'd laid out—a certain college, then business school while working in the family corporation, and he had a great gal in mind for him, too, the daughter of a board member. All that had worked on his older son, but not Brandon.

When Carson had become a private investigator working for the Oak Creek police department, Tug had offered him a small fortune to find his son and bring him home "just to talk." Tug had told everyone in town that he'd hired Carson to find Brandon, and when Carson and Brandon arrived on the Haverhill doorstep a few days later, word spread that Carson could get the job done. Unfortunately, Brandon had come only to tell his father he'd never live his life any way but his own. His father was furious and Brandon left again. Carson had felt for Tug Haverill, who never did let go of his need to be right. In the end, folks only remembered that Carson had found Brandon when no one else could. He'd been hired to find everyone from long-lost relatives to runaway dogs to deadbeat dads to people like Brandon, who simply walked away from their lives without looking back.

Carson had never got the message. You held on too loosely, you lost people. You held on too tightly, you lost people. There was a "just right," Carson supposed, but he'd never mastered it. He'd tried both with his ex-wife, then found himself awkwardly saying and doing things that hadn't felt anywhere near right, and none of that had worked, either. His wife had left.

She left her own newborn, too, his father had reminded him. *That's not about you. That's about her.*

Well, Carson has chosen her, hadn't he? He'd fallen in love with a woman who had it in her to walk out on her own baby—and supposedly because the baby was a boy and not the girl she wanted. A boy who looked like Carson instead of her and was so frail he needed to be in the NICU for six weeks. In those acid-burning weeks that followed, Carson had pledged to put his son before all else; if he ever fell in love again, it would be with Mary Poppins.

But Mary Poppins was fictional, so Carson had pretty much spent the last year and a half alone.

Also fictional? The nonsense Olivia Mack was spouting about her shrimp po'boys and chocolate cannoli having magical powers. The entire Mack family were clearly nut-jobs and there was no way in hell he was leading to his father to one of them.

Carson stood. Yes. He'd find Sarah Mack himself to keep his father from missing important events this week. He'd assess her and introduce her to his father, who'd feel absolutely nothing for the fortune-teller's gold-digging sister, and voilà.

He entered the name *Sarah Mack* into Google, then realized he didn't even know if Olivia's aunt was married or not. A simple search brought him many Sarah Macks, but they were all either too young or too old to be Olivia's aunt. He tried "Sarah Mack, hairstylist" and there were two, but both were under thirty.

It would be a lot easier to find the woman if he knew more about her. That was one of the keys of finding people, he'd learned—you needed to know the little details. Something Carson had discovered early on was that people liked to be reminded of home even when home meant strife or bad memories or they thought they were running as far from home as possible. Once Carson had a sense of what meant home for someone, figuratively speaking, it made it much easier to find them.

And to learn something about this Sarah Mack, he needed some information from Olivia.

He stood up, grabbed his jacket, let the sitter know he'd back by six, then headed for Blue Gulch and Olivia Mack's little yellow house.

Chapter Four

Olivia sat on the red velvet divan in the back room of her house—her mother's fortune-telling parlor. After Carson had stalked off, she'd tried to reach him a few times, but he wouldn't answer his phone. She'd been so disconcerted by telling him the truth about the mystery woman and by his expected reaction that she'd gone home after her shift and thought she'd soak in a bubble bath and try to think about how to go from here. But instead she'd been drawn to her mother's parlor.

Olivia had always loved and hated this room. Loved it because it was very much her mother. The rich velvets and satins, the small treasures from her travels around the country and the world. Miranda Mack actually did have a crystal ball. She'd found it in a secondhand shop owned by a tiny woman who'd celebrated her hundredth birthday the day Miranda celebrated her seventeenth and had come into the San Antonio store. According to Miranda she'd picked up the ball and it had glowed, and the shop owner had smiled and said Miranda should take it as a birthday gift from one birthday girl to another. It now sat in its bronze holder on the rectangular table in the "fortune nook," separated from the main room by heavy red velvet drapes. The nook was like a mini version of the main room, full of red velvet and treasures dotting the walls and sidebars. As a girl, Olivia had always felt very safe and protected in the nook.

But then she'd turned seventeen and knew that was when her own gift, passed down from the maternal side of the family, would make itself known, and Olivia had been freaked out. She wanted to be like Aunt Sarah, who claimed not to have a gift and insisted the family abilities must skip around. But Olivia's ability to heal with food had presented itself, at first, imperceptibly. Sarah always refused to talk about the family gifts and Miranda would shrug, but Olivia always thought there were family secrets being kept from her. If only she *could* read minds.

Sweetie, her mother's old cat and her cat now, jumped up on the sofa and curled up beside Olivia. She gave the cat a scratch behind the ears and reached for one of the many photo albums her mother kept on the coffee table. She stared at the last bunch of photos of Aunt Sarah, a tall, pretty woman with wildly curly auburn hair, her signature scarf tied around her neck. In one photo she wore a skin-tight black dress, the little tattoo visible on her ankle. In another photo, Sarah had her arm around Olivia and was smiling at her with such love in her warm green eyes.

What could have happened between the Mack sisters to make Sarah run off? To estrange herself from her only sibling and the niece she'd seemed to care so much about?

There was a knock on the door—the back door, where her mother would meet her clients. Surprised, Olivia jumped up. She moved aside the layers of gauzy curtain at the door to see Dory Drummond wearing a T-shirt, jeans and a long white wedding veil. Dory, recently engaged after a whirlwind courtship, was an old friend and often helped Olivia with cooking prep for her clients or in the food truck to make some extra money.

Dory's expression was a combination of worry and resignation, but there was a smidgen of something else…but what?

She wants to do what's right but she isn't sure what that is.

Whoa. The thought slammed into Olivia so forcefully she took a step back.

Olivia opened the door. "Dory, what's wrong?"

"I'm sorry to bother you at home. I stopped by the food truck to ask if we could get together to talk sometime soon, but a guy said you were off." Olivia noticed she held the telltale yellow paper bag from the Hurley's truck. "I have two smothered, chicken-fried-steak po'boys if you're interested."

Olivia smiled. "One of my favorite kinds, especially when I didn't have to make it." She gestured at the round table by the window and Dory sat down, Olivia across from her.

Dory stared at the yellow bag. "I've been dieting since I've been engaged. But you know what? A Hurley's Homestyle Kitchen smothered chicken-fried-steak

po'boy sounds amazing, which is why I couldn't resist ordering it. My mother used to make chicken-fried
steak and mashed potatoes in her incredible gravy
every Sunday night." Tears poked at Dory's eyes and
Olivia had to blink back her own. The losses of their
mothers was something they'd gone through together.
But over the past few days, since Dory had gotten engaged, Olivia had the feeling Dory was avoiding her.

"I miss my mother's cooking, too," Olivia said,
reaching over and giving Dory's hand a squeeze.
Granted, Olivia was the cook in the family, but when
Olivia was a little girl, her mother would make her food
into smiley faces on her plate, cut holes in pancakes
for strawberry eyes and a sausage mouth. And every
night for as long as Olivia could remember, her mother
would make them both a cup of lemon-ginger tea and
they'd watch TV together or sit on the little porch with
the cat in Miranda's lap. Olivia missed that so much,
but she still wasn't ready to have lemon-ginger tea.

Dory squeezed her eyes shut, then opened them.
"Okay, I'm just going to tell you. I have to tell you. I
don't know what to do."

"Of course you can talk to me," Olivia said.

"Your mother is the reason I'm here."

Oh, no. Not again. Carson Ford was enough to deal
with where Miranda Mack had been concerned.

Olivia sighed inwardly. She noticed Sweetie pad
over and stare up at Dory. "Sweetie is, like, eighteen
years old, but I'm afraid she might leap on the table
and swipe at your beautiful long veil."

Dory's mouth dropped open and she reached up and
felt the veil, her expression telling Olivia she'd forgot-

ten it was on. She looked around, clearly embarrassed, took off the veil and folded it neatly into her tote bag.

"It was my mother's," Dory explained. "I tried it on at home…to see what it looked like, to know what it would feel like, and I got so… I guess I ran out to go to talk to you without realizing it was on. I must have looked like the biggest idiot running through town in a wedding veil."

Got so…didn't sound so good, Olivia thought.

"I'm sorry to just barge in on you like this," Dory said, her blue eyes full of worry.

"That's okay, Dory. Really."

Dory opened up the bag and slid out the po'boy and took a bite. "I'm not supposed to be eating this. Beaufort's mother made an appointment for me with her nutritionist and personal trainer. I'm only supposed to eat whole foods so I look my best for the wedding." She took another big bite. More tears poked her eyes.

"Dory, what's going on?" Olivia asked. Beaufort was her fiancé. From one of the wealthiest families in town, Beaufort had his eye on running for mayor and then state senate.

Dory reached down to pet Sweetie as though to prolong saying why she was here. "I never told you this, Olivia, but I went to see your mother just two days before she died. I asked her to tell me what she saw for me, and she looked me right in the eye and said she adored me like a daughter, but she couldn't hold back the truth to spare feelings or hopes and that I wasn't in love with Beaufort Harrington."

"Oh, no," Olivia said, her gaze drawn to the three-carat diamond ring sparkling on Dory's finger. "Did she say more?" When Madam Miranda made her pronouncements, she usually didn't elaborate. *People know the truth about themselves deep down*, her mother had always said. *I tell the truth. Some people either can't handle the truth or don't want the truth and they do as suits. Others can't deny what's just below the surface.*

"When Beaufort proposed, I was so surprised," Dory continued. "I thought for sure he'd throw me over for a woman more like his family—rich and cultured and all that. I mean, it was always kind of obvious to me that Beaufort had a crush on me but he'd never asked me out until just two months ago. Then he proposed a few days ago and I said yes…for a few reasons."

Huh. "Is love one of them?"

Dory hung her head. "My mother didn't have health insurance. Her care took everything. I've been working 'round the clock to pay off those bills and keep the bakery going. Can you imagine, Olivia, losing my mother and my father—and then the family business? Drummond's Bake Shop has been in my family for seventy-five years. I can't lose it. I told Beaufort all this, that I was in a heap of trouble financially and that he wouldn't want to marry someone in such financial straits, and he said he'd make all my financial problems go away."

"Because he loves you so much?" Olivia asked.

"I'm not sure if he does or not. I always ask why an ambitious, handsome banker from a wealthy family would pick me, of all the women in Blue Gulch, and he just says I'm what he wants." She shrugged. "I don't know. We don't have all that much in common. I can't quite figure out why he *did* propose."

"Well, maybe the reason *is* love," Olivia said.

Dory nibbled the po'boy. "I don't think so," she

whispered. "I know this is going to make me sound terrible, but it kind of made me feel okay about saying yes. He doesn't love me but wants to marry me for some reason. I don't love him, but need to marry him for a reason. I suppose we're both doing the other a favor. But…your mom telling me what I already knew—what she must have known I already knew—is throwing me. She must have focused on that for a reason."

Olivia stared at Dory, this lovely, petite blonde with angelic blue eyes and a sweet manner. She wanted Dory to have everything—her family bakery, love, her financial worries gone. "Did my mother say anything else?"

Dory shook her head. "She only said that I wasn't in love. She said it again as I was leaving." Tears filled her eyes. "I'm all alone in the world, Livvy. And just like in a fairy tale, a knight in shining armor rides up."

Except Dory didn't love her knight in shining armor. *Sometimes people don't want the truth and they do as suits…*

Dory's use of her childhood nickname made her heart clench. As teenagers, they used to spend so much time talking about the kind of man they wanted to marry someday. Being madly in love with someone who was madly in love back was first on the list.

"I'm sorry I dumped this on you," Dory said, putting her half-finished po'boy back in the bag. She stood up, slinging her tote bag on her shoulder. "I just needed to say it out loud to someone who I knew wouldn't judge me or advise me. I just needed to get it out, you know?"

Olivia stood up and went around the table and hugged her friend. "I know. And I know you'll do what feels right to you, Dory. Whatever that may be."

As Dory hugged her back, the doorbell rang. "I'll let you go, Liv. Thanks for listening."

Dory left and Olivia went to the front door. Carson Ford stood there. She was relieved to see him. And barely able to take her eyes off him. How could she be so drawn to a man who was so…her opposite?

"Isn't that Dory Drummond?" Carson said, upping his chin at Dory, who was getting into her beat-up old car, which was even older than Olivia's.

"Yes, she's an old friend. Why?" Olivia asked.

"She just got engaged to a close family friend," Carson said. "Beaufort Harrington. Our fathers go way back."

Just figures, Olivia thought. She would definitely keep quiet about the fact that Dory had been a client of her mother's.

"Carson, look, I really am sorry about all this with my mother and my aunt and your father. But I promise you, there is nothing underhanded about it. My mother wasn't that kind of person."

"Then help me prove it," he said. "I intend to find this Sarah person myself so that my father's life isn't interrupted or upended. I'll find her, introduce them, my dad will feel absolutely nothing for this stranger and he can go back to his life and I can go back to mine."

"How can I help?" she asked. "I've been trying to find my aunt Sarah since my mother died."

"We can start with her last name, Social Security number if you know it, details that will narrow the field."

"I've tried all that. Well, not her Social Security number. I don't know it."

"Well, then we're going to take a road trip."

* * *

Carson stood on Olivia's porch, unsure if he'd really just said those words. A road trip with Olivia, who he barely knew?

"Do you have a day off coming up?" he asked. "We can make some calls, find out which salons employ Sarahs and go check them out."

She opened the door wider. "Come on in. Coffee?"

"Biggest mug you have," he said, stepping inside.

He glanced beyond the small foyer to see a tiny living room with a green velvet sofa, a well-worn oriental rug and all kinds of decorations, from masks to little statues. Madam Miranda clearly hadn't been raking in the bucks, given the old scuffed wide-plank floors and the unrenovated kitchen he could see through a doorway. Interesting.

"Did you grow up here?" he asked, following her into the small kitchen. She gestured at the round white wood table by the window and he sat down.

"I was born in this house. I've lived here all my life."

"Did you used to listen in when your mother was telling fortunes?" he asked.

"I tried not to," she said. "To give her clients privacy. But sometimes I couldn't resist." She poured chocolately-smelling coffee grounds into the coffee-maker and pressed a button. "One time, my middle school science teacher came to see Madam Miranda. Mrs. Flusky was the meanest teacher at the school, never smiled, barked at kids. I eavesdropped when she came. It took her a good five minutes to ask her question. She said, 'How can I go on with this pain of losing my daughter?' I don't think anyone knew that Mrs. Flusky even had a daughter. But it turned out her daughter was just twenty-two when she was hit by a car."

He saw Olivia wince just saying those words. "What did your mother tell her?"

"My mother told Mrs. Flusky that by going on, by living her life, by teaching with passion, by going back to the activities she'd given up, like her book club and her garden and traveling, she would be honoring her daughter by honoring *life*. Which would always have its share of crushing sorrow, its days of the status quo and, of course, joy. Madam Miranda then asked Mrs. Flusky how she thought her daughter would feel to know that she'd given up all she used to enjoy because of her grief. Mrs. Flusky said her daughter would hate knowing how small and sad her life had become, that they'd been planning to travel the South together that summer, but of course she wasn't going."

Carson leaned forward, curious what else Madam Miranda had said.

"And then my mother reached under the table and pulled out a small flowerpot," Olivia continued. "She told my mother to plant her daughter's favorite flower in the pot. When the flower bloomed, that meant it was time for Mrs. Flusky to honor her daughter by blooming anew, respecting the new person she was in the face of the changes in her life, but by doing what she enjoyed. She also gave Mrs. Flusky three flower seeds and said she'd bet her daughter would love it if she planted each seed in the three places they'd planned to visit in July."

"And did Mrs. Flusky change? Did she go on the trip?"

"I waited every day to see a difference in her. Finally, after a few weeks, she came into the classroom with the flowerpot my mother had given her. There was a green shoot. She put it on her windowsill in the sun. And she was different from that day. Not in any big way, but she was nicer. She even smiled sometimes. And I'll never forget how she said that when the school year ended she was going to Atlanta, Savannah and Charleston." She set out two mugs of coffee, along with cream and sugar.

He added cream and a spoonful of sugar. "You do realize there was no fortune-telling involved there," he said. "No hocus-pocus. Just compassion and insight."

She nodded. "I do realize that. I thought about that session for a long time. Before that and after that I'd heard my mother tell people their fortunes, what she saw for them. But with Mrs. Flusky, she told her what she *needed*. When I understood that, I knew for sure that my mother was the real deal, Carson. She wasn't a con artist. She cared. And I also began to realize that she did tell people what they needed—whether through a fortune or just common sense. If what she saw wasn't what they needed, she wouldn't put it out there."

"So my father *needs* your aunt Sarah." He leaned his head back.

"He must," she said. "Crazy as that sounds."

"As long as you know it does sound crazy," he said, surprised to find himself giving her something of a smile.

He could see her visibly relax, her shoulders drop a bit. He felt like a heel for making her so tense, for storming into her life and making his family's problem hers, especially when she must still be grieving her mother's loss. He wanted to get up and go over to her and press his hands on those shoulders and massage away her tension.

She wore a white T-shirt with a faded ad for Blue Gulch Animal Rescue, the silhouettes of a dog and cat on her stomach. Her skirt was some kind of denim-patch thing and she was barefoot, a silver ring around one of her toes. He followed her tanned legs from the toe ring up the toned calves to where the skirt ended. He'd been physically attracted to women before, of course, but something about Olivia Mack drew him in a way he hadn't experienced in a long, long time.

He cleared his throat for no reason other than to shake himself out of his sudden fantasy of walking over to her and kissing her. He pulled out the little leather notebook with its tiny pen that he carried everywhere. "Is your aunt Sarah's last name also Mack?"

She nodded. "She wasn't married when she left town. Her name was Sarah Mack, no middle name. But I've done many online searches for her, putting in all kinds of search words, like hair salons, her name, et cetera. Nothing ever comes up."

"You referred to your aunt as your estranged aunt," he said, sipping his coffee. "What's the story there?"

Olivia sipped her own coffee. "I don't know the whole story. There's a big family secret I've been kept in the dark about. But I do know that my aunt told my mother she was never, ever to tell Sarah her fortune— she didn't want to know, she wanted to do what felt right to her, make her own mistakes. Maybe there came a time when my mother couldn't hold her tongue?" She shrugged. "It's complicated, that's all I know."

Her aunt sounded levelheaded, so that was a plus. He

wouldn't want to know his supposed fortune or future, either. "Do you think she's still in Texas?"

"I don't know for sure, but I suspect. Sarah loved Texas. She was a big rodeo fan."

"Oh, yeah?" he said. "That's a good start. People tend to run away to what comforts them. Tuckerville is a bustling town full of shops and restaurants and it borders Stockton, where the rodeo championships are held. Seems a good place to start." Tuckerville was just an hour away. Two hours driving, two hours visiting salons. Half a day's work and hopefully they'd find her.

"So we're going to just get in your car and go visit hair salons in Tuckerville and ask for Sarahs?"

He nodded.

"I'm off tomorrow," she said. "But I need to cook tomorrow afternoon for Mr. Crenshaw. It's his chicken parmigiana and garlic bread night. He counts on it."

Carson had no idea who Mr. Crenshaw was. "I'll have you back home by three. How's that?"

"Mr. Crenshaw likes to eat at five thirty. Getting home at three will be cutting it very close."

"I'll help you," he said. "I'm a pretty good cook. I've had to learn these past eighteen months for Danny's sake."

She tilted her head and stared at him for a moment. "Okay, then. Most hair salons open at ten, so why don't we leave at nine tomorrow morning."

Half a day's work and this nutty situation would be resolved. He figured, anyway. But he was well aware that for someone who wanted this lunacy finished and done with, he sure was looking forward to spending time with Olivia tomorrow.

Chapter Five

Olivia sat on her porch at nine sharp, waiting for Carson. A shiny black SUV pulled into the driveway and he hopped out to open the passenger door for her. Gallant, she thought, offering him a smile as she got inside.

"I bought us coffee," he said as he buckled up and pointed at the two foam cups in the console cup holder. "One cream, one sugar, right?"

For a moment she felt flattered that he'd noticed and had tucked away how she liked her coffee, then she remembered it was his job to notice details.

"Thanks," she said, taking a sip and glancing at him as he started the engine.

The bright sun lit his dark hair and she saw shades of brown and copper. He slid on aviator sunglasses that made him look like a state trooper.

"So where's Danny this morning?" she asked as they headed toward Blue Gulch Street.

"He goes to a day care he loves three mornings a week. He has two best buddies there. My dad will pick him up today and keep him until I return."

"Your dad is so great with Danny. So loving. I never had grandparents. My mother's mother died before I was born and no one ever talked about my grandfather. I didn't know my father or his family."

He looked over at her. "I didn't know my grandparents, either. It's one of the reasons I'm so protective of my dad right now. For Danny's sake."

"I can understand that," she said. "Your son is lucky to have you."

He glanced at her again and was quiet for a moment, then said, "When Danny's mother walked out on us, I was so worried that I wouldn't be enough as a dad. I mean, I know I'm not a laugh a minute. Not that my ex was, either, but she was very outgoing and bubbly. Thank God my dad morphed into an award-wining grandfather."

His ex-wife walked out on them? Olivia couldn't imagine. Hadn't Carson said his son had been in the NICU for a couple of months? Had his mother left while Danny had been in the hospital? She wanted to know more about Carson and his past, but she wasn't sure she should pry.

There was suddenly a hard set to his jaw and shoulders so she figured she'd better keep the conversation to their mission. She already thought too much about Carson, wondered too much, noticed him too much. "Did you let your father know that you're looking for Sarah?"

A muscle worked in Carson's jaw and he shifted. "I did."

"And?" she prompted, sipping her coffee.

"He was a little too touched," Carson said. "Even though I made it clear I'm not doing this to find his supposed second great love. I'm doing it to prove that he'll feel absolutely nothing for this woman so he can go back to living his life."

"What if he *does* feel something?" Olivia asked. "Yes, I know, power of suggestion, blah, blah, blah. But you can't fake chemistry, a pull toward someone, a quickening of your pulse, an inexplicable draw."

She knew because she felt it with Carson. She couldn't stop stealing peeks at him, the strong profile, the broad shoulders, the muscular thighs.

"It would be pretty random for my father to meet some stranger and fall instantly in love. I have no doubt he'll feel toward Sarah Mack the way he feels when he meets anyone. The earth won't move."

"What if it does?" she asked.

He looked at her, clearly frustrated. "It won't."

She couldn't help a chuckle. "You sure are set in your ways."

"You are, too."

"Nope," she said. "I'm open to possibility."

He didn't respond to that. He reached into the inside pocket of his leather jacket and pulled out a piece of paper. "This is a list of every hair salon in Tuckerville and the surrounding towns. There are six in Tuckerville. And then four more in the bordering communities. I called ahead—there are four stylists named Sarah in four of the salons. Two in the bordering towns. My dad didn't come out this far in his search. We very well may find your aunt this morning."

She glanced at the list, her heart skipping a beat.

Was Sarah Mack in one of these salons? Tears poked at her eyes, and Olivia realized she wanted to be reunited with Sarah so badly that it was overwhelming.

"We're here," he finally said, turning onto a bustling main road and pulling into a spot in front of a bakery. When she didn't move, he glanced at her. "Hey," he whispered. "Are those tears?" He lifted up her chin and brushed away the wetness under her eyes with the back of knuckle. "We'll find her."

For a moment she was so startled by his kindness that she just stared at his hand, now resting on his knee. "We want to find her for very different reasons," she said. "You want to end something. I want something to begin."

He nodded, then gave her hand a squeeze. "Well, that may be true. But at least you'll have her back, right?"

Olivia froze. "What if she doesn't want to be found? I mean, she clearly doesn't."

Carson turned off the ignition and turned to face her. "You know what I've learned most in my business of finding people? That ninety-nine percent of people who walk away *do* want to be found, even if they don't know it, even if they're not walking around with it burning in their chest the way it can be for the people doing the looking. It's not easy living with something unsettled—on either side."

"Ninety-nine percent," she repeated, liking that number.

He nodded and was around the car to open her door for her before she could even hitch up her purse on her shoulder.

Feeling a bit better about what might happen, she

got out and looked around. The busy downtown was divided by a four-lane road, with shops and restaurants dotting both sides. Tuckerville was a lot bigger than Blue Gulch.

"Hair Magic is two shops down," he said, pointing left.

Hair Magic. Nope. No way. Aunt Sarah, who hated magic, hated talk of the family gift, would not work in a salon with the word *magic* in the name. That she was a hundred percent sure of. She was about to tell Carson they should cross it off the list, but there it was, Hair Magic, right between a heavenly smelling bagel shop and a bookstore.

And anyway, what did she know about her aunt, really? Maybe she did work here. Maybe the word *magic* was just another word. Aunt Sarah had never been superstitious or sentimental. And it had been five years since she'd seen her. Five years. She used to think she and her aunt were close, but Sarah had walked away from her. Olivia and Sarah had never had an argument; it wasn't fair, but wasn't that the old line about life?

Hair Magic had a storefront painted silver with silver drapes in the window. A bell jangled as they entered. There was a reception desk with no one behind it and six hair stations; two women and one man, all in various stages of their work, had customers. A Shania Twain song was playing from a speaker on a sideboard with magazines laid out across it.

"Are either of the women your aunt?" Carson whispered. "They look young."

She shook her head. Both women were in their twenties. Aunt Sarah was forty-eight.

"Can I help you?" one of the women called out.

"I heard there was a hairstylist who works here named Sarah who's great with men's hair," Carson said.

Olivia supposed that was his line to get info.

The man beamed, which told Olivia he was the owner and liked the word-of-mouth praise for one of his employees. He eyed Carson's hair, which was thick but relatively short. "Sarah doesn't come in until ten thirty. If you want to wait, I'm sure she can squeeze you in before her eleven o'clock client."

"Could you describe her?" Carson asked. "My friend said Sarah is in her forties. Auburn hair?"

"That's Sarah," the man said.

Olivia's heart squeezed. Aunt Sarah worked here. She was coming in a half hour!

"Bingo," Carson said. "That was easy," he added on a whisper to Olivia. "We'll wait," he said to the owner.

Could it really be this simple? Olivia liked simple, but when was anything this easy? Their first day out, their first hair salon, their first try? Aunt Sarah materializes through a Tuckerville doorway?

They sat down on the padded bench. Olivia watched the man pull a big round brush through a blonde's wavy hair, straightening the tresses. She glanced at the clock on the wall—10:02 a.m. The anticipation was too much. This would be a long thirty minutes.

Carson took a little notebook from his jacket pocket and flipped through it. He nodded a couple times, jotted something down, then returned it to his pocket.

"What's your aunt like?" he asked.

Olivia thought of tall, strong Aunt Sarah. "Well, she's a bit private and always kept to herself, but when I was growing up she'd come see me a few times a week, help me study, take me shoe shopping, bring me MP3 players loaded with songs she thought I'd like. When I was getting my catering business off the ground she would post flyers for me in shops and bulletin boards all over Blue Gulch County. She sent me quite a few of my first customers."

Carson glanced at her. "She sounds kind."

"She is." Olivia wanted to add, *See, you don't have to worry about your dad and Sarah, she's wonderful, really.* But Carson would just say there would be no "Dad and Aunt Sarah" and cross his arms over his chest and glower, so she kept that to herself.

They sat and watched a woman get her highlights wrapped in foil and listened to the chitchat. Olivia now knew all about an affair going on in the stylist's family, the client's teenaged son's struggles in language arts class and how many bottles of color number twelve the salon needed to order.

"Have any earplugs?" Carson leaned over to whisper.

Olivia couldn't help but smile. She actually liked all the chatter and gossip and chitchat. She always worked alone—for years in her kitchen, cooking for her clients, and for the last few weeks in the food truck. *It's lonely,* a little voice acknowledged. Before, she'd go home to her mother, who never stopped talking. Now she went home to a silent house and constant reminders of her losses. *I do want to find you, Aunt Sarah,* she thought suddenly. *Very much.*

The bell jangled, and Olivia almost jumped. She glanced up at the big clock on the wall—10:25 a.m. Aunt Sarah? She looked over at the woman who entered. She was tall, like Sarah Mack. Auburn-haired, like Sarah Mack, though her aunt's hair was curly and this woman's was pin-straight. Of course, a flatiron could have made that happen. Big black sunglasses covered her face.

Olivia hadn't seen her aunt in five years, but she felt sure that she'd know her aunt anywhere. And this woman…wasn't Sarah Mack.

Olivia stayed in her seat, disappointment prickling her heart.

"Sarah Mack?" Carson said, standing up.

The woman turned to Carson and took off her sunglasses. Dark brown eyes looked at him quizzically. "Sorry. I'm Sarah O'Dalley."

Carson's shoulders slumped. "Oh. Sorry to bother you. I was looking for a different Sarah." He asked if the stylists knew of any Sarahs who worked out of their homes, but no one was sure.

Olivia finally stood up and he glanced at her, his expression softening at the sadness she couldn't hide from her eyes, the dashed hope. He put a hand on each of her shoulders. The heavy warmth felt good.

"Sorry," he said as they headed for the door. "I should have asked the owner if her last name was Mack before we bothered waiting." They stepped out into the bright sunshine. "But then again, she may have married and changed it—or changed it even if she didn't marry. We'll find her, though."

"I don't know," she said. "If a person doesn't want to be found…"

"It's one salon," he said. "Three more to check with Sarahs, and we can go to the other two just in case she changed her name entirely. If she's not in this town, we'll just keep looking. We'll find her."

Olivia shrugged. She wasn't so sure.

He stared at her for a moment. "You really miss her, don't you?"

She nodded. "She's my only family. My mother didn't marry my father and he just sort of disappeared before I was even born. I mentioned I didn't have grandparents. For the longest time it was just me, my mom and Aunt Sarah." A chill snaked its way around her body.

"And now it's just you," he said.

She nodded, looking away. "I had no way of getting in touch with Sarah about my mother's death. And I tried very hard to find my aunt then. Maybe it's wrong to look for her. Maybe I should respect her wishes."

"Except now it's about your mother's wishes," he said gently.

Yes. That was exactly it. She felt so comforted by the fact that he understood that she almost threw herself around him.

Until she remembered he had his own reason for finding Sarah Mack. And it had nothing to do with the last promise she made to her mother on her deathbed.

"We'll find her," Carson repeated with conviction. "I promise."

That was a big promise. And she'd do well to remember he was motivated by self-interest—saving his father from possible heartbreak and financial ruin by finding his supposed second great love so that his father could see there was nothing between them. That Sarah was just a stranger.

An hour later, Olivia and Carson had visited the five other salons in Tuckerville. There were three Sarahs. None was Olivia's aunt. They stopped in a coffee shop to ask around if anyone knew of a freelance stylist named Sarah who worked out of her home, but no one did.

"For all we know, my aunt is working in a salon across the state, nowhere near a rodeo," Olivia said as they walked out of the coffee shop. "But it was a good try. She did love watching the rodeo."

Carson stared at her for a moment, gently pulling her out of the way of a man walking six dogs. "You know what we need?" he asked.

"What?" Olivia asked.

"Lunch."

She smiled. She was pretty hungry now that she thought about it.

He glanced around at the many restaurants and cafés on both sides of the main street. "Fancy or the bagel place for chicken salad on everything bagels?"

"The bagel place," Olivia said. "For tuna salad on a sesame bagel."

He nodded and took her hand, leading the way. His hand tight against hers felt so good she wanted to kiss him.

Grr. She had to be careful where Carson Ford was concerned. It was one thing to appreciate a man's handsome face and rock-hard body and deep voice and so on and so on, with Carson's many physical attributes. It was another to have her heart responding to him.

And it was, darn it.

As Carson turned on Blue Gulch Street, he remembered that he'd promised Olivia he'd help her cook for whoever this Mr. Crenshaw was.

"So what did you say we're making Mr. Crenshaw?" he asked as he pulled behind Olivia's car in her driveway.

"I won't hold you to helping me," she said. "If you need to get back to your work or go pick up Danny, I'll understand."

"I spent three hours early this morning on the case I'm working on. And my father complains he doesn't get enough time with Danny, so it's fine to leave them together for a couple extra hours."

"Well, then, we're making chicken parmigiana with garlic bread and a side of linguine in red sauce, one of Mr. Crenshaw's favorites. I make it from a recipe his wife had handed down from her great-grandmother."

As they headed inside Olivia's little house, she explained about her clients and their various dietary plans. Mr. Crenshaw was her secret favorite, she said. An eighty-seven-year-old widower who lived at the local assisted-living center but grumbled about the food. So Olivia cooked for him three times a week at a very big discount.

The moment Carson stepped through the doorway, the black-and-white cat weaved between his legs and he reached down to pet her. She rubbed her head against his shin, her long white whiskers stark against his charcoal pants.

Olivia smiled. "If my mother had witnessed that, she'd say you were okay, that Sweetie knows her people."

Carson raised an eyebrow. "A psychic cat. Just what the world needs."

She laughed, the sound making him happy. She hadn't laughed much today.

He followed Olivia into the kitchen, aware of the sway of her hips in her skirt, the way the late afternoon sun streaming in through the bay window lit the brown hair that hung in waves past her shoulders. She handed him an apron but he was so busy staring at her lips that he dropped it.

He scooped it up. "Olivia Mack, Personal Chef and Caterer" was embroidered in white script along the big red pocket.

"Put me to work," he said. "Should I be on linguine or chicken?"

"If you could take care of the linguine and the salad, I can focus on the chicken. My kitchen is yours, so just open the fridge and cabinets at will."

He wasn't really that much of a cook. He made breakfast and dinner for him and Danny every night. French toast was Danny's favorite so that was in heavy rotation in the mornings. As were homemade chicken fingers with sweet potato French fries for dinner. Then there was his mother's meat loaf recipe. Spaghetti in marinara sauce. Omelets stuffed with cheese and vegetables, which Danny gobbled up. He could handle linguine and a salad, though he doubted it would be up to a personal chef's usual level.

An array of pots and pans dangled from a rack above the stove. As he moved to the cabinets to search for the pasta pot, he brushed against Olivia, who was pulling the chicken breasts from the refrigerator. He wanted to take the chicken out of her hand, toss the pot and lean her up against the fridge and kiss her senseless. He wanted to but, of course, he pretended great interest in filling up the big pot with water. He glanced over at Olivia, and she glanced at him.

Had she felt the jolt, too? Had she felt nothing? He had no idea. Usually he could tell when a woman was as attracted to him as he was to her, but Olivia seemed very neutral to him. *Too* neutral, given what had brought them together and was still before them in finding her aunt.

He smiled. Maybe she was just as attracted.

"Thinking of something?" she asked as she covered the chicken in flour.

"I'm thinking that it's very comforting to watch someone cook. My mother was a great cook. She was obsessed with Julia Child and making her way through her giant cookbook. No chicken fingers for me as a kid. I was eating beef bourguignonne at three. Danny's probably lucky I'm not a great or adventurous cook. He hates mushrooms."

Olivia laughed. "Your mother sounds wonderful."

"She was," he said. "Did you learn to cook from your mom?"

She shook her head. "Madam Miranda wasn't much of a cook, but she had a few favorites that she learned to make. Cooking was never big in my family."

"Who taught you?" he asked as he set the back burner to high.

"I just always knew. When I was five, I could make a three-course dinner."

Her "gift," supposedly. Which Carson didn't want to think about or talk about. People had talents. Olivia's was cooking. End of story.

"Won't Mr. Crenshaw be disappointed when he tastes my rubber pasta and marinara sauce without enough pepper?" he asked as he salted the water for the linguine.

She eyed the pot. "You seem to know what you're doing. And besides, I'm watching. Closely."

He stopped stirring the linguine and stared at her. There was the slightest hint of flirtation in that last word. Her cheeks flushed and she turned back to her chicken. Suddenly she was very involved in making homemade bread crumbs and seasoning them. Hmm. Maybe she was as aware of him as he was of her.

He had the urge to walk up behind her and smell her hair. Breathe her in. Wrap his arms around her. When he used to think about what marriage would be like, he used to think about that. Doing boring everyday things, but while making out.

He turned his attention back to the water. Marriage. Ha. Marriage had gotten him all alone with a son who lately had been saying, "My mommy?" And because Carson knew exactly what Danny was asking, he wasn't going to pretend he didn't just because it was so damned painful to answer.

You have a mommy, he'd say. *But she had to go away.*

Mommy back? Danny would say, his hazel-green eyes just curious, not sad, not heavyhearted like his father's always were. Danny had never known his mother and at eighteen months, he was still young enough not to realize that something wasn't right about why his mother wasn't in his life.

All I know for sure is that if your mother knew you, she'd be unable to stay away from you, Carson would say, his heart feeling like it might implode. Explode.

Choc bunny? his son would say then, and relief would flood Carson's veins and he'd hand him the little chocolate bunny he'd bought as a treat and let Danny nibble an ear.

Danny's sweet face came to mind, his absolute trust in Carson. What was he doing, thinking about kissing Olivia Mack? Romance and love led to heartache and loss, and Carson had taken himself out of the running for that end result. He needed all the room in his heart for Danny.

Somehow he'd have to resist Olivia Mack. He'd make the salad, get the sauce going and then he'd leave. Olivia could handle the garlic bread.

Except as he was opening the fridge to find the lettuce, she was about to do the same and they collided. She was a half inch from him, flour on her cheek. Before he could think, he leaned down and kissed her, then took her face in his hands and deepened the kiss, opening his eyes when he dragged his mouth away from hers, dying to see her beautiful face.

She wrapped her arms around his neck and he kissed her again, harder, longer, and backed her against the counter, the scent of her soap and seasoned bread crumbs assailing him.

Sweetie the cat meowed so loudly that they both pulled back and stared down at the black-and-white cat staring up at them with her amber-stone eyes.

"You did say the cat was psychic," he said, stepping back. "So clearly it's a sign that we shouldn't be..."

"She's not really psychic," Olivia said and he tried to read the expression in her eyes, but all he got was *neutral*. She was good at masking how she felt. Or maybe this wasn't such a big deal. A hot kiss in a hot kitchen. That's all it was. He just didn't go around kissing women in kitchens or anywhere, for that matter. So it was a big deal. And he had the feeling it was for her, too.

"If I'm late with dinner, Mr. Crenshaw will pace the hall at the assisted-living center," she said. "So we should really get back to cooking."

He opened the fridge again and pulled out the lettuce. And a cucumber. And the tomatoes. He reached around Olivia's sexy form for a knife and began chopping and slicing. Once the salad was done, he asked Olivia about dressing, but apparently Mr. Crenshaw liked plain old olive oil and vinegar, which he had in his room. It turned out that Olivia had made the marinara sauce that morning, so he was done here.

"I guess I'll be in touch when I have some news about your aunt," he said. "Now that I have the basic information and the photos you gave me, I can work on my own."

"Oh," she said, the neutral expression back on her pretty face.

He might have thought she really didn't care either way, but the set of her shoulders, the way she held herself so stiffly, told him she did. He wanted to go over and massage them, tell her that he was just…what? Closed off? Closed, period? Refusing to start something he couldn't finish because he didn't want to hurt her? And that he would hurt her because he didn't believe in romance or love anymore? Yes. All that.

"Okay," she said, turning to face him for a moment before laying a piece of mozzarella cheese on the chicken. He could see the cloud in her eyes. "Thanks for helping."

He nodded. "See you around," he said and shot out of there. But he stood on her porch for a good long minute, wishing he could go back inside and prolong what they *had* started.

Chapter Six

Olivia had not heard from Carson in two days. She assumed that meant he hadn't found her aunt and was still looking. She also assumed that meant he regretted his impulsive kiss.

She didn't.

All day today and yesterday she'd hoped he'd come to the food-truck window, but he hadn't made an appearance. That kiss had been hovering in the air between them for a while and she thought it was better that it was acted on than ignored. *Ignoring the truth is among the worst things for your health*, her mother used to say.

So Olivia hadn't ignored the truth of her growing feelings for Carson Ford on all levels and when he kissed her, she kissed him back. Two days ago, while they'd been cooking together in her small kitchen,

she'd barely been able to concentrate on Mr. Crenshaw's chicken parmigiana. In fact, she'd been so focused on her feelings for Carson that she must have
infused the chicken with some passion because one of
the assisted-living nurses reported that Mr. Crenshaw
had asked a lady to dance at the weekly social for the
first time since arriving two years earlier.

She was sure she'd see Carson tonight at the engagement toast Dory's mother-in-law-to-be had quickly
put together for family and close friends in the Harrington mansion, where Olivia was now helping Dory
get ready. Like Dory, though, Olivia was used to being
part of the staff as a caterer in homes like this one, but
tonight, the party was in Dory's honor and Olivia was
a guest whose only job was to mingle and sip champagne. Since Carson had mentioned that his family and
the Harringtons were old friends, she was sure he and
his father would be here.

"Zip me up?" Dory asked, looking everywhere but
at her reflection in the ornate gold standing mirror
in the corner of Dory's "dressing room." Beaufort's
mother, Annalee Harrington, had insisted Dory prepare for the party at the mansion, as it was always referred to, in her own special "readying room." Dory
had called Olivia and begged her to come to the party
an hour early for support more than anything.

Olivia zipped up the back of Dory's stunning midnight blue velvet dress. She stood behind Dory in front
of the mirror, aware that her friend could barely look
at herself. "Dory, this is all happening so fast and you
seem to be getting swept up in it. If it's too fast, you can
slow it down. I can let Mrs. Harrington know you're

not feeling well and the party can be put off. You can have some time to really think about this."

Dory finally looked at herself in the mirror. "I have thought about it—a lot. I do like Beaufort. I'm sure I'll grow to love him. We have nothing in common, really, but soon we'll have family in common, right? And meanwhile, my family's bakery will be saved. After paying the last of my mother's hospital bills, I have two hundred and fourteen dollars left in my bank account. I had to let go of my last employee at the bakery because I couldn't pay another week. She was a single mother, Livvy." Tears glistened in Dory's eyes. "Beaufort picked me, the girl from the wrong side of the tracks with only a falling-down bakery to her name. That means something to me, even if it shouldn't. I think he does really love me. I'm sure I'll grow to love him."

Olivia looked at her friend's reflection. "Dory Drummond, you have a good head on your shoulders. I know you'll do right by yourself. If that means marrying Beaufort, so be it. If that means telling him you can't, so be it, too."

"Thanks, Livvy," Dory whispered with a nod.

There was a knock on the door.

"Come in," Dory called, lifting her chin and clearly trying to shake away her concerns.

Annalee Harrington swept into the room in her own exquisite dress, a tea length rose-gold silk. Her blond hair had been expertly put up into a chignon. How she walked on those four-inch heels, Olivia would never know.

"Dear, of course you'll wear *these* earrings," Annalee said, ignoring Olivia as she gestured at the dangling diamond-and-gold earrings on a velvet pad on the dresser. "I chose them specifically to go with the dress I picked out for you for tonight."

Dory reached her hands up to her ears. She glanced at the earrings on the dresser. "Those are gorgeous, Annalee, but my mother gave me these pearl earrings. I wear them for all special occasions."

Annalee frowned. "Dear, those are everyday pearls. And if I may be honest, they look a bit…" She leaned in close. "Are they even…real pearls?"

"I think so," Dory said. "Thank you for the dress and all this," she added, sweeping her arm out, "but I *am* wearing my mother's earrings."

Annalee stared at Dory long and hard, then her eyes lit up for a moment as if something had occurred to her. "I suppose it'll take some time." She glanced at Olivia and scooped up the fancy earrings and walked toward the door. "You're expected to make your entrance down the stairs at exactly six when you'll be announced as Beaufort's bride, Dory. Please don't be late."

"I won't be," Dory said, and Annalee left.

Dory frowned. "Did you feel the arctic blast in here or was that just me?"

Olivia still felt the chill in the room. "Well, you stood up to her about the earrings. So if you're going to marry Beaufort, at least we both know you won't be pushed around by Annalee."

Dory gazed at her reflection, reaching up to touch the pearls again. "Why do you think that the only thing your mother would tell me was that I wasn't in love with Beaufort? To make me acknowledge what I already know but don't want to think too deeply about?"

"Probably," Olivia said.

"I keep thinking about the difference between need

and want. I want real love. But I need to think about my present and future and make sensible decisions. How can I be sure I'll ever find real love anyway?"

It wasn't meant as a question. And it didn't matter what Olivia thought. People married for all sorts of reasons. Sometimes love was way at the bottom of those reasons. Olivia knew that one of her bosses, Annabel Hurley, had initially agreed to marry rancher West Montgomery in a deal. He'd save her family business, the restaurant, and she'd be the "perfect" stepmother his in-laws required so they wouldn't seek custody and try to take away his young daughter. They married and now were madly in love. But love hadn't brought them down the aisle. Maybe things would work out like that for Dory.

"What do you think Annalee meant by 'I suppose it'll take some time?'" Dory asked.

"I really don't know. Time for you to adjust to the big change in lifestyle?"

"That makes sense." She looked around the room. "Though I don't think I ever will. It's almost six. I'd better get ready for the big entrance."

"I'll see you downstairs," Olivia said. "You do look lovely, Dory."

Her friend smiled as best she could and Olivia slipped out of the room and down the beautiful, curved stairwell. On her way, she looked around for Carson and spotted him talking to his father and a small group of people, a few of whom she recognized as customers of her food truck.

Carson looked so handsome in his charcoal suit and red tie. Because she was staring at him, he looked over and headed her way.

"You look beautiful," he said.

"Thank you. You clean up well yourself." She had a flashback of herself pressed up against the counter in her kitchen, his lips on hers. If he was remembering, too, he showed no sign of it.

A bell jangled and everyone quieted. Annalee Harrington, flanked by her husband, stood on the first step of the staircase. "May I present my dear son's lovely bride-to-be, Dorothea Drummond. They are engaged to be married!"

Dory descended to much clapping. Olivia could tell by the look on her friend's face that she'd made some sort of peace with her decision, at least for tonight. She was engaged, the party was to toast that, and they would all do so.

After circulating a bit, Dory came up to Olivia and Carson. "I didn't know you two knew each other." Dory explained to Olivia that she and Carson had met at a fund-raiser Beaufort had taken Dory to.

"Olivia is helping me with a case," Carson said.

Reminding her that that was really all there was to them.

"Dory! Congratulations," Edmund Ford said as he walked over to join them. "Beaufort is an old family friend. His dad and I go way back to prep school, and, of course, we've been on the board together at Texas Trust for decades. I've known Beaufort since the day he was born. Good man you're marrying."

Dory smiled. "I recognize you from the bakery. How's that sweet grandson of yours? Bring him into the bakery tomorrow—I'm making his favorite rainbow cookies."

"Oh, I'll be sure to," Edmund said.

As Dory was swept away by others wanting to congratulate her, Edmund leaned close to Olivia and whispered, "Thank you for helping to look for my Sarah. I know she's your Sarah, too, and, according to Carson, you want to find her as badly as I do."

"She's the only family I have left," Olivia said before sipping her champagne. "I promised my mother I would deliver a note and a family heirloom. It means the world to me to make good on that."

"Your mother must have known you'd find her," Carson said. "Or she never would have made you promise."

Olivia almost dropped her glass. Yes. He was right. Of course her mother had known she would find Sarah. Miranda Mack would never have burdened Olivia with an unable-to-be-fulfilled deathbed wish.

"I suppose this means he's coming around," Edmund said, clapping Carson on the back.

Was that steam coming out of Carson's ears?

"I'm not coming around to believing in fortune-telling if that's what you're saying, Dad," Carson said. "But you're right—from what Olivia has said about her mother, Miranda wouldn't have made her daughter promise something she didn't think she could come through on. Simple deduction. Nothing to do with Miranda knowing the future."

"Well, whatever your reasons for finding my green-eyed hairstylist, I'm just grateful," Edmund said, his voice lower. "And it means a lot to me that you're on my side about something so important to me, Carson. Again, no matter the reasons why you're trying to find Sarah. Hope is a good thing."

Olivia could plainly see that Carson was conflicted. "That we can all agree on," she said.

But Carson placed his almost-full glass of champagne on a passing waiter's tray, said, "Excuse me," to his father and Olivia and walked away.

Carson was standing at the far end of the patio, staring at the lights that had been hung in the backyard, barely aware of the guests surrounding him, talking and laughing and sipping champagne. He made his appearance, he'd congratulated Beaufort and the family and now he wanted to go home to his son.

His father's crazy romantic quest, the engagement toast, the constant talk of love and marriage and happy endings all had Carson's stomach twisted. Every time he looked over at Beaufort and Dory arm in arm, he wanted to yell, *Don't do it! One of you will walk out on the other the minute something isn't perfect.*

The interesting thing was, every time he looked over at Beaufort and Dory, he could tell that something wasn't quite right *already*. They sure didn't look like or act like a couple in love. It was Carson's job to notice and pay attention, and body language spoke volumes. They didn't lean toward each other, into each other. They didn't stare into each other's eyes. Carson had known Beaufort Harrington a long time, since he was a kid. They didn't grow up in the same town, but their families spent a lot of time together, the two bankers glued to their phones while the boys explored backwoods and sneaked onto ranches to watch the huge bulls. For a long time, Beaufort had wanted to be a rancher but his father had said that no Harrington would be a two-bit cowboy and that was the end of that, despite the fact that Beaufort was now twenty-five years old. But every time Beaufort was around livestock and horses, his eyes lit up. The man's eyes didn't light up that way when he looked at Dory. And granted, Carson didn't know Dory, but this was not a woman excited about her pending nuptials, either.

Something was up about the engagement. He didn't know what, but it couldn't just be his so-called cynicism talking. The whole thing made him want to leave. Good love was bad. Bad love was bad. You couldn't win.

As he turned to head inside he saw Olivia talking to Dory and something shifted inside him. He felt it, an actual physical, tangible movement in his chest. She was beautiful in her pale yellow dress and strappy gold sandals, her long brown hair down around her shoulders, her full lips a pinky red. He'd avoided her for the past two days when all he was doing was thinking about her. But tonight was a reminder that he needed to just get this job done so it would be over. Including the time he'd need to spend around Olivia. He was starting to care about her—he did care about her—and he didn't want to. He was done with all that. It was him and Danny now, a unit, a twosome, and he'd devote his time and attention to his son, be the father he wished he'd had.

Olivia looked over at him just as his phone rang. His sitter.

Danny was throwing some kind of tantrum. He'd woken up screaming and yelling. Night terrors, the sitter thought. He let the sitter know he was on his way and would be there in minutes.

As he neared Olivia, he had every intention of just hurrying out toward the door but he found himself stopping.

Needing her.

What the hell?

"Danny is up and throwing the tantrum of all tantrums, according to his sitter," he whispered. "I have to go."

"I'll come help," she said and followed him out the door. "I'll text Dory that we needed to leave."

He didn't stop her, didn't say *I've got this*. For someone who didn't believe in much of anything these days, he sure did want her by his side right now.

Danny was indeed screaming his little head off. Olivia could hear him as she and Carson neared the front door of his house. The moment they entered, it was clear that the poor sitter seemed about to cry herself. As Carson took a screeching Danny from her, he tried bouncing the toddler on his hip and assuring the sitter it was all right, that Danny probably just had bad dreams or had an upset tummy. But Danny continued to cry his eyes out and kick.

Olivia watched Carson try everything in his arsenal to calm his son, but nothing worked. She wanted to take Danny herself and give something a try, but she was hesitant; she wasn't a mother and had zero babysitting experience. When the little boy let out a wail that almost split her eardrums, Olivia reached for Danny and, exasperated, Carson handed him over.

Olivia held Danny flat against her in his green footie pajamas, his head on her chest, and gently rubbed his back while singing a silly old camp song her mother used to sing when she was little about a meatball on top of spaghetti. Danny stopped fidgeting. He quieted down. When she was up to the second verse, Danny had stopped crying altogether. He peered at her, rubbed his eyes and seemed to be listening and fighting sleep at the same time.

"Again," Danny mumbled when she finished the song, his eyes closing and opening.

She was aware of Carson and the sitter staring at her as they stood by the door.

"Oh, thank heavens," the sitter whispered. "I'm so sorry I had to interrupt your evening. I should have been able to calm him down."

"It's no problem at all," Carson told her. "And you're wonderful with Danny. Sometimes it takes someone he barely knows."

That would be me, Olivia thought.

Carson said he'd see the sitter out to her car and would be back in a moment. By the end of the third run-through of the song, Danny was fast asleep. She held him against her, breathing in his baby shampoo, loving the sweet weight of him. She could hold him all night.

Carson came back in and smiled. "Baby whisperer."

She was about to say that the Mack women weren't known for that, but thought better of it. "Where's his room? I'll lay him down."

Carson led the way into the nursery. The room was painted a pale blue with stenciled sailboats lining the walls. Olivia gently lowered the toddler into the crib. He let out a sigh and continued sleeping.

They left the nursery, keeping the door ajar, and headed back in the living room. "I don't know how you did it," Carson said, "but I owe you. Big. Nightcap?"

"Actually, I'd love a cup of tea. Cream and sugar, if you have."

He nodded and went into the kitchen. She glanced

around, surprised by how cozy his house was. She hadn't known what to expect. It wasn't a mansion like his dad's house, but it wasn't a bungalow like hers. The home itself was a stately Colonial, white with a red door. The interior was toddler-friendly, with two big, plush sofas in durable brown leather, thick rugs, beanbags and floor pillows.

Carson returned with two mugs of steaming tea. She could smell the lemon from where she sat on the love seat.

"Thanks," she said, taking one of the textured blue mugs.

"I should be thanking you over and over. Now I know what song to sing him to calm him down."

She smiled and blew on the tea. *I want a baby*, she thought out of nowhere. *I want a baby of my own. A husband. A family.*

She did, she realized. She'd dated her last boyfriend for almost three years, and when he broke up with her out of the blue and proposed to a woman he'd met the week before—*when you know, you know*, he'd said— she'd been heartbroken. Her mother had tried to tell her, of course, but Olivia had refused to listen. Now, a year later, the ex and his wife were expecting a baby, per the announcement she'd read in the *Blue Gulch County Gazette*. At least he'd moved to his wife's hometown so she didn't have to see them all the time. Since then, she'd closed herself off to romance, cooking by herself, being hermit-like, determined not to meet anyone new and get her heart smashed again.

But she had met someone new. A handsome private investigator named Carson Ford. A divorced father of a little boy. And all those dreams had come roaring back to life. Marriage. Motherhood. Family. A unit.

To get the thoughts out of her head, thoughts that were dangerously veering toward a fantasy that the toddler she'd laid down in his crib was hers and that this handsome man sitting next to her was also hers, she blurted out the first thing that came to mind.

"So what case are you working on now? I mean, besides your father's."

He took a sip of his tea and set it down on the coffee table. "Well, the names are confidential, of course, but my client is a nine-year-old boy."

"Nine?" Surely Olivia had heard wrong.

"Nine. His father up and left three years ago. He left a note on the boy's pillow saying that he loved him but that the boy would be better off without him. He left a note on his wife's pillow, my client's mother, saying he was sorry but she always knew he wasn't cut out for this."

Olivia sighed. "'This' being adulthood?"

"Exactly," he said. "Marriage. Parenthood. Bills, responsibilities, not drinking himself drunk every night."

"The boy hired you to find his dad?" she asked.

Carson nodded. "He came to my office in Oak Creek. He put a shoe box full of one- and five-dollar bills on my desk and asked if it would be enough to hire me. I listened to his story and then told him that normally, no, his thirty-seven dollars in allowance and birthday money from his grandparents wouldn't be enough, but that sometimes, PIs took cases pro bono, meaning the client wouldn't have to pay. So I gave him back his shoe box and said he had himself a private investigator."

Dammit. The last of her flimsy hold on not falling hard for this man just...*poof*—vanished into nothing. Carson Ford was very kind.

"I let my young client know I'd need to talk to his mother, of course, and he said he was pretty sure she'd tell me not to bother looking for his dad, that the guy didn't want to be found. I went to see her and that's what she said, but if I wanted to waste my time trying to find him, fine."

"Any leads?" Olivia asked.

"He's off the grid, that's all I know right now. No arrests, no traffic stops, not using credit cards, hasn't applied for jobs with his Social Security number. If he's working, he's off the books."

She sipped her tea, the lemony heat soothing. "I suppose the boy knows you might not find him."

"Or that I will find him and it won't be what he expects. The man might not agree to come see his son even one time. Or he might be passed out drunk and unreachable. Sometimes you don't know what you'll find when you go looking."

She wondered what she'd find when they located Sarah. Would her aunt be bitter and cold? Unwilling to talk? Unwilling to accept the letter and family heirloom from her sister? Or would she be happy at the sight of her niece, whom she hadn't seen in five years?

Olivia had no idea how Sarah would react.

"It's brave of the boy to seek out his dad," Olivia said.

"It is, especially because his mother *did* prep him that he might not like what he finds." Carson leaned his head back against the couch, looking up at the ceiling. "Sometimes I think about Danny seeking out his mother someday. I don't know if she'll come back to see him on her own or if he'll look for her."

"I don't know how people just up and leave," she said, wrapping her hands around the hot mug to ward off the shiver that crept along her spine. "My aunt, your ex-wife, your young client's dad. It's sad enough that we lose people involuntarily. But to think about someone you love just walking away from you." She shook her head. "I'll never understand."

"Me, either," he said, reaching over to squeeze her hand.

He leaned his head back against the couch again and she couldn't take her eyes off the column of his neck, his strong jaw. She had the urge to reach up and run a finger across the hard line. "I used to think my father might as well have been gone," he said suddenly. "When I was a kid and teenager, nothing was as important to Edmund Ford as Texas Trust and the office. But he came home every night. Very late, but he came home. And he was never around on weekends and spent family vacations on the phone with the office. But every morning, every night, there he was."

"It's so hard to reconcile the man he is now with the father you grew up with," she said.

He picked up his mug. "I know. I want to be closer to him, but there's a brick wall there."

"That you built?"

He nodded. "I suppose it was a defense mechanism from when I was a kid, dealing with the disappointment of my father missing my birthday parties or school events or making promises to take me fishing and then canceling the morning of. That kind of thing."

"He sure is trying now," she said.

"That's true." He took a sip of tea. "I've narrowed down another couple of towns near the Stockton rodeo," he said, and she wasn't completely sure if he was changing the subject. Finding Sarah was about his dad, after all. "I called ahead and there are three Sarahs in the right age range. If you're free tomorrow afternoon, we could hit the road. I have a few leads on my young client's father in that area that I'd like to check out if you don't mind a brief detour."

"Tomorrow afternoon would be great," she said.

"Thanks again for everything you did tonight for Danny. Of course, now I'm going to call you at three in the morning when he wakes up with night terrors again or bad dreams or whatever this was."

Kiss me, she wanted to whisper.

But she didn't and he didn't kiss her. He did look at her, long and hard, and she thought he might be remembering their kiss in her kitchen.

"I'm sorry about the other day," he said. "When I kissed you. I have no business starting something I can't—"

"Can't what?" she asked.

"You're a really lovely person," he said. "I don't want to hurt you."

Ah. He either wasn't really attracted to her, didn't like her that way, or he just wasn't looking for something serious, and she struck him as the serious type. She had heard that one before.

"Maybe I'd hurt you," she countered.

"I'm impervious," he said and stood up.

Which meant he wanted her to leave. She swallowed back the little lump in her throat. She didn't want to leave.

Good Lord, she was falling in love with a man who'd just told her romance was off the table.

She didn't need Madam Miranda's crystal ball to know what was in her future if she didn't get a grip about Carson Ford.

Chapter Seven

The next day, Olivia had record sales of both po'boys and cannoli. She attributed it to both the day's specials—cheeseburger po'boys, a big hit with kids, and pumpkin-cream cannoli—and the gorgeous weather, a sunny, breezy fifty-nine degrees. The food truck had lines all morning into the afternoon, people with their faces tilted up to the sun as they waited.

Right before she was ready to turn over the truck to Dylan, the eighteen-year-old whiz-kid cook at Hurley's Homestyle Kitchen, a very handsome man with an adorable toddler on his shoulders came to the window and ordered a cheeseburger po'boy with lettuce, tomato and ketchup on one half, plain on the other.

"I'll bet the works half is for you, Danny," Olivia said to the little boy with a smile.

Danny grinned. "Burger!"

Olivia grinned back at her favorite toddler. "Some-one is in a better mood today," she said to Carson.

"He woke up smiling and raring to play."

"Well, one cheeseburger po'boy, half plain, half with the works coming right up."

As she worked on their po'boy, she wondered what she would be infusing it with. Happiness. Love. Hope.

She wondered if it would have any noticeable effect on Carson. He'd been immune to the last po'boy she'd made him.

She added the lettuce, tomato and ketchup and sliced the sandwich, and then handed it through the window. She tried not to take his money, but he insisted and refused the change from his twenty.

"You look very nice today," Carson said. And since she had garlic mayo on her shirt and flour on the ends of her hair, which was up in some lopsided bun-ponytail, he must have really thought so. "See you at three at your house for the trip to Stockton," he added. "I'm going to drop off Danny at my dad's, then I'll swing by."

She smiled and watched him walk over to one of the tables on the town green. He handed Danny the plain half, and Danny took a bite. She watched Carson take a bite of his half. Then another, then another, then another. If any big or small changes were going on within the man, she had no idea. Danny, on the other hand, still had three quarters of his half left and was adorably, saying, "Burger!" to anyone who passed by. When they finished and left, Olivia immediately missed them.

Penny Jergen, the local beauty queen and barista who'd been teary-eyed over her cheating fiancé last week, sashayed over to the food truck and ordered a veggie po'boy on whole-grain bread and announced she was now doing restaurant reviews for the *Blue Gulch County Gazette* and would be giving the food truck her highest rating of five stars. *Good for you*, Olivia thought, glad that Penny had found a new outlet for herself.

Finally, Olivia passed the reins to Dylan, zipped home for a shower and found herself putting on a little mascara and a touch of lip gloss. She looked through her closet for what to wear, something nicer than jeans but not dressy, something not sexy but not unsexy, then realized that just about everything she owned wasn't sexy, but was very much "her." Like her knee-length flippy yellow skirt with the tiny bulldogs all over it. Aunt Sarah loved bulldogs, and it seemed a good omen to wear it. A tank, a light white cardigan and her red ballet flats, and she was ready.

As Olivia waited on her porch for Carson, she scanned the newspaper. On the one-page People in the News section, which some folks in town called the society section, there were some photos of Dory and Beaufort's engagement toast gathering. In one of the photos was a close-up of Dory with the caption:

> Dory is wearing a dress her future mother-in-law bought for her as a welcome-to-the-family gift, but she sweetly accessorized the pricey frock with a pair of dime-store "pearl" earrings her mother gave to her for her sixteenth birthday back when they lived in the Blue Gulch trailer park.

Another photo showed the trailer Dory and her parents had lived in with the caption:

Blue Gulch mayoral hopeful Beaufort Harrington proposes to trailer-park gal, taking her from rags to riches.

Weird, Olivia thought, folding the newspaper and putting it aside on the porch. Dime-store earrings? Trailer-park gal? What was that all about?

As Carson pulled up, she took the *Gazette* with her into his SUV. "Did you see the paper? There are photos of the engagement party." With some very strange captions. "If you look very closely and squint, you can even see me in one of them."

"Actually, I did see the photos. I read the paper every morning—you never know what interesting little facts will present themselves, especially if you're looking for people. Police blotters, lottery winners, arrests that don't result in convictions—and photos of random people. Like there you are in a story about Dory and Beaufort's engagement. If someone were looking for you and had no luck, there you'd be."

She buckled her seat belt and smiled at the two cups of coffee in the holder. Carson really was thoughtful. "Huh. I hadn't really thought of all that."

"Simple, but effective. Some of the most complicated things come down to simple."

"I think that's true," she said. "Thanks for the coffee."

"I got us muffins, too," he said, pointing at the bag at his side. "Coffee-cake-lemon and cranberry-almond. Take your pick."

"Can we split them?" she asked.

"I was hoping you'd say that." The smile he shot her almost made her swoon. Happy, sexy, tender, dazzling.

She wanted to caress his handsome face and kiss him, but instead she busied herself by unartfully trying to split the muffins in two.

"I didn't know Beaufort Harrington was going to run for mayor," she said. "Dory didn't mention it."

"I think it's just talk and speculation right now. Getting his name out there, seeing if he can drum up early support. He has stiff competition."

"Dory as the mayor's wife," she said, trying to picture that. "She's not much of a spotlight seeker and is pretty shy."

"Folks like that, though," he said.

Olivia shrugged. "As long as she's happy."

Carson glanced at her. "Is she? I have to say, neither of them looked particularly happy last night. I can't really put my finger on it."

Well, Olivia knew why Dory didn't look like a blushing bride-to-be, but she wondered about Beaufort now. Maybe he did have his own reasons for proposing that had nothing to do with love, either.

"Well, maybe they just figured it was time to get hitched. If Beaufort's running for mayor, having a hometown wife is a plus."

"Romantic," she muttered, unable to help it.

"I don't know, Olivia. Maybe marrying for love isn't the be-all and end-all. Maybe marrying for purpose—whether because it's time to settle down or because someone meets the checklist—is smart. You know what you're walking into."

For Dory's sake, Olivia hoped so.

For the next hour, en route to Stockton, home of the rodeo championships, Olivia and Carson ate their muffin halves and sipped their coffee and looked out the window.

"Did you ever attend the rodeo with your aunt?" Carson asked as they pulled into a spot right in front of Wild West Hair, the first salon on Carson's list.

"A bunch of times. Right before she left town, Aunt Sarah and I went to the championships here in Stockton. She particularly loved watching the bull riders. Logan Grainger, the husband of Clementine Hurley Grainger, one of my bosses, used to be a champion bull rider."

"I didn't know that. I certainly couldn't last one second on a bull."

She tried to imagine Carson Ford on a bucking bull, but couldn't. She smiled at the thought. Carson was all man, but he was no cowboy.

A minute later, they were walking into Wild West Hair. The Sarah employed as a stylist was not their Sarah. Nor was their Sarah at Cut and Curl, or at Hair Parade. Stockton wasn't a big town and only had a small downtown that had grown out of necessity from the rodeo. Tuckerville, just five minutes away, had all the shops and restaurants. But they'd already visited the Tuckerville salons.

Dejected, they stopped in an old-fashioned coffee shop and sat at the counter and ordered coffee. Olivia smiled at the lady sitting one seat over and flipping her newspaper—and then her eye caught on a half-page advertisement.

Sarah Monk, expert hairstylist, is now at Style Mile in nearby Leeville! Over twenty-five years' experience. A master stylist of the whole kit and caboodle, including precision cuts, blow-outs, Japanese straightening, artful highlights, long-lasting color and quick cuts for fidgety children with overgrown locks. Hours: Tues–Thurs 10–6 and all day Saturday. Call for an appointment today!

Olivia's heart leaped. Sarah would use a phrase like *kit and caboodle*!

"Carson, look! Maybe Sarah's using the last name Monk. It's very close to Mack and is sort of apt. Maybe it's her."

"Excuse me, ma'am," Carson said to the woman with the newspaper. "Do you mind if we copy down the address from that ad?"

The waitress glanced over. "Oh, Sarah Monk? She's my stylist. Does my color every six weeks. Bet you couldn't even tell I wasn't a real blonde."

"I wouldn't have been able to tell," Olivia said, which was true. The color was very natural and soft. And Olivia liked the cut, kind of a long bob with bangs.

"She's the best," the waitress said, refilling their coffees. "I just love Sarah. And those green eyes of hers. Stunning. Tell her Lorraine sent you. Maybe she'll give me a discount on my color next time."

Those green eyes. Olivia and Carson locked gazes. He quickly jotted down the address of the salon, placed a ten-dollar bill on the counter, thanked the waitress and then they ran to his car.

"Leeville is just two towns over. A small town, not much there."

"Except maybe my aunt!" Olivia said, excitement building.

Fifteen minutes later, they'd arrived at Style Mile. The salon was between an apartment building and a real estate office. When they walked in, a woman with very green eyes stood up and put down her magazine. "Hi, how can I help you?"

"We heard Sarah Monk is working here now and does great work," Carson said.

Please don't say you're Sarah, Olivia thought. *Say that Sarah Monk of the stunning green eyes is in the back and will be right with you. And then Aunt Sarah will walk out, see me and run over and hug me. I'll have my aunt back.*

Please, please, please.

"I'm Sarah Monk," she said, and Olivia's heart plummeted.

"Sorry," Carson whispered to Olivia. "Um, we'll be back another time. My friend isn't feeling well."

She *wasn't* feeling well. At all. They were never going to find Sarah.

He led Olivia outside and wrapped her in a hug so warm and enveloping that she let herself droop against his strength. "I know it's disappointing. But I made you a promise that we'll find her, and we will."

She took in a breath and let it out. "I guess it'll just take time. You said you had a lead here about your young client's dad. Maybe we should turn our attention to that case."

He looked at her for a moment, as if making sure she was really okay. "We've hit all the salons in Stockton, so that's two more towns crossed off the list. I do like the notion of sticking close to rodeo or ranching towns. I have a good idea where to focus the search next."

She nodded. "So where to now for your young client?"

"His mom said we'd likely find her ex-husband either working the rodeo as a hand or at one of the ranches nearby. That's what he did for a living before they got married and he started drinking and got fired, leaving his ex to support the family. I called ahead to the rodeo and there are three Steve Johnsons working as hands. The manager I spoke to said the hands who don't have their own places bunk near the barns."

"Seems hard to imagine a man leaving his family to go live in a bunkhouse," Olivia said.

"I know."

Minutes later they were back in Carson's SUV and driving over to the rodeo. There weren't any events going on right now, so the place was pretty deserted except for employees. Carson parked and they wound their way over to the barns and walked through the field. When they passed a couple men, Carson asked if they knew "a Steve Johnson, late twenties," and one of the guys pointed to a man washing down a bull up ahead. Carson checked his phone, sliding through photos. Olivia could see it was the same guy.

"Are you going to talk to him?" she asked.

He shook his head. "My job is to find him. I need to let my client know I've done so, and then we can talk about next steps. If I go up to Johnson and introduce myself and let him know his son hired me to find him, that he just wants to see him, Johnson may bolt. I can't risk that."

Olivia nodded, her heart heavy. She crossed her arms over her chest as they walked back to his car, suddenly cold despite the warm afternoon.

"You okay?" he said as he opened her car door for her.

"I'm glad you found him and that it was easier than finding my aunt has been. I'm happy for your nine-year-old client. I guess I'm thinking about my own dad," she admitted. "My mother told him she was pregnant with his child, and he was gone the next day, never seen or heard from again. I've always known not to take it personally—I mean, it's not like he knew me, right? But still. I had a father for that space of time and he chose not to take on that title. I just don't get it."

"I don't get it, either, Liv," he said, and she was struck by the nickname, that he felt close enough to her to use it. "My dad didn't leave us but he certainly wasn't part of the family. I never got that, either. I can't imagine not being there for Danny, being very present and active in his life."

"Good," she said, reaching up and touching his shoulder, his navy blue Henley shirt warm from the sun.

He put his hand over hers and tilted her chin up with his finger and then kissed her. She closed her eyes, losing herself in how sweet it felt, how good. Her knees felt slightly shaky and she held on to him, wanting to stay in his arms forever.

But his phone rang.

"Blasted timing," he said, smiling at her. He glanced at the phone. "My dad. He's watching Danny so I'd better take this." He answered the call and listened for a minute, then explained to Olivia that his dad said he took Danny out for gelato at the new place that opened in Oak Creek and there was a hair salon right next to it. A stylist with auburn hair, green eyes and a tattoo on her arm was blow-drying someone's hair right by the window. "Does your aunt have a tattoo on her arm?"

"She didn't back then, but she might have gotten one."

"Dad," he said into the phone, "why not just go inside and ask her if her name is Sarah?" He listened for a moment. "Okay. We're on our way." He put down the phone and turned to Olivia. "Looks like we're going to Oak Creek to see if this woman is your aunt," Carson said. "For some reason, my dad doesn't want to ask her himself. I'm not sure what's going on with him."

Edmund Ford hadn't wanted to see a photo of Sarah Mack, though Olivia had offered to show him one. He'd said he wanted to be surprised, that he didn't need to know what she looked like until he laid eyes on her for the first time, that he'd feel something in his heart the moment he saw his Sarah and that was all he needed to go on.

"Case of the nerves, maybe?" Olivia said. "It could very well be her. Right next door to where we grew up."

Olivia's hope was back.

It took an hour, but they finally arrived in Oak Creek. Carson's dad had taken Danny to the playground in the interim and the plan was to meet back at the bench in front of the salon at 4:15 p.m. Edmund and Danny hadn't arrived yet.

Carson peered in the big bay window of the salon, Delia's Hair and Day Spa, but the glare from the sun made it difficult to see inside.

"This is one of the most expensive salons in the area," Olivia said. "But surely your dad called here when he first began his search, if not visited for one of his seven haircuts. And you said you called all the local salons to ask if any Sarahs worked there."

"Your aunt may have changed her name entirely. Maybe that's why she's been so hard to find. And who knows—maybe this stylist he noticed today wasn't working the day he came in to see if anyone matched the description."

Because of the setting sun and the glare likely streaming inside, the shades lining the windows had been lowered, but Carson could see a tanned arm with many silver bangle bracelets moving and a hand wielding a blow-dryer, while a woman sat in a big silver chair.

"Dada!"

Carson glanced left and there was Danny on his dad's shoulders as they headed toward the bench.

"That's the second time today I've seen Danny on the shoulders of a Ford," Olivia said to Carson, smiling at the pair as they approached.

"Hi, Liva!" Danny said, holding out his arms.

Carson glanced at Olivia, whose expression told him that her heart had just melted into a puddle. Danny had that effect on people.

Edmund effortlessly lifted Danny off his shoulders and handed him to Olivia, who scooped him into a hug.

"Meat song!" Danny said.

Olivia laughed. "How about one verse now and then the rest on the way home?"

"Top 'getty," Danny sang and started to giggle.

Now it was Carson's turn to laugh. Olivia sat down on the bench, Danny cuddled close against her chest, and she started to sing-whisper about a meatball all covered in cheese.

"Okay, now we have to go see something inside this place," she told Danny, "but after, I'm going to sing the rest and you can help me sing it."

"Cheese!" Danny sang.

Olivia laughed and stood back up, Danny in her arms. "Edmund, may I ask why you didn't want to go in and ask her name?"

Edmund took a breath and let it out. "Because… well, I did go in and I looked right at her and she does have lovely green eyes. But—" He stopped, as if weighing something, thinking something over.

"But what, Dad?" Carson asked.

"I looked right at that woman with her auburn hair and her green eyes and her tattoo and I didn't feel a thing," he said, disappointment clouding his features. "Madam Miranda told me that when I see my Sarah, I'd know it. I didn't know anything when I looked at this stylist. I didn't feel anything at all."

Carson could have done a cartwheel. "Dad, *of course* you didn't feel anything. Why would you feel the earth move and your heart start beating like a teenager over a total stranger? Like I've been telling you for weeks now, it's all just make-believe. Nice to hear but with no basis in reality."

His father's expression—and Olivia's—told him he might have gone a little too far. Dammit.

"Dad, I just mean that you get your life back," he said quickly. "Olivia gets her aunt back. Everything goes back to normal."

"Normal?" Edmund repeated, glaring at Carson. "How dare you," he added on a harsh whisper, mindful of his grandson. "I like my prediction. And I intend to see it fulfilled. With or without you."

Olivia stepped forward, Danny in her arms, the boy looking from his father to his grandfather. "Why don't we go in," she said to Carson. "And see if it's my aunt." Olivia reached out her arms to transfer Danny to his grandfather, whose expression softened the moment he held the boy. "Danny, I can't wait to sing you the rest of the song! Your dad and I are going to go inside this shop but we'll be back in a minute."

Edmund turned away and began pointing to cars. "What color is that one, Danny?"

"Blue!" Danny said.

"Dad, I—" Carson began. But what was he going to say? If it was Sarah Mack inside, she *would* be just a stranger to Edmund. Was his father really expecting to be shot with Cupid's arrow and to fall instantly in love? How could his dad really put so much stock in a fortune? Carson didn't get it.

His father didn't even turn back around. He held up a hand in Carson's direction, then faced Olivia. "Please let me know if it's your aunt."

"I will," she said, shooting Carson a death glare before walking up the three steps to the front door of the salon.

As they entered, he *felt* Olivia's frown, felt her entire body turn inward, which meant the stylist was not her aunt. But she was a green-eyed hairstylist—that he could see with his own eyes—and her name *was* Sarah, evident from the engraved silver name tag pinned to her sleek black bolero jacket. She had three visible tattoos, wrist, arm and a small one behind the left ear, a starfish, if he was seeing correctly at this slight distance. She could easily have another on her ankle, which was covered by shiny black glued-on pants.

"She's not my aunt," Olivia whispered, "but I didn't think she would be."

Carson stared at her. "Because the moment my father does encounter your aunt, you expect him to have hearts shooting out of his chest like the love-struck raccoon on the cartoon Danny watches?"

She crossed her arms over her chest. "It doesn't matter anyway. She's not my aunt."

"Your mother never told my father that the Sarah of his prediction was your aunt. Just that she was a green-eyed hairstylist named Sarah with a particular tattoo. Since that tattoo is of common symbols of the trade, this very woman herself might have that same tattoo. Your mother might not have been talking about her sister at all. This woman *could* be my father's predicted bride."

She shook her head as though that was ridiculous. "Carson, come on."

"Excuse me," Carson said to the stylist. "We're looking for a specific stylist who works here named Sarah, but we were told she'd have a tattoo on her ankle of a blow-dryer and brush."

The woman smiled. "That's me." She leaned down and began lifting the hem of her pants on her left leg.

Victory! Yes! This was the predicted green-eyed hairstylist named Sarah with the tattoo. And his father felt zippo, nothing, nada! It was all a dumb little game and it was over. His father would be disappointed, sure, but now that he knew he did want love in his life, he could look for someone he liked—instead of someone a "fortune-teller" *told* him he'd like.

"I think we're done here," Carson whispered to Olivia. But as the stylist continued to roll up her pants, a tattoo taking up half her calf began to reveal itself of black blow-dryer and a black brush. Shoot. Dammit. "What color did you say that blow-dryer and brush were?" he added to Olivia.

"The blow-dryer is hot pink and the brush is silver," Olivia said. "And the tattoo is very small and just above the ankle bone."

"Guess I'm not your Sarah then," the woman said and went back to blow-drying her customer.

He was glum. Olivia was glum.

And through the door, he could see that his father had Danny up on his shoulders and was pointing out the different kinds of cars that were parked.

Instead of waiting with bated breath for them to come out, to learn if the woman was his predicted great love, his dad was focused on Danny. That was the man he'd become.

Suddenly Carson felt terrible about hoping to disappoint his father, about hoping this woman he felt nothing for, had no attraction to, would be his predicted great love.

What the hell was wrong with him? Was this the kind of father *he* wanted to be?

Dammit, dammit, dammit.

"Well, what's the verdict?" Edmund asked as Carson stepped outside. "From your expression, Carson, I'm hopeful that she's Olivia's aunt. You look...disappointed."

Knife. Twist. "She's not Olivia's aunt," he said. "She's not your predicted second great love."

He watched relief cross his father's features, and then realization of some kind that Carson must have turned some figurative corner about the whole thing. He hadn't, not about the prediction and fortune-telling.

"I do want you to be happy, Dad," he said.

Edmund clapped him on the back. "I'm glad to hear that."

So why did Carson feel so…conflicted? What was burning in his gut? Something didn't feel right. Something felt very wrong.

Olivia finally came down the stairs, disappointment etched on her face, and he wanted to scoop her up into his arms and assure her again that they'd find Sarah Mack. As he took a step toward her, Danny said, "Liva!"

Olivia's entire face brightened. She rushed down the steps to Danny and beamed at him.

His dad put Carson's son before his own feelings. Olivia put his son before her own feelings.

It was time for Carson to start putting others before his own cynical heart.

But the more he watched Olivia sing the meatball song and then one about an itsy-bitsy spider as she made spiders out of her fingers, the more he realized this was all going to be over be soon and she'd be out of their lives.

He always put Danny before himself. Which meant saving Danny from another woman in his life walking away. Once Carson found Sarah Mack, Olivia would go her way, Carson would go his.

Except if her aunt was really her father's predicted love, Sarah Mack would be part of their lives. Which meant Olivia would be, too.

Suddenly this was getting more complicated. Either

way, someone was going to get hurt, and he wasn't sure who.

His phone rang. The Blue Gulch PD, who often hired him to help out on cases.

"Carson, this is Detective Nick Slater. You asked me to let you know if a Sarah Mack came up in the system. I was just looking for leads on a suspect and I noticed a woman named Sarah Mack was stopped for a traffic violation on Blue Gulch Street at three o'clock today."

Huh. "Date of birth and address?"

Slater read off the information. The DOB matched the right age for Olivia's aunt. And even if she went by a different name professionally, the name Sarah Mack was on her license. Unfortunately, the address on the license was her old place in Blue Gulch; she clearly didn't live in Blue Gulch anymore.

"What was the violation? Speeding?" Carson asked.

"Actually, she was going too slow. Five miles per hour in a thirty zone. She had people honking at her. She was let go with a warning."

"I owe you one, Detective Slater. Thanks."

"You've done so much for the Blue Gulch PD. It's my pleasure to help you out." Slater was married to one of the Hurleys of Hurley's Homestyle Kitchen, the family who owned the food truck that Olivia worked in.

After getting the make, model and year of the car, plus the plate number, Carson put his phone away. He looked at Olivia, now singing a different song to Danny a few feet away on the bench in front of the salon.

He was afraid to get her hopes up again. But he had a feeling that he would be reuniting Olivia with her aunt today.

If Sarah Mack was still in Blue Gulch, the car would

be easy to spot. Not many old yellow VW Beetles on the road these days. If she'd come and gone, that was another story. But it was just a matter of time—not if.

"Hey, you two," Carson said, heading over. "I've got some news you're both gonna like."

Chapter Eight

Olivia felt it in her bones; she would be seeing her aunt very soon. She just knew it. But as quickly as the good feeling had come, it faded to nothing. She shivered inside Carson's SUV despite the unusually warm February day.

Edmund had taken a sleepy Danny back to his house for a nap, and Olivia and Carson headed over to Blue Gulch to search Blue Gulch Street and the one hotel and B and B for a yellow VW bug. Her aunt hadn't had that car when she lived in Blue Gulch, but the style of car sounded like something her aunt would like.

"The traffic stop was two hours ago?" Olivia asked, craning her neck to look for the car as Carson turned onto Blue Gulch Street, the main drag of town where the shops and restaurants were, including the Hurley's Homestyle Kitchen food truck. "I wonder if she's still in town. Maybe she just passed through." Huh. Maybe she wouldn't be seeing her aunt so soon, after all.

"There's only reason someone goes five miles an hour on the main road in town," Carson said. "Because she's looking for someone on the street or for someone in store windows."

"You think my aunt was looking for me? Why not call? Why not come by? Why not leave a note in the mailbox?"

"Maybe she just looks for you," he said. "Maybe she drives through Blue Gulch often, hoping to spot you, just get a glimpse of you."

"But that would mean she still cares about me," Olivia said.

"I'm sure she does care. Sometimes, people leave your life for reasons that have nothing to do with you. They're consumed by something else and it drives them away."

"Like your nine-year-old client's father, most likely," she said.

"Exactly. I always say I don't get it, but I guess I do. I mean, I understand, intellectually, why some people walk out on their lives and families. But I'll never get it emotionally."

She nodded. "You look left, I'll look right." But no-where that she could see, on the street or parked in the spots, was a yellow Beetle.

"You have no idea at all what caused the estrange-ment between your mother and aunt?" Carson asked.

They passed the library and the coffee shop and the food truck, which had a nice line. Olivia scanned the parking lot by the town green. No yellow Beetle.

"I know that my aunt never wanted to talk about

fortune-telling or the family 'gifts' and that there was a secret. I'm not sure whose—my mother's or my aunt's. I once heard the tail end of an argument and my aunt saying, 'Don't you ever bring them up again,' but that was the last I heard of that and when I asked my mother what 'them' referred to, she just waved her hand dismissively. Three weeks later, my aunt sold her house, which I discovered because of the sold sign on the lawn and she was gone. No goodbye. Nothing. That was five years ago. My mother wouldn't talk about it or speculate. I finally stopped asking."

"The argument must have been about something important to drive your aunt away," he said gently.

"I know. I just have no idea what it involved. When my mother got sick, I started looking for my aunt but couldn't find her. I was sure Sarah would want to know, to be there to make amends. And in the days before the funeral, I doubled my efforts to find her. Having that to focus on was the only thing that kept me from falling apart. But I didn't find her. She doesn't even know her sister is gone." Olivia burst into tears, unable to help herself or stop herself. She covered her face in her hands and sobbed.

Carson parked the car and drew her into his arms. She resisted at first, miserable, sad, tears falling down her cheeks, but then she gave in to the comfort and held on to him, gave in to depth of her sadness. The loss of her aunt, the loss of her mother, the loss of the father she never knew. Hell, she was even crying for Danny and the loss of his mother. For Carson's young client, and the loss of his father.

She felt him put his head down on top of hers, resting his cheek as he stroked her hair, one hand tight around her shoulders.

"You've lost a lot, Olivia, but you're about to *find,*" Carson said, tipping up her chin.

She looked into his hazel-green eyes and felt better, stronger. "I'm mortified that I just started blubbering."

"Don't be," he said. "Best way to deal with strong emotions is to let 'em rip."

"Well, thanks for letting me literally cry on your shoulder."

He leaned forward, taking her face in his hand, and kissed her, wiping away the tears under her eyes. Then he dropped his hands to his lap and turned to face forward. "I've got to stop doing that."

"Or keep doing that," she said.

"Olivia, I'm not…"

"Looking for romance. So you said. Yet you keep kissing me. Interesting."

He smiled, then laughed. "I just don't want to mess up here, Olivia. You're a good, kind person and I don't want to hurt you."

He was guarded, but she was a grown-up and either she'd bust through those walls of his or she wouldn't. *Love would out*, as they said. Or it wouldn't.

Feeling better and stronger, Olivia sat up straight. "Let's drive past the hotel and B and B, and check for my aunt's car," she said, deftly changing the subject.

The car wasn't at the hotel in the center of Blue Gulch Street or at the B and B on a side street near Olivia's house. Carson did another drive-by of the main road, but they didn't see the yellow Beetle.

"That she was here is a sign that she's ready to come out of hiding," Carson said. "Do you think she knows you're looking for her? If she has the family gift or whatever."

She glanced at him. *That* was a sign that he didn't find it as far-fetched as he had before. "It's possible. She wouldn't talk about her gift. I don't know what it is or even if she has one. And my mother would never talk about it."

"Well, maybe she senses you're looking for her and she came to town today to see if she'd run in to you."

Olivia shrugged. "She knows where I live."

"The two of you will reunite. That I do believe," he said, giving her hand a squeeze. "I'll take you home. It's been quite a day."

It had been. She squeezed his hand back, missing the warmth and strength of it as he put it on the wheel.

Olivia's mother's face came to mind. She wished Madam Miranda was here to tell her whether she was setting herself up for a broken heart.

An hour later, Carson was sitting in the Johnson living room, his nine-year-old client, Joey, sitting straight up on the sofa next to his mother, whom Carson had called earlier after dropping off Olivia at her house. He'd let Tara Johnson know he had located her ex-husband at the rodeo, where he worked as a ranch hand. They'd made arrangements for Carson to stop by at six o'clock.

"I didn't say anything to your father," Carson said to Joey. "He doesn't know that you hired me or that you're looking for him. I wanted to locate him first and let you know where he is so that you can decide how you want to handle the next steps."

"My mom and I talked about it," Joey said, brushing his long, sandy blond bangs away from his eyes. "If you're willing, will you come with me to talk to him?"

Carson hadn't been expecting that.

"It just seems more official if the private investigator I hired to find him is there, you know?" Joey explained. "I feel like he'd more willing to tell the truth. I don't know."

"Well, I'm happy to take you to see him, if that's okay with your mom."

"It's fine with me," Tara Johnson said. "And I appreciate what you've done for Joey. It's a hard situation. My only concern is Joey's feelings. You can tell his dad that I'm not looking for him to haul him into court or anything like that. I know he has problems. I know he has no money. I know he's probably working for room and board. I only care that Joey has a relationship with his dad."

Tears glistened in Joey's eyes and he leaned his head against his mother's arm. Hell, now Carson felt a tear poking at his own eyes. "I did find out his work schedule for the week," Carson said. "If you want to go after school or on the weekend, he works then. We can catch him just as his shift is ending so he'll be free to talk."

They arranged to go in two days, when Joey's school had a half day and he didn't have baseball practice.

"You're a brave kid," he said to Joey as the boy walked him to the door. "I had some issues with my dad but I was always too bottled up inside to confront him. I admire you."

The boy looked up at Carson with such open brown eyes that it took everything in him not to hug him tight. He put out his hand and Joey shook it. "See you in a couple days."

"Thanks for finding him," Joey said. "If you want to

know a secret," he added on a whisper, "I'm just glad he's alive. I wasn't sure if you'd come back and say he wasn't. My mom warned me about that."

"I know what you mean," Carson said.

Outside, on the doorstep, he couldn't help wondering if Danny would be having a conversation like this some day. Wondering where his mother was, if she was still alive, *why* the big question. Heavyhearted, he got into his car. He couldn't get home to hug his son soon enough.

The next morning, Dory was helping out in the food truck since there was a sidewalk sale on Blue Gulch Street and people would be out in droves. Olivia had done a lot of the prep work this morning, but even with Dory taking orders and dealing with the cash register and Olivia cooking, Olivia still only had two hands for cooking.

While she was sautéing shrimp, she couldn't help but notice that Amanda Buckman, harried mom of twin four-year-old boys and twin eight-year-old girls, had just bites left of her eggplant-parm po'boy and her expression and body language had changed. Where before she'd been slumped and tired-looking, she now sat up straight, her face tilted to the sun, and she smiled at her daughters doing cartwheels on the green while the boys finished their kid-size chicken-finger po'boys and swung their legs. Miles Fincello, the pharmacist at the drugstore, who'd ordered a pulled-pork po'boy with extra barbecue sauce and a mini vanilla-cream cannoli with pistachios, had come to the window with worry etched on his face; now, he was chatting on his cell phone, smiling. And Molly Euling, whose house was on the corner of Blue Gulch Street and Golden Way, Olivia's street, and was always snapping at dog walkers to keep their "mutts" off her grass, was now petting the loud pug she was always complaining about.

A good day's work—regarding both Olivia's special ability and sales. The Hurleys would be very pleased with the day's receipts, that was for sure.

"Pardon me, excuse me, excuse me," a loud voice said at the food truck window. "Dory, smile for me, will you?"

"May I help you?" Dory said to the pushy man who Olivia didn't recognize.

"I'm Hal Herbert from the *Blue Gulch County Gazette*. I'd like to get a few shots of you for the paper and our website. Can you hold the order pad a bit higher so it can make the frame?"

"Why on earth would you want to get pictures of me taking orders in the Hurley Homestyle Kitchen food truck?" Dory asked. "I'm just helping out a friend."

"Just doing my job, miss," the man said. "There's going to be a feature on Beaufort Harrington." He consulted his own little notebook. "Your fiancé. Apparently he's throwing his hat into the Blue Gulch mayoral race." The guy took a couple more pictures, then scribbled something in the notebook.

"Yes, I know that," Dory said. "But why are the newspapers so interested in *me* and *my* life?" she asked, looking at Olivia in confusion. "This morning, when I was up early at the bakery to get the breads done, another reporter stopped by to take pictures of me sliding the loaves in the oven. I didn't even have time to get the flour off my face."

"I guess that's the world of politics," Olivia said. "Maybe candidates' brides-to-be sell papers?"

Dory shrugged. "How did you know I'd be here, anyway?" she asked the reporter.

The man consulted his notebook. "Looks like a Mrs. Harrington has been calling in your schedule."

"Annalee?" Dory said after the man had taken more pictures and gone. "Olivia, why is Annalee Harrington so interested in having photos of me working here and at the bakery in the paper? And did you see the captions of the photos from the engagement toast gathering? My mother's 'dime-store' earrings? I was so angry about that jab."

"Maybe you should talk to Beaufort about what's going on," Olivia said.

"I absolutely will." She glanced out the window. "Oh, the gals from the library are heading our way. And a bunch of teachers from the middle school, too."

"I'm ready!" Olivia said.

Olivia got back to work, but she couldn't help peering out the window of the food truck, looking for two people in particular.

Carson, who was a no-show, and whose handsome face she missed.

And her aunt. She supposed it was silly to think Sarah would just walk up to the food truck and say, "Oh, hi, Olivia, it's your aunt" after five years of radio silence. But if she'd been around yesterday, maybe she would do just that. Maybe Sarah was ready to talk again. If so, where was she? Olivia had stayed up past midnight expecting the doorbell to ring, her aunt to be on the other side. But the doorbell hadn't rung once.

Olivia turned her attention back to the stove and

sauté pans. She had five orders of the special po'boy of the day, a scrumptious meat loaf, if she did say so herself, and seven other kinds to make, plus a bunch of cannoli.

She had wrapped up the final tuna-melt po'boy when she heard a sharp voice say, "Dory, you don't need to work here."

Olivia glanced past Dory's shoulder to see her fiancé, Beaufort Harrington, standing there with some of his coworkers from Texas Trust. Edmund Ford was not among them.

"Dory, you're my fiancé. You don't have to work at all. You know that. You don't even have to work in the bakery—you can hire someone to manage the place for you and all the extra employees you need. You're going to be a Harrington, for God's sake."

"I'm helping out my friend Olivia," Dory said. "I told you about Olivia Mack. I've been her assistant with her catering business in the past."

"Sweetheart, there's no need to assist anyone," Beaufort said.

"Let's talk about this later," Dory told him. "There's quite a line, as you can see."

Beaufort ordered a shrimp po'boy. He didn't look happy.

Olivia wondered what would happen to Beaufort's mood after he ate the po'boy she was making for him. She spread on the remoulade, layered the shrimp and wrapped it up.

As the line died down now that it was past two, she kept an eye on Beaufort Harrington. He finished the po'boy, stood up and came back over to the truck.

"Dory, I just meant that you're going to be my wife.

You don't need to work. You're going to have a lot of social engagements, especially once my candidacy is officially announced."

If her po'boy had any effect on Beaufort it was to make him more emphatic about Dory *not* working.

"Beau, why would your mother send reporters to take pictures of me working at the bakery and here, then?"

Beaufort's cheeks turned pink. "Oh, you know my mother."

"What do you mean?" she asked.

"Gotta run, sweetheart. See you later. Great po'boy, Olivia," he called out. Then he hurried away.

"What do you think is going on with Annalee Harrington?" Dory asked.

"I don't know. But it looks like you and Beaufort have a lot to iron out before you get married. You've made it pretty clear you intend to run the bakery yourself, not hire someone to keep it going."

Dory nodded. "I have made that clear. Maybe Beaufort thinks I'm more interested in the money than the shop. But he's wrong."

"I think you two just need to talk. If this is primarily a business arrangement, the business has to be ironed out."

Dory brightened. "You're right." She glanced at Olivia. "Hey, I know you just made a thousand po'boys, but before you put away the ham, can you make me a good old-fashioned ham-and-cheese with your amazing honey mustard? No one makes a po'boy like you."

"Of course," Olivia said.

As Olivia made one last sandwich and Dory helped her clean up and get the truck ready for the dinner shift that Dylan would be taking over, Olivia had a bad feeling that things with Beaufort might not go as Dory had thought.

She watched Dory eat the po'boy, her friend's shoulders rising, her chin lifting. Dory's eyes narrowed. She took the final bite of the sandwich and nodded to herself as if making some kind of decision.

"Olivia, I've got to run. I have someone to see before closing time."

Hmm. Just what had she infused Dory's sandwich with?

Chapter Nine

After making dinner for himself and Danny, Carson settled the toddler in his car seat and hit the road to Blue Gulch to look for Sarah Mack's car. No sign of it. He did see his dad walking and window-shopping, a bag from Blue Gulch Toys on his arm. He pulled over and surprised Edmund Ford. The look on his father's face at the sight of Danny never failed to stop Carson in his tracks. Pure love, thrill, delight. The way a parent's face should light up. Danny was overjoyed by the stuffed panda Grandpa had picked up for him.

Carson's phone rang—Beaufort Harrington. The man could barely speak.

"I wanted you to hear it from me instead of the local press or gossips," Beaufort spluttered, his voice broken. "Dory called off the engagement. One minute we're engaged and the next we're not. I saw her just a couple hours ago at the Hurley's food truck—she was helping out the woman who runs it. And suddenly an hour later, she hands me back my ring."

He froze. The food truck. Olivia. Had her "ability" somehow interfered?

Come on. That would be crazy. She made po'boys and cannoli. She didn't have special abilities to "lift hearts" or break them with her food. She was just a good cook and people liked to eat. Add those together and you got smiles. End of story. Whatever had happened between Dory and Beaufort had nothing to do with Olivia or the food truck. "Oh, man," Carson said. "I'm really sorry."

"Me, too. My parents are here now—I'd better go. Talk to you soon."

What the heck happened?

He let his dad know what was going on and took Edmund up on his offer to bring Danny home and put him to bed so that he could talk to Olivia. Beaufort was an old friend, and to hear him so torn up was heartbreaking. And something told him there was more to the story than anyone knew.

Olivia had spent a long morning and afternoon at the food truck. After her shift she made Mr. Crenshaw chicken Milanese with a side of fettuccine in light cream sauce and delivered it, sitting awhile with him to catch up on his romance with widow Eleanor Parkerton who lived one floor up. Then she'd made another client's Weight Watchers–friendly meal of exactly eight points, delivered that and finally was curled up with Sweetie on the divan in her mother's fortune-telling parlor, looking through family photos.

Aunt Sarah on a bicycle, her auburn hair blowing back in the wind, a joyful smile on her face. Her mother with the enigmatic expression in her eyes as she sat on the porch of their house, Sweetie in her lap. Their grandmother, also a fortune-teller, a woman Olivia hadn't had the chance to know, with her two daughters as teenagers. And one of Olivia's father, the only photo there was of him in the album. She stared at it, always surprised to see a bit of herself in the man's face, as though she should look nothing like the stranger he was. She used to think about seeking him out, but decided against it long ago. He'd left before she was born, and Olivia didn't even know his last name. Her mother had told her that the man had been utterly irresistible to her. Even though she knew he'd break her heart and she'd never see him again, she thought she could use her strong will to conquer what would happen. Miranda had told Olivia she wouldn't have willingly gotten pregnant knowing the father of her baby wouldn't stick around; she *would* have resisted him and not have had their short-lived few weeks together. But all Miranda's attempts to keep him in her life had failed, and Madam Miranda had further accepted that she couldn't rewrite the truth, no matter how badly she wanted to.

Olivia didn't like any of that. What the hell was the point of anything, then, if you couldn't write your own destiny, be the captain of your own ship? She pressed her face against Sweetie's fur, the old cat's purring a comfort. Sometimes she believed what her mother had—that life had a plan for you and all the little detours were part of that plan. The things-happen-for-a-reason point of view. And sometimes she was like

Carson—pragmatic, logical, about the here and now and what made sense. The you-decide team. Carson would say that if her mother had supposedly known Olivia's father wouldn't stick around, then she could have chosen not to sleep with him and create a life. But she had anyway and, oh, look! Then again, Carson seemed to be coming around—slowly—to the idea that her mother *may* have had special abilities.

What Olivia believed was this: her mother had fallen in love, had known it was doomed, but also had known there would be a daughter who she would love more than anything. In a way, her mother had both broken her own heart and healed it.

"I don't know, Sweetie," she said to the cat, giving her a scratch on the head and taking a sip of her tea.

The doorbell rang, startling Olivia. She went to the front door to find Dory standing there.

"Dory, is everything okay?"

Before Dory could answer, a black SUV pulled up to the house. Carson.

He came up to the door and saw Dory. Looking a bit uncomfortable he said, "Sorry to interrupt. To be honest, I just got a call from Beaufort and he's pretty broken up." He turned to walk back down the porch steps. "I'll let you two talk."

"No," Dory said to Carson. "I know you're a good friend of Beaufort's and close with Olivia. And I know Olivia won't feel comfortable breaking a confidence and telling you what I told her, so I'll tell you myself."

"Come into the living room, both of you," Olivia said. She led the way and gestured for Dory and Carson to sit. Carson chose one end of the sofa; Dory sat on the chair across from it. Olivia bit her lip and sat next to Carson.

"Carson, what you might not know," Dory began, "is that the reason I accepted Beaufort's marriage proposal after dating such a short time was because he offered to save my family business, Drummond's Bake Shop. My mother died recently and her bills took my accounts. There's nothing left and the shop is next to go. But Beaufort said he would save the shop if I married him."

"I'm very sorry about your mother, Dory," Carson said. "To have your family business in jeopardy on top of a such a loss must be very painful and very difficult."

Olivia found herself reaching over to touch Carson's hand. That was a kind thing to say.

Dory nodded, the sadness in her blue eyes heartbreaking. "Tonight I found out why Beaufort proposed. It was part of a whole plan to present me as his wife from the wrong side of the tracks, so that he'd look less privileged and more accepting, more like a regular guy instead of a wealthy one-percenter type. His 'people' wanted him to have a wife with a certain look—petite, blonde, nonthreatening with a good backstory. Who knew my growing-up in the Blue Gulch trailer park would be so appealing to a future politician?"

Carson frowned. "That doesn't sound like Beaufort."

Olivia didn't know Beaufort Harrington well, if at all, but he'd always seemed like a follower rather than a leader. Perhaps his mother was behind all the plans. Based on the news articles and photos, Olivia wouldn't doubt it.

"Well, he has his ambitions," Dory said. "And I can't fault him for picking and choosing his wife based on all that when I said yes so that my family business would be saved."

"But now your family business won't be saved," Olivia said. "What are you going to do?"

Dory pulled a folder from her tote bag. "My hopes are in here. A business plan. Six months ago, when I saw the writing on the wall about the bakery, I presented a plan to my bank for a loan and was turned down. But after seeing how you and the Hurleys run the food truck, why it's so successful, I have new ideas. I wrote up a new plan tonight and I'm going to present it to my bank tomorrow. I have a good feeling about it."

Whether Olivia's ham-and-cheese po'boy with honey mustard helped spur Dory to rely on herself or whether Dory just realized what she really wanted and needed, Olivia was happy for her friend.

"In any case, Olivia, your mother was right. I don't love Beaufort. You know what I do love? My bakery. I need to do this myself. I'm going to save Drummond's Bake Shop." She stood and stopped for a moment to pet Sweetie, who was weaving between her legs, then headed for the door.

"Good for you, Dory," Olivia said, hugging her friend.

"Best of luck to you with the shop and the loan," Carson said.

Dory smiled and left, and Carson narrowed his eyes at Olivia.

"So your mother was the one who put it in her head not to marry Beaufort?" The frown was back.

"Carson, that's the least of what happened. Dory

doesn't love Beaufort. Beaufort doesn't love her. A marriage based on a deal has been canceled. That's all."

He leaned back on the couch. "So we have people making important decisions with legal and lifelong significance based on a fortune-teller's prediction. We have people making decisions based on necessity. What the hell ever happened to getting married because you fell in love?"

Olivia sat down beside Carson. "I'm holding out for that."

"I should hope so," he said, crossing his arms over his chest.

"Huh," Olivia said. "So you do have faith, after all."

He frowned. "Faith? What are you talking about?"

"You do believe in love."

"I believe in marrying for the right reason," he said. "The right reason is love. That doesn't mean I believe in love anymore. I don't. I used to, but not anymore."

"You love Danny. You love your dad." *I wish I could add myself to that list*, Olivia realized, her heart clenching.

"I believe in facts. I believe in people walking the walk. My son has my unconditional love—you bet he does. My father changed. He earned my respect back. He earned my love back."

Olivia glanced at him, the hard set of his jaw, the flash of intensity in his eyes.

"When my son was so frail in the NICU at birth and the doctors weren't sure he'd make it, I kept caressing his tiny fingers through those window holes in his incubator and thinking over and over if only his mother were still there, Danny would know it, he'd feel her there, feel her love, and he'd get better. I thought the reason he was getting worse was because he knew his mother had given up on him and walked out."

Oh, Carson. She bit her lip and wanted to put her arms around him, but he looked like he might bolt at any moment so she stayed quiet. This was a time to listen, not talk.

"But you know what happened?" he said, turning to face her. "Danny did start getting better. Because I was there, because his grandfather was there. Because of the fantastic nurses and doctors. He got better and I realized his mother being around or not had nothing to do with it. He'd be fine. And so would I."

She got it now. This wasn't about faith or love or lack thereof regarding either or both. This was about Carson Ford's refusal to let himself need anyone or anything.

"When my ex-wife was pregnant," Carson said, "she had her fortune told at a carnival in Oak Creek. For ten bucks she was told she'd have a daughter who would be perfect and look just like her. Jodie ran around buying pink layettes and nursery decorations. Instead, our *son* was born eight weeks early and sickly and looked exactly like me. I don't think Jodie ever got over the 'betrayal.'" He shook his head. "I loved Jodie, but after that it was easy to let go of the love."

"I can understand that," she said, reaching over to squeeze his hand. And now she knew a bit more why her mother's profession and his father being involved with a fortune-teller affected him the way it did.

"Tell me something, Olivia. Why didn't your mother tell you who *your* great love would be?"

Talk about a change of subject. A subject she didn't want to discuss—not with Carson. Not with the man she loved. Olivia glanced away. "She must have had her reasons. She did tell me my last boyfriend wasn't the one. And he wasn't."

"Self-fulfilling prophecy? You dumped him?"

"He fell in love with someone else and proposed, like, a day later," she said, wincing at the memory. "That was the end of us."

"I think your mother never told you who your great love is because she had no idea. The way it should be. No knows these things in advance. My dad will find that out when we finally find your aunt."

"I think my mother did know," Olivia said slowly, testing out the words on her heart. Could Carson be the one? Her great love? If he was, he sure was making it difficult. "There was no need to tell me who. No need to lead."

"Like your mother did with my father," he muttered. "She *led* him right to your aunt. And now look how close we are to finding her. A total setup. I'm still not sure what all that means, Olivia. But I know you're a very honest, good person. And from everything I've learned about Madam Miranda, she was, too."

Olivia nodded, appreciating that. "My mother must have had her reasons for putting it the way she did to your dad, the clues to Sarah's identity. And I think the reason was that she knew it was time. In that she was running out of time herself, and because it was time for Sarah to come home. Time for Sarah to be with her own great love. And time for your father to find his. They happened to be one and the same."

Carson closed his eyes. She could feel him internally shaking his head even though he sat ramrod-straight.

"This is what I know about life and how it works, Olivia," he said. "If you're *there*, if you show up, if

you do the work—you might get what you want. That's
how things happen. Period. Not via a crystal ball."
And this time he did bolt up. He ran a hand through
his thick, dark hair and let out a breath. "I need to get
home to my son."

She didn't know how to argue with what he was saying. There was no argument. He was right. But he was
ignoring the whole other side of the coin. Hope, faith,
love—need. All things you couldn't see or touch. You
felt those things.

She walked Carson to the door and opened it. She
half expected him to rush out without saying goodbye,
but he stopped in the doorway and turned. He reached
up his hand and touched her face, and then gave her
something of a nod before walking to his car.

Unsettled, her heart heavy, Olivia shut the door and
sat back down on the couch. She pulled Sweetie up
onto her lap and held her close and knew with total
crystal-ball clarity that she'd fallen in love with Carson
Ford. She picked up Sweetie and walked past the red
velvet curtains into the fortune-telling nook. The real
crystal ball in its holder sat on the table. She leaned
over to look inside it but saw nothing, just her reflection and Sweetie's face. "Is Carson the one for me or
am I headed for heartbreak?" she asked.

She didn't expect an answer and didn't get one.

Until Sweetie let out one meow and nuzzled her
cheek.

"Is that a yes or a no?" she asked the cat.

Sweetie nuzzled again. Olivia liked to think that
was cat for *yes*. But a moment later, Olivia was back
to "unclear at this time" like from the old Magic 8 Ball
she and her friends used to play with at sleepovers.

She wasn't so sure she would ask again later, though.
Maybe sometimes it was better not to know a thing
about what would happen.

Chapter Ten

Carson spent the next morning with his son. After making Danny his favorite chocolate-chip-and-banana pancakes for breakfast, they went to the playground, then the library for story hour, then home for a nap. When Danny woke up, they played hide-and-seek in the backyard and a little T-ball, then headed in to await the sitter. Carson didn't want to leave the little guy. He gave Danny a big hug, very aware that he was about to pick up Joey Johnson for the trip over to confront his father.

I'll always be here for you, Carson thought, giving Danny a kiss on the head before heading out.

He'd needed today. Much of it spent with Danny and now on his work. Some time away from Olivia and fortune-telling seemed the ticket, until he realized all he was doing was thinking about her. At the playground, he heard a caregiver singing a song to a toddler falling asleep in her arms, and he'd found himself wishing Olivia could be there with them. And when he'd pushed Danny on the toddler swings, he felt strangely bereft, like something was missing. Someone. Olivia. He wanted her beside him, singing that meatball song and wearing that skirt with the bulldogs on it.

What he really needed was a bracing cup of coffee and to focus on his work, which this afternoon meant taking Joey to the rodeo barns. He had no idea what to expect, how this was going to play out, and he'd made sure to call Joey's mom last night to make sure she knew it might not go well and that Joey needed to be braced for that.

When he arrived at the Johnsons', Joey was waiting for him on the steps. Carson waved at his mom, who was standing at the window, and off they went. Joey was silent in the car on the way there, holding a letter in his hand from his mom to his father. Joey had explained the letter said that his mother wanted nothing from Steve Johnson except for him to open his life to let Joey in, that she would drive him out to visit once a week or more, depending on what they were both comfortable with.

As Carson pulled into a spot at the rodeo grounds, Joey fell apart. The boy's shoulders began quaking and he just sat there crying, holding his letter.

Carson turned off the ignition and turned to face Joey. "Hey. You know what the most important thing about today is? No matter what happens? That you're here. That you tried. No matter what happens, Joey, you'll always know that. Trying is everything."

"But what if he doesn't even recognize me?" Joey

asks. "Or what if he does and he just walks away?" Tears fell down the boy's freckled cheeks.

His heart clenching, Carson repeated, "You'll know you tried. That's all you can do sometimes. But that way you'll have no regrets because you did what you could. You're a great kid, Joey."

Joey wiped under his eyes and took a deep breath. "Is it time?" he asked, looking up at Carson, then at the dashboard clock. His father got off work in a few minutes.

"It's just about time," Carson said. "Let's go."

Every figurative finger crossed, he walked Joey out to the barns. Two men came out first, their Stetsons pulled down low against the bright sunshine, and he could feel Joey practically jump beside him. Neither man was his father, though. Then another cowboy, and a cowgirl carrying a saddle.

Finally, a couple minutes later, as he and Joey were just steps from the barn, another man came out. Steve Johnson. He was carrying a knapsack over his shoulder and wearing a black cowboy hat.

Joey stopped in his tracks. "Dad?" he said, almost in a whisper.

Steve glanced over their way and froze. "Joey? My God, Joey?"

Joey nodded and the two walked toward each other, Steve throwing down the knapsack and running over to his son.

The cowboy hugged him tight. "I can't believe it's really you."

"It's me," Joey said.

Carson explained who he was and that Joey had hired him to track him down solely so that the two could have a father-and-son relationship, that this wasn't about anything else. Joey handed over the letter, and at the obviously familiar handwriting, Steve froze, then opened it and read it. He put in his pocket.

"I'm sorry for just leaving you," Steve said, looking down at the ground. "I didn't mean to stay away. I just had some problems I had to take care of. And then one day became a week and then a month and then a year, then more. And I never felt like I could come back."

"Why?" Joey asked. Carson could tell from the boy's expression that it was the question he wanted answered more than anything else.

"I guess because I'd been gone so long and thought you hated me. You'd have every right."

"I don't hate you," Joey said, his voice breaking. "I miss you."

"I've missed you like crazy," Steve said, pulling him into another hug.

Carson directed the two to a picnic table by the barns to talk privately. A half hour later, they came over to where Carson waited. Steve said he was going to call Joey's mom and make arrangements to pick up Joey every Saturday. Carson was so damned happy for Joey he almost did a fist pump. Sometimes, things really worked out. Carson liked those times.

He extended his hand and Steve shook it. "I'm very glad to hear it."

The entire way back home, Joey talked nonstop about the things his dad had told him, how he'd learned how to be a cowboy and had even won a few bronc-riding competitions. He'd asked a ton of questions about Joey, how he liked school and what he was learning and what he liked to do after school.

"Wow, can you imagine if I didn't hire you to find him?" Joey asked, his manner, his voice, his whole bearing completely different than on the way over. "He'd still be gone and I'd still be always wondering about my dad. Now he's coming to pick me up on Saturday for a whole day together."

"You were incredibly brave," Carson said. "I've got to hand it to you. And I'm very happy with how things turned out."

Joey Johnson was exceptionally brave. Carson thought about all the times he'd wanted to confront his dad, who'd been physically there, sometimes, anyway, about always canceling their plans or not turning up to birthday celebrations or traveling on holidays for business, but he'd always felt too proud to let anyone know how disappointed and hurt he'd been. So he'd kept it all bottled up inside, giving himself stomachaches. His mother had known; she'd been able to tell by his expression, but Carson had never opened up to her much about it.

But here, a nine-year-old had gone all out, risking everything to *try*. The afternoon could have gone very differently, very painfully. As a PI, Carson had experienced quite a few of those reunions. There were some people, like his old neighbor's son, who really didn't want to be found.

But some people, people who drove right into Blue Gulch, clearly did. And so it was time to find Sarah Mack once and for all and he would if he had to drive down every road of every street in the county and surrounding ones. He'd find that little yellow car; he'd find Sarah, and he'd give Olivia what she needed: her aunt.

As he turned onto the road toward Oak Creek, he

realized something. He suddenly wanted to find Sarah Mack more for Olivia's sake than to prove to his father that the woman wasn't his second great love, that he'd feel the same nothing at the sight of her as he had for the stylist in the Oak Creek salon.

Which meant he'd come to care about Olivia Mack way too much.

And that a nine-year-old kid was a hell of a lot braver than he was.

Carson dropped off Joey and talked with his relieved mom a bit, then hit the road, starting with the main street of Oak Creek to look for the yellow Beetle. For all they know, Sarah Mack lived in Oak Creek, just a town away from Blue Gulch. But he didn't see the car and driving through town got him nowhere, too. He was going to try the town to the east, then decided he'd try Blue Gulch again. If Sarah had gone there once— who knew how many times she'd driven around Blue Gulch, really—she would go back. He had no doubt that the woman had driven through town to catch a glimpse of her niece.

The car wasn't on Blue Gulch Street or in any of the parking spots or lots. But when he turned onto a side road and pulled into the parking lot behind the library, there it was, way in the back, the last spot, between the brick wall of a building and a minivan. He checked the plate to make sure—it was definitely Sarah Mack's car.

Yes! Thank you, universe.

Adrenaline coursing through him, Carson parked and headed inside the library, which wasn't very crowded, but there was no sign of a woman matching Sarah's description. He did another sweep, just in case he'd missed her. As politely as possible he excused himself from the children's librarian who'd come over to say hello and ask how Danny was. Normally, he'd love to talk about his favorite subject—his son—but he had an aunt to find.

He headed out through the front door of the library and looked around, trying to spot a tall, forty-eight-year-old woman with long auburn hair, probably curly, per Olivia. Blue Gulch Street was crowded today with people walking around for day two of the sidewalk sale, so spotting anyone wasn't easy. His dad's closest neighbors were heading into the Blue Gulch coffee shop with lots of shopping bags in their hands. And there were the Hurleys—Essie Hurley, owner of Hurley's Homestyle Kitchen and the food truck that Olivia worked in, and her three granddaughters with their husbands. Annabel and West, with a baby in a carrier on his chest, and their little girl. Georgia and Nick—the detective who'd called him about Sarah Mack's car in the first place—with a baby in a stroller. And Clementine and Logan with a pair of cute young twins and a girl around nine or ten. The big family, whom Carson had met at Nick's wedding, was setting down blankets on the town green, picnic baskets as corner weights. A few yards away, one of Danny's day care mates and his family were trying to teach a puppy to sit. He scanned the crowded green, looking for anyone who fit the bill.

Wait a minute. Could that be her?

Sitting across the square, on one of the small boulders that dotted the far edges of the town green and doubled as low seats, was a woman who looked to be in her midforties, tall, wearing huge black sunglasses and a gray cap. An auburn ponytail lay on one shoulder. She was alone and seemed to be people watching, but she was sitting across from the food truck just on the other side of the square. Because she was trying to catch a glimpse of her niece? She wore a casual gray dress—maybe so she wouldn't stand out.

He had a pretty good feeling the woman was Sarah Mack. He pulled out his phone and pressed in Olivia's telephone number, his heart beating ten miles a minute.

Olivia hurried out of her house, Carson's phone call just a moment ago echoing in her mind. He was ninety-nine percent sure that her aunt was sitting on the town green, looking toward the Hurley's food truck. Olivia lived just a couple minutes away by foot. *Please don't be gone when I get there*, she thought.

At the corner of Blue Gulch Street, she saw Carson standing in front of the coffee shop, sipping from a take-out cup. He nodded across the green and she followed the direction of his gaze.

Every molecule in her body seemed to speed up and slow down at the same time. The woman sitting there in the huge sunglasses was Aunt Sarah. She'd know her anywhere, big black lenses covering her face or not.

As she walked toward her aunt from the right, away from where Sarah was looking, she could see the silver glint of the tattoo on her ankle. The brush. As she drew closer, she could see the hot pink blow-dryer. Aunt Sarah. She was really here.

She walked closer, unsure if she could call out or just present herself.

Finally, she was just steps away.

"Aunt Sarah," she said softly.

Sarah started and turned and whipped off her sunglasses. "Olivia. Olivia!" She rushed over and enveloped Olivia into a hug.

"I can't believe you just found me," Sarah said, her green eyes glistening with tears. "I've been hanging around town the past few days, looking for glimpses of you. I wasn't ready to just knock on your door. I heard in town from bits here and there that you run the food truck, so I thought I'd catch a glimpse of you working."

"Why have you come now?" Olivia asked. "I mean, was there a specific reason you chose now?"

"I can't explain it," Sarah said. "I just had this overpowering urge the last few weeks to see you, even from a distance."

"Mom died," Olivia said on a whisper, barely able to say the words.

Sarah's expression clouded over. "I know. I...felt it, I guess. And because of that, I looked for the obituary until there it was. I did attend the funeral in disguise. I just wasn't ready to see you."

"But why?" Olivia asked. "I don't understand. I've never understood."

Sarah took a deep breath. "Let's talk about this in private."

While her aunt sat on the sofa in the living room of Olivia's house, making baby talk to Sweetie about how much she missed the dear old cat, Olivia put together a cheese-and-cracker plate in the kitchen, thinking that Sarah and Edmund already had the warm-hearted baby talk in common. She smiled, imagining the two meeting for the first time, thunderstruck at the sight of each other.

But there was a lot to get through before she'd even

raise the subject of Miranda's prediction. Such as what had kept her aunt away for so long. She poured two glasses of white wine and set everything on a tray, her hands trembling a bit with anticipation of finally learning what had come between the sisters.

As she was bringing the tray into the living room, she half expected to find her aunt gone. But there she sat, her beautiful green eyes giving nothing away, her curly auburn hair in a long ponytail off to one side. Again, Olivia's gaze locked on the little tattoo on her ankle. Her aunt, now forty-eight, hadn't changed a whit in five years.

She handed Sarah a glass of wine, and they clinked. She'd hoped her aunt might make a toast—to their reunion, to the future—but she didn't. Perhaps Sarah felt toasts might be better saved until everything was said.

"Will you tell me why you left five years ago?" Olivia asked as she sat down across from Sarah.

Sarah took a deep breath and let it out. She sipped her wine, put it down and crossed her arms over her chest, as if protecting herself from what she was about to say. "A very long time ago, when I was just sixteen years old, I discovered I was pregnant. The father, my then boyfriend, immediately broke up with me and insisted it couldn't be his. My mother, very firmly, told me that for the sake of the babies, I had to give them up for adoption and that there would be no discussion."

"Babies?" Olivia whispered. Not baby. *Babies.*

She nodded. "Yes, babies. My mother knew before I did that I was pregnant with twins. She sent me away to a home for pregnant teenagers in Houston. I never held the babies or saw them. But I did hear one of the nurses say that they were boys. Fraternal twins."

"I had no idea," Olivia said, thinking of Sarah at only sixteen, pregnant, sent away. How scary it must have been.

"I came back home and never talked about it," Sarah continued. "My mother refused to discuss it, never brought it up, not once, and my sister was only fourteen. Miranda asked questions, but I always cut her off and eventually she stopped. I just turned inward and tried to pretend the whole thing had been a dream."

"Oh, Aunt Sarah. It must have been so hard. You were so young."

She sipped her wine and looked away as if trying to stop a memory. "When I was seventeen and my gift was supposed to make itself known, it didn't. I thought I was being blamed for getting pregnant, for giving away the twins. I shut down even more." Sarah stood up and walked over to the windows, looking out at the backyard.

"Did your gift ever materialize?" Olivia asked.

Sarah turned to face her. "No. I don't know why. My mother said that sometimes it skipped a generation or a person, that her aunt didn't have a gift. But when Miranda turned seventeen and it became clear she had the gift of predicting the future, I felt so jealous. I kept my distance from her and told her she was never, ever, to tell me anything about my future or I'd never speak to her again. So she never did."

"Until five years ago?" Olivia asked, her heart in her throat.

Sarah nodded. "Until five years ago. Miranda told me that she knew, just knew, that one of the twins—who'd been adopted separately—was desperately trying to find me and having no luck. I told her to stop, that I didn't want to hear it. I reminded her that she promised me she'd never tell me anything about my future, and she said it wasn't *my* future—it was the boys'. I was so upset with her. This was my business, not hers."

"But she didn't stop?" Olivia asked. Her mother could be relentless when she felt strongly about something. She must have felt *very* strongly about what she was telling her sister.

"Miranda kept telling me to just check with the adoption agency, that I'd find contact information there, that she *knew* it was important I do so. I told her to mind her own business, that I didn't want to hear more, that I couldn't handle it. She said I *had* to handle it. That night, I packed my things and left."

"Oh, Aunt Sarah, it must be hard for you to even talk about. I'm so sorry."

Her aunt's face crumped for a moment. "It's very hard. For so long I didn't let myself even think about being pregnant or all my hopes and dreams that somehow, I could just run away and have the twins. But I was so afraid. I had no one. I was just sixteen. My mother was so firm about how things would be. The night I gave birth, when it was all over, I literally felt something inside my chest shutter closed."

Olivia rushed over to her aunt and wrapped her arms around her. Sarah stiffened, but finally she embraced Olivia and allowed the hug, the comfort.

"Until five years ago, I never allowed myself to think about that night. The loss. The heartbreak. I'm so sorry I left you behind, Livvy. I was so unfair to you. When I knew that Miranda passed away, I began feeling terrible shame and guilt that I hadn't listened to her, that I let my own fear keep me from helping the boys—or one of them. But I was so shut down about it."

Olivia could well imagine how scared and alone her aunt had felt—thirty-two years ago and five years ago. And now, as well. "I understand, Aunt Sarah. I really do."

"And lately," Sarah continued, "these past few weeks, I can't explain it, but I feel ready to check that registry and see if they…or one, anyway, is looking for me. I've been worried that maybe Miranda's insistence was because she knew one or both needed a blood relative for something health-related." She shook her head, tears glistening in her eyes. "What if I'm too late?"

"Aunt Sarah, maybe she just thought it was time for you to make peace with your past. Perhaps she foresaw that the twins simply wanted to find their birth mother, which is natural."

"Perhaps."

Olivia waited for Sarah to continue, but her aunt remained silent and turned back to the window again.

Olivia sensed that her aunt needed a break from the conversation. "Where do you live?" she asked.

Sarah turned around. "In Tuckerville. I'm still a hairstylist. When I first moved there, I made up a phony last name and worked off the books in a busy salon, and when I built up a following in a few months, I began working out of my home. I have an over-the-top stage name that I go by professionally—Starlight Smith. I was trying to make myself difficult to find— by anyone." She turned away again and her shoulders started shaking.

Olivia wrapped her arms around her aunt, who began sobbing. "I'm so glad you told me. And that you're here. No matter what, Sarah, we're family and we belong together."

Sarah squeezed her hand. "I think I need to rest. Is the guest room still a guest room?"

Olivia nodded. "Yup."

As Sarah headed down the hall, she turned and said, "I promise I won't flee. I do feel a little shaky about talking about the twins. They're thirty-two years old now. Grown men who very likely have families of their own." She closed her eyes. "I'd better go lie down for a bit."

She disappeared into the guest room with Sweetie following.

Olivia sank down on the sofa, starting to process everything she'd learned. If her aunt really did want to track down the twins, Carson could help.

What she would give to unload to him right now, feel his strong arms around her.

"Olivia?" Sarah called.

Olivia went into the guest room. "Do you need something?"

"Your mom knew I loved her, right?" Sarah asked, tears glistening again. "I just need to know that she did."

Olivia sat on the edge of the bed. "She did know. She told me that constantly. When you first left, I kept pestering her to tell me what happened, that I'd heard the tail end of an argument. And she'd always say, 'We did have an argument and Sarah needs to process it in her own way on her own time. She loves us, even though she left. Always remember that.'"

Sarah reached over and squeezed Olivia's hand. "I

knew she'd understand. Even if she didn't agree. I feel a lot better about that."

"While she was dying, she asked me to promise to find you so that I could deliver a letter and a family heirloom. I assured her I would. Would you like the letter and heirloom now?"

"Okay," she said.

Olivia rushed to her bedroom and retrieved the letter and the box with the gold bangle bracelet that had both sisters' names engraved on it. It had been their grandmother's.

The letter was sealed with red wax but it wasn't very long since the envelope was so thin. Olivia had always wondered what it said, but she wouldn't ask unless Sarah wanted to share it.

She left her aunt alone to read the letter. Ten minutes later, Sarah came into the kitchen, where Olivia was tidying up.

"Do you want to read the letter?" Sarah asked, handing it over. Olivia almost gasped when she realized her aunt was wearing the gold bangle. The letter must have done its job.

Olivia nodded and took it. The letter was handwritten on thin white stationery in black ink.

Dear Sarah,

I'm sorry that I drove you away. It's always been a fine line for me to know when to stay silent. I should have respected your feelings. I hope you'll forgive me. If you do, I'll know it.

All my love,

Your sister, Miranda

"I do forgive her," Sarah said, brushing tears from under her eyes. "And you know, I do think she knows it," she added, looking toward the ceiling.

Olivia hugged her aunt, then put the letter back in the envelope.

"I was thinking about hiring a private investigator to help me find the twins," Sarah said. "If they have been looking for me, I want them to be able to contact me. And if they haven't been looking, well, I'll just leave my contact information so that they can find me if they ever decide to do so. I suppose I could start with the adoption agency and the registry, but I think I would rather have someone I trust go through the steps and arrange things for me."

Olivia smiled. "I know just the guy."

Chapter Eleven

Over dinner, Olivia explained the whole story to her aunt, about Carson barging up to the food truck, the prediction about his father's second great love being a green-eyed hairstylist named Sarah with a small tattoo of a brush and a blow-dryer on her ankle and the road trips to find her.

The more she talked, the more Olivia became aware of her aunt's stricken expression.

"I want no part of this," Sarah said through gritted teeth. She stood up and grabbed her tote bag and then rushed out the door.

Oh, no. No, no, no.

"Sarah, wait!" Olivia called, rushing after her. She saw her aunt hurrying toward the town green.

Olivia stepped back inside and closed her eyes. Why hasn't she anticipated that her aunt wouldn't want any part of her mother's fortune-telling or prediction? Aunt Sarah was clearly uncomfortable with all that. Especially because Miranda had "seen" something regarding the twins, or one of them, anyway, and it had driven Sarah away. Olivia should have known Sarah would react negatively to being a part of Miranda's prediction.

Head against the wall, she thought, very tempted to thunk her forehead against the front door. She should have handled this better. But she'd simply told the truth. She couldn't *not* tell Sarah about the prediction, particularly since the one private investigator Olivia knew— and trusted with all her heart—was the son of Sarah's predicted great love. Ugh. Why would Sarah be comfortable with that? Of course she wouldn't be.

What a mess. Just like it was in the beginning, when Carson *had* barged up to the food truck, full of preconceived notions.

She grabbed her phone and called Sarah, thanking her lucky stars that her aunt had given Olivia her cell phone number and address while they were cooking together. She pressed in the number. Voice mail.

"Sarah, I'm sorry I was so insensitive," Olivia said. "I know you don't like any of this. Please don't leave again. Can we please just talk?"

She put the phone away, unsure what to do. Edmund Ford came to mind—that wonderful, kind, doting grandfather. Meeting his Sarah meant everything to Edmund. What if Sarah came back and said there was no way she was meeting some man her sister thought was her great love? She had every right not to, but now Olivia felt for Edmund Ford.

She pulled out her phone again and called Carson. She wouldn't betray her aunt's confidence about the twins, certainly not concerning such a personal subject, but she needed to hear his voice, get his perspective. He'd found Sarah for her. Maybe he could find her again.

He answered immediately. "Let me try talking to her," Carson said. "I don't know what the big argument between the sisters was about, but I do know how *I* feel about the prediction and my dad. Once she hears what I have to say about the whole thing, she may agree to meet my dad just so I can be proven right and we can all get on with our lives, and you and Sarah can rebuild your relationship."

We can all get on with our lives... Her heart clenched as she gave Carson Sarah's address and telephone number.

"Would you mind watching Danny while I go to her house?" he asked.

"Of course," she said. "I'll come right over." She paused, realizing she had to tell him something, something he might not like hearing. "Carson, if Sarah will talk to you and she agrees to meet your dad, you do need to accept that it's going to be love at first sight. My mother's predictions were rarely wrong."

"I'm hardly worried about that, Olivia. Power of suggestion. People make things so. You can make yourself believe what you want. My dad might be affected by the prediction and all starry-eyed and full of hope, but clearly your aunt wants no part of it. She won't be walking into the situation expecting to be blown away by love."

My aunt knows that her sister's gift was very real, though, Olivia wanted to counter. From the time Miranda was seventeen until five years ago, Sarah had witnessed her predictions come true constantly. But Olivia knew to let it go for now. "We'll see," she said gently.

"Yes, we will."

If he could convince Sarah to meet Edmund in the first place. Olivia wasn't so sure about that.

"I can't believe she's gone again," Olivia said when Carson opened the door of his house and let her in. "I just got her back."

He squeezed her hand, his heart going out to her. "Let me see what I can do." He looked over at Danny, who was sitting in his playpen, squeezing his new stuffed panda that sang a silly song. "Danny, look who's here to play with you while I go do some work."

Danny stood up. "Liva!"

Carson loved watching Olivia's expression go from worried to pure happiness at the sight of the toddler holding out his arms for her to scoop him up.

She hurried over to Danny and picked him up, giving him a cuddle. "I'm so happy to see you, Danny. Want to do a puzzle?" she asked, pointing at the four-piece puzzle of a dolphin.

"See you two later," Carson said, kissing the top of Danny's head. "Everything will be okay."

"I didn't think you believed in that kind of thing," she said with a bit of a sad smile.

He narrowed his eyes at her. He wasn't going to say that it was just something people said because he didn't go around making platitudes about important things. He really did think this would work out okay. He'd state the facts to her aunt, who seemed levelheaded, and she'd agree to meet his dad to get it out of the way and off the table. Sarah and Edmund would feel absolutely nothing for each other, and that would be that.

"Instinct. Gut reaction. Those have validity," he said.

"Thanks for doing this." With Danny in her arms, she smiled at the little boy, who was twirling a long lock of her silky brown hair.

His own smile faltered. He was doing this so that he could put an end to it. But at least he'd bring Olivia and Sarah back together again. That was what this was all about.

For the past twenty minutes, Danny had sat in Olivia's lap on the overstuffed rocker by the window as she read him the same picture book four times, pointing at the pages and giggling. A talking monkey who liked hamburgers was very funny stuff to a toddler.

As she closed the book, grateful that Danny didn't ask her to read it a fifth time, she wondered what was going on with Carson and her aunt right now. Had Carson gotten ahold of Sarah? Had she refused to talk to him? Carson could be pretty persuasive. Hadn't he gotten her to agree to come to his father's house that first day he stormed up to the food truck?

"Monkey?" Danny asked, scrambling off her lap and looking around his toy area in the family room. "Monkey?" he said, picking up stuffed animals and tossing them aside. "Monkey?"

"I'll help you look," she said, getting up from the rocking chair.

She missed the feel of Danny against her. She loved the way his hair smelled, like baby shampoo. She loved the little weight of him. She loved the way the expres-

sion in his big hazel-green eyes changed every other
second with worry or delight as the monkey in the book
gobbled up every hamburger in town and got a belly-
ache. She loved *him*.

So what was going to happen now? What was Olivia
supposed to do with all this…love? Carson didn't seem
to want it. Danny wasn't hers to give it to. And if Carson
had his way, the three Fords would be out of her life in
a matter of time, once he got his father and Sarah together to prove—supposedly—that there was no spark,
no connection. No great love happening.

Her cell phone rang and Olivia grabbed it out of her
pocket, keeping an eye on Danny as she kept looking
for the stuffed monkey. It was Dory.

"Guess what!" Dory practically screamed in her ear.
"I did it! I got the loan. I'm going to save the bakery
on my own."

Olivia's heart leaped for her friend. "I'm so happy
for you! Let me know when you're free to celebrate
with one of your amazing cupcakes, on me, of course."

"Thanks," Dory said. "And thanks for being there
and listening. I had a long talk with Beaufort about
everything—and I mean everything. Do you know that
his mother threatened to sue me for public humiliation
and the cost of the engagement toast gathering? Beaufort managed to calm her down."

Olivia could just picture Annalee Harrington with
steam coming out of her ears. "His mother must be
scrambling to undo all the publicity she generated."

"Well, it's the strangest thing, Olivia. When I told
Beaufort about the loan—of course, I didn't use his
bank, Texas Trust—he was truly happy for me. He
said our whole romance might have been put on the

fast track by his ambition-crazed family, but that he has real feelings for me. He asked if we could get together to talk, maybe start over from scratch and see if there is something real underneath everything—no photographers or reporters or mothers. I reminded him that I planned to work every day in my bakery, that it's as important to me as running for mayor is for him, and he finally got it."

Olivia smiled. "Do you think there's a chance for you two?"

"I honestly don't know. I do like Beaufort an awful lot. But I'm not in love—as your mother made me focus on. All this time I thought she was saying that he wasn't the one for me. But she was just telling me to look into my heart, to acknowledge my feelings or lack thereof. I started things with Beaufort for the same reason he started things with me—because we could each help each other out. Now, we want to see what's there with no eye at the future. Just each other."

"That's great, Dory. I'm doubly happy for you."

As Dory said goodbye and Olivia pocketed the phone, she realized her friend was right; her mother had never said Beaufort wasn't "the one" for Dory. He could be. But before, Dory wasn't listening to her heart, which had been telling her to fix her life herself and not exchange herself and that heart so that someone else could make things all better.

Her mother was a smart cookie. Insightful. She just *knew*. Based on what Miranda had told Dory and her refusal to say anything else, Olivia had the feeling that Beaufort Harrington might well be the one for Dory and that Madam Miranda had put Dory on the path to questioning what she was doing. Now Dory had rescued herself—and might still get the handsome knight.

If only I *knew what would happen in my own life*, she thought, again wondering if Carson was talking to Sarah that very moment.

"Monkey!" Danny said, pointing down the hall. He took off running.

She followed, pausing as Danny raced into his father's bedroom. Olivia didn't think she should be going into Carson's room, but she couldn't exactly let Danny run around unattended. She stood in the doorway as he looked around the large room for the stuffed monkey.

A king-size bed was against the back wall, centered between two end tables, a short stack of books on one. As Danny climbed onto the bed, she saw that a pile of stuffed animals was wedged between the pillows. Including a yellow monkey. In the corner of the room by the windows was a little play area with a foam interlocking mat decorated with letters and numbers. Building blocks, toys, more stuffed animals. This wasn't exactly Carson's bachelor lair or sanctuary. He was a dad through and through.

Danny flopped backward on the bed, holding up the yellow monkey and making him dance. Olivia sat down next to him, sinking into the plushness of the navy-and-white comforter. She couldn't help imagining Carson coming out of the master bathroom, naked, damp, his dark hair slicked back.

She allowed herself to push away all that was on her mind and just think of Carson kissing her.

Until a yellow sock monkey started dancing on her thigh. "Hi, Liva! Monkey!"

She blinked away thoughts of a naked Carson to focus on the here and now.

"Catch?" Danny asked, scrambling off the bed so slowly that she could have caught him in two seconds. He went giggling out of the room.

"I'm gonna get you!" she said, chasing him in slow motion.

You've already caught me, she thought. *And so has your dad.*

It was a hell of a lot easier to find Sarah Mack when number one, Carson knew her address, and number two, she was sitting on the steps of her house, a small yellow bungalow that reminded him of Olivia's. His relief at seeing her there didn't go unnoticed by him. He wanted to make Olivia happy.

As he approached, Sarah was looking away, a worried look in her eyes.

"Sarah? I'm Carson Ford, Olivia's...friend. I'm the son of the man who's supposed to be your great love."

She turned toward him, squinting a bit at the setting sun. "The private investigator?"

He nodded. "I'm sure Olivia told you that I don't want any part in this prediction business, either. To me, it's nonsense and make-believe and the power of suggestion. The only reason I barged into Olivia's life was to ask her to tell my father that her mother was a scam artist."

"She wasn't, though, Carson. My sister was the real deal. That's why I estranged myself from her and her daughter. Did Olivia tell you about that?"

He shook his head. "I only know that you and your sister had an argument and you left five years ago."

"My sister had the gift of knowing. She would get a feeling and simply know. When she told me, five years ago, that one of the twin boys I gave up for adoption at age sixteen was looking for me, that it was important that I contact him, I—I just couldn't handle it. I shut down that part of myself for so long."

"I can understand that," he said, sitting down beside her, keeping enough distance between them. He made sure to give her space, to not bombard her with questions, to let her talk at her own pace.

"I'm not interested in the prediction my sister made to your father, Carson. I don't want any part of that. It's taken me this long—five years—to finally accept what my sister told me about the twins. I'm ready to start the process to find them. I wasn't ready then."

"If you're ready, I can help you," he said. "It would be my pleasure."

She glanced at him, suspicion in her eyes. "Because you want me to meet your dad, right?"

"I would help you regardless, Sarah. But yes, I do want you to meet my father only to put an end to this fortune nonsense. You say your sister had a gift, Olivia says she had a gift. There are supposedly hundreds, thousands of people who believed she had a gift. Well, I don't believe in any of that mumbo jumbo. I believe in reality and facts and, yeah, I rely heavily on my instincts, but that's not seeing into the future. That's about trusting yourself."

"Carson, I'm not sure it's a good idea that I meet your father. I'm sorry, but I would prefer not to."

He got it, he really did. He wished he didn't have to push it; the woman had enough on her mind. For one, she'd just reunited with her niece. Now she'd be undertaking something that would be very emotional for her, push all kinds of buttons: finding the twins she gave up for adoption decades ago. But his father was counting on him. If Carson could just get the love prediction off the table, everyone could focus on their lives again.

"I just need five minutes of your time, Sarah. That's it. Five minutes for you and my dad to take one look each other and feel absolutely nothing. Yeah, he'll be disappointed since he's put so much stock in this green-eyed hairstylist named Sarah being his second great love, but when he sees it's meaningless, that he feels nothing, he'll be free to pursue love with someone *he* chooses, someone he falls for naturally."

Yes, he thought. That was really the point here. He wanted his dad to be happy and find love—his second great love. He truly did. And Edmund would find it once he realized there was nothing between him and Sarah Mack.

"Carson, I really don't want to be put in the position of having to disappoint your father. That seems unfair. So why not just leave it alone? I've got so much on my mind about the possibility of meeting the twins that love and romance are the last things I want."

It finally dawned on Carson that Sarah was saying that she knew his father would fall instantly in love. Because Madam Miranda had said they were destined for each other.

Oh, come on. Was everyone crazy but him?

"My father meets a lot of women in the course of a day," Carson said. "He will meet you and feel the way he does about the vice president of sales or the barista at the coffee shop or the children's librarian who helps him pick books for my son. Please, Sarah. It's all he can think about lately—the mystery woman he's meant to be with. Just let him see it's not meant to be and that will be that."

"It's not meant to be—*for me*," she said. "I guess I can help on that end, since I have no intention of getting involved with any man right now."

Finally. "So you'll meet him? Perhaps you can come for dinner tomorrow night at my house? Neutral turf. Six thirty?"

"And you'll help me find the twins?" she asked.

He nodded and they both stood up.

"Carson, the family gift seems to have skipped me. But my sister *did* have the ability to see beyond. That is just the truth. Not mumbo jumbo or nonsense. The truth."

He stared at her. "Right. So when you meet my father, there'll be fireworks exploding overhead and parades marching and instant love?"

Sarah raised an eyebrow. "I'm just saying that since my sister predicted that I'm the one for your dad, he will very likely feel those fireworks and hear that parade when he meets me."

He won't, Carson thought. *Not a single boom or clang of the cymbals. And come on, she's so sure my dad will fall for her, but she doesn't seem worried one bit about resisting him.* "So it doesn't work both ways? You can be the one for him, but he may not be the one for you?"

"Oh, it works both ways," she said. "But that doesn't mean I have to give in to it. I'm a very strong-willed person, Carson. Clearly. And as I've said, I'm not interested in love. I just want to reconnect with the twins I gave up, have some peace by knowing that they're all right, and then I'll move on. I'd like to keep up my relationship with Olivia, though. I feel terrible that I estranged myself from her. And I should have been there for her these past two months since she lost her mother."

"Well, you're here now." He pictured Olivia, playing with Danny, singing to him, hoping that Carson was able to convince her aunt to come back. He didn't want Olivia hurt. He wanted to be happy. He gave her his address. "Six thirty, tomorrow night."

"I'll be there. But I'm not sure you're going to get what you want. You may end up with a bigger problem."

"Meaning?" Carson drew in a deep breath.

Sarah Mack stood up and lifted her chin. "Might as well wait till you cross that bridge, as they say."

He didn't want to cross whatever bridge she was referring to.

Chapter Twelve

"Dad?" Carson called out as he let himself in his father's house in Blue Gulch the next morning.

He had no idea how this was going to turn out—tonight, dinner at his house. With his father. Sarah. And Olivia, of course.

"In the kitchen," his dad called back.

Carson entered the kitchen to find his dad trying to frost a very lopsided cake. Except every time Edmund swiped the rubber spatula against the side of the vanilla sponge, the frosting took off a slab of the cake.

"Yesterday I promised Danny I'd bake him a cake for his half birthday," Edmund said, frosting all over the striped apron he wore and a glob on his shearling house slipper. "It might not *look* good, but it'll *taste* good. That's what counts."

Carson froze, staring from the cake to his father.

What would he do without this man? What would Danny do without him? "You're a great grandfather," he said, looking at the ridiculous cake again. Carson wouldn't be surprised if it caved in on itself. "Danny is very, very lucky to have you."

Edmund lifted his chin, the way he did when he was touched by praise. "Maybe I'm trying to make up for what I didn't do the first time around. When I had a terrific eighteen-month-old of my own running around my house in Oak Creek and I was too busy with my work and committees and the town council. I let you down and I let your mother down." He dropped the rubber spatula on the counter, another glob of chocolate icing splattering against his apron. "I won't let Danny down."

"Dad, you know what I've been realizing? When I was a kid, you did what felt right to you. You worked. Hard. The way you saw it, you were supporting your family and so you put work ahead of everything so that nothing would interfere. I never understood that before."

"That doesn't make it right. I wasn't there for you, Carson. And I wasn't there for your mother." He took a deep breath. "I've been doing a lot of thinking the past couple of days. I'm calling off the hunt for Sarah. After the way I lived my life when I had everything a man could want, I have no business trying to find a second great love. I had my chance the first time around and I blew it. Right now, I'm going to focus on Danny. He only has one parent. I'm going to make up for everything he doesn't have."

Carson's stomach twisted. "Dad, you *do* have a right to a second chance and a second love. You're a completely different person than you were when I was growing up. You're here, one hundred percent for both me and Danny. When Jodie left and I realized she wasn't coming back, *you* were there in the NICU. You were there when I was scared to death that my newborn son might not make it. And you've been by my side ever since, for eighteen months. You've been more than an amazing grandfather. You've been an amazing *dad*."

Edmund grabbed him in a bear hug. "You have no idea how much that means to me. How much *you* mean to me. I know you know how much I love Danny. But I also love you with all my heart, Carson. I always have since the day you were born. I'm just better at making it clear these days."

Carson could feel decades' worth of old resentments ungluing from the cells of his body.

Suddenly, Carson wanted his father to take one look at Sarah Mack and hear those parade cymbals clanking and drumbeats, and for fireworks to go off over his head. He wanted cartoon hearts pouring out of his chest as he staggered around, shot by Cupid's arrow. He wanted his father to feel what Carson felt every time he looked at Olivia.

Oh, God.

What?

He loved Olivia?

He loved Olivia.

But he couldn't love her. He'd shut himself down, off, wasn't letting anyone in. Final answer.

And just because you felt something didn't mean you had to give in to it. Wasn't that what Sarah Mack had said last night? She'd meet his dad, and if she felt anything for him, she'd simply not act on it. She wanted to focus on finding the twins she'd given up for adoption. And on her niece, with whom she'd just gotten reunited. She'd closed herself off to love, like Carson, and would simply *not go there*. It was that easy.

Feeling better about everything, except the part about his dad possibly getting hurt, Carson picked up the spatula. "Want some help frosting this cake?"

His dad would not get hurt. His dad would meet Sarah, feel absolutely nothing, be a little disappointed that the prediction was silly nonsense and find his second great love on his own. He'd meet a lovely woman whom *he* chose. Everything *would* work out just fine.

Edmund smiled. "I sure do. I might be good at being a grandfather, but I'm a terrible baker."

"Dad, the reason I stopped by is to tell you that I found Sarah Mack."

His dad stared at him. "What?"

"I found her, Dad. And she's agreed to come to my house for dinner tonight to meet you. I'll warn you—she's not looking for love." *Just like I'm not.*

"I wasn't necessarily looking for love, either," Edmund said. "But the idea presented itself. It's funny—once it did, I couldn't stop thinking about. A second chance. A fresh shot. A new beginning."

Carson frowned. All things he was refusing to take for himself. "Well, just be forewarned that she's got a lot going on right now and doesn't seem very interested in romance."

"I'm not worried," Edmund said. "Madam Miranda said it was so and it'll be so. You can't ignore destiny."

"Well, you can."

"You can *try* to ignore destiny, Carson. There's a big difference."

Carson swallowed.

* * *

Six thirty came and went. So did six thirty-five. Now, as Olivia glanced at the grandfather clock against the wall of the living room in Carson's house, she realized that Carson and Edmund were doing the same thing.

What if her aunt changed her mind? About everything? What if she'd gone back to her incognito life? Although now, Olivia had Sarah's address and telephone number. Of course, that didn't mean her aunt would answer the door or the phone or ever speak to Olivia again. Last night, after Carson had called Olivia and let her know he'd talked to Sarah and that she'd agreed to come to dinner tonight, Olivia had left her aunt a voice mail message. She'd said only that she'd missed her so much the past five years and couldn't bear to lose her again, and that no matter what, to call when she was ready to talk.

So far, she hadn't heard from Sarah. Not last night, not all day today.

"The suspense is killing me," Edmund said. "I'm going to check on Danny."

Danny had been so tuckered out from a fun afternoon of playing with his grandfather that he'd fallen asleep on the car ride over to Carson's and had been effortlessly transferred to his crib.

As Edmund headed down the hall, Olivia peered out the windows. No little yellow car.

Now it was six forty.

"We have to accept that she might not come," Carson said, sitting down on the leather sofa. "She's skittish, that's for sure."

"I can understand why," Olivia said, too jumpy to

sit. Based on what Carson said, even if her aunt fell instantly in love with Edmund, she was going to fight it to focus on her own mission. And to continue to ignore her sister's ability, something she never made peace with.

There was a knock at the door, and Olivia's eyes widened. Carson leaped up.

"She came," Olivia whispered, relief flooding her.

Carson opened the door, Olivia standing behind him.

And there was Sarah Mack, wearing a navy blue dress, her hair in a low ponytail. She carried a small yellow box from Drummond's Bake Shop. One day, if it ever seemed like the right time, Olivia would tell her aunt all about Dory and her own fortune.

"Thank you for coming," Carson said to Sarah. "It means a lot."

Olivia slipped past Carson and hugged her aunt. "I'm so glad you're here."

Sarah smiled at her. "I still can't get over how good it feels to see you, Olivia. Five years without and suddenly now, twice in two days. I've missed you so much."

"Me, too," Olivia said, a little lump forming in her throat.

Sarah handed Carson the box. "Cookies from my favorite bakery in Blue Gulch." She glanced past Carson, looking around the living room. "Is your father here?"

"He's upstairs, checking on my son," Carson said. "Danny's eighteen months. Sometimes my dad says he's going to check on Danny while he's napping and he ends up just sitting there, staring at him sleeping, marveling at his features. I've caught him doing it and it always makes me choke up a little. When you witness love."

Olivia stared at Carson, dumbstruck by what she'd just heard come out of his mouth. Choking up? Witnessing love?

"He sounds like a nice man," Sarah said, her expression a bit strained.

"I'm not trying to make his case, I promise," Carson said. "I just see him differently now so I guess I'm Team Edmund now."

"Wait," Olivia said. "Make his case? Suddenly you're hoping my aunt *does* fall for your dad?"

He took a breath and let it out. "All I know is that I want my father to be happy. I was missing that piece before. There's no scam involved—I know that now. So all that's left is…feelings."

Sarah glanced at the floor. "Or a lack thereof."

Footsteps sounded from the stairs and then down the hall as Edmund's voice carried into the living room. "Of course, I got caught up watching Danny's little face—"

He stopped speaking as he rounded the corner into the living room archway. He stared at Sarah, who was staring at him.

Olivia looked from her aunt to Edmund and back again as though at a soccer match; Carson stood across from her doing the same. Sarah. Edmund. Sarah. Edmund.

"Dad, this is Sarah Mack. Olivia's aunt," Carson said. "Sarah, my father, Edmund Ford."

Edmund stepped into the room, his gaze never leaving Sarah. He was neither smiling nor frowning. His expression was completely neutral, as was Sarah's.

Huh. Maybe there was nothing here. Or maybe there would be no great spark in the first moments but they would work up to falling in love. If they did.

Of course they would. Miranda Mack had predicted it.

Edmund stopped in front of Sarah and extended his hand. "The longer version. My name is Edmund Ford. I'm a widower of five years. This is my son, Carson, who you've met, of course. And my grandson, Danny, is asleep upstairs. I'm a banker at Texas Trust, where I've spent the past thirty years. About two months ago, I went to Madam Miranda to have my fortune told. She said my second great love was a green-eyed hairstylist named Sarah. She said I would know her right away, but that she had a small tattoo of a brush and blow-dryer on her ankle. I've been looking for her ever since. And now here she stands before me."

Sarah hadn't taken her gaze off Edmund, either. She lifted her chin as he clasped both his hands over hers.

"I understand from Carson that you're not comfortable with or particularly interested in your sister's prediction," Edmund continued. "So I'd like us to just forget that and have a nice dinner, welcoming you back into your niece's life. That's what this dinner will be. A welcome home celebration. Nothing more."

Olivia could tell her aunt liked that; Sarah's shoulders relaxed and she accepted a glass of wine from Edmund. They all sat down, Sarah and Edmund across from each other on the two couches, Olivia and Carson beside each other on the facing love seat.

They spent the next ten minutes making small talk about Tuckerville, Oak Creek, Blue Gulch, the rodeo, hairstyles, toddlers and Hurley's food truck. But it was very clear to Olivia that her aunt could not take her eyes off Edmund Ford. And the same went for Edmund.

Carson excused himself to the kitchen to check on dinner, and Olivia popped up to help.

"Olivia," Sarah said, worry in her eyes as she sat up very straight, staring at her niece.

"What's wrong?" Edmund asked, looking from Sarah to Olivia and back again.

"Please tell me the truth, Olivia," Sarah said. "Did you make dinner? Did you help?"

Ah. Olivia knew what her aunt was asking. She was worried that Olivia had infused dinner with amorous vibes. She hadn't cooked, helped or even stepped foot in the kitchen tonight.

"I promise you that I did not," Olivia said.

Sarah nodded. "Okay. Sorry for being so anxious."

"I must be missing something," Edmund said, confusion in his expression.

Olivia explained about her gift in as few words as possible so as not to make her aunt uncomfortable—and requested that Edmund keep it a secret. "I've never been all that comfortable with it myself, but I've come to accept that I do seem able to mend spirits with my cooking. At the least, I seem able to affect people positively."

Edmund grinned. "Well, no wonder you have lines for the food truck every day. Aside from the delicious po'boys. Who can't use a boost?"

"You feel differently about special abilities than your son does," Sarah said to Edmund.

"I've always been a realist," Edmund said. "But my mind and heart are open. I think that's the key to life."

Sarah bit her lip and sipped her wine but didn't respond.

"Well, I'll just go help Carson," Olivia said.

In the kitchen, Olivia practically slumped over at the counter. "I didn't even realize until this moment that I needed to come up for air."

Carson smiled as he slid the pasta carbonara, which looked and smelled amazing, into a serving dish. "You okay? I had the same reaction when I came in."

"I can't tell if there's anything between them," Olivia said. "I can see that they can't stop looking at each other, but no one's flirting or giving anything away."

Carson kneeled to peer into the oven, then shut it off and took out the garlic bread. "I know. My dad wears his heart on his sleeve these days but I'm not getting anything. Not a sign."

He wasn't gloating. He wasn't even smiling. Olivia took a knife and cut the garlic bread into pieces. "Could my mother have been wrong? I can't even imagine it."

Maybe her aunt didn't feel anything for Edmund Ford and vice versa. Maybe her mother *had* been wrong—this time. Maybe Carson had been right all along and this was some kind of a ruse for Edmund Ford to use his time and resources to find Aunt Sarah and bring her back to Blue Gulch for Olivia's sake?

No. Olivia just couldn't see her mother doing that.

"Dinnertime," Carson said, picking up the pasta and heading for the door. "Who knows, Olivia. They're both being so cagey. Maybe they'll announce their engagement by the first bite."

Olivia smiled. Carson sure had changed his tune.

By the time Carson was ready to serve dessert, chocolate-almond gelato, he still couldn't tell if there was anything between his father and Sarah Mack, but he knew the woman felt comfortable around Edmund because she'd opened up about her new willingness to look for the twins she'd given up for adoption, five years after her sister had told her that one of them had begun the process to find her. His dad had listened intently, asked questions without being too personal, and offered to help in any way he could.

"Dad, help me get dessert, will you?" Carson said.

His father excused himself and they headed into the kitchen.

"I have to say I'm almost a little let down," Carson said as he pulled out the gelato from the freezer. "Based on Olivia and Sarah insisting that Madam Miranda was the real deal, I was expecting firecrackers to be exploding across the ceiling, but I guess Miranda had it wrong."

Edmund peered through the archway, then leaned close to Carson. "Are you kidding? Madam Miranda was anything but wrong. I'm completely crazy about that woman."

Carson stared at his father, seeing the far-off dreaminess in the man eyes. "What? You haven't been acting like you're madly in love."

"For Sarah's sake. I know she's not looking for love. I know she's skittish and has a lot on her mind. And I know she's probably fighting what she may feel— if anything. I don't want to scare her out of my life."

"So what does it feel like?" Carson asked. "Attraction? Intrigue? Interest?"

"Much more than that," Edmund said. "It feels like I just met the woman I'm going to marry."

"Really?"

Edmund nodded. "Trust me, I was expecting to feel like I did back in high school, a wild crush, that kind of thing. But the feeling that swept over me when I laid eyes on Sarah Mack for the first time, and as I've gotten to know her a bit over the past hour, it's like I've known her my entire life. It's a depth of feeling I can't explain, Carson. But it looks like it's one-sided."

"But you're her great love, Dad. I'm sure she feels the same way—she's just fighting it like I told you she said she would."

Edmund shook his head. "I'm not so sure. Madam Miranda said that Sarah was *my* second great love. That doesn't mean I'm *hers*. You can be madly in love with someone who doesn't love you back. Isn't that the basis of most love songs?"

Carson had thought of that last night when he'd been talking to Sarah in front of her home. But hadn't Sarah said the fortune worked both ways?

And that she'd fight it?

Dammit. Had he gone through all this only to finally come around and then deliver the woman straight into father's arms when she'd break his heart, after all?

"She's just stunning," Edmund was saying in a dreamy tone, staring at the wall. "Those green eyes. And her voice. So melodic. She has such a fierce intellect, too. And despite the complicated quest she'll be embarking on, her sense of humor shines through. What a woman."

Carson stared at his father. Good grief. The man *was* in love. After fifty minutes.

"I miss her just being in here," Edmund whispered.

Whoa, boy.

"So, Aunt Sarah," Olivia asked as Carson and Edmund were busy in the kitchen. "Was Mom wrong? You don't seem to be very taken with Edmund."

"Are you kidding?" Sarah whispered. "I'm fighting my attraction to that amazing man with every fiber of my being. He's so handsome! And kind. There's such complexity to him. And the way he talks about his grandson is so sweet. Did you notice he has one dimple?"

Olivia laughed. "Yes. His son has the same. The grandson, too."

"But," Sarah said, her smile fading, "I'm not here for romance. The timing just isn't right. I want to find the twins, Olivia, and I don't know how I'm going to feel when I do. It's been so long since I allowed myself to think about those babies. And suddenly I'm going to meet them? I might not be able to handle it."

"You've been so strong, Sarah," Olivia said. "You'll be able to handle it. I'll be with you every step of the way, if you'll let me."

Sarah took her hand. "I'd like that. It means so much to me that you'd support me after I abandoned you the way I did. I wasn't even there for you when you lost your mother." Tears glistened in Sarah's eyes.

"I understand what happened, Sarah. I know how sometimes blocks can keep people away, how fear can grow and become a wall. But you're here. You're back. That's all that matters to me—the present and future."

Sarah leaned over and hugged Olivia. "Thank you."

"I understand what you mean about not wanting to acknowledge how you feel about Edmund," Olivia said. "But to push love away? Especially when you need it the most?"

"One thing at a time," Sarah said. "I've fought my feelings for the past thirty-two years. Literally repressed them. I'm a master at it, unfortunately. I can fight my feelings for a man I just met."

"Your predicted great love," Olivia clarified with a smile. "That's a little different than 'a man you just met.'"

Carson and Edmund came back into the dining room just then, Carson holding a tray with four fancy dishes of gelato. Olivia wondered at the conversation the two Ford men had had in the kitchen. If her aunt was smitten with Edmund, he must be smitten with her. He was very likely keeping himself in check so he wouldn't send Sarah running for the hills. Smart man.

After dessert and coffee, Carson said that he would start the process of finding the twins tomorrow morning.

Sarah nodded and stood up. "It's been quite a day and evening. I think I'll head home."

"I'd love it if you stayed with me," Olivia said. "Carson may need you in the morning to verify information or look at records."

"I'd like that," Sarah said.

As Olivia and her aunt headed to the door, the Ford men followed.

Sarah thanked Carson for dinner, and then told Edmund how nice it was to meet him. Olivia had the overpowering desire to stay, to convince her aunt to stay and linger with these two men they both clearly wanted to be with.

But her time with Carson was coming to an end. Had come an end, really. He'd done what he said he was going to do.

"Thank you," Olivia whispered to Carson, fighting the urge to lift her hand to his cheek, to kiss him.

And then she and her aunt were out the door, heading down the bluestone path to their cars in the driveway.

As they reached Sarah's car, her aunt said, "Tomorrow morning may change my entire life. Even the thought of having the twins' contact information scares me. I'm so damned afraid of not knowing what to expect." She shook her head. "Isn't *that* ironic. I suddenly wish I had a crystal ball."

Olivia squeezed her aunt's hand. "We'll face tomorrow together. You and me."

Sarah squeezed back. "Looks like there's already a 'you and me' where you're concerned," she said, upping her chin at the door, where Carson and Edmund both stood, watching them approach their cars. "You love that man. I know you do. I know it without having a shred of special ability."

She did love him. And it was *her* heart that was going to get broken in all this.

Chapter Thirteen

At one thirty in the afternoon the next day, Carson and Olivia waited in the reception area of Adoption Connections in Houston, the agency that had handled the twins' case. Carson had called first thing that morning to make an appointment for Sarah, and she'd been behind closed doors with the assistant director for almost a half hour.

"How does it work?" Olivia asked Carson, staring down the hallway. The pale yellow walls were lined with photographs of babies and children of all ages and races and shapes and sizes. "Will my aunt receive the names and addresses of the twins?"

Carson glanced at Olivia, who sat fidgeting beside him on the padded chair. He picked up her hand and held it for a moment. "The assistant director told me over the phone that once a clear match was made between adoptee and birth parent, that both would receive the contact information left by the other. So Sarah should receive a name and telephone number at the very least of the twin who initiated contract. Maybe at this point, both twins did."

"I wish I knew what was going on in there," Olivia said, straining her neck to see down the hall. "I wish we could have gone in there with her, but I understand that she wanted to talk to the assistant director alone."

Full circle, Sarah had said. She knew she had the support of Carson and her niece, but she wanted to be strong and come full circle. Carson felt for her as she'd walked down the hall alone. He'd wanted to stand up and tell her that she didn't have to be so tough, that she did have their support—and the support of a great man waiting for her in Blue Gulch, if only she'd open up her heart.

But who was he to talk about opening hearts?

The drive up to Houston had been tense, to say the least. Carson had picked up Sarah and Olivia at nine that morning, with coffee and muffins, but both women had been too nervous to partake. Sarah had mostly looked out the window. He'd been so aware of Olivia in the seat next to him. She wore a denim skirt and a pale pink blazer, her hair in a low ponytail like her aunt's. He'd held her hand throughout most of the long drive, and the fact that she'd let him was more startling than the realization that he cared that much about her. He knew he did, but every time he caught a glimpse of their hands intertwined, a strange chill would run up his spine, then settle, then sneak up again. Still, he'd left his hand where it was.

"I think I hear a door opening," Olivia said, standing up.

Carson stood, too, as footsteps came from down the hall. He could hear Sarah thanking the assistant director, and finally, she appeared, clutching a document and an envelope. She looked a bit stressed, but hopeful at the same time.

"Only one of the twins had initiated contact," Sarah said. "He left this letter for the file," she added, looking at it and biting her lip. She handed the envelope to Carson. "Will you read the letter, Carson?"

He nodded and they sat back down, Carson between the two women. He opened the envelope and took out a piece of white paper and began reading.

"I can't address this letter since I don't know your name or what to call you. Dear Birth Mother sounds too cold. I've often thought about you, but ever since I discovered I have a twin brother I never knew existed, I've decided to try to make contact. Please write back, email or call.
"Jake Morrow
"Black Bear Ranch
"RR 8
"Mill Valley, Texas"

"Jake Morrow," Sarah repeated, tears in her eyes.

It was dated five years earlier and included a telephone number and email address. Carson handed the letter to Sarah, who read it herself, then put it back inside the envelope.

"Jake Morrow. It's a nice name," Olivia said. "You okay, Aunt Sarah?"

Sarah twisted her lips. "Right before I gave birth I asked one of the nurses if the twins were going to be adopted together but I was told that was classified. Now I know they weren't."

"Do you think this is what my mother knew?" Olivia asked Sarah. "That one of the twins was trying to find the other?"

"Probably," Sarah said. "I'd like to help him do that, but I'm not sure how I can."

Carson had a feeling that Sarah wasn't ready to pick up the phone herself. "Mill Valley is just a couple of hours from Blue Gulch County," he said. "I could call Jake and arrange a meeting, if you'd like."

"I appreciate that. Although I'm not sure how much I can help with locating his twin."

"I can get started on that," Carson said. "Plus, even though the twins were adopted separately, Jake may have more information that he realizes. Parents, grand-parents, old records, attics—you never know what you'll find or what's right in your house."

"In a matter of days I might actually be in contact with one of those tiny babies," Sarah said, her expression a combination of hope and wistfulness. "I almost can't believe it. My mother insisted it was for the best that I put it behind me and never speak of it. I wonder if she was trying to protect me by doing that, by acting as though none of it ever happened."

"But it did happen," Olivia said gently.

Sarah nodded and squeezed her niece's hand. "Yes, it most certainly did. And as strange as it feels to suddenly have it be the focus of my life, it feels good, too. And right. If I could know that the twins are okay, I would be at peace."

Olivia slung her arm around her aunt. "Well, we're here for you, Sarah. You know that right?"

Sarah nodded. "Thank you, both. From the bottom of my heart." She stood up. "Let's head home."

Carson noticed that Sarah kept the letter from Jake in her hand instead of putting it in her purse. She felt a connection to him and was letting herself feel it, which was good. She wasn't shutting down or off. Carson had a good feeling about all this.

Finally, three hours later, they arrived back at Olivia's house, a huge bouquet of wildflowers waiting in a round basket on the porch. Olivia plucked the card. It was addressed to Sarah.

"For me?" Sarah asked, taking the card. She read.

Dear Sarah,
   I hope today went well. I recall you said last night at dinner that wildflowers always made you feel better. If you could use an ear or a distraction, I'm available. 555-2345
Yours,
Edmund Ford

Sarah breathed in the colorful bouquet, a soft smile on her face. "That was thoughtful and very kind. I'll call to thank him." At the door, she turned to Carson. "Thank you again for everything."

"My pleasure," Carson said, watching Sarah head inside.

Olivia wasn't surprised at his father's gesture. That was his dad.

"Come in for a cup of coffee?" Olivia asked on the porch. She knew he probably wanted to get home to

Danny, but she wanted to prolong his leaving for just five more minutes.

"I should get home," he said. "But after six hours in the car today, I could use a strong cup of coffee."

Good, she thought. *Me, too*. In the kitchen, Olivia lifted an ear toward the doorway and smiled. "I still hear her talking," she whispered to Carson. "Maybe she's loosening up on her stronghold against love."

"I hope so." If anyone needed love in her life, Olivia thought, it was Sarah Mack.

"Now she's laughing," Olivia said. "That's nice to hear."

Carson nodded. "A huge weight was lifted off her chest. She did something she's probably been thinking about, fretting over for five years. All that had been blocking her before may naturally lift away. She may be readier for a relationship than she realizes."

And you? she wanted to ask. *You are, too, and just don't know it.*

Or was that wishful thinking?

Her aunt acted and was getting results. She was taking charge, doing something. It was time for Olivia to do the same. She loved this man and she was going to show him. She was going to ask for what she wanted. *Him.*

She slid her arms around Carson's neck and kissed him, backing him against the counter.

At first, he responded, deepening the kiss, his hand weaving in her hair, down her back, his other hand sliding up her tank top toward her bra. Every nerve ending was on delicious fire. She pressed herself against him, her hands against his muscular chest, never wanting this moment to end. Carson, Carson, Carson.

But the moment did end.

He slowly pulled away, shaking his head. "I want you so bad, Olivia. You have no idea. But—" He stepped farther away, straightening his shirt, his expression...wary, and her heart crumbled.

She turned her face away so that he wouldn't see how disappointed she was. She moved to the coffee-maker, pretending great interest in lining up the creamer and sugar bowl. *But I don't love you and don't want to hurt you.* She had no doubt that was the rest of the sentence.

"I—" he began, but said nothing else.

Oh, hell. "I appreciate what you're doing for my aunt," she said, trying to keep her voice even. "She'll keep me informed about Jake and your progress locating the other twin, so..."

So... Don't leave, she wanted to scream. *Stop me from trying to save face and make this less uncomfortable for you. Tell me you love me and I'm worth blasting through your wall for.*

She could feel him staring at her, and she glanced at him, his hazel-green eyes flashing with an intensity. She thought he might say something, but he just nodded and left.

From down the hall, she could hear her aunt telling Edmund Ford a funny story about the time she colored her own hair a bright orange. The sound of her aunt's light laughter was like a soothing balm against her own crumbling heart.

Carson had spent a restless night tossing and turning and thinking about Olivia, about the expression on her beautiful face when he'd walked out last night. Didn't she know how badly he wanted her? That he loved her but couldn't face it and so would rather just ignore his feelings by not acting on them.

Like her aunt was. Who he knew was making a huge mistake by doing so.

Why was his life not making sense? This was nuts. Why could he see it for Sarah and not himself.

Because she's not you, dummy, he told himself. It's easy to think this or that about someone else and a lot harder to practice what you preach.

And while he'd been calling himself a fool for knowing what was what and still refusing to do anything about it—such as go get his woman and tell her he was a dope and that he loved her and wanted to spend his life with her—he'd stayed put on his couch. Not doing any of the above. Paralyzed with… "I can't-itis." Then his father had kept him on the phone for an hour, sounding like a dreamy romantic who couldn't stop talking about the woman he loved. Apparently, Edmund and Sarah had spent almost two hours on the phone, talking about everything. His father sounded so happy, so lighthearted, so hopeful that his second great love was going to open her heart to him, after all, that Carson had almost called Olivia and asked her to come over since Danny was sleeping.

But the thought of Danny stopped him in his tracks again. Danny. Left by his mother. Now here Carson was, about to open his life and home and heart to another woman. He'd trusted the first time around, thought he'd had everything he wanted, thought his family would be forever.

But it wasn't.

For himself, for Danny, he'd stay a lone wolf.

Now, he sat in his home office, taking another sip of the very strong coffee he'd made and watched the clock finally hit 9:00 a.m, a reasonable time to make telephone calls.

He picked up his cell phone and pressed in the number Jake Morrow had left in the letter. Carson had easily found his home telephone number, as well.

A deep voice answered. "Hello."

"Jake Morrow?" Carson asked.

"Speaking."

"My name is Carson Ford. I'm a private investigator in Blue Gulch County. Your birth mother, Sarah Mack, asked me to contact you. Via Adoption Connections of Houston, she received the letter you sent five years ago about your interest in finding your biological twin brother. She'd like to meet you and help locate him, if she can."

Jake Morrow was silent for a moment. "I appreciate the call," he said. "But that was five years ago. A lot's happened in that time. I'm no longer interested in contact with either my birth mother or my twin brother. Thanks for calling, though. Goodbye."

Click.

Oh, dammit.

Though she wasn't due at Hurley's Homestyle Kitchen food truck until eleven thirty, Olivia headed over at nine thirty, needing to get out of the house, plus she wanted to give Sarah some privacy. She heard her talking to Edmund on the telephone again this morning. There was flirtation. Laughter. Happiness. Olivia's heart had leaped for her aunt, but she herself was down in the dumps this morning. She'd had a horrible night's sleep, unable to get comfortable, waking up and thinking about a certain sexy private investigator who was acting like his own worst enemy.

Unless he just didn't return her feelings. Maybe she was giving herself too much credit, thinking he loved her deep down when he didn't.

But she knew he loved her. She felt it every time he looked at her. It was in how he spoke to her, his expression, the way he brought her coffee just the way she liked it, how he'd helped her aunt, driving all the way to Houston and back. The man loved her!

Right?

She'd moped for a good five minutes, then had gone into her mother's fortune-telling parlor, hoping to soak up some truths in the air, but all she felt was her own truth—that *she* loved Carson.

She was almost at the food truck when her cell phone rang.

Carson. "I spoke to Jake Morrow this morning. He said he changed his mind about making contact with his birth mother or twin brother and hung up."

She stopped in her tracks. Oh, no. "Carson, now what? That'll break Aunt Sarah's heart."

"Let's talk it through. Can you stop by this morning? I've got Danny with me."

So she could break her own heart even more? "I'll be right there."

She headed back home and got in her car and drove over to Carson's. He and Danny were waiting for her on the porch, Danny holding his yellow monkey in one hand and a cheese stick in the other.

"Hi, Liva!" Danny said.

She tapped his nose. "Hey, sweetie."

"Come on in," Carson said. "Danny, want to build Olivia a tower of blocks?"

"Yes!" Danny said and went running for his play area in the family room.

Olivia followed Carson into the kitchen, sending Danny a smile as he worked on his tower. He handed her a mug of coffee—just the way she liked it, of course.

He sipped his own coffee as they headed into the family room and sat down on the plush sofa. "I think your aunt should write Jake Morrow a letter and send it to his home. Explain herself, in her own words, anything she'd like to say. At least she'll be a real person rather than an idea in Jake's mind. What do think?"

"It's a good idea. Plus, it'll give her something proactive to do. It's been five years since Jake sent that letter—with no contact from his birth mother. I think Sarah will understand that he might have been put off by that. I'll talk to her."

Carson's cell phone rang. "Maybe Jake Morrow calling back? Changed his mind, perhaps."

Hope blossomed in Olivia's chest. "You answer your calls. I'll play with Danny."

Carson headed into his office to answer the phone, and Olivia went to Danny's play area.

Danny stood in front of his tower of big blocks, almost as high as he was. "Meatball," he said, giggling and pointing at the top block.

"To put on top? All covered with cheese?" Olivia said, ticking the little goofball.

Danny laughed. "Top 'getti," he sang, then doubled over in laughter.

Olivia scooped up Danny into a hug, smelling his

baby shampoo–scented head. She never wanted to let him go.

She loved this little boy. And she loved the man down the hall.

And she was going to fight for them.

"Danny, I'm going to put you in your playpen for a few minutes with your talking panda while I talk to your daddy, okay?"

He rubbed his eyes and yawned. "'Kay."

She picked up the sleepyhead and set him down in the playpen, giving him a kiss on the head, then marched into Carson's office and shut the door.

"Was that Jake?" she asked.

"No. It was actually Joey Johnson letting me know his dad came to his Little League practice this morning and then took him out for breakfast and he had a great time."

"Aww," Olivia said. "I'm very glad." She cleared her throat. "Danny's in his playpen. I'm going to head home to talk to Sarah about writing that letter to Jacob. But before I go, I want to tell you something."

He stared at her. "Okay," he said, as though bracing himself. He stood up from his desk chair and leaned against the window.

"I want to speak my mind, Carson, because if I don't, I'll always wonder if telling you would have made a difference."

"Tell me what?" he asked.

Do it. Tell him. She sucked in a deep breath. "That I love you. That I'm in love with you. I love you and I love Danny and I want us all to have a future."

He was quiet for a moment, then said, "Olivia. I…

trusted in love once and it blew up on me. I can't do this again. I'm very sorry."

Not good enough, buster, sorry. She squared her shoulders and lifted her chin. "And if you'd gone to see Madam Miranda and she told you I was your second great love? Then what?"

"Olivia. I never would have gone to see your mother for a reading of my fortune, so it's a moot point."

"But if you had. If she'd told you."

"That we were destined for each other?" he asked. She nodded.

"I don't believe in that, Olivia. Reality is Jake Morrow hanging up in my ear. That's life. There's no guarantees about anything."

"Carson," she said.

"I think your aunt should write that letter," he said, his tone making clear he was done with the conversation.

No. He was not dismissing her again. She knew this man loved her. She knew it in her heart, mind and soul. "Carson—"

He moved away from the window and came around the desk until he was standing just inches from her. "I wouldn't need a crystal ball to tell me that we belong together, Olivia. I already know it. I feel it in every cell of my body. I feel it running through my veins. I feel it here all the time," he said, pressing his hand over his heart.

She gasped. "But—"

"But I'm fighting it. I've been fighting it and I'll keep fighting it. So that Danny and I never have to go through that kind of pain again. Weren't you the one who said, Olivia, that people do all kinds of things even when they know the truth? You could be madly in love with me and destined to be with me and—"

He stopped and turned away.

"And what, Carson?" she asked gently.

"And I could lose you anyway. Destiny gives, destiny takes."

"Carson, the only thing I can guarantee you is that I love you and your little boy with all my heart. But, yeah, life can pull some fast ones. I'd like you to be by my side when they happen."

"Liva? Daddy?" a little voice said through the closed door.

"Danny's calling," he said, heading to the door. He seemed very relieved by the interruption. "I'm sorry, Olivia," he added, turning to face her for a moment. He tilted his head. "I really am sorry. Let me know when your aunt sends the letter."

Dammit, he was frustrating. How the hell was she going to get through to this man?

Chapter Fourteen

An entire week had passed since Carson had seen
Olivia. He'd taken on two new cases, a complicated
one for the Oak Creek police department involving a
potential burglary suspect who'd skipped town, and the
other for a middle-aged high school English teacher
convinced that her husband was cheating on her, but
wanted some kind of proof before she "did anything
reckless." Carson had always avoided the spying-on-
spouses jobs, but he was in a bad mood this week and
the client had caught him on his worst day, so he'd
taken the case.

Yesterday he'd trailed the husband to an Italian restaurant in Tuckerville, where the fiftysomething man
met a young woman who spent the next forty-five minutes giving him Italian lessons. Then he followed the
man to a bookstore, where he purchased two travel

guides to Rome and a birthday card with a cover that read "For my beautiful wife." When the man took the card over to the little café area, Carson ordered a coffee and sat at the table beside him, glancing over as the man wrote inside the card—"My beloved Carla" and a bunch of romantic stuff—then put in what looked like boarding passes for an airline flight. Considering that Carson's client's name was Carla, Carson had figured he could call it a day. He'd called his client right away to inform her that he was one hundred percent sure her husband was not cheating. That night, the client texted him that Carson was right; her husband had just surprised her with a trip to Italy and even knew how to say a bunch of Italian phrases.

The whole thing had given Carson a headache. He hadn't been expecting the case to turn out that way. Score one for love and marriage. Carson: zero.

His doorbell rang and for a moment his heart sped up when he thought it might be Olivia, but he'd done such a great job of pushing her away that he was sure it wasn't her. Dammit, he missed her. The sight of her pretty face and crazy skirts and the sound of her voice and how soft her lips always looked, and the way she turned his head around, made him want to join the world instead of staying behind lock and key. But a week later, he'd stayed where he was, working, stewing, taking care of Danny and watching his father fall more and more deeply in love with Sarah Mack.

Though Sarah still insisted she wasn't looking to get involved in a romance, she and Edmund had gotten together every day since the return from the adoption agency. Edmund had seen her through the first couple of days of heartache when Olivia had let her aunt know that Jake Morrow had changed his mind about contact. And Edmund had been there when she was ready to start writing the letter to Jake. According to his father, Sarah had spent days working on the letter, thinking about it, deleting it, rewriting it; and she and Edmund had taken long walks into the woods, Edmund silent by her side so she could think, his father simply a source of support, of friendship.

Last night, his father had called him at midnight to report that he'd asked Sarah if he could kiss her goodnight after their date, and she'd finally said yes, and all the fireworks and clanging cymbals had made their noise. Edmund Ford was deeply in love.

Even if she breaks my heart, it was worth just feeling the way I do right now, his dad had said.

The fortune had come true. His father had found his predicted second great love and destiny had taken its course. How else could Carson look at it? Yesterday, he'd tried falling back on his preferred power-of-suggestion explanation. His dad had been told he'd feel a certain way about a certain someone, Sarah had made it all the more stakes worthy by being truly "hard to get," and his dad had fallen hard.

Except that didn't sound or feel right to Carson, either. What had happened between Edmund and Sarah was very real. And, yes, Carson had to admit, beautiful.

He still didn't believe in the whole fortune thing, well, not completely, but it was staring him in the face every time he looked at his father, every time his father talked about Sarah. All Carson really knew for sure was that he was happy for his dad. Edmund Ford deserved all the love and happiness in the world.

Carson opened the door to find the man himself standing on the porch, holding an envelope.

"Sarah finally wrote the letter to Jake," Edmund said. "She thought you might like to read it."

Carson raised an eyebrow. "That's all right. I'm sure it's deeply personal."

"Sarah wants to make sure you think she handled it just right," his dad said. "You've been there with her throughout and have experience with hitting the right notes so that someone you're seeking doesn't run away. Drop it off at the post office when you're done, will you?"

Edmund held out the letter, and Carson finally took it. "Give Danny a hug for me," his father added as he headed to his car. "Remind him that Sarah and I are taking him to the town carnival at four."

Carson nodded and watched his father walk away, the old skip in his step. The man exuded happiness. Honestly, he didn't know how his dad could take it, handle it, deal with such a tentative relationship when he felt so strongly about Sarah. The woman was a bit fragile and could bolt at any time. She'd basically said as much from the get-go and, according to Edmund, reiterated that every day. And still, his father acted like all was well. Carson could never deal with that kind of uncertainty.

Uncertainty. Huh. It struck him how ironic that was. If only he could be sure that Olivia wouldn't pull a fast one on him and Danny… Despite a complete lack of evidence that she ever would. Despite her telling him that she loved him. Was in love with him. Loved Danny. He still couldn't…let go enough to let her in.

He closed the door and walked upstairs to Danny's nursery to check on him. His son was sound asleep in his crib, clutching his yellow monkey. Carson went back downstairs to his office and sat behind his desk, wanting to read Sarah's letter in an official capacity instead of a personal one. He was her PI, after all. This was business. Even if she was his father's great love. And the aunt of the woman he refused to allow himself to love.

He slid the letter from the unsealed envelope. It was handwritten in black ink.

Dear Jake,

My name is Sarah Mack. When I was sixteen years old, I gave birth to fraternal twin boys on February 15, thirty-two years ago. I never saw you or your twin, I never had the opportunity to hold you. And although I tried very hard not to think of you both over the years in order to protect my heart, I thought about the two of you every day.

If you would like to meet, to ask questions, for closure, for anything I may able to tell you so that you can locate your twin, I would be happy to do that. I apologize for not availing myself to the registry five years ago when you first sought me out. I wasn't ready then. But I am ready now.

One thing I've learned lately is that holding yourself back from your own happiness and well-being, especially because of fear or anger, hurts others just as much as it hurts ourselves.

Your birth mother, Sarah Mack.

It was a good letter, just right, Carson thought. But instead of putting it in the envelope and sealing it up to mail, he kept staring at that last line. *Hurts others just as much as it hurts ourselves...*

He hadn't wanted to hurt Olivia.

And not only had he hurt her, but he'd also hurt Danny, who asked for "Liva" and the spaghetti song every day.

Joey Johnson's tear-streaked face came to mind, the boy sitting in his car, scared to death over confronting his dad, with no idea if his father would reject him. Then Carson's own dad's words floated through his head. *Even if she breaks my heart, it was worth just feeling the way I do right now.*

But Carson didn't want to feel the way *he* did right now: alone, heavyhearted, with one sixteenth of the bravery of his nine-year-old client. Even Sarah had come around by saying yes to a good-night kiss—choosing love over fear.

Carson sealed the envelope and when Danny's sitter arrived, he headed out. He had a very important letter to mail. And then a very important errand to run. And finally, a very important woman to see.

Olivia handed her teary-eyed customer the tuna-melt po'boy with extra cucumbers that she'd ordered, and watched the woman sit down at a table. She took a bite. Then another. The another. She lifted her chin. Then ate another bite. She bit her lip, pulled out her phone and pressed in a number, then had a conversation Olivia couldn't hear.

Suddenly, a guy came running down the street toward the food truck. The young woman stood and went running toward him like in a slow-motion TV commercial. The two embraced and walked off, hand in hand.

Ah, Olivia thought with a smile. A rueful smile, though, these days. *If only my own ability worked on me. Or Carson.* She wouldn't want Carson to come into her life via any kind of magic other than the natural kind, but a little head start? She'd take it. A head start for Carson would come in the form of a tiny pickax to knock away at the armor.

As Olivia prepared today's special po'boy, a good old-fashioned Italian, she noticed the three Hurley sisters coming up to the window. With them was a pretty brunette she didn't recognize.

"Hi, Olivia!" Georgia called out, flipping her shiny brown hair behind her shoulders. Georgia was the eldest and baked for Hurley's Homestyle Kitchen.

"Got a second?" Annabel, the middle sister, asked. "We'd like to introduce you to our cousin and new part-time cook, Emma Hurley."

Emma smiled and held up a hand at Olivia.

"Emma here is not only a whiz in the kitchen, but she's proving herself to be a great baker, too," Clementine, the youngest and a waitress, said.

Georgia nodded. "Yesterday Emma helped me make six apple pies—I was told they had the best crust ever." Since Georgia was the baker for the restaurant, that was high praise. Olivia always loved how warm and welcoming and kind the Hurley sisters were; they never looked at people as competition, worrying that Olivia would start her own food truck and leave them in the lurch, or that great baker Emma would steal thunder from Georgia. Olivia owed the Hurleys a lot. She'd never forget how they'd given her a fresh start when she'd needed one. Olivia had come to really love the Hurley's Homestyle Kitchen food truck.

She came outside, the warm, breezy March air refreshing.

Emma extended her hand toward Olivia. "I really appreciate the job at Hurley's Homestyle Kitchen. I'm new in town."

Olivia shook the woman's hand. Emma looked to be in her midtwenties with big blue eyes and soft, wavy golden-brown hair to her shoulders...and a secret, Olivia sensed. She had a good feeling about Emma, though.

"Emma's mostly going to be working at the restaurant," Annabel said, "but we thought she could learn the ropes of the truck so that she could help out during rushes or pinch-hit if you or Dylan are sick. I know your busy time is about to start, Olivia, so could you use a hand?"

"I'd love the help," Olivia said, smiling at Emma.

Fifteen minutes later, Olivia had just finished giving Emma the lay of the land and going over the recipes for all the po'boys and cannoli when a crowd came out of Texas Trust and headed for the food truck. Then the real estate office crew walked over.

Olivia gestured with her chin at the people coming their way. "We're about to get as busy as Annabel said."

"I'm ready!" Emma said, rolling up her sleeves.

Olivia smiled. Emma might have a secret up those sleeves, but she liked her and was grateful for her very competent help.

By the end of the lunch rush—almost two hundred po'boys and over a hundred cannoli—Olivia could finally sit down at the little desk by the driver's seat and clink a lemonade toast with Emma to a rush gone well. As she made a mini strawberry cannoli for Emma,

Olivia was struck by the notion that Emma Hurley had a big secret to share with someone—someone she was having trouble finding.

She tried to ask her new assistant a few questions about herself, but Emma was a bit cagey and Olivia realized that the woman probably didn't want to be asked questions. Emma helped clean up like a champ and then Olivia said she might as well clock out for the day.

A shadow loomed at the window and at first Olivia thought Emma was back, but it was Carson.

Her heart moved. He looked so damned handsome. He wore a navy blue Henley shirt and sexy jeans and his brown cowboy boots. She hadn't laid eyes on him in an entire week, but she'd sensed she hadn't seen the last of Carson Ford. He needed time, to think and process and mull—and miss her. She didn't know how long that would take, but she was sure glad to see him now. It definitely meant the *missing* part had begun.

He took off his aviator sunglasses. "I'd love a shrimp po'boy."

She smiled. "That's what you ordered the day I met you."

"I'm trying for a do-over," he said. "I wasn't very nice to you that day. And that night, you told me about your gift when I was walking you home from my dad's house. I didn't believe you, even though I saw some evidence of it since. Like with that pushy lady."

"I remember," she said, reaching for the container of shrimp that Emma had helped her season. He was simply "making nice." Her aunt and his dad were an item, and it made sense for Carson to be on good, friendly terms with Olivia.

"If you do have a gift," he added, "I'd appreciate it

if you'd infuse my po'boy with a little assurance. A lot of assurance, actually."

She moved closer to the window. "Assurance for what?"

He disappeared from view and the door to the food truck opened. He stepped up inside. "That the woman I love will forgive me for being so stubborn."

A rush of happiness zinged from Olivia's toes to the top of her head.

"I love you, Olivia Mack. I love everything you are." He opened a little velvet box; a beautiful diamond ring sparkled. "The sales guy at Blue Gulch Jewelers told me this ring was destined for my bride. That was the exact word he used."

She laughed. "You don't believe in destiny."

"But I believe in how I feel about you. I'm just going to run with that. That's what I want to teach Danny. To love, to be open, not to run away. I *love* you, Olivia," he said.

"I love you, too."

He kissed her, then pulled back. "I wasn't sure about proposing here—if you'd want to remember that you got engaged in a food truck. But this is where we met, after all."

Happy tears poked at her eyes. "There's no place that could have been more special."

"I guess it was destiny," he said, kissing her again.

Epilogue

Four weeks later, on a breathtaking, warm and breezy late-March evening, Olivia stood with Dory Drummond in the beautiful backyard of Edmund Ford's mansion, admiring the twinkling white lights strung among the trees. Hundreds of guests at Edmund and Sarah's engagement party mingled, sipping champagne and trying appetizers that uniformed waiters appeared with on round silver trays.

"If I could have your attention," Edmund said, standing in front of the weeping willow and clinking his glass with a spoon. Aunt Sarah stood beside him, looking so lovely in her pale yellow dress and strappy sandals, her curly auburn hair down around her shoulders. "I'd like to thank you all for coming to share in my good fortune." He shot a wink at Carson, who was standing a few feet from Olivia with Beaufort Harrington. "Until very recently, I never thought I would find a second chance at happiness. But this wonderful woman changed all that. I'm very happy to announce that Sarah and I have set a wedding date for September and you're all invited."

There was a big round of applause and excited chatter as guests crowded around the happy couple. Olivia excused herself from Dory and rushed up to her aunt, wrapping her in a hug.

"When Edmund first proposed last week," Sarah said, "I was so flabbergasted, but my answer was in my heart. A very big and sure yes. My fiancé has been asking what kind of wedding I'd like, and I was thinking maybe we'd elope, but I don't want such a big and special day to pass without you there. Or Carson. You're both family."

"I wouldn't want to miss your wedding, Aunt Sarah," Olivia said, so thrilled for the woman. "Just think, by the fall we'll both be married women."

"I just might join that club, too," Dory said as she joined them, her expression all dreamy as she gazed at Beaufort. "What a difference a month makes. Now that Beau and I have gotten to know each other apart from any expectations, we're madly in love."

"I'm so happy for you, Dory," Olivia said, hugging her dear friend.

The huge Hurley group came over to meet Sarah, and Olivia made the introductions. There were Annabel and West, Georgia and Nick, Clementine and Logan, and even seventy-five-year-old Essie Hurley had a date, the charming and dapper owner of the independent bookstore on the far end of Blue Gulch Street. Love was most definitely in the air in Blue Gulch, Texas.

Sarah's cell phone rang, and she reached into her little sequined purse for it. "Unfamiliar number," she said. "Hello?" She listened for a moment, her left hand flying to her mouth. She looked like she might cry.

Oh, no. What was this? Olivia wondered.

Sarah turned and walked a few feet away, standing beside the weeping willow as if to talk in private. Wait, was she smiling now? Suddenly the hand was back at her mouth. She was pacing a bit, talking, then listening. Then smiling. Then just standing very still, staring out at the night.

Finally, she put the phone away and came over to Olivia. "Let's go find Carson and Edmund," Sarah said. "I have some news to share."

Wondering what was up, Olivia scanned the crowd. "There's Edmund. He's standing with Carson and a few others."

They walked over to find Edmund and Carson listening to one of the men telling a very long story about a Texas Trust deal; they both looked a little bored, so Olivia figured it was a good time to steal them away. She gestured them over.

The four of them walked across the yard and stood behind another tree.

"I just received a telephone call from Jake Morrow," Sarah said. "It's been a month since I wrote that letter to him, and I'd pretty much given up hope that he'd want contact. But he said he'd spent some time thinking things over and he would like to meet me."

"That's great!" Olivia said, squeezing her aunt's hand. "I'm so glad he responded." Over the past month, every day that the mail hadn't brought a letter and the phone hadn't rung with a call from Jake, Olivia had noticed a bit of sad wistfulness in the air around her aunt. But now, there was joy on her face.

Edmund wrapped his fiancée in a hug. "I'm so happy for you."

"I had a feeling he'd come around," Carson said. "Jake started the ball rolling five years ago, then stopped it, so the want—the need—was there. Is he coming to Blue Gulch or will you travel to his ranch?"

"He's coming to Blue Gulch next Saturday," Sarah said. "He said he'd like to see where he began, under- stand a little about his birth family. And he *is* hoping I can help him locate his twin brother. So far, he's had no luck with that."

"Well, I'll certainly help if I can," Carson said, his arm around Olivia.

Olivia noticed her aunt was looking at her as though wondering something, trying to figure out if Sarah should say what was on her mind.

"Sarah?" Olivia prompted.

"I was just thinking," she began, glancing at Ed- mund and Carson, and then back at Olivia. "Since we're both engaged to these wonderful men here, and they're family and we're family, wouldn't it be nice to have a double wedding?"

Olivia gasped. "I'd love it!"

"We're already each other's best man," Carson said, looking at his dad, "so that works."

Olivia smiled. "And Danny can be our ring bearer. I can just see him in his little tuxedo."

"Two dads down the aisle with our beautiful brides," Edmund said. "Count me in."

With the people she loved most beside her and the stars twinkling overhead, Olivia felt her mother's presence more strongly than she ever had these months without Miranda.

"Want to know something?" Carson whispered as the foursome began heading back to the party.

"What?" she asked, unable to drag her gaze away from Carson's handsome face, his hazel-green eyes.

"When I kissed Danny good-night before heading over to your house to pick you up, he said something I think you're going to like."

She couldn't imagine being any happier than she was right now. "What did he say?"

"He said, 'Liva mama?'"

Olivia's heart flip-flopped. "He did? He said that?"

Carson nodded and stopped on the grass, holding her close.

"I am going to be his mama," she whispered, her cup running over to the point that tears were threatening.

"I owe this all to a fortune, destiny, stubbornness, reality, life and hard work," Carson said. "All of that. It all played a part. I'm just glad it did."

She leaned up to kiss her fiancé. "Me, too. Because *love* played the biggest part of all."

* * * * *

A CONVENIENT SCANDAL

KIMBERLEY TROUTTE

Dedicated to the strong women I call my friends.

History of Plunder Cove

For centuries, the Harpers have masterminded shrewd business deals.

In the 1830s, cattle baron Jonas Harper purchased the twelve-thousand-acre land grant of Plunder Cove on the now affluent California coast. It's been said that the king of Spain dumped the rich land on the American because pirates ruthlessly raided the cove. It is also said no one saw a pirate ship after Jonas bought the land for a rock-bottom price.

Harpers pass this tale on to each generation to remind their heirs that there is a pirate in each of them. Every generation is expected to increase the Harper legacy, usually through great sacrifice, as with oil tycoon, RW Harper, who sent his children away ten years ago.

Now RW has asked his children to return to Plunder Cove—with conditions. He is not above bribing them to get what he wants.

Harpers don't love, they pillage. But if RW's wily plans succeed, all four Harpers, including RW, might finally find love in Plunder Cove.

One

Jeff Harper pressed his forehead to the glass pane of his floor-to-ceiling living room window and watched the mass of reporters swarming below.

They couldn't get a good shot of him at this height, since he was twenty-two floors above Central Park, but once he stepped outside his building they'd attack. Every word he said, or didn't say, would be used to bury him—shovel after shovel piled on top of his rotting career.

Dammit, he hated to fail.

Before this week, Jeff had been able to live with the invasion of his privacy and had learned to use the cameras to his advantage. The press followed him around New York because he was the last unmarried prince of Harper Industries and a hotel critic on the show *Secrets and Sheets*. Paparazzi photographed his dinner dates as if each one was a passionate love match. His name had appeared on the list of America's Most Eligible Bachelors for the last three years running. When pressed during interviews, he always said there was no special woman in his life and he was never getting married. The author of the article inevitably wrapped up with some bogus statement about "Jeffrey Harper just needs to find the right woman to settle him down." Which was a big *hell no*.

Why end up like his parents?

He'd mostly put up with the press until he'd seen his own

backside plastered across tabloid front pages with the headline "Hotel Critic Caught in Sex Scandal."

Sex scandal. He wished.

He'd been set up.

And the incriminating video had gone viral.

The show he'd created and nurtured was canceled. Everything he'd built—his career, his reputation, his lifelong
passion for the hotel industry—had exploded.

Just like that, Jeff was done.

If he didn't fix this, he'd never regain what he'd lost.

Only one person might hire him at this point. Of course,
he was the one person Jeff had vowed never to beg.

Grimacing, he dialed the number.

The phone rang once. "Jeffrey, I've been waiting for your
call."

Not a good sign since Jeff never called.

"Hey, Dad. I was wondering…" He swallowed hard. This
was going to be painful. "Is the family hotel project still
on the table?"

A year ago, when Jeff's brother had returned home to
Plunder Cove, their father had offered to put Jeff in charge
of converting the Spanish mansion into an exclusive five-
star resort. He liked the idea more than he'd dared admit.
Hotel design, development and management had been his
dream career since he was old enough to put blocks together,
and he'd steadily worked to become an international expert
in the field. But it was more than that. He couldn't put into
words why turning his childhood home into a safe place was
important. No one would know why using his own hands
to reshape the past meant everything to Jeff. Yet…he'd de-
clined his father's offer because RW was a mean, selfish,
poor excuse for a father, and he'd never respected Jeff.

But beggars couldn't be choosers, and all that.

"You've reconsidered." RW stated it as fact.

Did he have a choice? "The network pulled my show.
I've got time on my hands."

"Wonderful."

Strange word to use under the circumstances, but his father sounded pleased. The tightness in Jeff's chest loosened a bit when he realized he didn't have to beg for the job. He'd half-expected his father would make him grovel. "I'll be there tomorrow."

"There's one condition."

He should have guessed that. Those three words lifted the hairs on the back of Jeff's neck. "Yeah? What?"

"You've got to improve your image. I've seen the video, son."

Jeff paced his living room. "It's not what it looks like."

"That's a relief because it looks like you had a quickie in the elevator at Xander Finn's hotel with a hotel maid. Low-class, son. Harpers pay for suites."

Jeff ground his molars together. "I paid for a suite."

He just hadn't had time to use it while he was undercover exposing a social injustice.

Jeff cared about people and used the power of his name and his show to set things right. The great RW would never understand why Jeff went out of his way to expose the mega-rich like Xander Finn.

Weeks earlier, Finn had threatened bodily harm to the *Secrets and Sheets* crew if they stepped inside the gilded doors of his most expensive Manhattan hotel. The threat had made Jeff wonder what the man had to hide. He'd filmed the episode himself, and the dirt he uncovered would show viewers how badly customers were being ripped off by one of the richest men in New York.

Little did Jeff know that *he* was about to become the one to "break the internet," with ridiculous GIFs and memes.

The latest one said, "Those who can, run a hotel; those who can't, become sex-crazed critics."

"Success is all about image," RW was still talking over the phone. "Yours needs an overhaul, Jeffrey. Didn't you know hotels have video cameras in the elevators?"

"Of course, I do. I was set up!" Jeff slammed his teeth together to keep from blurting out what really happened in the elevator. His father hadn't shielded him from abuse when he was six; why would he shield him now?

No, except for this job offer—with conditions—Jeff was on his own. Always had been.

"Wait." A flicker of foreboding licked up Jeff's spine. "How did you know I was in Finn's elevator? Did he send you the entire video?"

"Xander and I go way back. He's always been a pain in the ass. No, I haven't seen it all, but he promises me it gets worse. I get the sense you don't want the public to see what happens next. Am I correct?"

Jeff let out a slow breath. The small digital slice encircling the internet was bad enough. If the rest went public, there would be no coming back. "What does he want?"

"I bet you can guess."

Jeff rubbed the back of his neck. "The recording I made of his hotel."

"Bingo. And a televised statement that his hotel is above reproach. The best damned hotel you've ever seen." RW paused. "Xander wants you to grovel."

"I'm not doing that. It was one of the worst I've ever seen. Think about the people who save for years to vacation at his fancy hotel. No. It's unacceptable. No one can bully me anymore, Dad."

"Then we have a problem," RW said.

"We?"

"Harper Industries has a reputation to uphold and stockholders to please. We can't go around hiring a sex-crazed—"

"Dad! I was set up."

"Blackmail only works because you were caught on tape. You screwed up." There. That was the father he'd expected when he picked up the phone. The superior tone and words dripping with condemnation were signature RW Harper.

"Blackmail only works if I roll over. I won't do that," Jeff snapped.

"Think carefully," RW said. "He's threatening to release bits and pieces of your damned sex video for eternity unless you agree to his terms. With a constant stream of bad press, you'll never work in New York's hotel industry again. Or anywhere else for that matter. Not even for me."

Jeff pinched the bridge of his nose. "Then he's got me."

"Not if we stop him with good PR. It must be done quickly to keep your train wreck from derailing the entire Plunder Cove project. I promised the townspeople their percentage of resort profits and I intend to keep my word."

"The people in Pueblicito not getting their share. *That's* what bothers you the most about what happened to me?"

"The Harpers owe them, son."

Jeff shook his head. Harpers were pirates—takers, and users. The family tree included buccaneers and land barons who'd once owned the people in Pueblicito. RW was just as bad as past generations because he only cared about increasing profits for Harper Industries.

Greed had destroyed his family.

And now Dad wants to donate profit to strangers? What's the catch?

Jeff didn't believe the mean oil tycoon had grown a charitable heart. It wasn't possible.

"Why now?" Jeff pressed.

"I have my reasons. They're none of your concern."

Deflection. Secrets. Now *that* was more like the father Jeff remembered, which probably meant the old man was stringing the townspeople along in an elaborate con. The RW Jeff knew was a master schemer who fought dirty and stole what he wanted.

"You have a choice. Agree to Xander's terms or agree to mine." RW paused for effect. "Together we can beat him at his own game."

"I'm listening."

"We offer the public a respectable Jeffrey Harper, an upstanding successful hotel developer. You'll again be a businessman everyone looks up to. The shareholders will have undeniable proof that you've settled down and are prepared to represent Harper Industries in this new venture."

"How?"

"With a legal contract signed in front of witnesses."

Jeff frowned. "What sort of contract?"

"The long-lasting, 'until death do you part' sort."

Oh, hell no.

Jeff sat heavily on his couch. "I'm not getting married."

"You can't be a playboy forever. It's time you settled down. Started a family."

"Like you did? How'd that work out for you, Dad?"

It was a low blow, thrown with force. Jeff would never forgive his parents for the hell they'd put him and his brother and sister through.

RW didn't respond. Not that Jeff had thought he would. The silence was a hammer pounding all the nails into the bitter wall lodged between them.

After a long minute RW said, "I'm hiring a project manager at the end of the week. When the hotel is ready, I'll hire a manager for that, too. You agree with my terms and you've got both jobs. Don't agree and you'll be scrounging on your own in New York."

I've been scrounging since I turned sixteen and you kicked me out of the house, old man.

"Think this through." RW's voice grew softer. "The hotel you create on Plunder Cove will be a family legacy. I don't trust easily, but I have faith you'll do it right."

Those words floored him.

He'd never heard anything like them before.

Jeff stared at his size twelve loafers. He wanted to believe what his dad said, but the reality of who RW had always been was too hard to forget—as was the "one condition."

"Come on, Dad. You can't expect me to get married."

"I'll give you a few days to think about it," RW said.

In a few days, another million people would share those damned GIFs and memes. The social media attack would never stop—unless he fought back.

Dad's ridiculous plan was the only thing that made a lick of sense.

It pissed him off, but still he growled, "Have your people start the search for a chef. A great one."

"You want to marry a chef?"

"No, I want to hire one. An exclusive resort needs a five-star restaurant. That's how we'll get the ball rolling. A restaurant is faster to get up and running than a hotel and the best ones get the word out fast. Find me a group of chefs to choose from. Lure them from the world's top restaurants and offer them deals they can't refuse. I'll assess their culinary skills and choose a winner."

"A contest? You'd pit them against each other?"

"Call it part of the cooking interview. We'll see which one can handle the heat. My chef has to be capable of rising above stress."

RW produced a sharp whistle through his nose, the one he used when he was not pleased. "You *must* marry, Jeffrey. That's my only stipulation. I don't care who as long as she makes you look respectable."

Jeff didn't want a wife. He wanted a hotel.

He needed to make Plunder Cove the best locale in the world, and then he'd have his dignity back. And a touch of something that might resemble a survivor's victory.

A plan started to form.

The producer of *Secrets and Sheets* had hounded Jeff for years to do a segment on the Spanish mansion and its pirate past. He'd always said no. Why glorify a place that still gave him nightmares? But now, his childhood home could be the only thing that would help him reboot his career.

"Fine. My crew can film the ceremony in one of the gardens or down on the beach. The reception will be filmed inside the new restaurant. You can't buy better advertising for the resort." The press would eat it up.

"Now that's thinking big. I like it," RW said.

Yeah? Well, hold on because it's only the first part of the plan.

Dad didn't have to know that Jeff was going to dangle the televised wedding to his producer in exchange for something far more important—the final, edited episode of *Secrets and Sheets*. Jeff wished for the fiftieth time that he hadn't given the raw footage to the show's producer. He hadn't thought to keep a copy and now he was empty-handed against Finn. But not for long. Once Jeff had the recording, he'd release it on every media outlet possible. The blackmail would stop and the world would finally know what Finn had done to his customers, and to Jeff.

No one attacked the Harpers and lived to tell the tale.

For the first time that week, Jeff actually smiled.

Michele Cox snuggled next to her sister on the twin bed at the group home and softly read Cari's favorite picture book. *Rosie's Magic Horse* was about a girl who saves her family from financial ruin by riding a Popsicle-stick horse in search of pirate treasure. Michele didn't know which Cari loved more—the idea that a girl could save the day while riding a horse, or that something as small as a used Popsicle stick could aspire to greatness. Whatever the case, Cari insisted that Michele read the book to her at bedtime every night.

Tonight, Cari had fallen asleep before Michele got to the part about the pirates. Michele kept reading anyway. Sometimes she needed her own Popsicle make-believe. When she closed the book, she slipped out of the bed carefully so as not to wake her snoring sister.

Kissing Cari's forehead, Michele whispered, "Sweet dreams, cowgirl."

Michele's heart and feet were heavy as she went down

the hall to the staff station. "I'll call in and read to her every night," Michele said to one of Cari's favorite caregivers. "You've got my number. Text immediately if she gets the sniffles." Cari was susceptible to pneumonia and had been hospitalized several times.

"Don't worry, she'll be fine. She knows the routine and is getting comfortable here. We'll take good care of her."

The pit in Michele's stomach deepened. It had taken six months for Cari to learn the ropes at this home. Six long, painful months. What would happen if Michele couldn't pay the fees to keep her here?

"Thanks for taking care of her. She's all I've got." Michele swiped the tear off her cheek.

"Oh, hon. You go have a good time. You deserve it."

Deserve it? No, Michele was the one who'd messed up and lost the money her sister needed. She was heartsick over it.

She drove to her own apartment, poured herself a glass of wine and plopped down at the table in her painfully silent kitchen. God, she felt so alone. She was the sole provider and caretaker for her sister after Mom had died six months ago. Her father had passed when Michele was only ten. Cari needed services and health care and a chance to be a happy cowgirl, all of which required funds that had been stolen by her so-called partner.

There was only one way to fix the horrible mess she'd made.

She picked up the envelope sitting on top of her polka-dot place mats. "Harper Industries," it said across the top in black embossed letters. Pulling out the employment application, she reread the lines, "Candidates will cook for and be judged by Jeffrey Harper."

Her stomach flopped at the thought.

Michele wasn't a fan of his show. That playboy attitude of his left her cold. She'd had her fill of arrogant, demanding males in her career. She'd given everything she had to the last head chef she'd worked with and where had that left her? Poor and alone. Because of him, she'd lost her desire to cook—which was the last connection she had to her mother.

Mom had introduced her to family recipes when Michele was only seven years old. Cooking together meant tasting, laughing and dancing in the kitchen. All her best memories came from that warm, spicy, belly-filling place. While the rest of the house was dark and choked with bad memories—cancer, pills, dying—the kitchen was safe. Like her mother's embrace.

As a young girl, Michele had experimented with dishes to make her mom and Cari feel better. Mom had encouraged Michele to submit the creations in local cook-offs and, surprisingly, Michele had won every contest she entered. The local paper had called her "a child prodigy" and "a Picasso in the kitchen." Cooking had been easy back then because food was a river of color coursing through her veins. Spatulas and spoons were her crayons. All she had to do was let the colors flow.

But now she was empty, her passion dried up. What if her gift, her single moneymaking talent, never returned?

If Michele Cox wasn't a chef, who was she?

She tapped her pen on the Harper Industries application. Could she fake it? Jeffrey Harper was an infamous critic who publicly destroyed those who didn't meet his standards. Would he know the difference between passionate cooking and plain old cooking? If he did, he'd annihilate her.

But if he didn't…

The Harper chef job came with a twenty-thousand-dollar up-front bonus. Twenty thousand! With that kind of money, Cari could continue riding therapy horses. Hippotherapy was supposed to be beneficial for people with Down syndrome but Michele had been amazed at how her sister had come alive the first time she'd touched a pony. Cari's cognitive, motor, speech and social skills had blossomed. But riding lessons weren't cheap and neither were housing and medi-

cal bills. Michele's rent was two weeks late and she barely
had enough money in her account to pay for Cari's care.

Her options were slim. If Harper Industries didn't hire
her, the two of them might be living on the streets.

She signed the application and went on to the final step.
She had to make a video answering a single question: *Why
do you want to work for Harper Industries?*

Straightening her spine, she looked into the camera on
her computer and pressed the record button. "I want to work
for Harper Industries because I need to believe good things
can happen to good people." Her voice hitched and she
quickly turned the video off.

Shoot. Where'd that come from? She'd almost blurted
out what happened at Alfieri's. "Get it together, Michele.
If you spill all the sordid details, they'll never hire you."

She scrubbed her cheeks, took a giant inhale and tried
again.

"I am Michele Cox, the former chef at a five-star restaurant,
Alfieri's, in Manhattan. I will include articles about my
awards and specialties but those highlights are not the most
important aspect of being a chef, nor are they why I cook.

"Food, Mr. Harper, is a powerful medicine. Good cuisine
can make people feel good. When the dishes are excellent,
the patron can ease loneliness with a bite of ricotta cannelloni.
That's what I do. I make patrons feel happy and loved.
I can do that for your new restaurant, too. I hope you'll give
me a chance. Thank you."

Well. That wasn't so bad. Before she could change her
mind, she pressed Send on the video and sealed the application
packet to be sent by overnight mail along with the
glowing newspaper articles she'd promised. Today was the
day she'd put Alfieri's behind her and search for her cooking
mojo.

A good person should catch a break once in a while.

All she needed was one.

Two

Michele ran as fast as she could through the parking lot while trying not to break her neck on her high heels or snap the wheels off her luggage. She'd arrived in Los Angeles yesterday and spent the night at a nearby hotel to be on time for today's flight to Plunder Cove. The taxi driver had dropped her off in the wrong wing of the airport, making her late. He didn't seem to believe that a woman like her actually did mean she should be dropped off at the private jet terminal.

Her heart was pounding out of her chest when she arrived at the guarded gate. "Please tell me… I'm not…too late."

"Name," the guard said.

"Michele Cox. A jet from Harper Industries is supposed to take me to—"

The gate opened. "You're expected."

"Over here." A woman wearing a blue suit waved to her. "Oh, dear. Your cheeks are pink. Come, there's ice water inside the private suite but there's no time for a shower. Mr. Harper is ready to leave."

Her first thought was *A shower in a private suite in the airport?* The second was *Jeffrey Harper is inside?* She could only guess how she looked after her panicked run in the Los Angeles sunshine. No doubt her cheeks were more scarlet than pink. She finger-combed her blond hair and hoped for the best.

A door opened and Michele found herself in a ritzy lounge complete with cream-colored sofas, hardwood floors, recessed lighting, deep navy curtains, game tables and a cherrywood bar. Five women were chatting and drinking champagne.

"Miss Cox?" A deep voice called out from the end of the corridor. "I almost left without you."

Her heart skipped a beat until she realized it wasn't Jeffrey Harper. The man was handsome—of the tall, dark, broad-shouldered variety. He was also married, with a shiny new band on his left finger. Other than that, she had no idea who he was or why he knew her name.

"Sorry!" And…there went the wheel on her luggage. She grabbed the suitcase by the handle and kept hustling toward him. "Thanks for waiting. The International Wing was full of people and—" Her heel broke and she nearly twisted her ankle. "Shoot!"

"The International Wing? That's a good mile. You ran that whole way?"

"Only one?" She struggled to catch her breath. "Felt like two."

"Let me take that." He handed her luggage to an agent while she collected her broken heel.

She scanned the room. When she saw a beautiful woman speaking French over by the bar, her heart plummeted. It was Chef Suzette Monteclaire, the queen of French cuisine. What was she doing in the Harpers' private suite?

"Now that we're all here." The man raised his voice above the chatter. "Let me introduce myself. I'm Matt Harper, Jeff's brother and your pilot to Plunder Cove. Before we get on the jet, do you have any questions?"

The women looked at each other. A bad feeling slithered into her belly. Michele raised her finger.

"Yes, Miss Cox?"

"Are we *all* applying for the chef job?"

Matt shrugged. "Looks like it."

"I don't understand. I thought there was only one position open."

"Me, too," another woman agreed. "Why are we all here?"

A woman in the center of the group chuckled. She had thick dark hair and hooded green eyes. "Isn't it obvious? It's a contest. The winner gets to work for sexy Jeffrey Harper." She winked at Matt.

"Is this part of his show? I have not seen this on *Secrets and Sheets*," a soft-spoken woman said. Michele thought she was Lily Snow, the chef from Manhattan's upscale Chinese restaurant—The China Lily.

"He's creating a cooking show, no?" another woman asked, in a Swedish accent. Her hair was strikingly white-blond. Her large eyes were like sapphires against a milky pale complexion. She was tall, svelte and gorgeous. Everything about her screamed perfection and wealth. Lots of wealth.

Michele tried to inconspicuously wipe the sweat off her upper lip. Jeffrey Harper was going to turn her misery into a cooking show. Would she be able to pretend she was the chef she used to be not just for him but with all of America watching?

Matt shook his head. "I don't know what the hell this is, I'm only supposed to fly you all into Plunder Cove. If this is not what you signed up for, I'll give you the chance to back out gracefully. I'll arrange for a driver to take you back to your terminal and I will pay for your return flight."

Seeing all the talent in the room, Michele's legs twitched to start running back to New York. But she needed this—for Cari, for herself.

She didn't move. None of the other women did either.

"No takers?" Matt shrugged. "Right. Follow me to the jet."

Three hours later, a stretch limousine filled with six chef candidates turned up a long lane. Beautiful purple-flowered trees lined a wide driveway. Michele had never seen trees like that before.

"There it is!" One of the women squealed. "Casa Larga."

Michele looked through the tinted car window and saw a mansion straight out of a magazine spread. It was way bigger in real life. Imposing.

The women all started talking at once—something about Jeff's sister being Yogi to the stars—but Michele could only swallow hard. Why did she think she belonged here with these famous chefs and celebrities? She should've listened to Matt Harper and walked away gracefully. On her broken heel with her broken luggage.

"Jeff is a seriously hot man," one of the ladies said.

Michele didn't disagree but what did it matter? She didn't want to be hit on. And she didn't want a playboy or an arrogant critic for a boss. She needed Jeffrey to hire her and stay out of her kitchen. It hadn't gotten past her that Jeffrey Harper was only interviewing women. Why wasn't there a male chef candidate in the bunch?

The limo parked and the women piled out.

"Welcome to Casa Larga at Plunder Cove," a woman wearing a yellow skirt said in a voice that was soft, melodious. "I'm Jeff's sister, Chloe Harper. It's my job to get you settled inside. You'll be sharing. Two ladies to each room tonight. Tomorrow...well, we'll see how it all plays out. Follow me and I'll give you the tour."

They walked through large double doors and into a huge entryway. Michele looked up at the largest chandelier she'd ever seen.

Chloe continued, "I'll give you a schedule for when you will be called to the kitchen to cook a meal. It should be a signature dish that highlights what you do best."

The woman with the white-blond hair held up a perfectly manicured finger. Michele had learned her name was Freja. "Wardrobe and makeup, first, eh? My fans will be seeing me in Sweden. They can vote, too, no?"

An avalanche of panic made Michele's limbs weak. She hadn't suspected this would be a competition, much less a televised one. She didn't know if she could cook a master-piece and if she failed with the entire world watching, her career would be over.

Chloe looked startled. "This is not a reality show, it's a competition. At the end, Jeff will choose one of you as his chef. Fans will not be voting."

Michele's heart started to beat normally again until Chloe went on to add, "We'll have a television crew in here once the restaurant is completed. Whomever Jeff chooses should expect lots of cameras that day."

Even knowing that, Michele wanted to be the chosen one. She had to be. This job was the path to financial stability, the only way she knew to make sure Cari was healthy and happy. It was the kick in the backside that she desperately needed. She had to convince Jeffrey Harper that she was the right one for the job. Somehow, she had to get her cooking mojo back.

Jeff stood shoulder-to-shoulder with Matt on the upstairs landing and watched Chloe lead the women through the downstairs corridor. They all had one thing in common—they were fantastic chefs. That's all he really cared about.

"You sure about this plan, bro?" Matt asked. "You're get-ting married when the restaurant is done?"

Jeff grimaced. "I don't have much of a choice. That's the deal."

"You and Dad are big on deals. It's stupid. Marriage is not a business contract. When it's right, you connect on a deep level, deeper than you'll believe. Julia touches me in places I didn't know existed."

"Sounds like good sex to me."

"Shut up." Matt socked him in the shoulder. "You should give yourself a chance to find love, man. That's all I'm saying."

Jeff could take all the time in the world, but he'd never find the sort of connection Matt had found with his wife, Julia. Jeff wasn't wired for it.

The chefs walked below him, a slow parade of beauty and talent, chatting as they went. They seemed oblivious to him standing above them. He was fine with that. He really didn't want to make contact until he judged their dishes. Why waste time with small talk if he wasn't impressed with their culinary skills?

As the last woman passed by, she stopped and looked up as if she'd sensed him. Her eyes met his. She tipped her head to the side slightly, and the light on the chandelier sparkled like diamonds across her long blond hair.

She raised one hand.

He raised his in return.

She smiled and hell if he couldn't see her dimples from where he stood. It was the purest sight he'd ever seen. If he had to choose one word to describe her in that moment it would be *sparkly*.

All too quickly she turned and hustled to catch up with Chloe's tour. She was gone two full beats before he looked away.

Matt thumped him on the head. "Earth to Jeff."

Jeff turned to face his brother. "Was she limping?"

"Did you not hear a word I said? That's what I was telling you, yes, she's limping because she broke her shoe running to catch our jet."

Jeff was still thinking about her smile. Can't fake dimples like that, right?

"She ran at least a mile in those high heels. I don't know about the other women in this competition, but that one has strength. A backbone." And then Matt butchered a handful of Spanish words.

"What?"

Matt grinned. "Good, huh? My wife is teaching me Spanish. It means 'she has the heart of a bull.'"

"You like saying that word, don't you?"

Matt tipped his head. "Which one?"

"Wife."

Matt had that look on his face—the "sneaking cookies and eating them in bed before Mom caught him" look. "Oh, yeah. You could enjoy saying the word, too, if you allowed yourself to find the right lady. You don't let anyone get close, Jeff. Start putting yourself out there. Be real and you'll find love. I swear it."

Jeff exhaled deeply. "Lightning doesn't strike twice in one family. And I'm not like you. Never was. You and Julia were meant for one another, you've known it since you were, like, ten. Another woman like Julia doesn't exist."

"You haven't found her because you need to open up. Show her who you are without the smoke and mirrors. No stage lighting. No props. Just two real people being…normal."

Did he want normal? What did it even mean?

"You could start with the lady you were making goo-goo eyes at. Along with her backbone, and pretty face, there's something sweet about Michele Cox."

"That was Michele Cox from Alfieri's? She made me one of the best chicken cacciatore dishes I've ever tasted. I still have daydreams about that chicken."

"Can I pick 'em or what?" Matt grinned and threw his arm over Jeff's shoulder.

"You've got it wrong. I'm not marrying any of these women, but I might hire Cox. I watched her on a cooking show once. Hell, she handled her kitchen with such passion, such flair. Spice and color all mixed together. I've never seen anything like it. She was poetry in action."

Matt cocked his head. "Poetry in action? Seems like you've thought about her a bit."

Had he? Sure. After seeing her on television, he'd made a point to visit her restaurant a few times. One night he'd even asked Alfieri if he could go back to the kitchen to meet the chef, but she'd left before he got a chance. The next time he'd gone in, he was told Michele had left the restaurant altogether. He'd been disappointed.

"I see it on your face. You like her," Matt said.

"I've never met her."

"So now is your chance. Ask her out. I dare you."

Jeff shot him a dirty look. "What is this, middle school? Dares don't work anymore. I'm not interested in searching for love. I just need a chef, and a wife who'll satisfy Dad's terms."

Matt shook his head, his voice sad. "You'll never feel it that way."

"Feel what?"

"Lightning."

Three

Michele scoped out her beautiful bedroom. It had a sitting area, a desk, two televisions, two queen-size beds, Spanish tile and a balcony. The decor was tasteful and lightly Mediterranean. The room was twice as big as her bedroom at home. Heck, maybe it was bigger than her bedroom and living room combined. She opened the French doors and stepped onto the balcony.

"Oh, hello!" The petite chef from The China Lily was sitting on the veranda. "Lovely view from here."

Michele looked out over the gardens below and let her gaze drift out to sea. "It's beautiful."

"And overwhelming. This bedroom is almost as large as my flat in Manhattan."

"Mine, too." Michele stretched out her hand. "We weren't formally introduced. I'm Michele Cox, from—"

"Alfieri's." Lily took her hand. "I know. May I say I love your lasagna? It's the best Italian dish I've ever tasted."

"It's my own recipe. The secret's in the sauce." Michele brought her finger to her lips. "And your dim sum is to die for."

"Ah, we're a mutual admiration society." Lily motioned to the other lounge chair. "Join me?"

Michele sank into the plush cushions and exhaled deeply. She was tired, jet-lagged, and her feet hurt from running in heels. "It feels like I haven't sat down in years."

"It has been a long day. I didn't know there would be a competition. Did you?"

"No. I might not have applied," Michele said softly, thinking about how the competition complicated her plans. "Do you know any of the other chefs?"

"Not personally, but I recognized Freja Ringwold, the gorgeous tall blonde? She's very famous in Sweden with her own cooking show. Tonia Sanchez, the curvy brunette with green eyes, owns three high-end Southwestern restaurants in Arizona. Suzette Monteclaire is well-known for—"

"French cuisine. Yes, I know." Michele felt like a fish out of water. A really small, unqualified fish. "What about the dark-haired chef with amazing skin? Nadia something."

"I've never seen her before. But—" Lily held up her finger and took out her cell phone "—Google will know." A short time later, she smiled. "Nadia is an award-winning Mediterranean chef in Saudi Arabia, oh, and her father is a sheikh. There's a picture of him and RW Harper taken about fifteen years ago. So, she might be a shoo-in, with her connections."

Great. What were Michele's chances with this group? "That's all of us, then. An eclectic bunch. What is Jeffrey looking for?"

"A fantastic chef. Any of us would fit the bill," Lily said.

Except she wasn't the chef she used to be.

"If you do not mind me asking, why did you leave Alfieri's? It seemed like you had a good situation there. I read there was some sort of—" Lily ran her slender hand through the air— "shake-up?"

Michele sighed. "You could call it that."

"Sorry. I shouldn't pry."

Michele studied the woman who was her competition and didn't feel any sort of maliciousness in her. It had been a long time since she'd had a friend to talk to. Mom was the person she had confided in her whole life and now that she was gone… God, her heart was so heavy.

"It's okay. Alfieri was—" how to describe the man who'd destroyed her? "—difficult. I couldn't stay. Don't get me wrong, I owe him my career. He took me in as a young apprentice. He was a great teacher, a fabulous chef who took a chance on me. When things were good, they were really good. I miss what we had together. What we created." That last bit came out choked.

"Oh," Lily said softly. "You were in love with him?"

The creative genius? She adored that part of him, but the rest terrified her.

She shook her head. "He is fifteen years older than me and so full of life and experience. I was an innocent girl from Indiana who ventured to New York to hone my cooking skills. Alfieri became my mentor. Because I owed him so much, I overlooked—" she winced, remembering the night he'd tried to scald her with boiling sauce because it was too salty "—I tried to ignore his faults. Until things got too intense."

Her throat was dry. She reached for the mineral water on the table with trembling fingers. Damn that man! He still got to her. She tried to wash the memories down.

"What happened?" Lily's eyes filled with concern.

She didn't know if it was the fact that she was so far from home and missing her sister—and, of course, Mom— or because Lily had such a gentle way about her, but Michele felt like she could confide in her. Now that she was talking, she couldn't stop. "I threatened to leave because parts of me, the best parts, were disappearing." Now, thanks to him, she still second-guessed herself every time she stepped into the kitchen. Alfieri's caustic words had dammed up her colorful river. "He apologized for his behavior, promised to go to anger-management therapy, and begged me to stay. Then he offered me a partnership. He was opening a second restaurant and said I could be the head chef there. We'd rarely have to see one another and I'd have full reign over the second location. It seemed like a dream come true. I agreed and gave him my life's savings as my share of the partnership. I trusted him." She looked Lily in the eye. "Fatal mistake."

"Oh, no."

"Long ugly story cut to the chase—he hired another chef for the second location without telling me." Another young woman to idolize and belittle. "I quit and demanded my money back. He said he didn't know what I was talking about but I could hire a lawyer if I wanted. He knew I didn't have money for lawyers. I was such a fool to trust him."

Michele didn't realize she was crying until Lily got up from her lounger, went inside and came back with a wash towel.

"You poor dear." Lily handed her the towel. "I hope Alfieri gets his just deserts for treating you like that."

Michele wiped her face, grateful for the kindness. Lily was the first person she'd confided in about this. She didn't talk about Alfieri much, because she was deeply ashamed. She should've left his restaurant long ago but she'd been in such awe of his brilliant mind that she'd made excuses for his behavior. As if cruelty was acceptable, even expected, from a head chef.

What she hadn't realized was that cruelty would eat goodness and destroy beauty. It had wormed under her skin, stealing the special gift her mom had given her, and even after that, she'd believed Alfieri.

She should've known better than to put her trust in a condescending, egotistical man. She'd never make that mistake again.

The door opened to the balcony, making Michele jump.

"Here you two are." Jeff's sister stepped outside. "Lily, you're the first chef to cook tonight. Please come downstairs to the kitchen in thirty minutes. Michele, you'll be cooking tomorrow. Good luck to both of you."

Good luck she needed desperately, and she would work her backside off to get it.

* * *

Jeff paced the large kitchen.

What in the hell was he doing?

The first two chefs had created culinary masterpieces. He'd personally judged them both and gave them five out of five stars. Either one of the dishes would be perfect for his new restaurant. The chefs were both talented and intelligent. There wasn't anything wrong with either of them. The problem? He hadn't…*connected* with either one.

There was no poetry.

Who was up next? He looked at his clipboard and read the names. The second name from the bottom caught his eye. *Michele Cox.*

A tiny spark zinged in his gut.

He picked up his cell phone and dialed Chloe's number. His sister had come home recently, too, and was helping with the candidate selection. Right now, he needed a clear head.

"How's it going?" Chloe asked. "Ready for Tonia?"

"Skip ahead to Michele Cox."

"She's not up until lunch tomorrow."

He couldn't wait that long. He had to know if the zing in his core was real. "Move her up."

"Sure. I like her. She's so, I don't know…"

"Sparkly." The word left his mouth before he could shut it down.

"Yes! That's it. Her eyes, her dimples, there's a shine there. Do you know her?"

"Not really. Do not tell her I said that either. If her culinary skills don't match my expectations I'll send her home like the other two."

"You're dismissing them already? Don't move. I'm on my way." Less than a minute later, Chloe rushed into the kitchen. "Seriously? Just like that, they're done? You didn't give those first two chefs much of a chance and one of them was Dad's pick—the sheikh's daughter."

"Dad isn't making the decisions here. I am. Why waste their time and mine?" He leaned against the counter, crossing his arms.

"Because this is just another example of how you don't spend much effort getting to know people. Do you ever let anyone in, Jeff?"

"What's that supposed to mean?"

"I worry about you. When was the last time you made a real connection with someone? Anyone?" She pressed her hand to his chest. "Here."

Never. "I don't have time for real connections."

"You need to try or you'll wake up one day, grumpy, old and lonely. There's more to life than work, Jeff. More to relationships than three minutes in an elevator." She softened the zinger with a smile.

He wasn't going to discuss the sex video with his kid sister. It had been more than three minutes, but few people knew what had really happened in the elevator and he wanted to keep it that way.

"I'm fine."

"Are you?" Her gaze pored over his face, her expression sad. "After what Mom did to you? Of the three of us, you had it the worst. I still have nightmares about that night in the shed."

Suddenly, he felt cold, his heart pounding. "How? You were, like, three."

"I remember."

He squeezed his hands into fists. He was not going to talk about this. "I'm fine. You can stop worrying about me being old and lonely. Didn't you hear the news? I'm getting married."

She shook her head. "Not funny, Jeff."

He lifted an eyebrow. "Don't believe me? Ask Dad."

She mimicked his pose right back at him. His little sister never backed down from a challenge. It ran in the family.

"Stop teasing. When we were kids, you swore you'd never get married."

He shrugged. "People grow up."

Her eyes widened. "You're serious."

"As a heart attack."

"I can't believe it. This is great. Who is the lucky bride? Please tell me it isn't the one from the elevator."

"Hell, no." His insides shuddered. "No one from New York."

"A local sweetheart? Is that why you changed your mind and agreed to come home?"

He frowned. "I'm not Matt. No one has ever waited for me."

"Then who?"

"Beats me. Got any ideas?"

She cocked her head. "I don't understand."

"The great RW Harper proclaimed a marriage to be so and…" he raised his hands in surrender "…I'm tying the knot. Once a bride shows up and agrees to a loveless marriage."

"No. You can't get married without falling in love. That's…not normal."

"Must run in the family. Doubt Mom and Dad cared for one another."

"And look how that turned out!" She gripped his elbow. "Please, Jeff. Reconsider. I want you to be happy."

He patted her arm. "I don't have a lot of options right now. In case you didn't see it, there was another meme released this morning. It's brutal."

"I saw it." She leaned against his shoulder. "I'm so sorry."

Her small act of kindness tugged on the anxiety in his gut and made him question whether he should tell her what had really happened in the elevator.

Would she understand?

"You're a good person who deserves to be loved. I'll do whatever I can to help you find your soul mate, Jeff."

"That's not happening," he grumbled.

"All you need to do is open your fourth chakra—your heart space. I'll help you unblock it so you have a chance."

Did she think he was emotionally constipated? Hell, maybe he was. "Give it up, sis. I'm a lost cause. Besides, I've managed this long without love, why find it now?"

"Oh, Jeff." Her eyes were wet. "Managing is not happiness. I learned that the hard way. I can teach you how to let your feelings flow. To heal you."

He didn't want to offend her, but yoga wasn't going to fix his problems. She was lucky she hadn't acquired Mom's "incapacity to love" genes like he had. Damned lucky.

"I've got a chef to hire and a hotel empire to build. And on that note—" he pushed himself off the counter "— tell Michele Cox to come down in twenty minutes. She'll be the last one tonight."

"Okay." Chloe started to walk out of the kitchen but turned back to give him a big hug before she left.

Jeff made sure no one else was around and then pulled up the application videos on his computer. He played the one labeled "Michele Cox."

"…When the dishes are excellent, the patron can ease loneliness with a bite of ricotta cannelloni. That's what I do. I make patrons feel happy and loved. I can do that for your new restaurant, too. I hope you'll give me a chance. Thank you."

Her voice and words were strong. Confident. So why did he get a sense that Michele was fragile?

He played it again. "I want to work for Harper Industries because I need to believe good things can happen to good people." He pressed Pause so he could study her. Zoomed in closer. There. In her light brown eyes, he saw a look he'd seen in his own reflection.

It made his heart beat faster.

Michele Cox was a survivor, too.

Four

Michele stood alone next to the island in the Harper family kitchen and pressed her palms against the cool marble countertop.

She closed her eyes and silently breathed in, *I am a cooking goddess. Amazing and talented.* And exhaled, *I will create greatness.* And then she threw her arms up in victory. It was a superstitious ritual, one she'd done before big cooking nights at Alfieri's to focus her thoughts. It used to work. Tonight? Not so much.

Bad thoughts kept rushing in. Broken fragments of anxiety looped through her mind like a terrible song she couldn't stop hearing.

Why do you think you can do this? You'll mess this up.

It was Alfieri's voice. She opened her eyes and squeezed her fists together.

She couldn't make a mistake tonight.

Biting her lip, she debated long and hard before she finally gave in and pulled up her recipe on her cell phone.

That's right, you have to cheat. You are nothing without me.

"Shut up, Alfieri!" she whispered.

Using her own recipe wasn't cheating. She'd created it after all, but she usually didn't need to look at it. She used to be able to cook by her senses, her mood and something she called "Mom's magic." Lately, though, she second-guessed herself about everything. Her mom and all the magic were gone.

Michele put the phone on the counter in front of her where she could see the recipes and began.

The sage-rosemary bread was baking and the pan with lemon, olive oil and Italian white wine and spices was heating up nicely. The kitchen smelled divine. She stuffed squid with prosciutto, smoked mozzarella and garlic cloves and gently placed them into the pan. Lightly, she drizzled the squid with her secret homemade truffle sauce. Her special linguine noodles cooked on the back burner and the arugula-basil-chardonnay grape salad with light oil and lemon dressing was up next. Everything looked perfect...except... something felt off.

She had a sinking feeling she'd forgotten to fill the last squid with garlic. It wasn't hot yet. If she hurried, she could snatch it back and fix her error. She turned the heat down and used a slotted spoon to carefully recover the squid from the pan. The truffle sauce made the darned thing slippery to handle and it plopped out of the spoon and into the pan again. She wasn't wearing an apron because all of hers had Alfieri's name on them, so when the oil splashed up, it spotted her silk blouse. The one people said brought out the amber color in her eyes.

"Gah! Thanks a lot, you slimy sea booger!"

"Miss Cox?" A deep voice came up behind her.

The surprise caused her to jerk the spoon and catapult the squid from the pan into the air. She lunged and caught it before it hit the floor tiles. Cupping the drippy squid behind her back, she straightened her shoulders and rose up to face...*him*.

Jeffrey Harper's large frame filled the space, blocking the exit. There was no way she could flee or pretend he hadn't seen her glaring faux pas. The way he was looking at her? He'd definitely witnessed her launch food into the air and catch it with her bare hand.

"Mr. Harper. You startled me."

He stepped closer and her heartbeat kicked up even more. He wore a white linen shirt—unbuttoned just enough so she could glimpse glorious red chest hair—and jeans that molded perfectly to his legs.

The casual version of the man was sexier than the one she'd seen on television.

"My apologies. I didn't mean to interrupt your conversation with…" He cocked his head toward the pan and a beautiful copper-colored bang fell onto his forehead. He tossed his head to move it back into place. "Slimy sea boogers."

Could a person die from failure?

She steeled herself to be the recipient of his disgusted look—the one he used in the episode when he'd seen rats running across a cutting board in a hotel's kitchen. Instead, she saw...*amusement*?

"I wasn't having a conversation with all of them. Just this one." She produced the squid that she'd been hiding behind her back. "He was behaving badly."

Instead of berating her and kicking her out of his kitchen—as Alfieri would have—the corner of Jeffrey's lips curled.

He had beautiful lips.

"I see. What are you going to do about him?" He kept coming closer.

He was so tall. She had to tip her head to gaze into his eyes, which were an amazing powder blue with a golden starburst in the irises. Simply mesmerizing. It was easy to understand why women lusted after Jeffrey Harper.

She looked at the misshapen squid. Alfieri would've scolded her. *That mistake will come out of your paycheck.*

"Throw it away?" she said.

"Why? Cook it up. I'll eat it."

Her hands were shaking when she shoved a garlic clove inside, rearranged the stuffing, dropped the squid in the pan with the others, and turned up the heat. The pan started sizzling, which didn't come close to the electricity she felt when Jeffrey stood so close. His woodsy cologne smelled better than the food but having him watch her cook made her nervous.

"I don't see chicken." He sounded disappointed.

Did he expect all the chefs to serve chicken? Had she missed that part of the fine print in the contract she'd signed?

"It's pan-seared and stuffed squid with my special truffle sauce. The linguine noodles and bay clams are almost ready," she said, her voice tiny.

He crossed his arms, his body language expressing disappointment. "Miss Cox, the chef position for my restaurant is highly competitive. I expect to be impressed by each meal."

Now *that* sounded more like Alfieri. The condescending tone stirred up her anger. "What more do I need to do, Mr. Harper? Juggle clams and catch them with my teeth?"

His mouth dropped open. She'd surprised herself, too, since she usually didn't speak up to a boss and never in a job interview. She waited for him to ask her to leave.

Instead Jeffrey Harper surprised *her*.

He laughed.

It was a good, hearty sound that rolled through her core, loosening the bitterness inside her. She couldn't help but smile.

He had a really great laugh.

"No, Miss Cox. Just excite me. I'm looking forward to being transported."

What did that mean? The way he looked at her, like they were sharing some sort of inside joke, was unnerving. She didn't get the punch line.

"Chardonnay?" he asked.

"Sure, if that's what you like to drink. But I'd probably suggest a nice light-bodied, high-acid red wine, like a Sangiovese, or perhaps a white Viognier?"

"I'll see what we've got in the cellar." Watching him stride out of the kitchen, it struck her that Jeffrey Harper was not as cocky as he seemed on television. She liked him better this way. Plus, he hadn't yelled at her.

She took the bread out of the oven, wrapped it in a colorful towel, and placed it in a basket. Checking the recipe again to make sure she hadn't forgotten anything, she plated up the meal. Four stuffed squid were dressed with the light sauce and adorned with a sprinkling of spices. The linguine and clams were cooked perfectly. The salad was a lacy pyramid of arugula and basil leaves and decorated with sweet chardonnay grapes. The dressing was another secret recipe that never failed. The meal was not a work of art, but it looked good, it smelled good, and she was sure it would taste good. That was the best she could do tonight.

She sighed. Good wouldn't cut it here, not by a long shot. The other chefs would be excellent.

"I have both wines." His deep voice rumbled behind her, sending shivers up her spine. "Which would you prefer, Miss Cox?"

She glanced over her shoulder at him. He waved two bottles at her. "Me?"

"I'm not drinking alone."

She folded his napkin into a flower shape. "Oh, okay. Um, I like white. Thank you." She carried his plate to the table.

"Viognier it is." He poured her a glass and placed it at the table across from him. "Sit."

Apparently, she was supposed to watch him eat. Was he going to tell her bite by bite how she'd messed up or how the food didn't *excite* him? Would he throw the entire plate at her head and order her to clean up the mess like Alfieri would?

She glanced at the table and realized she'd forgotten the salad. Another rookie move. What else would she mess up tonight? "I'll be right back."

When she returned with his salad plate, she was surprised to see he'd split his entrée onto two plates.

"What are you doing, Mr. Harper?"

"Join me. I hate to eat alone." His smile was more sincere than cocky and there was something about the look in his eyes that tugged at her. Sadness? Loneliness?

She hated to eat alone, too. Uneasily, she sat across from him.

He sounded relieved when he said, "Thank you."

She heard those two words so infrequently that she checked to make sure he wasn't being sarcastic. He wasn't.

"Eat," he ordered.

Huh. Somehow, she'd scored an impromptu date with America's Most Eligible Bachelor. It wasn't a bad way to go out after the worst job interview of her life. Not bad at all.

He lit two candles and moved them so he could look at Michele Cox's pretty face.

Jeff had never met a chef like her.

When he first came into the kitchen, he hadn't been impressed. There was no poetry in action. No color or fluidity. She seemed stiff and uncertain. And why was she looking at her cell phone so much? Was she using someone else's recipe?

Then she'd verbally threatened her food. That was strange enough, but chucking it into the air and catching it as if nothing had happened? Her cheeks had flushed with embarrassment and her gorgeous honey-colored eyes had sparked with worry, and still she'd sassed him. That took balls. And wits. Two things he wanted in his chef.

Two things that made him want to know more about her.

He cut through the squid and garlicky butter oozed out. He popped the bite into his mouth and chewed, slowly, deliberately. She met his gaze, and in her expression, he saw hopefulness. She wanted to win this battle. Badly. A flicker of something lit up in him, too, though he wasn't ready to name it.

He took a bite of the linguine and the salad, making her

wait for his verdict. Not because he was cruel, but because he wanted to savor this moment—his eyes locked with hers, the two of them eating together.

"Here, you've got a little—" He shook out the napkin she'd folded into a flower and wiped a bit of butter off her chin.

"Thanks." She gave him a taste of those deep dimples. Foreplay with the chef. He liked it. So much so that he almost forgot he was judging the meal.

"It's good," he said, chewing the last bite. The second squid, the misshapen one, seemed to have twice as much garlic as the first. Inconsistency was a bad sign.

"I know." She looked at the food on her plate and her dimples disappeared. "Good. Not magic."

She felt it, too. Something was missing. "I enjoyed it. Why didn't you make your signature dish?"

"My chicken cacciatore?"

"Hell, yes. I had it in New York. It was seriously one of the best dishes I've ever tasted." If she'd made it for him, she would've been a shoo-in for the job and yet she went with seafood? She didn't know how risky that was.

"I created that dish for Alfieri's. I won't make it anymore."

"Why not? It was fantastic."

"I'm sorry… I just…can't." Her voice choked and she gulped the rest of her wine.

Was it his imagination, or had her cheeks gone pale? Wait. Were those tears in her eyes?

What the hell had he said?

"Miss Cox, is there something wrong?"

She put her glass down and looked him in the eye. "It's nothing. Thank you for being so kind. I'm not used to it."

No one had ever called him *kind* before. "I'm honest."

She waved her hand over the table. "The candles? Sharing your food? Your wine? It's a sweet thing to do when we both know I'm not getting the job."

That gave him pause. Why was she trying to talk herself out of the position? "Have you changed your mind?"

"No! I desperately need…" She pressed her lips together, cutting off her thoughts. "I want to work for Harper Industries. I really do. I'm just…this is embarrassing. I didn't cook an award-winner tonight. I'm not sure I know how to anymore."

He couldn't fathom why, but his senses told him that whatever she was hiding scared her. Was she in trouble? "You're selling yourself short."

"No, I'm not." She bit her lip. Was it quivering?

Was she that sensitive about her food? Chefs needed to be creative and strong, bold and thick-skinned. Tears in the kitchen wouldn't work.

"If you'll excuse me, I'll clean up the dishes for the next contestant." She reached for his plate.

He stopped her by putting his hand on hers. "Miss Cox? *What* do you desperately need?"

She froze. Her expression seemed serious and troubled as if the answer was the key to everything. "To find what I lost so I can take care of my sister."

What the hell did that mean?

As he tried to decipher her words, she pulled her hand back and reoffered it as a handshake, "Thank you for the opportunity, Mr. Harper. I wish you luck in finding the perfect chef. I'm sorry I wasted your time."

Shaking her soft, delicate hand produced a stab of disappointment. He said nothing. He couldn't. She had the right to walk away from the job; people walked away all the time.

So why did it feel like she'd just quit *him*?

He watched her leave and drank his wine. Alone.

Five

Michele berated herself all the way back to the room she shared with Lily.

How could she have made such dumb mistakes in front of a world-renowned critic like Jeffrey Harper? One bad word from him and she would never cook again. He had the power to ruin her career for eternity.

Well, if *she* didn't ruin everything first.

She knocked on the door and was surprised to see Lily was already in her pajamas. "Sorry, did I wake you?"

Lily yawned. "No. I am getting ready to go to bed, though. I'm exhausted from jet lag. Aren't you?"

Actually, no. She was still pumped from her time with Jeffrey. A wild mix of emotions—disappointment, embarrassment and attraction—boiled in her blood. She liked Jeffrey more than she'd expected she would, which made crashing and burning in front of him even worse.

She walked into the room and snagged her purse. "I need to make a call before bed. I'll take my conversation somewhere else."

She'd promised Cari she'd read her the bedtime story every night over the phone. She would've done it earlier but she'd been called to the kitchen tonight instead of tomorrow. Hopefully, the assistant at the home had reminded Cari that Michele might be calling later than usual. Cari couldn't tell time, but she'd have a sense that it was late in New York.

"Before you go…" Lily sat on her bed. "Please tell me how your interview went. I was confused by mine."

"Why? What happened?" Michele came and sat on the bed, facing Lily. "Didn't he like your cuisine?"

"Oh, yes. He said it was excellent. The best dim sum he'd ever tasted."

A sharp spike of jealousy pricked Michele's insides. *Excellent*. Not *good*.

That proved it. Jeffrey hated her squid.

"What's confusing about that?" Michele asked. "Sounds like you impressed him."

"During my interview, Jeffrey was… I don't want to say cold, exactly. But very businesslike, almost as if his heart wasn't in it. He only asked me one personal question and then thanked me and left."

Jeffrey hadn't been cold during her interview. Remembering the way he'd smiled at her still made Michele warm and tingly. "Didn't he invite you to eat with him in the dining room?"

Lily's brown eyes widened. "No. He ate over the sink in the kitchen. Didn't even sit down. He didn't want me to leave until he was finished and then he excused me. He asked you to join him for dinner?"

"Oh, well, he must've felt sorry for me. I really bombed my dish."

"Jeffrey doesn't give me the impression that he'd feel sorry for anyone creating unsatisfactory cuisine. Incompetent service seems to really annoy him on the show."

Michele thought about it. Lily was right. The guy she'd watched on TV would've asked her to leave the moment she'd showed him the deformed squid in her palm. Alfieri would have thrown whatever was in his hand at her and ordered her out of his kitchen.

More confused than before, Michele hoisted the purse with the book inside over her shoulder. "I'm going to make that call. I won't wake you when I come in."

* * *

Angel Mendoza was the only woman RW Harper loved, the only one he couldn't keep. He poured champagne into her favorite crystal flute and seltzer into his own mug.

He'd stopped drinking the moment she'd come into his life. He needed to be alert, awake. He needed to not slip back into that nightmarish hole she'd dragged him out of. It was as if she'd fashioned a new heart for him out of dead, tattered tissue, and was teaching it how to beat. How to feel.

She'd come to him as a therapist, and her therapy had saved his life. Now he was doing everything possible to keep from screwing it all up. He had to make sure that she could live her life, too.

He joined her on the balcony. "To you," he said, handing her the flute.

Turning her face away from the orange-pink sunset, she melted him with her deep brown eyes. Damn, Angel was gorgeous. Sundowners with her were his favorite evening ritual, one he would sorely miss if she left him.

When she left him. Again.

He knew they were sharing a slice of borrowed time. It had taken a lot of coaxing to bring her back two months ago, and he suspected she'd given in only to bring Cristina and her young son to Plunder Cove for protection from the gang that was hunting all three of them. Her return had nothing to do with him.

Still, he didn't want to let her go.

Taking the champagne in one hand, she cupped his cheek with the other. Her hands were soft and cool. "You are an amazing man. Thank you for protecting them, RW. I don't know what I would've done—" She shook her head, banishing ugly visions that he didn't want to imagine, either. She took a sip as if to drown the quiver in her voice.

Right. As if he could not hear her fear and pain. He was hypersensitive to all things Angel Mendoza. Right now, her breathing was too shallow, her soft cheeks pale, her sexy laugh lines drawn too tight.

"How are our guests? Everyone settling in?" he asked, hoping to take her mind off the past that still haunted her.

"Do you mean my guests, or Jeffrey's?"

"I assume Jeffrey is getting acquainted with the chefs we located for him. Quite an amazing amount of talent out there. I have no idea how he'll choose one. Maybe he'll marry one, too."

Cool ocean breezes blew over the edge of the balcony. Angel wiggled under his arm for warmth. He loved when she did that. He pulled her in tight and hung on.

It might be the last time he touched her.

"Are you sure that's his intent? Maybe he simply wants the best chef for the restaurant."

RW inhaled, breathing in her scent. "How would I know? The boy has no bridal prospects in mind and always loved the kitchen. Can't tell you how many times I found him asleep in there as a child and had to carry him back to his bedroom. It makes sense he would marry a chef." RW didn't mention how much the staff had taken care of Jeffrey when his own mother wouldn't.

"You're still going to force him to marry?"

"That was the deal," he said firmly. "He needs to change his ways. Repairing his reputation is the only way I can save him from Xander Finn. Jeff knows it, too."

"Well, if that's the case, Jeff simply needs to let himself *feel* which chef is the right fit…for whatever he is planning," she said. "He should follow his heart."

"It took me four decades to locate that organ in my chest. What makes you think he'll find his and trust it in a few weeks?"

She smiled up at him. "Because we'll help him."

He doubted Jeffrey would listen to his old man when it came to affairs of the heart—not after RW had so badly botched things with Jeffrey's mother—but Angel was a force to be reckoned with. She was the only reason RW had learned to get in tune with his own emotions. Lately, she had been trying to teach him how to forgive himself for all the sins of his past.

He rubbed her arm, to warm her, yes, but mostly to touch her. He touched her every chance he could get.

"How about your friends? Are they comfortable?"

"From the dirty streets to Casa Larga is a mind-blowing trip. Cristina is still jumping at every shadow. It's hard for her to believe that she's safe here," she said.

Twenty years ago, Cristina had joined the gang because she was a young, filthy and hungry runaway. Angel, who had been a teenager herself, had looked out for the girl until Angel left the gang, in fear for her life. She'd begged Cristina to go with her but the young woman was too scared. Leaving Cristina behind had been tough. So, when Cristina called three months ago, Angel did not hesitate. She'd rescued the young woman and her four-year-old son and now she was doing everything she could to keep them both hidden and safe. If the gang found them, they would find Angel and her family.

Angel would not let that happen.

"Cristina and her son are safe. You've got to trust me." He spun her around to face him. "I won't let Cuchillo find her or you. I'm going to break that bastard."

Angel swallowed hard. "I know." There it was again. The worry in her voice was killing him.

He pulled her back into his arms, shielding her, hoping to prove that he would always protect her. He wasn't supposed to fall in love with his therapist—she'd made the rules clear from the start—but that new heart she'd given him? It felt things it shouldn't.

Even if she left, *when* she left, he'd still feel those things. He didn't have a choice in the matter.

After a long silent moment, he asked, "What about the little boy? Is he scared, too?"

"Sebastian is four years old and confused. Living with the gang is all he has ever known. He doesn't understand why we brought him here. He's too little to know we saved his life. He's throwing a fit to go back home and is driving Cristina crazy when she's already on edge." Angel let out a deep breath. "It's going to take some time."

"What can I do to make him happy? Can I give him something?"

"Hmm. Stock options are out of the question, but…" She lifted her finger. "I might know a way to help both him and Jeffrey."

He lifted his eyebrow. "*This* I've got to see."

She picked up her cell phone. "Hi, Jeffrey, it's Angel."

"Hey, Angel. What's wrong? Is everything okay?" RW heard his son's voice through the receiver.

"I was wondering if you could ask one of your chef friends for a favor?" she said.

"A favor?"

"Our little guest is sad. A grilled cheese sandwich might perk him up. Since the regular kitchen staff is on vacation while you're running the cooking competition, I was hoping you could get one of the chefs to help me out."

"Any particular chef?" Jeff asked.

"It doesn't matter, just pick a nice one."

"A nice one? What does that—"

"Thanks, Jeffrey. Appreciate it," Angel interrupted him. "Gotta go." She hung up.

Angel smiled at RW. "Let's see who he chooses to help that little boy. That will be the one closest to his heart."

"Devious." RW kissed the top of her head. "I like it."

Michele sat on a bar stool and stood the picture book up on the island she'd recently used to stuff her career-ending squid. The kitchen was one of the only rooms she knew how to find in this gigantic house without a map. Besides, it was quiet and warm and just as clean as she'd left it. Apparently, she'd been the last contestant to cook tonight.

She spoke softly into her cell phone. "You're still awake. Don't you know all cowgirls need their sleep?"

"Can't sleep good without my story," Cari whined. "Why were you so slow?"

"I'm working, remember?" *At least, I was.* "Are you tucked into bed?"

"Yepee."

Imagining her sister burrowed under the covers with a plastic pony in each hand warmed her heart. "Okay, then. Let's find out what that Rosie is up to tonight…"

Jeff ran his hand through his hair. "Pick a *nice* one?" he grumbled. Why did it matter? Any line cook or fry guy could make a grilled cheese sandwich.

Hell, I could do it.

That idea sounded more appealing than approaching six women and grabbing one for Angel's job. No wait, there were only five now since Miss Cox had bailed. He didn't know the first two chefs very well, and they were on their way out. He had yet to meet the last three. How could he possibly pick a nice one out of the bunch?

No, it was less stress to do it himself. *I'll show you grilled cheese, little man.*

He headed into the kitchen, but stopped short two strides in. Someone was sleeping with her head on the kitchen island. Long, blond hair draped over a thin arm that held… what? He leaned closer to see. A picture book?

That hair looked so damned soft. He lifted it off her face and whispered the one name he'd been thinking about all day, "Miss Cox."

Michele jerked up, her eyes wild with fear. "Cari!"

"It's Jeff. You're safe here." When he realized his hand hovered over her back, itching to comfort her—to touch her—he stepped back.

He shoved his hands in his pockets. "Was your bed not to your liking?"

Awareness came into her face. She rubbed that pretty mouth of hers and sat up. "Sorry. I had to make a phone call and didn't want to disturb my roommate. It's so warm and comfortable in here, I guess I fell asleep." She pushed her hair back, inadvertently making it stick up on one side.

Damn, she looked adorable.

He took his hands out of his pockets and sat on the bar stool beside her. "I used to do that all the time as a kid. When my parents were fighting, this was the best place in the house to get any sleep."

She faced him. "Your parents argued a lot?"

"Only every day and twice on Sunday. I grew up thinking all parents hated each other and cursed the day they had kids."

"I'm sorry. That must have been terrible for you."

People didn't usually say nice things to him unless they wanted something, like a job or a good critique. None of that was the case with Miss Cox. She'd quit.

And she was different. *Warm.* He didn't talk about his past, but something inside him slipped when her honey eyes dripped with concern.

"My brother, Matt, took the brunt of Dad's fury. It was bad. But Matt was tough and took the mental and physical abuse. Sometimes I envied him because Dad at least noticed him. I was the little redheaded kid everyone ignored. Forgot. I broke the rules and threw balls in the house in the off-limits areas in the hopes of breaking something just so someone would remember I existed. God, I broke Mom's Ming." He threw up his hands. Knowing about rare Chinese ceramics now, he wanted to punch himself in the nose for that stupid trick. "Who got punished for the vase destruction? Matt. He lied to protect me." His hands were shaking. He ran them through his hair. "Why did I tell you all of that?"

"I promise I won't tell anyone. I signed a nondisclosure agreement, remember?" And then she smiled.

Those dimples did it. He took her hand in his. Gently, he placed a kiss on her knuckle. "Thank you."

Her mouth opened in surprise and he released her hand.

"Um. Why did you come in here, Mr. Harper? Are you hungry already?"

"Jeff, please. You know my ugly secrets."

"Only if you call me Michele."

Michele. His mind rolled her first name around like a shiny toy.

"So? Fess up. You hid the squid under your napkin and now you're starving."

He laughed. "Why won't you believe me? I told you I liked the squid. Ate every last crumb of your meal, Miss, um, Michele. I'm only here to make a grilled cheese sandwich for a friend."

"For a friend, huh?" She acted like she didn't believe him.

"Yep. He loves grilled cheese." That's all he would say.

Only a few people knew about the mother and child hiding here at Casa Larga and Jeff intended to keep the secret. Hell, everyone in Plunder Cove could be at risk if someone leaked the news. And then he remembered Angel's request to find a nice chef to make the sandwich.

"Would you consider making it for him?" he asked.

"Of course." She rose. "Maybe I'll recover a little dignity after the flying squid debacle. Call it my finale. What do you want—the kid or adult version?"

When she stepped away from him, coldness rushed in like a wave. It was a weird sensation that reminded him of the time when he was ten and he and Matt had raced out to the buoy in the boating lane. Ocean temps were incredibly cold that day and it was a dumb idea to swim out, but a challenge was a challenge. Jeff never backed down.

With Matt far ahead, hypothermia had set in and Jeff's arms and legs didn't want to work right. He'd treaded water, gasping for air, as wave after wave dragged him under. The buoy he was desperate to cling to moved farther away. Matt had saved him that day, dragging Jeff back to shore as a lifeguard would. But it had taken days to really warm up. When he was low, part of him felt like a layer of frostbite was still stuck to his bones.

But not now.

Michele embodied warmth. How else could he explain it? Sitting beside her heated his blood. His cells, one after another, thawed. It was irrational and damned stupid, especially since she'd already quit on him, but one idea kept washing over him. Dragging him under.

She needs to stay.

Six

Jeffrey Harper really got to her.

Sure, he was as sexy as the day was long, and smart, and confident and…did she say sexy? But he was also sensitive. That story about his childhood made her heart hurt. She couldn't imagine breaking valuable artifacts just so her mom would notice her. Not that they'd had any valuable objects in her childhood home. They'd had bills. Lots of them. Mom's cancer medicines and Cari's special schools came first. She hadn't had a father for most of her life so there was no use waiting for a man to show up and save the day. If Michele wanted anything for herself, she'd worked for the money.

Making a sandwich for Jeff was a nice thing she could do before she went home. It was her way of saying thanks. It had nothing to do with wanting to hang out with Jeffrey Harper a bit longer. Nothing at all.

He followed her to the pantry, closing the gap between them again. Her insides took notice of the heat coming from him. Or was that coming from her? She always felt hot near the man. There was a slight curve to his lips. Most women would have to rise up on their tippy-toes to kiss that mouth.

"What's the difference?" he asked about the grilled cheese sandwiches.

"For children, I go with the sweet grilled cheese. For a guy like you…" The humor in his starburst blue eyes made her reckless. What did she have to lose? "I'd go with heat. Roasted peppers. Habaneros, maybe."

"A guy like me?"

She tapped his chest. "A spicy guy like you could take it."

His gaze followed her finger and then slowly rose up to meet her eyes. She saw what she'd done. She'd flipped a switch. The playfulness in his expression had become dangerously intense.

She had no business stoking his fire, so why did part of her really want to?

"I can go with sweet." The way he said it, deep and low, like she could be on the menu, made her throat dry.

"One of each?"

He nodded, crossed his arms over that broad chest of his and leaned against the counter.

"Okay, but you're going to want to step back. The fumes will make your eyes water," she warned.

"Then you'd better wear these." He put a pair of mirrored navigation sunglasses on her and combed her hair back from her face with his long fingers. She stood very still and enjoyed the sensation. She'd missed feeling wanted, desired. Something about Jeffrey Harper brought out those needs. She supposed she wasn't any different from the rest of the women in America who lusted after Jeffrey Harper.

"Now you're ready to fly," he said, breaking the moment.

She saluted him and began roasting the peppers in a little bit of olive oil. It only took a few minutes for the fumes to make her cough.

He reached over her and turned on the fan. "Better?"

"Much. Thanks." *And, yes, I was just imagining your arm around me.*

When the peppers were nicely blackened, she took them out of the pan and put them on a plate to cool, leaving the pepper-oil in the pan. She cut a thin slice from the pepper and minced it finely. She mixed it and raspberry jelly into the pepper-oil and spread the spicy mix on two slices of focaccia bread.

"What about the rest of the habaneros?" he asked. "Aren't they going between the slices of bread?"

"Do you have a death wish? They'd blow your head off in this sandwich. Save them for another day."

"You said I was spicy enough to take it."

She blushed. "No one's that spicy. Those things are wicked. This tiny slice and the spicy oil will give the right amount of kick. I promise."

She spread cream cheese on the bread and grilled the whole sandwich in a mixture of olive oil, garlic salt and rosemary.

"Looks great. Can I eat it now?" he asked.

She nodded and took the glasses off.

He took a bite, chewing thoughtfully. When his eyes rolled toward the ceiling fan, she knew she'd done her job right. It gave her a zing of pleasure, something she hadn't felt in months.

"That's the best grilled cheese sandwich I've ever tasted." Two seconds later, he went in search of water. "Spicy."

"Told you."

He took another bite. The sounds he made while he ate could have come from an X-rated movie. Wickedly, she wondered what sounds he'd made in the filming of the elevator video.

"I'll leave you to enjoy it." She made the second sandwich with mild cheddar cheese, grape jelly and plain white bread. He watched her every move.

"My sister loves this sandwich. Sans the crust of course." Carefully, she sliced off the edges.

"She's the one you were reading to. Cari, is it?"

Michele nearly cut her finger. "Yes. How did you know?"

"You said her name in your sleep."

"Huh."

He leaned over and pointed at the bread. "You missed a spot."

"Sometimes I leave a spot, you know for the pain-in-the-neck critic." She smiled at him.

"Great. Thanks. Go on."

"You don't take an exception to my description?"

"Nope. Entirely accurate."

She shook her head, smiling. Who knew making sandwiches could be so much fun? It had been weeks since she'd been this comfortable in a kitchen. It felt good. Right.

"Now for every kid's favorite. You'd better come a little closer. This is the tricky part."

"An apple?" He put his hand on her shoulder, as he leaned in. His breath lifted the hair on her neck, sending a shiver up her spine. Her core heated up shamelessly.

"You see an apple? I see a jolly red apple man." She picked up a knife.

Out of nowhere, uncertainty struck again. *You're going to mess this up in front of him. You can't cook anymore. Not without me.* Alfieri's voice was back. Her hand shook just a bit when she held the knife above the apple.

"Michele." Jeff's voice drew her gaze to him. "What's wrong?"

"I'm a mess." She put the knife down. "I shouldn't have applied for this job. You don't want me for your chef."

She turned away so she wouldn't witness the disgust on his face. Or whatever his reaction would be to her admission. Jeffrey Harper was not the kind of man who put up with weakness or failure.

"Relax," he said softly, without an ounce of his cocky television voice. "You're not being judged now. Just breathe. Let it out slowly."

She exhaled.

"That's what I do when the nerves catch up with me on the show. Again. Deep inhale."

She did as told.

"This time with the exhale say, 'This is what I do best. I'm going to kill this sonofabitch apple.'"

That did it. She laughed out loud.

He grinned. "Go get it, tiger."

Still chuckling, she picked up the apple and began carving the first eye. She made a pupil and even added a starburst to the iris. "You get nervous on the show?"

"The more nerves, the better the show." He leaned closer. "That's an eye! Amazing, Miss Cox."

"Michele," she reminded him.

The excitement in his voice delighted her. He liked it. She went to work on the other one as Jeffrey stood beside her. Pushing on, she used a piece of red apple skin to roll up into a nose. Carefully, she cut out a smiling mouth with sweet full lips. After adding the apple stem hat, it was done.

"I did this once for my sister so she'd eat her lunch. Now, she wants all her apples to become jolly red men." She placed it in his hand. "I hope your friend enjoys it."

"That's unbelievable." He turned it in his hand as if it was art. "I've never seen anything like it."

The words of encouragement were a balm to her damaged heart. No boss had said anything like that to her in... well, she couldn't remember.

Critical words were more common in Alfieri's kitchen than compliments. He was a powerful head chef who'd used despicable behavior and abuse to "train" her to become one of the best chefs in New York, second only to him. In truth, he'd ruined her.

She closed her eyes and blocked out Alfieri's angry eyes, his shaking finger, the cruel turn of his lips.

"Michele." She opened her eyes to see Jeffrey leaning in close, studying her. "I don't know what problems you're having, but you should trust your talent. You are amazing."

That did it.

She rose up on her tippy-toes and kissed his spicy lips.

* * *

Michele Cox was full of surprises. Funny, sexy, sweet, kind, smart and…insecure. That last one didn't match up with the rest of her personality. Something bad had happened to her, he was sure of it. He wished he knew what it was and how to fix it.

Without a word, she rose up and softly, gently, pressed her lips to his. Fully unprepared, he stood still, cautious after what had happened in the elevator. Given one more moment, he would have swept her up in his arms and deepened that sweet kiss. But before he could, she stepped back.

"Sorry." Her beautiful golden-brown eyes were wide with…what? Had she surprised herself, too? "That was unprofessional. I don't normally…" She was pressing her hand to her lips. "I'll just leave. Good luck!"

Before he could stop her, Michele Cox rushed through the kitchen door and out of his life. Again.

Seven

Michele awoke with the sense that something was wrong. It was the same feeling she'd opened her eyes to every morning since she'd left Alfieri's. This morning was worse.

All night, her mind did the play-by-play critique of every mistake she'd made in front of Jeffrey Harper. Including that kiss. She pulled the pillow over her head in embarrassment. He must've thought she'd lost her mind.

What was that sound? She lifted the pillow, pushed the hair out of her eyes and listened. Sniffling? Sitting up, she noticed Lily's bed was empty.

Tying her robe around her, Michele followed the soft sounds to the closed bathroom door. She knocked lightly. "Lily? Are you okay?"

The door opened. Lily held a tissue to her nose. "He doesn't want me. I've been asked to pack my bags and go home."

"No. When?"

"I was doing my early morning Tai Chi in the gardens and Chloe joined me for what she called sunrise meditation and yoga. After we were both finished, she gave me the news. She was nice about it."

"Oh. I'm sorry, Lily." Michele's heart sank. She really liked Lily. Since they were both New Yorkers, and had bonded quickly, Michele had hoped her new-found friend would win the competition. Jeffrey deserved to have such a kind chef working for him. "Maybe we can call a taxi and leave together. Let me pack up and—"

"Miss Cox?" Chloe called to her from the doorway. "You've been asked to join the remaining chefs in the great hall to discuss today's schedule and what happens in the next stage of the competition."

Lily shot her a surprised look. No one was more shocked than Michele.

"Um, I think there's been a mistake. I quit the competition yesterday," Michele said.

Chloe turned her head and her long blond braid fell over her shoulder. "You don't want to be here?"

Oh, she wanted to stay. Desperately. The bonus money alone would save her. And cooking those grilled cheese sandwiches was the first time she'd felt like herself in the kitchen in a long while. Plus, there was a gorgeous, red-headed hunk she liked, more than she dared tell his sister, more than she wanted to think about. She'd kissed him for goodness sake! That's why she should bow out gracefully before she made a bigger fool of herself in front of him.

"I don't deserve to be here with these other great chefs," she muttered.

Chloe smiled. "My brother disagrees. You impressed him last night."

When? Based on her performance with the squid, she wouldn't hire her; would he?

"It is up to you, Miss Cox. If you want to leave, we'll make the arrangements for your flight back to New York. No problem. Jeff wants you to be happy with your choice, whatever it may be. The other chefs are gathering in the great hall. Join us, if you decide to continue on."

Chloe closed the door behind her.

"Wow, that's just…" Michele sat on the edge of her bed. "I didn't expect he'd want me to stay."

"I'm glad. If I can't win, I hope you do. He should have a great, kind chef." Lily smiled sweetly. "I'm rooting for you."

* * *

Jeff waited for Chloe to come around the corner. "So? What did she say?"

"Who?"

He gave her his deadpan look.

She laughed. "Just teasing. Michele was a little surprised. She thought she'd quit the competition yesterday."

"She did."

Chloe cocked her eyebrow, a typical Harper expression. "Sounds like she doesn't want to be here, Jeff. Why don't you let her go and continue this challenge with the other chefs?"

"Is that what she said? Michele doesn't want to be with me?" He cleared his throat. *Damn.* "*Work* for me?"

Chloe's lips quirked. "If you want her, why don't you end this competition and go after her? Ask her out. Woo her. See what happens."

"It's not that easy. She's not like the other women I've dated. Michele is…different." And struggling with something he didn't understand. She needed to be treated with care. He understood more than he dared admit. "Did she say she wants to leave Casa Larga?"

"Not exactly. She feels like she doesn't deserve to be here."

"That's insecurity talking. She's a damn fine chef, just as good as the other ones here. Did you convince her?" He was pacing now. "Is she staying or not?"

"I left it up to her. We'll know what she decides if she comes to the great hall, which is where I am supposed to be right now." Chloe kissed his cheek. "Good luck!"

Luck. He didn't believe in it, otherwise he'd have to ask what he'd done to piss off the universe.

"Good morning, ladies," Chloe's voice echoed from the great hall.

Part of him wanted to peek his head in to see if Michele had decided to stay. The other part of him reminded himself to cool his jets. He didn't want to do anything that might scare Michele off. It was obvious she was conflicted about staying. But damn, he wanted to look.

A workout. That's what he needed.

He started toward the gym to burn off his frustrated energy. It was laughable. A week ago, if he'd felt like this, he would've asked a lady or two out on a date. Now he was trying to get away from them.

"Mr. Harper?" a voice called.

Damn. It was a chef he'd already excused.

She hustled to catch up with him. "It's Lily. May I speak with you?"

He ran his hand through his hair. "My decision had nothing to do with your dinner. You are a fine chef, Lily. I meant what I said. I loved your dim sum."

"Thank you. That means a lot coming from you. I've watched all your shows. Some of them three and four times." She wrung her hands as if she was nervous and her cheeks turned pink. "I feel like I know you."

He pinched his nose. Was this some sort of hero worship? He was no hero. "I'm not that guy from the show. I'm just…a guy."

"No, no. You are a professional. What happened to you and to the show was very unfair."

He agreed with her assessment. "Thank you for your support and for coming here. I'm sorry it didn't work out. Best of luck in your job search." He tried to walk away, but she stepped in front of him.

"You deserve success and happiness, Jeffrey," she said. "Be careful about who you choose. Some of these chefs might be here for the wrong reasons."

Hold up. Lily had roomed with Michele, hadn't she? What had they talked about? "I'm going to need more information."

"I don't have more to say. Just…be careful."

That told him absolutely nothing but triggered his internal warning alarms because he, too, was cautious. Michele said she needed the job but something had spooked her so badly that she felt she didn't deserve it. That flicker of fear in her eyes? It hit too close to home. As a child, his heart had been broken by people who were supposed to love him. Had Michele encountered something similar?

Hell, these thoughts were depressing.

He needed to sprint on the treadmill or pound the hell out of the boxing bag.

Before the cold seeped in through the cracks.

Eight

The next morning, Tonia cooked him breakfast, Freja made lunch and Suzette rounded out the day with dinner. His taste buds were impressed but none of the meals captivated him as much as that single carved apple.

Michele had an artistic flair rarely seen in any discipline. Hell, in a matter of minutes she'd created an iris in the apple's eye that shockingly resembled his own. Michele possessed something he'd never experienced before. Magic? Is that what she'd called it? Unfortunately, it seemed to come and go for her, which was bad news for his restaurant. A five-star dining experience demanded consistency and near perfection for every dish. Betting on Michele Cox was foolhardy and, still, he couldn't bring himself to excuse her. Not yet.

She seemed to have worked her magic on him, too, with one gentle kiss.

When he wasn't judging meals, he worked with the building contractor and crew. The goal was to have the restaurant ready to open in six months. It was an ambitious time frame, but he wanted the restaurant in full swing as quickly as possible so the Harper marketing team would have good news to release, to hopefully counteract all the bad news still going around about Jeff.

Even though RW's lawyers had sent cease and desist orders, Finn was still doing his damnedest to ruin what was left of Jeff's reputation. The woman from the elevator was threatening to speak out as well. Lawyers had been dispatched to her home to try to reason with her.

The universe kept dumping on him.

In the early evening, Jeff took off his construction hat and joined Matt in the guesthouse for one of their brotherly, cutthroat games of pool.

"Married yet?" Matt handed him a beer.

"Asshole."

"What? I didn't sign up for this gig. That's all on you, brother."

"It was Dad's idea, not mine. Forget about a wife, I'm having a hard enough time choosing a chef."

Matt put a hand on his shoulder. "You can end it now. Tell RW to take a flying leap and live your own life. Go be happy."

"Happy. Everyone talks about that, but what the hell is it?" Jeff sipped his beer. "I like what I'm doing here. The restaurant construction plans are ambitious and, if I sit on the crew, they'll be done on time. I like that I'm creating this place from the ground up. If I walk now, I throw away my chance to make the hotel all it could be. RW will find someone else."

And Finn would release the rest of the video and Jeff would be done.

"This is not your only chance at building your dream. It's a restaurant and a hotel, man. You can do that anywhere, anytime. Building a strong relationship, a strong marriage? That's a lifetime achievement. Give yourself a chance to get it right."

Jeff racked the set. "You going to keep chapping my balls or take your shot?"

Matt didn't understand. Jeff's brother had everything he wanted—a beautiful, adoring wife, a son and a job he loved. Jeff didn't have any of that. Might never have any of it. The career he loved was at least attainable, here and now. He couldn't let it go or he'd have nothing.

"Oh, I'm taking my shot. Be prepared to pay up. I'm feeling hot tonight." And as promised, Matt's first shot launched two balls into the side pockets.

Jeff rolled his eyes. It was going to be a quick, demoralizing game.

Chloe opened the sliding glass window and stepped inside. "Thought I'd find you two here."

"Yep. Boy Wonder is hiding out from four gorgeous chefs," Matt said, and missed his shot.

"That's Karma for teasing your brother," Jeff replied.

"Looked like Karma to me. No decisions on a chef yet?" Chloe hitched herself up on the counter.

"Nope." Jeff's ball exploded into the hole.

"Whoa. Take it easy. You want to buy us a new table?" Matt complained.

"Sorry." Jeff glanced at Chloe. "Why don't you choose one?"

Chloe shook her head and her long braid fell over her shoulder. "No way. That's not my specialty. I'm just helping out until the hotel is up and running. Dad promised I'd be the Activities Director once we have clients."

"You aren't going back to your yoga studio in LA?" Matt asked.

"No. I'm done with the fakeness of Hollywood. And I could use a break from Mom."

"Yeah, no kidding. Jeff and I have taken a decade-plus long break. What's she up to these days?" Matt said.

A shiver rolled through Jeff.

"She's on a yacht in Europe with…" Chloe started, and then seemed to notice something in Jeff's expression that made her pause. She shook her head. "Let's not talk about her tonight. Jeff, I say choose the chef that appeals to your tastes. You won't go wrong."

Tastes. Michele's lips came to mind. He shot the next

ball harder than he meant to. It careened over the felt like a missile and rocketed straight toward Matt's head. Matt ducked just in time. The ball hit the wall with a loud bang, knocking a chunk out of the wood paneling.

"Holy smokes. You trying to brain me?" Matt asked.

"Jeff, are you okay?" Chloe asked.

"I guess I'm a little…frustrated."

"Just a little? I'd hate to see you all worked up." Matt motioned for Jeff to sit on a bar stool. "Plant your ass before you bruise my pretty face."

Jeff exhaled deeply and sat with Chloe.

"What can we do to help you?" Chloe asked softly.

Jeff tossed his hair out of his eyes. "Either you guys choose the chef or I'm going with the eeny-meeny-miney-mo method."

"I hear they're all great, but don't you like one more than the others?" Matt asked.

Jeff did, but he couldn't have her. Michele might ruin everything.

He had three goals at the moment: choose a great chef, finish the restaurant, and find a wife who didn't love him. That was it. He just needed two women who didn't make his head spin or his heart ache. But with Michele… His head was spinning and his heart pounded.

He was drawn to her more than he should be for lots of reasons, not the least of them being that nice girls like her shouldn't make spicy sandwiches for a bastard like him. It was too much fun, too easy, far too hot. And shouldn't happen again, or he'd really start regretting that he'd promised Dad he'd get married.

Hell, it was Dad's fault that he was this conflicted.

Why hadn't RW chosen male chefs to judge? A bunch of guys would have made the choice far easier. "I don't know them well enough to make that decision yet. And time is running out. Help me, Chloe. Pick one."

She smiled. "I won't choose for you, but I can help. Matt, let's save this poor boy from his misery."

Matt cracked his knuckles. "Yep. We can do this. Who's left standing?"

"Refined Freja from Sweden, toned Tonia from Arizona, spicy Suzette from France." Chloe had nicknamed them all.

"Scratch the last one. She's not staying. Her food was amazing—probably the best of the bunch—and she knew it. She came off haughty and super conceited," Jeff said.

"Yep, she has to go. Can't have two people who are full of themselves in one restaurant." Matt sipped his beer.

"Shut up." Jeff slugged him. "I'm knowledgeable, not full of myself."

"You keep telling yourself that, bro."

"Oh, I almost forgot the last one," Chloe said with a twinkle in her eye. "Sparkly Michele."

"What, no alliteration for her?" Matt asked.

"No need. Jeff has his own description."

"No, I don't. Michele is out, too." He didn't want to diagnose why those words were so hard to say. He wanted her to stay, but deep down he knew that was not a reason to keep her. She was the wild card in the deck, too risky for such an important project. Why was he tempted to trust her and rely on her to make his restaurant great when she admitted she wasn't cooking as well as she should be? Just the fact that he wanted her to stay despite her inconsistencies was a red flag that his head wasn't on straight when it came to Michele Cox. He walked back to the pool table and lined up to take his shot so that his sister couldn't see the emotion swirling in his eyes.

Chloe put her hand on his elbow, stopping his shot. "I thought she'd decided to stay."

He spun around to face them both. "Yes, but I can't let her. She's insecure, inconsistent and I heard she's here for the wrong reasons."

"Wrong reasons, like…?" Matt motioned with his beer bottle for Jeff to go on.

"Hell if I know. She said something about needing to help her sister. I don't know what that means."

"I might," Chloe said softly. "Dad showed me the report. He did a background check on each of the chefs."

"Any reason why Dad didn't show *me* the report?" Jeff was livid. His father obviously *still* didn't respect him. He felt like a kid again, being ignored by the old man.

"Did you ask for the report? I assumed Dad's team would've researched the candidates during the selection process, so I asked. No way Dad went into this thing blind," Chloe said.

"Oh." And now Jeff felt like a dumbass because he hadn't asked for the report when he should have. He could only blame his whole life being upturned for the oversight. Blackmail could mess with a guy's head.

"What did the report say about Jeff's Michele?" Matt asked.

"She's not my anything," Jeff grumbled but he looked at Chloe and waited for her answer.

"Michele takes care of her sister, who has Down syndrome. Medical costs. Housing. Everything. Her sister lives in an assisted community for adults. That can't be cheap," Chloe said.

Jeff had not expected that. When he'd caught Michele with the picture book, he hadn't imagined she was reading to an adult with neurotypical differences. His heart melted a little.

"Oh, man. I knew I liked her," Matt said.

Jeff did, too. He more than liked her. But should that matter? No. "This is a business. The restaurant cannot achieve five-star status without a great chef."

"Miss Sparkle is not as good as the others?" Matt asked.

Jeff exhaled deeply. "That's the thing. I believe she is the best, or was. Something happened to make her doubt herself. She lost... I don't know...the passion for it?"

Chloe leaned in. "I've worked with artists and actors in my yoga studio in Hollywood who were just like Michele. Something crushes their spirit and it's hard to recover. Some never do. What happened to her?"

He didn't know, shouldn't care. "Not my business." But that look in Michele's eyes on the application video—the survivor's spark—made him want to find out.

Matt patted his back. "My two cents? Don't quit on Michele so soon. See if she can recover her passion."

"She quit on me." Jeff swallowed his frustration with the last sips of beer.

"But she came back. You said it was her insecurity talking, remember? I'm with Matt. Give her another chance," Chloe said.

The idea of keeping her around another day lit a fire in his chest. It's what he wanted, even though he knew he shouldn't. "Fine. I'll give her one more day in the competition. If she can't cut it, I'll have to let her go."

"Okay, where does that leave us?" Matt asked.

"With three potential candidates. Michele, Freja and Tonia. I'd be cautious of Tonia—she's got knockout curves and knows how to use them," Chloe said.

"You can't fault her because she's smoking hot," Matt said.

"We're trying to improve Jeff's image. It's too easy to imagine Tonia faking it in one of Jeff's elevator videos," Chloe explained.

Jeff's head shot up. "Wait! You knew the maid in the GIF was faking it?"

Chloe laughed. "Seriously? Doesn't everyone? I highly doubt she was a maid, though. Porn star?"

He hadn't stuck around to ask. "Someone hired her to jump me in the elevator. I'd never seen her before." Jeff put the cue stick down on the table so they wouldn't see his hands shaking.

"Jumped? As in a stranger groped you?" Matt asked.

"Don't…want to…talk about it." He ground out the words through his clenched teeth.

He'd been the brunt of daily internet jokes, but he cared about what Matt thought and wouldn't be able to take it if his big brother laughed at him. Jeff's muscles bunched, ready to throw a punch. If Matt so much as cracked a smile, he'd lose a tooth.

"Some woman just…" Matt shook his head. "Wow. That's jacked up. Does that happen to you a lot?" His tone was serious, not at all teasing.

Matt believes me. Jeff released the air burning his lungs.

Chloe covered her mouth in horror. Her eyes wide with shock and filling up with tears.

Dammit, he couldn't do this now.

"Next subject!" he barked.

"I'm sorry, Jeff. I didn't realize what happened or I wouldn't have joked about it." Chloe rubbed his back. "It would do you good to talk to someone about this. If not with us, how about Angel? She's really helped Dad."

"I don't need a therapist." So what that his heart was pounding and his forehead was sweating? Big deal that he had an urge to snap the cue stick in two. He was fine. Would be fine. "I need to work and put it all behind me."

A silent look passed between Chloe and Matt.

"Just remember we're here for you, bro. All the time," Matt said.

"Fine. Can we get back to the chefs?" Jeff said. "You two are supposed to be helping me choose one, not psychoanalyzing me."

Chloe nodded. "Sure. We were talking about Tonia. If she's the one you want, Dad's image people will do what they can to tone down her sex-kitten vibe a bit for the cameras. It'll be fine."

Did he want a toned-down employee working for him? Did he want fake and surface level? With every chef so far, he'd wanted a connection. He wanted real for a change. Michele and her dimples popped into his head. And then her curves, closely followed by her soft lips. Damn, he wanted to kiss her again.

No.

He couldn't fantasize about the way she sassed him with that pretty mouth of hers. Or how much he wanted to taste the sweet spot below her ear and see if she would shiver with delight. He'd agreed to give her one more chance, but if she couldn't get her act together, he'd send her home.

"Now Freja is tall, regal, elegant and supermodel gorgeous. She has a stellar reputation in Sweden. Her entrées are supposed to be amazing. But…" Chloe trailed off.

His sister's assessment was spot-on. Freja was a real looker and her Swedish venison meatballs were both sweet and savory. "But what?"

"Don't take this the wrong way, but why is she here? She's famous in her own right in Sweden. Freja has graced more magazine covers than you have, Jeff. Why leave all that to come here to work for you? What's in it for her?"

"Way to crush a guy's ego, sis," Matt said.

"She's right, though. And before Lily left, she told me to be careful. Maybe someone is here under false pretenses," Jeff said.

"Did Lily say who to watch out for?" Matt asked.

"No. I wondered if it was Michele, but I guess it could be any of them. Or all of them."

Chloe leaned forward. "Why don't we test each chef to find out their true motives."

"Test them? How?" he asked.

Chloe sat back on her bar stool. "Leave that to me. I'll arrange outings for each of them tailored to give you a chance to connect with them personally, to find out why they're really here."

Jeff pinched the bridge of his nose. "We already determined that I don't make real connections."

"Fake it until you make it. And trust me. This next step in the competition will tell you who you should choose," Chloe said.

Matt grinned. "Sounds like a dating show."

Jeff slugged him, just because.

Nine

Michele got up early and called the billing department at Cari's group home to beg for an extension.

Even with careful fiscal management, she'd come up short. She didn't have enough for the rent. If she didn't get the chef job, she'd have to scramble for something else and fast.

But when the bookkeeper told her that all of Cari's expenses for the month had been paid for by Harper Industries, she gasped. Jeffrey Harper was full of surprises. She had no idea how he knew about Cari's group home fees but she was grateful.

Rushing downstairs to thank him for his generosity, she ran into Chloe.

"Good morning, Michele. You're up early. Still on New York time?"

"I'm an early riser." And a night owl. Working at Alfieri's meant being the first to arrive and last to leave the kitchen.

"Well, you should relax today. I am organizing individual outings with Jeff so he can get to know each one of you a little better. To see if your personalities mesh. The other two chefs are going to be with him for most of the day. I'm planning something for you that might take place tonight, but that one is still sketchy. I'll let you know when it's all settled."

This was the strangest interview...process? Contest?

Competition? "Okay. So, I might not see Jeffrey at all today?"

Chloe cocked her head and studied Michele for a second. "I don't think so, unless he runs into you like I just did. He's very busy. You go and enjoy the day. Use the pool. Walk the gardens. Go to the beach. If you get hungry for good Mexican food, I'd suggest visiting Pueblicito and going to Juanita's Café. Give them Jeff's name when you order and tell them who you are. We have a tab set up for you ladies in case you want to buy any food in the market or restaurant. As long as you're here, everything is paid for by Harper Industries."

Michele teared up and hugged Chloe. "Thank you for my sister's rent, too."

Chloe pulled back and smiled. "That wasn't me. Last night Jeff mentioned he had some online banking to do before he went to bed. He must have paid your sister's rent then. He comes off cocky and gruff, but there's a mushy heart under all that muscle. I hope you give him a chance."

She blinked. Give him a chance? Wasn't it the other way around?

Somehow, he'd given her a second chance at the opportunity of a lifetime and she was determined not to blow it.

Chloe patted her shoulder. "Enjoy your day off."

It was her first vacation in the last five years. And here she was in sunny California, staying in a sexy billionaire's mansion. It was a little mind-blowing. Suddenly she wanted to kiss Jeffrey again and it wasn't just to thank him for paying for her sister's fees.

On her way back to her room, Michele saw Suzette dragging her luggage out the front door. Holy moly! Jeffrey had excused the queen of French cuisine. It made no sense that Suzette was going home and Michele was still in the running. Why was Jeffrey keeping her here? She had a sense that she was dangling by one thin rope and had better figure out how to climb.

Tying up her walking shoes and zipping her sweatshirt, she headed out to explore Plunder Cove. She had barely started down the long driveway when a sleek silver car came from the house and pulled up next to her. The driver, a balding older gentleman, rolled down his window. "Want a ride, miss?"

"I'm not sure. How long does it take to walk to the town?"

"For me? It's a good thirty minutes one-way to Pueblicito since my legs aren't what they used to be. It is mostly downhill. You'd make it in twenty."

"I'll walk, then. The sunlight and sea air might do me some good."

"May I make a suggestion? If you buy something in town—food and whatnot—call me to come pick you up." He handed her a business card. "I wouldn't want a nice lady like you exerting yourself walking back up the hill."

She read the card. There was a phone number on it, plus a description that made her smile.

Robert Jones, Driver Extraordinary for Harper Industries
For Pickup, Call Alfred's Batcave

"Thank you, Robert. Or would you prefer to be called Alfred?" she asked.

He seemed very professional, somewhat stiff and formal, but his lips twitched before he answered. "Whichever you prefer, miss. Jeffrey calls me Alfred. But if you do that, you must request the Batmobile."

Jeffrey was into Batman? She had not expected that. The realization made him even more tempting. She'd loved DC Comics as a kid. She'd pretended she was a superhero who had the powers to save her mother and sister from illness. Michele's mother had made Halloween costumes for both of her daughters until she was too weak to sew. Man, she was devastated when she'd finally outgrown her Cat-woman costume.

"Will do. I'm Michele, by the way."

"I know, miss." He saluted her, did a U-turn in the drive-way, and drove back to what Michele now knew was the Batcave.

Michele smiled, imagining Jeff and his brother chasing each other through the spacious rooms and running through the gardens playing caped crusaders. It should have been a fun house to play in but then she remembered Jeffrey had said his parents wished they'd never had kids. Maybe this wasn't such a perfect place to grow up in after all. She was honored he'd confided in her about his childhood. It touched her. She had a sense that he didn't like to talk about himself much and had surprised himself by opening up. His can-didness and kindness made her want to trust him and prove that she could do the job he needed. The more she thought about Jeffrey Harper—his grin, those blue eyes, his wide chest… Okay, maybe she was thinking about him far too much. But the more she did, the more she wanted to stay.

"What the hell?"

Standing next to his sister, Jeff watched Freja stroll down the boat ramp as if it was a model's runway. She wore long crepe-like pants, a flowery blouse, a silk scarf, a large hat over her platinum-blond hair and four-inch heels. It was the strangest fishing getup he'd ever seen.

Chloe gave him a tiny elbowing and mumbled, "Not a word. Have fun!"

Untying the rope from the dock, he started up the motor and pushed off. Less than an hour later they returned.

Chloe must have seen them coming into the bay from the house, for she rushed down to greet them on the dock. "That was fast. Did you… Oh, dear, what happened?"

Jeff offered his hand to help Freja off the boat. She

pushed it away with a huff. Her hat was soggy, her clothes dripping. His weren't any better.

To Chloe, Freja said, "A head chef does not hunt for de food. It ees brought to her!" She stomped past them both in her squeaky heels.

"She's not wrong about that." He tipped his head to get the water out of his ears. "You owe me a cell phone."

"What happened?" Chloe asked.

"I'll put it to you this way, if I ever start acting like a prima donna just because I've been on television, slug me."

She punched him in the arm.

"Ow. Not funny. I mean it. Freja acted as if there were cameras everywhere. She was constantly turning to present her 'best side' to the invisible lens. Hell, if she'd just sat still and held the rod like I taught her, she wouldn't have lost her balance and gone ass-backward into the drink. And I wouldn't have had to rescue her."

He could see his sister was trying not to laugh. "Does she think we are secretly filming the chefs?"

They walked back toward the house. "Apparently. I tried to tell her the truth but she doesn't want to buy it. She thinks she's the only one in the competition who knows what's really going on."

"So…you didn't get to connect with her on a personal level."

"I saved her life and her giant floppy hat. Does that count?"

Chloe shook her head. "No, but it does give us a little insight. She's here for the spotlight. That might not be a bad thing. She knows how to work the cameras to improve your image and promote the restaurant. Her fan base in Europe is substantial already. And she is beautiful. Unless you can't stand her personality, I don't think we should count her out yet."

"I didn't say I couldn't stand her," he grumbled. "It's hard to communicate with her, though. She doesn't listen to my stories and she sure as hell didn't make me laugh." He flipped his wet hair off his forehead and wanted to slap himself. Since when did those qualities matter in a chef?

Michele Cox was ruining him.

"Get a hot shower. You're meeting Tonia at the stables at one o'clock," Chloe said.

Up at dawn at the building site, the morning spent fishing and performing ocean rescue, and horseback riding in the afternoon. Was his sister trying to kill him?

"Fine, as long as I get to soak in the hot tub tonight. I haven't ridden in so long, I might not be able to sit for a week."

He had a vision of Michele joining him in the warm bubbles and shook it off. He shouldn't see her in a bathing suit or he'd never be able to send her home.

"Sure, after the dinner party," Chloe said. "Dad says he can't make it to the California Restaurant and Lodging Association legislative meeting and dinner. You'll have to do it for him."

He gave Chloe a dark look. "No way, I'm not going to that." He wasn't ready to get sliced and diced in public yet. He didn't have a stellar restaurant to speak for him yet and the hotel was still in the planning phase. It was too soon.

"Dad thought you'd say that. He had hotel mock-up brochures made for you to wave around. They're awesome, Jeff. And you are the perfect guy to talk up the resort. This will be good for you, to get out there and show everyone that the stupid video hasn't fazed you. You're running this show, just like you always do. You'll see."

Was he running the show? Sometimes, it didn't feel like it. What happened in that video had knocked him back, but he'd gotten up and was working to be smarter, stronger, unfazed.

Like Michele.

Ten

It had to be the smallest town she'd ever seen. The main road had a few stores, an old adobe church, a miniature post office, a gas station and a couple of mom-and-pop stores. There were zero stoplights. Three roads with Spanish names jutted off toward the residential section of town. She strolled down one of the side roads in search of beach access and passed quaint old houses that looked to be at least a hundred years old.

A man washing a motorcycle in a small driveway looked up when she passed. "Miss Cox! Are you lost?"

It was Matt, Jeffrey's older brother. He lived here? "I'm looking for the beach."

He pointed. "Go back a quarter of a mile and you'll find the access road. Follow the signs and stay out of the snowy plover hatchery."

"Will do. How about lunch? Any place you recommend?"

"Not to your caliber of fine dining, but the best Mexican food is at my mother-in-law's place. Juanita's. You can't miss it."

Mother-in-law? Interesting that a rich boy would leave Casa Larga to marry someone from this small town and then live here. "Thanks."

"Oh, and, Miss Cox? I'm rooting for you."

Her chest warmed. It felt good to have someone believe in her again. Maybe she could do this. "Thanks."

Walking back down the main street, she found Juanita's Mexican Market and Café. The smell of barbecued meat made her stomach growl. She hadn't eaten breakfast and it was already close to noon. There were a handful of tables outside on the patio, full with people laughing and eating. Each table had baskets of tortilla chips and bowls filled with what seemed to be homemade salsa. Michele's mouth watered. Since there were no available tables, she thought she'd have to order a meal to go.

"Hey, lady. Wanna join us?" An older woman called from a table.

"Yeah, come on, we don't mind sharing. Well, Nona does," a second woman said.

The third woman had just dipped her chip into a small bowl of guacamole. "I told you to order your own. I don't like double-dipping." She pointed to the one available chair and said in a demanding voice, "*Por supuesto, siéntate.*"

Michele didn't think she had a choice. She sat down. "Thank you. I'm Michele."

"You're one of Jeffrey's fancy cooks. I'm Alana, she's Flora and the guac-hoarder over there is Nona. We're sisters."

"I like to keep my germs to myself," Nona complained.

"My sister and I used to fight over food, too," Michele sighed. "I miss that."

Flora's hand went to her mouth and Alana made a little squeak.

"We lost our sister once. Thank God she's back for now," Nona said. "May your sister rest in peace." All three women made the sign of the cross over themselves.

"Oh, no. She's in New York. She's fine." Sort of. "It's just that I am used to seeing her every day. This separation is difficult."

Alana nodded. "Don't know what I'd do without these two picking on me every day." She pushed the basket of chips toward Michele. "Eat up. We'll get the waitress to take your order."

"How's the competition coming? I hear it's down to three chefs," Nona said.

Michele chewed a chip and marveled at how fast word spread in a small town. "The competition is amazing. Though I don't have much of a chance."

"Why would you think that?" Nona said.

Without going into the long story, Michele said simply, "I seem to have misplaced my confidence and my talent."

"You should learn from Jeffrey. He's talented and self-assured. Amazing, no? After how his mother treated him, it's a wonder he didn't end up crazy like his father," Alana said. "Those two were the worst."

"*Cállate*," Nona admonished hissed Alana. "That is private business."

"Jeffrey told me his parents fought," Michele said.

"It surprises me that he shared any of it. He must trust you, but I don't think we should add fuel to the fire." Nona gave both of her sisters a strong look to keep their mouths shut.

"*Claro*." Alana lifted her chin defiantly. "We wouldn't want anyone to know the evil mother ignored that sweet boy for days and screamed at him for no reason."

"That's awful," Michele said.

"A friend in the Harpers' kitchen said she had to make sure Jeffrey had enough food to eat," Flora pitched in.

"That woman is the worst mother ever," Flora said. "She didn't deserve those three beautiful babies. And that Jeffrey was so adorable with his copper hair and freckles. Who wouldn't love him?"

Michele's heart broke. She'd always known her mother loved her. She'd even said so with her last breath.

Alana nodded. "Holy Madre, she is terrible. I hope she never comes back here."

Nona's thin shoulders rounded and she seemed to cave

in. "She told everyone that I beat little Matthew. If I hadn't taken the brush from her hand, I don't know what would have happened..." Nona squeezed her eyes shut on the memory.

"Now I understand why that beautiful house seems so dark and cold. I'm glad his mother is no longer in the picture," Michele said softly.

"We are all glad of that. Things are getting better." Nona brightened. "Angel is there to help RW heal. She's convinced him to seek forgiveness from everyone he's harmed in the past. Believe me, it is a long list. But because he wants to change, he has asked the three kids to come home. We'll see if they forgive him or not, but it is great to have them all here."

Michele didn't know who Angel was or why RW needed healing, but she kept those questions to herself. What she really wanted was to know more about Jeffrey. Maybe she could help him before he sent her home. It was the least she could do after he'd paid her sister's expenses.

Michele ate the last chip and said, "It's amazing to me that his childhood was bad because he is so—"

"Handsome," Flora interrupted.

"Strong," Alana added.

"Smart," Nona said.

"Yes. All those things, but I was going to say 'sure of himself.' I wish I had an ounce of his confidence."

"Sure, sure he is confident but he is alone. He needs someone to take care of him, like his family never did. If we could only find him a wife—"

Three heads swung toward her.

Michele lifted her hands. "I'm just trying to be his chef."

She needed the job Jeffrey was offering, not a husband. Her sister depended on her to provide a stable income and life for the two of them. Getting romantically involved with a playboy who'd publicly declared he'd never get married? That would be the opposite of stability. Besides, she was not ready to trust any man with her heart after Alfieri had betrayed her.

The three women meant well, but marrying sexy Jeffrey Harper was not in the cards.

Besides, with all the women Jeffrey dated, how could he ever be alone?

RW stood on his balcony and looked out over his estate. It was beautiful, no denying it. His thousands of acres of gardens, pastures and grassy knolls all stretched out gracefully to the private beach that dipped into the sea. In the distance, he could see his nine oil derricks formed into a horseshoe in the sea. They were lit up like Christmas trees. Some would say he was successful and had created quite a legacy for his kids.

RW knew better. None of the toys, land or business meant a damn. The only things that truly mattered were setting things straight with his kids and winning the heart of the woman he couldn't seem to live without. And protecting them all.

Angel knocked on his open door and came on in. "Is everything okay?"

"Hell, yes. Now that you're here."

"Your text said come right away." She studied his face in her subtle way, looking for signs of distress. He knew all her tricks.

He grinned. "I figured you needed a break from that screaming kid."

"Cristina's boy is a bit of a handful. But I don't blame him. He misses his little friends and…" she swallowed hard "…the others."

He knew her dark spots, too. It killed him every time her sweet expressions twisted in momentary panic, which happened only when she thought about her ex-boyfriend, Cuchillo, and his gang. She had barely escaped those killers when she was a pregnant teenager. She'd been on the run, hiding in Plunder Cove for years with a secret identity and job as the local Mexican restaurant owner. Since she'd helped Cristina and Sebastian to escape to Plunder Cove, Angel was thinking about her ex more often. RW would fix that. He picked up the remote and pressed the button. Mexican music started playing.

Stretching his hand toward her he said, "*Baila conmigo.*"

"Randall Wesley Harper! You're speaking Spanish."

Now that look of surprise was good. He loved impressing her. "People who call me by my full name are usually pissed off. I love the way you say it."

She turned her head, listening. "My favorite song since I was a little girl. How did you know?"

"A little birdie told me."

She smiled. "Henry."

"Yep, don't tell grandkids any secrets unless you want them broadcasted." He wiggled his fingers at her. "Come on, *bella. Baila conmigo.*" She took his hand and he spun her into his embrace. "That's more like it."

She felt so good in his arms. Heart to heart. Body to body.

This meant something, though he didn't dare name it.

Angel was a dream he didn't want to wake up from. It was going to hurt in the end. He might not survive it.

Pressing her cheek to his, she played with the hair at the base of his neck. They swayed together in perfect rhythm. He sang softly in her ear.

"You know all the words?" She pulled back and he could see the shock of delight. "Do you understand them?"

He lifted his eyebrow and gave her one of his cocky grins. Jeffrey might have been famous for a grin just like it, but he'd learned the smug look from his old man. "I'm not just another pretty face, Angel."

She chuckled. "Go ahead, then. Translate."

He looked into her eyes and spoke the words he'd learned from heart. "Little mourning dove, my love, my heart. Do not fly away from me. I could not endure without your love. Cannot breathe without you with me. My heart beats only for you. You are my world. My everything."

Her eyes welled.

He kissed her with all the passion in his damaged heart. It beat strong when it was close to hers.

She held on to his neck and matched him kiss for kiss while he ran his hands down her lovely shoulders to her back. He pressed her against him and silently begged her to stay.

"RW." Her voice was breathy. "Close the door."

Eleven

Michele's hands were full of groceries. She'd bought all sorts of interesting and authentic ingredients at Juanita's Mexican Market and Café but had not gotten a chance to meet the owner herself. Too bad. She would've liked to have asked a few questions about the Harpers.

What those three sisters had told her seemed impossible. It was mind-boggling that a family so wealthy and famous could have such terrible troubles. Poor Jeffrey. She admired him for working to become successful after being raised like that and then being kicked out of the house when he was only sixteen. Her childhood had been a piece of cake by comparison. Even though her dad had died when Michele was only ten and her mom had to be both parents after that, she always knew she was loved. Her mother had been the best mom on the planet, even if cancer had cut her life far too short. The love her mother had given her made the situation Michele was in that much harder. She had to be the mom now for Cari and make sure her sister had everything she needed. She couldn't afford to get involved with Jeff or any man until she had her responsibilities under control.

Michele found a spot on the sidewalk that was out of the foot traffic to put the grocery bags down and dug into her purse for her cell phone. Smiling at the business card in her hand, she dialed.

"This is Michele Cox. Am I speaking to Alfred at the Batcave?"

A deep chuckle came through her phone. "Yes, yes, you are. Would you like a ride, miss?"

"I would. Thank you. I'm standing outside Juanita's," Michele said.

"Very good. We'll be right there."

We? Her heart beat a little faster.

Was Jeffrey coming, too?

She expected the long car that Alfred had been driving in the morning. She did a double take when a bright yellow Bentley convertible pulled up beside her with the top down. Alfred wore a plaid British ivy cap over his bald head while his passenger sat in the front seat with her long blond hair flowing in the wind. Chloe, not Jeffrey.

"Hi, Michele. Thought I'd tag along so we can stop at a shop along the way. I'll move to the back," Chloe said. "Alfred, take us to Carolina's."

Michele handed her bags to Alfred who loaded them in the trunk. "Carolina's?" She'd seen pretty much everything the little town had to offer but didn't remember that store.

"It's a one-stop dress store for baptisms, *quinceañera* parties, proms and weddings. Lots of color and yards of frill and lace but I've got my fingers crossed they have at least one gown that will work for you tonight."

"I don't understand," Michele said.

"For your outing with Jeff. It's been firmed up. Each one has been a different way for Jeff to get to know the chefs better. Freja, for example, went fishing with him this morning. And Tonia and he rode horses."

"I've never been on a boat before and love riding horses. Those outings sound lovely."

"Well, they were illuminating, that's for sure." Chloe smiled. "The other two chefs had adventures in Plunder Cove but yours will be up the coast in another little ocean-side town just south of Big Sur called Seal Point. Matt is flying Jeff up there for a meeting with the California Restaurant and Lodging Association. There is a dinner party afterward with lots of big shots and some press. He really doesn't want to go to this event, but it's important to get the word out about the Plunder Cove hotel. And let's face it, a conservative dinner party with a respectable date can help improve Jeffrey's public image. All you two need to do is show up for the dinner and then you both can leave. Alfred will drive you back home together."

Date?

She needed to keep her eye on the prize—the job, not the sexy man. Going on a date with him would be dangerous. Even as warning bells were going off in her brain, her lips were itching for another chance to taste Jeffrey's full lips. A real date could be more temptation than she could handle.

"This is an important night for my brother. Please say you'll help him," Chloe said. "We have to do something to fix his damaged image."

Schmoozing at dinner parties. Talking to big shots. Wearing a gown. All these things were so far outside Michele's wheelhouse that she didn't know where to begin. She was more comfortable behind the scenes and in the kitchen than outside where the VIPs ate. But she would go to this event to prove to Jeffrey that she could represent Harper Industries in any environment and convince him to choose her.

"Just tell me what I need to do." Her voice sounded meek, unconvincing. She cleared her throat. "I want to help him, any way I can."

"My brother likes you." Chloe touched her arm. "Be yourself, Michele. And have a nice time."

Trying not to yawn, Jeff shifted in his seat to ease off his sore backside. Tonia had sucked at horseback riding and had only wanted to ask him about his family—his brother, his sister, his father…and anyone else that lived at Casa Larga. Thankfully, they'd cut the adventure short before he'd had to come up with answers for her, or listening to the governor's speech right now would be even more painful than it already was.

He looked around the conference hall. It was packed with all the big boys in the California hotel industry plus a few tiny fish trying to make a splash for themselves. Where did he fit in? Jeff might be a small fish after having his reputation decimated, but he was working for one of the biggest companies in the world. When he made eye contact with some of the attendees, he could tell he was hated by some and idolized by others. Story of his life.

He checked his phone. No new GIFs. He should be grateful. Instead, it worried him. Had the lawyers convinced Finn to cease and desist, or was he working on the next series of damning videos?

Just then Chloe texted him.

Oh, brother of mine, you owe me. Big-time.

Why?

You'll see. How's the meeting?

Kill me now before the boredom does. What do I owe you for?

Tonight's adventure.

He frowned.

No more damned adventures today. I'm beat. As soon as this never-ending meeting wraps up, I'm going home and falling into bed.

You can't. Dad asked me to make sure you stay for the dinner party.

No.

His sister knew why he hated to eat alone. Eating with a group of strangers was not much better.

Come on. It's important for you to mingle and spread the word about our hotel. Show them the brochure. Talk it up. Besides, your date is on her way.

His pulse kicked up.

My date?

Don't worry, I packed your tux on the plane and Matt brought it to the hotel. They're holding it for you in the lobby. Have a nice time! Alfred will bring you both back to the Batcave when you're ready. Gotta run. You can thank me tomorrow.

Who's my date?

There was no response.

Chloe!

The texting had stopped. Dammit, his sister was toying with him. And now he had the rest of the meeting to wonder who would show up tonight. Was this supposed to be a real date or was it part of the interview process?

Hell, *who* was his date?

He'd already spent time with Freja and Tonia. Would it be pretty, sweet, kind Michele?

He'd missed seeing her today. She was the only chef he'd connected with on a personal level, and quickly, which made him wary. Plus, he couldn't stop thinking about the kiss in the kitchen. And how he wished he'd pressed her up against the kitchen island and kissed her back.

He honestly hoped it wasn't Michele because he would be distracted by her. When she was close it was hard to concentrate on anything but the light catching in her hair and eyes, and the way her smile crinkles tugged at a soft spot in his chest, the rise and fall of her breasts when she breathed... damn. He was in big trouble if his date was Michele.

Worse. If the big boys at the dinner party intimidated her, bringing out her insecurities, she'd be going home tomorrow. He had a job to do and couldn't make any more excuses for her. He'd have to cut her loose. And that would be the worst.

Michele felt a little funny sitting in the back of the limo while Alfred drove, but he said he wouldn't have it any other way. "You look like a movie star, Miss Cox. And you'll be treated like one tonight. You just relax. The drive up the coastal highway is beautiful."

He wasn't kidding. The highway meandered and curved along the blue-green craggy-rocked Pacific Ocean. It was breathtaking.

"And here we are. Seal Point," Alfred said, as he pulled up to the lobby of a two-story building.

She'd expected something larger, more ornate, and was pleasantly surprised by the rustic wood-sided lodge atop the rocky cliffs. Torches lit pathways through gardens and into groves of lacy dark green Monterey pines. It felt intimate, somehow. The sun was an orange ball of wax melting into the Pacific Ocean. The sea breeze softly caressed her skin. It was a beautiful night, fragrant and warm. The setting was so romantic. And inside the lodge was the man who had the power to make her professional dreams come true and tempt her into destroying everything. She wanted him and knew she shouldn't act on her desires.

Alfred opened her door. "Ready, miss?"

As I'll ever be.

She'd never had her makeup professionally done before today, nor her hair swept up so perfectly. The dress Chloe had purchased for her was pale pink and clung to her curves like a cloud.

For the first time since she'd left her hometown to work for Alfieri, Michele felt beautiful. Special. Even if it was just a fantasy for tonight. She was at a stunningly romantic place, but she wasn't here for romance. It was her job to make Jeffrey Harper look respectable, which meant she wasn't going to gaze into his pretty starburst blues or let his deep voice delight her, and she was certainly not going to kiss his full lips.

This was a business dinner, nothing more. She could do this because Jeffrey needed her. And if she proved capable here, perhaps he'd choose her for his restaurant.

You'll fail like you always do. You'll embarrass Jeffrey in front of everyone.

"Shut up, Alfieri!" she mumbled under her breath.

"Miss? Did you say something?" Alfred still stood by the door waiting for her to get out.

Her legs seemed unable to move. "If I asked you to drive me back to the Batcave, would you do it?" Her voice was shaky.

Alfred leaned closer and whispered, "Is that what you want, miss?"

If I leave now, I might as well fly straight home to New York.

She swallowed. "No. I'm just a little nervous. I'm not used to parties like this." Or being on a date with a famous, wealthy man. Who was she kidding? Any man. She hadn't been on a date in years. "Where do I go?"

"I believe the people in the lobby can direct you to the restaurant where the dinner party is taking place."

She nodded. "Sure, okay."

"Miss Cox? I'll be out here waiting for you and Jeffrey. Say the word and I will drive you back to Plunder Cove. But I believe you will be great tonight. Do as Chloe said and simply be yourself."

"Thank you, Alfred." She took a deep breath and walked toward the lobby, all the while wondering what word she needed to say to get a ride out of here should things go terribly wrong.

Michele didn't ask the people at the front desk for directions. She simply followed the sound of piano music and laughter. The restaurant was beautiful. Lots of windows, tables with white cloths and candles. She searched the room and found...*him*.

Holy wow, he looked great in a tux. His broad shoulders nicely filled out the jacket. The thin black tie dipped inside behind the single button he still had buttoned. The perfectly tailored tux highlighted his thin waist and long legs. Her mouth watered.

Jeff was scanning the crowd, too. Looking for her? When his gaze met hers, she lifted her hand to wave. His mouth opened in what seemed like surprise. He rose to his feet and lifted his hand back at her. His lips formed one word. *Wow.*

Her breath caught in her chest, her heart pounded, her lips turned up of their own accord. All the other people in the room, including the pianist, disappeared. There was only Jeffrey and that smile on his lips.

It was just like the first time she'd seen him. The way he looked at her heated up her insides.

Respectable business dinner, she reminded herself, even as she wondered what his kiss would taste like.

Twelve

At first, Jeff wondered if he'd been stood up. He suspected people were all asking themselves the same question he was asking: Where was his date?

The better question: Who was his date?

Dinner was about to be served and he was running out of small talk to use with the people at his table. He was disappointed by the lack of intelligent conversation and frustrated with the power plays. The organizers of the event had snubbed him and put him at a table with low-level hotel management—the flunkies. The big guys, the movers and shakers in the hotel industry, were all sitting together at the front of the restaurant next to the windows with the ocean views. They drank and laughed loudly, while he was at the back with these jokers, clenching his fists under the table. If his date didn't show up soon, he'd leave.

And then he saw her.

Michele walked into the room wearing an amazing pink dress that bared her shoulders and accentuated her breasts, waist and hips. Her blond hair was swept up into an intricate twist, exposing her sleek, long neck. One gold chain, with what looked like a heart, dipped into her cleavage. His gaze followed that heart and then traveled slowly back up to her parted glossy lips and smoky eyes. Lots of kissable skin.

"Wow."

She'd come to be by his side during a boring business

dinner. That was all. But he was aroused just by looking at her. His heart pounded out a distress signal, a warning not to get in too deep. And then she raised her hand and smiled and things suddenly got real.

Someone at his table asked him a question, but he ignored it. His aching body was drawn to her and he was striding in that direction before he realized he'd risen from his chair.

"God, you look gorgeous." He took her arm without even thinking about it.

"So do you." Her cheeks pinked and she looked at him from under her long lashes. Her voice was husky, and soft enough that only he heard her. No flirtatious tone. She said those words like she meant them.

Hell, he was going to have to sit down.

Guiding her to his table, he wished they could leave now and go somewhere quiet to be alone, but the food was arriving and she'd come all this way for him. To help him represent his dream to the industry movers and shakers. He needed to at least feed her before he whisked her away.

He pulled her chair out and she kept her gaze on his. "Thank you."

Sexy without trying. He was in big trouble.

He sat quickly and introductions were made around the table. Michele smiled and shook hands with each person and offered appropriate comments as she did so. Like she was really listening.

"I ordered steak for both me and my date. I didn't like the other option." When he scooted his chair in, his thigh bumped hers under the table. The sudden touch was electric. She didn't move away, so he kept his leg right where it was.

"Ah, so you were going to eat mine, too." She smiled. "I might share if you're good."

Michele looked at him for a beat too long and then, as if she had to collect herself, she turned back to the lady next to her. "Tell me about your hotel. Does it have a restaurant?"

The food arrived and Jeff silently chewed his steak,

watching Michele. Her whole body seemed to absorb what each person had to say. She laughed easily and gave restaurant advice. Calling each person by their first names, she seemed to remember what each one had told her about themselves. She interacted with them as if she was the one here to represent Harper Industries, not him, and she even added a few plugs for Casa Larga, as if she really cared about the place. The way she described the grounds and the private beach made *him* want to vacation there.

Hell, she was amazing.

Michele, in her gracious, easy way made him realize a cold hard truth—he was being a superior, egotistical ass. Like Finn.

And RW.

The thought that he was turning into his father made Jeff shift uncomfortably in his chair. He'd sworn to himself that he would never be arrogant, unfeeling and cruel like his father. He'd fought hard against those family genes for most of his life. That's why he'd created *Secrets and Sheets* in the first place—to stand up to the arrogant bastards who thought they owned the world. Sure, Jeff was cocky and funny on television, but he wasn't a superior jerk.

Was he?

Music started up outside and people left their tables and went out on the patio to dance.

She leaned over and whispered in his ear, sending chills bumps into his scalp. "Are you okay? You haven't said a full sentence in over an hour."

He scooted even closer and whispered back, "I'm an idiot."

They were eye-to-eye, breath-to-breath. She blinked and he could see confusion in her expression. "Did I do something wrong?"

"No, sweetheart. You're doing everything right."

She studied his expression.

"I swear, it's not you. I'm just…off tonight," he said.

"You're allowed. I don't expect you to be perfect."

Damn. She'd done it again.

Michele had a remarkable talent for surprising the hell out of him. Most people he knew did expect him to be perfect—his agent, producer, fans, dates and RW. As a kid, he was never good enough. For the show, Jeff was supposed to be at the top of his game and improving his performance every episode.

Before this moment with Michele, he hadn't realized how exhausting his life was.

"It happens to the best of us," Michele went on. "If this party isn't working for you, we could leave now, or..." She cocked her head toward the music. "We could shake out the sillies on the dance floor. That's what my sister does when she's feeling...off."

He lifted an eyebrow. He'd never heard that expression before. "Oh, it might be a lot sillier than you think. I don't know if you've heard the rumors, but the truth is, only one of the Harper men knows how to dance and it isn't me. Sure you want that kind of embarrassment?"

"No worries. My standards are really low. The first and last time I danced was at my junior prom. And I'm not sure you could call that dancing."

He stood to pull her chair out and whispered in her ear, "A dancing virgin, then."

Her lips quirked. "I guess so."

When she rose, she gave his arm a squeeze, sending off an alarm that reverberated low and deep in his psyche. "I didn't have time to mention it before, but I want to thank you for paying my sister's fees. I will pay you back. I promise."

"That's not necessary."

"I think it is. But I am grateful for the gesture." She kissed his cheek. "Dance with me."

She turned to walk outside, expecting him to be right behind her. He wasn't.

Suddenly, he regretted agreeing to dance. What if he

couldn't hold her, touch her, feel her velvety skin on his, without wanting more?

Without wanting too much.

He exhaled slowly through his nose and stiffly followed her outside.

"Over here," she called to him. "I thought I lost you. Isn't this place beautiful? The Monterey pine grove and the moonlight shining on the water?"

He couldn't talk. All he could do was feel.

He wanted this, needed her.

The music slowed at that moment and he took Michele in his arms and held her close.

He didn't want to let her go. He had to keep reminding himself that this was business, not a date, not the start of something he couldn't finish. A woman like Michele would want more than he could give her. She deserved more than him.

Michele put her head on his chest and he pressed the small of her back, holding her against him. She felt good in his arms, really good.

"How do my moves compare to those at the junior prom?" he asked, his voice sounding surprisingly normal.

Gazing up at him, she smiled. Her dimples drove him crazy. "You, Jeffrey Harper, are so much better. This is definitely dancing."

Michele had one hand on his shoulder while the other was wrapped around his waist. As they swayed to the love song, he listened to her breathing, felt her heart beat against his chest.

Slowly, he ran a finger over her bare shoulder. Silky and soft. He wanted to kiss the curve of her there, the hollow, and work his way up to her delicate earlobe.

"Michele?"

"Hmm?"

"My closest friends call me Jeff."

Her breath caught. "Jeff," she said softly.

The sound of his name on her lips lit a fire in his groin. Feelings he had not felt in a long time burned through his blood.

He wanted this, to hold someone who was compassionate and real. He wanted to experience…something. Everything.

Was this what his siblings had meant by feeling a real connection?

"Remember when you kissed me in the kitchen?" he asked.

She stopped swaying and buried her face against his chest. "I don't know why…that was so…embarrassing."

"Yes. It was…for me." He tipped her chin up so he could see her eyes when he said, "I really messed it up. Will you please do it again?"

Her lips parted in surprise and then turned up into the sweetest smile he'd ever seen. "I promised myself I wouldn't kiss you again."

"Pretty please? What do I have to do, Miss Cox? Juggle clams and catch them in my teeth?"

She burst out laughing and then covered her mouth. She cut her eyes to see if she'd bothered anyone on the dance floor. He was sure she'd only bothered him.

Her laughter did amazing things to him.

"You got me," she said and smiled.

He liked the sound of that.

She put her hand on his cheek and rose up on her toes. This time, when her lips touched his, he kissed her back. Not gently.

It had been too long since he'd kissed a woman he cared about and his body reacted with a landslide of need, ache, fire. It felt good. Real.

He deepened the kiss, diving in, tasting, touching, wanting. He pressed her body to his. Enjoying the sensation of her breasts against his chest, her thighs touching his. He stroked her shoulder with his free hand. God, her skin was so soft, her lips perfect.

He'd come to this event to make a good impression on the other hotel owners and now he didn't give a damn about any of them. He kissed Michele as if he'd never kissed a woman before and still he wanted more.

He felt like he could never get enough.

The band played a faster song and he reluctantly pulled away to look at her. Her cheeks were flushed, her eyes hooded. Sexy. Her hips moved to the sensual beat. He liked it.

He liked her.

Putting his hands on her hips, he tried to follow along, not quite catching up. She raised her eyebrow and slowed the movement, rubbing against him as she did, pressing, teasing. Hell, he liked that more. Cupping her jaw, he kissed her again, soundly.

Out of the corner of his eye, he saw a woman dressed in a black sequined gown pass by, puffing on her cigarette. She turned around and took a long look at Jeff kissing Michele.

"You're disgusting," she snarled at Jeff. "First the maid in the hotel and now this? Stay away from him, honey. He's a pig." The woman threw her cigarette on the patio, ground it out with her heel and stomped away before either one of them could say a word.

Anger boiled inside him.

"Dammit!" How dare Finn's manipulations ruin this, too.

"Ignore her," Michele said softly. "She doesn't know you. People only see what they want to, not what's true. You are so much more than a stupid GIF."

He turned his head and studied her. Was *she* for real? Could she see him—past the show, the press, the GIF?

Matt's words rushed back to him.

Show her who you are without the smoke and mirrors. No stage lighting. No props. Just two real people being... normal.

And suddenly he wanted normal. Wanted real.

More. He wanted real *with* Michele. The thought alone

should have scared him. He should've pushed himself away because he knew he'd only hurt her in the end. But he was too caught up in the heat and her sparkle to do anything except pull her into his arms and kiss her like no one was looking. The little sound of contentment she made at the back of her throat went straight to his groin. He lifted his head to look at her. She still had her eyes closed and the sweetest smile on her face. This had nothing to do with the chef job—he'd have to figure that out later—it had everything to do with the sensations pulsing through him. He couldn't hold back the tidal wave of want that overtook him.

"Let's take this off the dance floor." His voice was little more than a growl.

Breathing heavily, she nodded.

"Tonight, the chef competition is on hold. Our date has nothing to do with that."

"I didn't believe it did."

"Good. I had activities with the other women, but nothing like a date. I wouldn't want you or anyone else to think this is how I operate."

"No. Of course not."

He led her down the torch-lit pathway, away from the restaurant and patio dance floor and past the Monterey pine grove. He was on the hunt for a quiet alcove far away from the dinner party and prying eyes, any place to be alone with Michele and not have to think or be judged.

"What's that?" She pointed toward the redwood structure perched like a beacon high above the rugged Big Sur coast.

"A wedding pagoda. Couples come from all over to be married under that canopy."

"It's lovely. I can just imagine the bride and groom standing there, gazing into each other's eyes, with the waves rolling in, whispering sweet promises below."

"You're a romantic."

"And you're not?"

"Not about weddings, no. My parents blew that institution sky-high."

"Ah, so that article I read about you was true. You will never get married."

"Don't believe everything you read. I will get married, but it sure as hell won't be for love."

Her jaw dropped. "What would it be for? A business arrangement? The trading of camels? A joining of kingdoms?"

She was joking. He wasn't.

"Something like that. I wouldn't want my bride to fall in love with me. I'd just hurt her like my parents hurt each other."

"It doesn't have to be that way. My parents married for love and rarely argued. They raised me and my sister in a great home before they passed away. What if you fall in love with your bride and you both live happily ever after? It could happen."

"Not to me. I don't have the chemical makeup for it."

She blinked. "You can't fall in love?"

"No. And I won't hurt anyone because of my screwed-up DNA."

"I don't believe that."

"That's because you aren't like me. You're warm and caring. Sweet. I see you going for the wedding pagoda and the happily-ever-after, Michele. I hope it sticks for you. I'll take the no-drama, no-stress business contract in front of a judge. It's better that way."

"That seems so...unfeeling."

Yeah, that's what he was trying to tell her. No matter what was happening between them tonight, he didn't have any of those feelings. Never would.

He was cold.

"Let's find a fireplace," he said.

He didn't tell her that he'd already agreed to a loveless marriage when the restaurant was completed.

Why ruin the best date he'd had in years?

* * *

Michele sat beside Jeff on a couch in front of a rock fireplace. They were alone and far from the dinner party. An owl hooted in a tree nearby.

"Cold?" He took his tuxedo jacket off and wrapped it around her shoulders. Not with him sitting this close. Her body was still humming from his kisses.

She put her head on his shoulder and looked up at the stars. "So beautiful."

"Got that right." He was looking at her.

It surprised her. He'd dated so many gorgeous women, did he really think she was beautiful?

She laced her fingers with his. She really wanted to touch him. All over.

With her head still on his shoulder she whispered, "Can we just stay here forever?"

"What about the restaurant I have to finish? And the world-renowned recipes you're going to create?"

She sighed. What if she couldn't create any recipes anymore, world renowned or otherwise? She knew the answer. This would be her last night with Jeff unless she could find the magic.

"Well, if we have to go back to reality tomorrow—" she started.

"Let's make this a night to remember," he finished and punctuated the thought by cupping her jaw and kissing her lips.

He was such an amazing kisser. When he sucked on her bottom lip she moaned with delight. She turned her head so he could have better access. He gripped her hair and pinned her in place. His tongue thrust in and out. In and out. She imagined that tongue doing wicked things between her legs and she moaned again.

"Pull up your dress," he growled. "I want to touch you."

She hesitated. The man had just told her that he couldn't fall in love. He wasn't interested in a real marriage, only one that was advantageous to his business. He was a play-boy who dated anyone he wanted. And he was right, she wasn't like that at all. She wanted to love, to feel every-thing, and to make a life and family with her soul mate, like her mother did.

But the expression on his face—dark, determined, needy—was her undoing. No one had ever looked at her like that before and she longed to feel sexy, just once. She stood and crinkled up the material from the hem of her dress until her legs were exposed.

"More," he said.

She swallowed and pulled her gown up further until he could see her pink panties. They matched the dress and probably looked almost nude in the light of the fire.

"Come here, sweetheart." He crooked his finger at her.

Her brain kept trying to tell her that Jeffrey Harper was the opposite of her soul mate. He was sexually experienced and hot enough to burn her to ash. He was a one-night guy and she didn't do one-night stands, and she didn't sleep around at work either. It wasn't in her chemical makeup to shut feelings off and walk away. And it certainly wasn't like her to hook up with a take-charge kind of a guy who had the power to hurt her professionally and personally. But part of her was drawn to the sadness in Jeff, the deep pain he tried to hide.

There was a heart in that wide, muscular chest. Jeffrey just didn't know it. Maybe if she could show him how to love…

She came toward him and he pulled her on top of his lap. She straddled his legs, the only thing between them were her panties and his tuxedo pants. He was so deliciously hard. He ran his hand up her leg starting at her calf and going higher, higher.

"Kiss me," she whispered.

"Oh, babe, your wish is my command."

He kissed her shoulder, her neck, along her jawline.

When he finally made his way to her lips she met him with her tongue. He opened to her, letting her lick his lips, taste, explore. He sucked in a sharp breath and she knew she was doing something right.

One of his hands rubbed, petted, traveling up her legs, driving her wild. Their tongues danced. She'd never been kissed like that before. When he got to her glutes, he gave them a squeeze. Her heart pounded hard in her chest. The world was spinning around her. She gripped his shoulders to stabilize herself, enjoying this man and his incredible lips. His finger ran underneath the elastic of her panties. She stilled in his arms. Was he really going to—the thought was cut off when his hand was suddenly touching her inside her panties.

"Okay?" he asked.

She nodded. More than okay. She hadn't felt like this in years.

He petted her, making her wet.

A voice in her head tried to remind her that she was outside a party where anyone could walk by, anyone could see what he was doing to her. But what he was doing was far too good.

Her own moans blocked out any inner voices.

"You like that?" he asked.

"Oh, yes."

He kept petting. Kissing. Driving her wild.

His finger went inside. He tugged gently, hitting a sweet spot she didn't know she had.

"Oh. " Was all she could muster. He felt so good. Before she knew it, her hips were moving with his hand's movements. Her breath and heart beat racing.

"Come for me," he growled against her neck. "Let go."

The words, hoarse and encouraging, undid any reserve she'd been clinging to. She threw her head back and rode him up and over the abyss. Moaning as the feelings—raw, rich, delicious—rolled through her.

Just then, a flash went off.

"Thanks, Harper!" a man shouted and ran off.

She blinked in surprise.

Jeff cursed while quickly lifting her off his lap. "Head down," he said in a clipped sharp tone. He brought his jacket up to cover her face. But it was too late. A photographer had snapped a picture of them in a decidedly unrespectable dating moment. And…there was the fact that she'd oh-so willingly flown over the abyss with her potential boss. No one would know that they mutually agreed this date had nothing to do with the chef position.

She'd thrown gasoline on his already damaged reputation, setting fire to everything.

Jeff pounded his pockets, coming up empty. "Do you have a cell phone?"

She handed him hers.

"Alfred, come to the side lot and get Michele the hell out of here," Jeff barked into it.

Paparazzi *here*? In the middle of freaking nowhere? Why wouldn't those bastards leave him alone?

He glanced at Michele. She was pale and still had his jacket held up to her neck as if she wanted to disappear. Hell, she looked so…beautiful. He'd never seen anything more gorgeous than Michele letting go in his arms. He longed to pull her back, nuzzle against her neck and whisper how much he wanted to have her come again and show her how much he still wanted her. Damn the paparazzi! He'd lived with the press long enough to know that the one night would have consequences for both of them. Sweet Michele—a woman who was already fighting insecurities—was about to have her reputation destroyed, too.

Unless he did something.

"Stay here. When Alfred arrives, climb in the limo and lock the door. He'll get you home safely," he told her.

"What about you? Where are you going?" Her voice was

small. Hell, he'd messed this up for her. He was pissed at himself for wanting her so much. He should have had better control, been stronger. But even now he wanted her and was nearly desperate to throw caution to the wind.

"I'll stay here as long as it takes to find that photographer and make him delete the photo. I'll get my own ride home. Don't worry, Michele. I'll handle it."

Her eyes widened. "How will you handle it?"

He wanted to beat it out of the guy, but he knew how these things worked. Jeff couldn't afford an assault and battery charge on top of everything else.

"The way Harpers do. With money." He spat those last words out. He really was becoming his father.

The limo pulled up. Alfred raced out of the car faster than Jeff had ever seen the old guy move and was quickly opening the door for her.

"Get her home safely," Jeff demanded.

"We can figure this out together. Please come with me." Michele reached out to him, but he stepped back.

"I can't." He was stepping back because he didn't want to hurt her. And he would, he was sure of that. A lady who wanted to get married for love would eventually hate him.

He couldn't love.

But his thoughts got messed up around her. He wanted to make love to her more than anything he'd ever wanted and wasn't sure why. He'd been with many women. Why was Michele different? Why did he need to touch her so badly? As if to prove the point, his hand was already on her shoulder before he could stop himself.

"Let Alfred take you back. This is my fault. I'm sorry."

Her crestfallen expression ripped a hole in his chest. "I'm not."

Damn. He wanted to kiss her so deeply that she'd never doubt how special she was. She made him want to be more than he could be. He wanted to feel. To be real. To fall in love. To love Michele deeply with everything he was not.

He exhaled slowly. "Don't misunderstand. I'm not sorry for our time together. That was...amazing. No, I'm sorry that I can't be a better man. You deserve more.

"Go. Now," Jeff finally managed.

"Jeff, please!" Michele called after him, but he didn't stop, wouldn't turn around.

He didn't understand why all the pieces he'd held together for so long were shattering like a bashed-in chandelier. Only one thing was crystal clear—he needed to protect Michele.

From himself.

Thirteen

Michele got up early to find Jeff. Had he come home at all?

She wanted to tell him that she wasn't mad at him. Concerned, confused, yes, but not angry. He'd given her the best night she'd had in a long time. She wanted to be with him again, in spite of everything, and she wanted to help him. If she could find him.

He wasn't anywhere in Casa Larga.

She wandered outside and found both Tonia and Freja sunbathing by the pool.

"Look who's here, Miss Sex Kitten," Tonia said.

"What?" Michele asked.

Freja pointed to the newspaper. "You made de front page."

Michele snatched up the paper. Sure enough, there she was on Jeff's lap with her dress hiked up to her thighs with the caption, "Who is Jeffrey Harper's New Sex Kitten?"

"Oh, no." Her heart sank. She sat on a lounge chair and read the scathing article. It painted him in a terrible light but the writer didn't know who she was.

"Good chefs win by their talents," Tonia snarled. "I can understand why you would try sleeping with the boss."

"A bad picture. Ees you, no?" Freja asked.

"Of course it's her. She wasn't here last night." Tonia gave Michele a withering look. "I demand you be disqualified from the competition. I guess Jeffrey won't do it, so I'm going to look for RW right now."

Tonia grabbed her cover-up and marched into the house.

Freja tsked. "Too bad. I like you better than that one, but she ees right. Ees best if you quit."

They were both right.

God. She'd messed things up. She really, really liked Jeff. A lot. And she'd let him down. The one night she was supposed to help improve his reputation, she gave in to her desires and let herself go on his lap. Even though it was one of the best dates of her life, she'd hurt his reputation even more. She'd been selfish and lost the job that would save both her and her sister while hurting the first guy she'd dated in a long time. Who does that? Feeling terrible, she decided she'd go clear the air with him, make sure he was okay, and then...she'd leave.

Angel was heading down the hallway in RW's private wing when she saw a woman opening doors and peeking inside each room.

Who was she? What was she looking for? And where was the guard?

Cautious, Angel stepped back inside RW's room and closed the door. The woman didn't seem to be dangerous. She was barefoot and wearing a pool cover-up, for Pete's sake, but Angel couldn't take any chances. Not with Cristina and her little boy hiding here from Cuchillo's gang. Angel had made many mistakes in her life, including trusting the wrong man and staying with him when she should have left. She wasn't that girl anymore. She was a woman who had escaped all of that. Now she had to protect everyone—RW's family and her own.

She called security. "A young woman is wandering the halls in RW's private wing. Please escort her back to wherever she is supposed to be. And make sure the guard is stationed at his post in the next thirty seconds, or RW will fire him."

Not even a minute later, Angel heard a commotion in the hall.

"*Idiota!* Get your hands off me," the young woman yelled. The voice sounded familiar. Was she one of the chefs? Had Angel made a mistake by calling security?

Angel was about to go and correct the situation when her phone rang in her hand. "*Hola?*"

"Oh, Angel. Good, I'm glad you answered." It was Chloe. "Can you come to Matt and Julia's house? Dad's here, too."

RW left Casa Larga and went to Julia's house? Something was wrong. With her heart in her throat she asked, "RW… is he…okay? Is Julia? What's going on?"

"It's about Jeff. Another picture has popped up in the newspaper this time. I'm worried this will convince Jeff that he can't have a real relationship and he'll marry for the wrong reasons. We need to figure out a way to convince Jeff that he is not like Mom and Dad. Please come here so we can talk. We need your help."

Jeff was on the restaurant work site, hammering nails with the rest of the framing crew.

He didn't want to think, or talk; he just wanted to pound nails. Over and over until his muscles screamed louder than his brain. He couldn't stop seeing the anguish on Michele's face after he'd forced her to walk away. After he'd given in to temptation and landed them both on the front page.

He hadn't been able to find the jerk who'd snuck up and interrupted the best thing Jeff had experienced in years. He still craved Michele more than anything. A cold shower, two cups of espresso and a terrible night's sleep hadn't dampened his desire for her. If anything, time had made his need for her grow, like an unquenchable thirst. The intensity of his desire for him scared him.

But that was too freaking bad because he couldn't have her, especially not now.

Everyone had seen the photo of Michele in his lap at the convention. They would assume he couldn't keep it in his pants. And they'd take Michele down with him. He was glad no one knew who she was and he planned to keep it that way. He wouldn't tarnish her career with his own smutty one.

This whole fiasco only proved his point about how different they were. This was why he couldn't marry someone who loved him or love them in return. No matter how good Michele felt in his arms, how amazing her lips tasted, he couldn't touch her again. He'd only ruin her.

He pounded nails as hard as he could.

By midday, Chloe showed up at the work site. She was about to duck under the chain when Jeff called to her, "You can't come in here without a helmet. Construction site rules."

"Then you come out!"

Hell, no. "Can't. Busy."

She gave him the stink eye. "Hey, can you throw me your helmet?" she asked a worker who was taking his lunch break.

"Sure, pretty lady. As long as you bring it back."

Plopping the helmet on her head, she swung her leg over the chain and stomped toward Jeff. "You aren't returning my calls. What's wrong with the new phone I bought for you?"

"I turned my phone off. Too many crazy women calling for a good time." He wasn't joking. He held a nail between his teeth while he hammered another one.

"Come on, Jeff. Stop, so we can talk about what happened. I feel terrible."

She looked terrible. Hell, he didn't mean to hurt her, too. He put the hammer and nails down. "It wasn't your fault." No, this whole thing started and ended with him.

She pulled him away from the other workers before saying, "I'm worried about you. You've got to stop thinking you can't connect with people. Feel. By that picture in the paper, it looks like you feel something with Michele."

He narrowed his eyes. "You don't know what you're talking about."

She put her hands on her hips just like she used to do when she was a little girl. "That might be the official story, but I know it's bull. You did make a real connection with her. I can see it in your reaction."

He couldn't look her in the eye. "Everything is fine."

"Really? Then talk to Michele. The poor girl doesn't deserve to be ignored."

He looked down at his hands. They still ached to touch her. They still belonged to a man who could turn Michele's life into a media circus. "I can't be near her right now."

Chloe let out a deep breath. "Because you like her. A lot. And you're scared."

He didn't respond.

"So, what are you going to do about the chef competition? Those three women are waiting for your answer. Which one will you choose?"

He still had no idea. He knew which one he wanted, but was she the best one for the job? Everything was even more confused than before.

"I haven't decided."

"Fine," she huffed. "One more event. We could invite the townspeople from Pueblicito to view the plans and the building site. The chefs can prepare their finest hors d'oeuvres and we'll see which one comes out the best."

It wasn't a terrible idea. The sooner he decided who the chef would be, the faster the marketing team could start the promo machine and drum up interest.

The sooner Michele would be gone...or permanently a part of the dream he was creating. "Okay."

"This coming weekend Dad has something going on,

and he'll want to be at the event. How about the weekend after that?"

"Yeah. If the chefs are okay with staying that long. I suggest having Dad increase their bonus." Twelve days. He could throw himself into his work and not have to think about anything until then. Not even Michele's soft skin. The memory of her on his lap crept into his thoughts. Since he didn't have a nail, he pounded his thigh to obliterate the vision.

Chloe shielded her eyes from the sun and studied him. "You should talk to Angel, or...someone. I really think it would help."

"I'll keep that in mind." He rose to go back to work, but then turned around. "Check in on Michele. Make sure she's doing okay. I didn't mean for any of this to happen."

"Or you could talk to her yourself."

He walked away.

He'd find someone else to date tonight. Someone he couldn't hurt.

It was time to start looking for a bride.

Michele was coming to grips with the fact that Jeff was avoiding her. It hurt.

She thought they'd had something special, but apparently, she'd read the situation incorrectly. She'd only been a one-night fling for him. And it hadn't even been a full night.

Part of her had known that truth at the time and yet she'd climbed on his lap anyway, because his lips and touch had felt oh-so good. She'd allowed herself to believe she could heal a playboy's heart. She'd risked her dreams and responsibilities on that hope.

Playing with fire only seemed to make her burn for more sizzling kisses, more caresses, more Jeffrey Harper.

He was the opposite of what she should be focusing on—taking care of her sister, learning how to cook again, finding a man to love her, starting a family.

But what she felt for Jeffrey didn't matter. She needed to put her energy into the one thing that *did* matter—landing this job.

There was one final competition, a sort of winner-take-all. She'd been asked to prepare hors d'oeuvres for a large party to show off the restaurant project. She knew this was a big deal for Jeff and was determined to do her best.

Sitting in her room, Michele scoured the internet looking for good Italian recipes, not finding anything that grabbed her. Nothing was good enough for Jeff's special night.

Closing her eyes, she whispered, "Help me, Mom. I need a little magic."

A light breeze came in through her window, lifting her hair off her face. Suddenly, she smelled sage, and rosemary. Opening her eyes, she squealed.

She knew what she was going to make.

Michele spent most of the next week in the Harpers' kitchen. It wasn't easy cooking meals next to the two other chefs she was competing against. They kept bumping into each other and fighting over the utensils, stove and ovens. All three chefs were making practice foods, getting them right.

Michele noticed that Freja was making a seafood cioppino. "You might want to rethink that one. Jeff hates seafood."

Freja pulled her white-blond hair up in a beautiful twist. "How ees dis possible? He took me fishing, said he loved water. He even swims like a fishy."

"Don't listen to her," Tonia said. "She's just trying to get into your head."

"I don't lie," Michele said.

Tonia shrugged. "We all know how you cheat."

Michele shook her head. "Suit yourself. Make all the fish hors d'oeuvres you want."

Freja looked at her ingredients, bit her lip and then put the fish back in the refrigerator. "I make something else."

The day of the event finally arrived. Michele had practiced enough. It was as if Jeff had flipped a switch inside her. All that sensual energy he'd awakened had to be channeled somewhere and she poured it into her cooking. She sampled each of her hors d'oeuvres. They were fantastic.

She went upstairs to get ready. Would it be the last time she'd see Jeff? She was incredibly sad at the thought. But he'd moved on, apparently, and she should stop driving herself crazy and move on, too. They were two different people who wanted different things.

He'd said it by the wedding pagoda. *You aren't like me. You're warm and caring. Sweet. I see you going for the wedding pagoda and the happily-ever-after, Michele. I hope it sticks for you. I'll take the no-drama, no-stress business contract in front of a judge.*

Well, she hoped he was wrong. She wanted him to find happiness and love someday, too. Even if it was with someone else.

Michele showered, applied her makeup, dried her hair and put on her flowing black pants, pale blue halter blouse and matching strappy sandals. Jeff seemed to like her bare shoulders. And she liked when he kissed them.

Shut up, Michele! she yelled at herself. Jeff wasn't going to kiss her anymore. And she shouldn't be wanting him to.

She was here to be a five-star chef. Period.

Downstairs, people had started to arrive. She hustled to the kitchen and found Freja and Tonia had plated up their trays and were outside feeding the guests already. Darn it! They'd left her the two smallest, least attractive trays. She hurried. The first tray was for the fried giant ravioli stuffed with Italian sausage, spinach, parmesan, mozzarella, cherry tomatoes and a mixture of fresh Italian spices. In the center of the tray she had a tomato-and-red-wine-based dipping sauce that was to die for.

On the second tray, she placed her crostini, made with her homemade Italian bread. She'd kneaded savory fragrant spices, some of which she'd purchased from Juanita's, into the dough and had toasted the slices perfectly. She'd spread a thin layer of olive oil and goat cheese on top of the toasted bread. Purple and black dry-cured olives with rosemary and orange zest came next. The crostini were gorgeous and reminded her of a midnight sky. They made her think of the stars she and Jeff had looked at together. Arugula topped the olives. Around the edges of the tray, she carefully placed delicious prosciutto-, mozzarella-and risotto-stuffed fritters.

Everything smelled good, looked good, and would taste great.

Her magic was back.

She was ready.

Angel sat on the couch in Cristina's bungalow and checked the watch RW had given her for her birthday. They were late. RW and his family had already gone downstairs for Jeff's restaurant unveiling. Angel's sisters were coming, too, but Julia and Matt had stayed home because Henry was sick. Angel thought about Jeff's predicament. Chloe, Matt and RW had all told her about Jeff's childhood. Jeff had refused to join what he called "an intervention" and claimed he didn't need their help.

From what the others told her, it was clear that Jeff did need some sort of help. Therapy was not a bad idea. Each of the Harper kids had their own crosses to bear because of the way RW and his ex-wife had raised them. The only role models Jeff had growing up were two adults who acted like they hated each other. Jeff had never known love and therefore thought he was incapable of giving love. But Angel knew differently. Hadn't RW proved that he was a loving man to her? Jeff could do the same. He just needed a gentle hand to guide him toward the feelings he was bottling up. Maybe Michele was the nice one he needed.

Angel glanced at her watch again. If Cristina didn't hurry, they would miss Jeff's big speech.

"Come on, Cristina. What's taking so long?" Angel's patience was growing thin. It was stressful having the woman and her child staying in Casa Larga. Protecting so many people kept Angel on edge.

Cristina walked out of the bedroom and closed the door behind her. "Sebastian doesn't want to go. Maybe I should stay here."

"No, you need to get out of this bungalow and have some fun. I'll get someone to watch Sebastian so you can take a break."

Angel instructed one of the maids to babysit. She knew Cristina needed more than just a break for one night. The young woman craved the same things Angel did—a free life with her family outside the gang. But Cristina and her son *could* go somewhere else and be happy and safe. Over time, Cuchillo would lose interest in wanting to make Cristina pay for deserting the gang. And since Cristina hadn't personally witnessed Cuchillo's sadistic crimes, not like Angel, she wouldn't be a strong witness for the prosecutor. Cuchillo wouldn't have to hunt Cristina down and seal her lips forever.

Angel wished she could be that lucky.

Fourteen

"Thank you all for coming." Jeff stood next to the newly framed restaurant, the sky peeking through the bare wood bones. He lifted his voice so everyone in the crowd could hear him while searching the faces for Michele.

Even though he knew he shouldn't.

He wanted to see her.

There had to be fifty people from Pueblicito there to take a look at the new building and taste the food from the competing chefs. *Shareholders*, Dad had called the townspeople. It appeared that RW Harper was going to donate a percentage of the hotel and restaurant profits to them after all. At least, Jeff hoped that was the case, otherwise his father had suckered him into lying to these people.

"As you can see, the restaurant is coming along nicely. We expect to be open for business right on time." It was going up fast and even in its early stages, it looked amazing.

The crowd cheered.

Pride bloomed in his chest. This was what it felt like to be proud of his accomplishments. Damn, he'd missed this feeling. It surprised him that he was so thrilled with a project that involved the home he used to hate. Working with his father had been better than he ever dreamed possible.

"The plans for both the restaurant and the hotel are pinned up on the wall for you to review at your leisure, but let me set the mood first. Pretend you have just arrived in Plunder Cove, weary and hungry. You walk up those steps…" He pointed to a grassy hillside. The steps had yet to be made. "…and see this wood-sided building, both rustic and charming, with views out to the Pacific Ocean. The shape, the wood, makes you think of—"

"A pirate ship!" someone in the crowd interrupted.

He nodded and one of the old women in the crowd, called out, "Knew you'd do this right. We've got faith in you, Jeffrey."

He pressed his hands to his chest and made a tiny bow. Then he went on to describe his vision for the restaurant. Freja passed by him with a half-empty tray. Tonia was on the other side of the patio surrounded by a group of hungry people. "And please, eat up. We have three of the finest chefs in the world here with us tonight. Enjoy."

He scanned the crowd.

And then he saw her.

Standing off to the side holding her tray, Michele was watching him. The look on her face resembled pride—in him. It made him want to grab her, press her up against the wall and kiss those pretty lips. Ignoring all the warnings going off in his brain, ignoring everything he'd told himself as he'd stayed away from her for days, he strode toward her, determined to pull her away and get a taste.

He'd drink until he was full and then he'd think about the reasons why he shouldn't have her.

A man bumped into him. "Water!" the guy choked.

Another person started coughing, and another. Someone behind him said, "We need flan, or milk. This stuff is too spicy!"

Jeff looked around. One guy had tears running down his face while his wife tried to console him. What was going on?

"I thought it would be sweet." A woman walked up to Michele and pointed. "My husband can't eat spicy peppers. He might have to go to the ER because of you!"

Michele blanched. "What?"

The three sisters from Pueblicito came to her aid. Nona said, "I love the sauce. Habaneros are my favorite."

"Me, too," Flora nodded.

"Just the right kick," Alana added.

"Habaneros?" Michele looked at Jeff, her face pale. "I didn't put peppers in the sauce."

"Are you sure?"

"No, I…don't think I did…" She bit her lip, indecisive. She tasted the sauce and her face went eyes widened. "There are peppers in this sauce."

Jeff ran his hand through his hair. Every molecule in his body, especially those below his waistline, screamed at him to ignore the mistake and give her a chance. Let her stay. No, make her stay. But would he let Tonia or Freja continue in the competition if they messed up as badly as Michele had with the sauce when it wasn't her first mistake? Maybe not.

Deep down he knew he wanted to forgive any mistakes Michele made because he wanted her. He couldn't be objective about Michele. With her he was in a constant state of need. He shouldn't feel needy when he was supposed to be in control. She was ruining him in more ways than one. His gut burned as if he'd swallowed a whole habanero chili.

He had to grow up, be the boss he was supposed to be and let her go. He turned to the serving staff and asked them to bring water and milk right away.

"Michele, I don't know what in the hell happened, but this is unacceptable. You know how important this night is for me," he said. "I need a chef who is consistent." Disappointment and sadness gripped him. He had to cut her out of the competition, which meant he might never see her again.

"I know, Jeff. I'm sorry. This won't reflect on you. It's not your fault, it's my responsibility. I'll clean it up before I go." The sparkle he loved so much was gone. She raised her voice. "Ladies and gentlemen, I apologize that the sauce was too spicy. Anytime there is a mistake in the kitchen a good chef always makes it right. Please do not leave yet. I will create something special for you to cool your tongues."

Before she ran back to the kitchen her gaze met his. "I'm sorry."

The three sisters from Pueblicito cornered Jeff.

"You were too hard on her." Nona eyed him ferociously.

"Yeah, she's a nice lady who makes great food," Alana agreed. "Did you try those giant ravioli? I'm gonna be dreaming about them for weeks."

"I like the ball things and the olives. Michele was my favorite. Those other two chefs?" Flora shook her head. "Not even close."

"I can't have a chef who makes mistakes like that," he said to them. "It's business."

"I see. You never made any mistakes." Nona's expression was all too knowing. As if she'd witnessed some of the hell he'd lived through. "No one ever counted you out? Treated you like you were dirt and then kicked you to the curb?"

His jaw dropped. How did she know all of that?

"Nona's right. Give her another chance," Flora said. "She's the one for you."

Alana smacked her lips. "You think she has any more of those ravioli in the kitchen?"

The old women were right. Michele's food tonight was sparking with magic. She was consistent with every dish except the dipping sauce.

Why had she messed it up? It didn't make sense.

Michele was beside herself. What had happened? She hadn't used habanero chilis since the night she made the grilled cheese sandwich for Jeff. Someone had put those peppers in her dish.

She quickly rushed to make a specialty that the crowd would love. The only secret ingredients in the dessert would be the love and grief she was feeling right now. The passion for cooking had come back to her because Jeff had brought the magic back into her life. She was full of gratitude for that fact alone. But it was more than that. She was falling for him, hard. She knew he didn't think he could give her what she needed, but part of her wanted him anyway. Okay, most of her wanted him anyway. Even if she couldn't have him. And now she wouldn't have the job she needed, either. Jeff was sending her home.

She blinked back tears. How had things gotten so messed up?

At least the dessert was delicious. She tasted it to make sure and decided it was time to bring the guests in. The only number at Casa Larga that Michele had in her cell phone was to the Batcave.

Alfred, will you please tell Jeff to send the guests to the great hall?

Sure, Miss. I'll send up the Bat Signal.

The group came into the hall, filling it quickly. She was relieved that they'd all stayed because she was scared she'd ruined things for Jeff. She'd been so proud of him as he talked about his project. It was clear he was meant to create hotels, just as she'd been meant to create great food. Even if she'd lost track of herself along the way.

Michele stood behind the long table and encouraged the crowd to come forward to take a bowl. "This dessert is called 'zabaglione.' It is an Italian custard with some of my own special spices and marsala wine. Don't worry, nothing hot in this, just sweet and—"

"*Delicioso*," a woman said after taking her first bite. "This is amazing."

People started talking at once.

"Oh, my."

"This is the best thing I've ever tasted!"

"Fantastic. You've got to try this."

The rave reviews continued until someone in the crowd clapped and soon the room erupted in applause. They loved her dessert. Her heart melted. She'd made something everyone loved.

"Hey." Jeff stepped up to the table. "Can I talk to you?"

Her eyes welled. She blinked quickly, determined to keep things professional even as she walked out the door. She'd gone from needing this job financially, to wanting to help Jeff succeed in his grand and wonderful adventure. And now all of it was over.

"Of course. Take a bowl of zabaglione, too."

He took a bite. The look that spread across his face was mesmerizing. It was like a wave of happiness and joy. She wished he always looked like that.

What she didn't see? Shock. It was as if he'd known she could cook like this and had just been waiting for her to figure it out.

"Tastes like light, creamy heaven. Simply poetic. Welcome back."

She blushed with delight. "Thank you."

He took her hand. "Come with me."

It seemed like they were leaving the great hall. Was this it? Jeff was escorting her off the property?

They passed Tonia eating a bowlful of zabaglione in the corner. Her pretty face twisted with white-hot anger.

"Wait for me," he said to Michele. "I need to talk to Tonia."

Oh. Michele understood what this meant—Tonia had won the chef's competition. Michele was heartbroken. She wanted Jeff to have the best chef but something about Tonia made her feel like she had to watch her back. She'd lost the chance to be Jeff's chef. It was over. Did this mean she would never see him again? Never touch him. Listen to his deep voice, his laughter. Kiss his beautiful lips.

Walking over to Tonia, she heard Jeff say, "You don't like the zabaglione?"

"Not one bit. Why did Miss Nicey-Nice get a do-over?" Tonia spoke loudly to ensure that Michele heard her.

He crossed his arms. "My competition, my rules."

She scowled. "I didn't mess up my hors d'oeuvres, and yet I didn't get to make a dessert. She gets special treatment, has since night one. That's not fair."

"You mean fair like when you lied to me about being able to ride horses? It was clear you'd never been on a horse and yet you told me you rode them on your grand-father's ranch every summer." His tone was loaded with sarcasm.

"That was different. I explained it had been a while. I was rusty. I thought you understood."

"About the horses, yes. Not the habaneros."

Tonia put her hands on her hips. "Excuse me?"

"How did you know to use those specific peppers to sabotage Michele's dish?"

Michele could see the hardening around Tonia's eyes. She was furious. "What are you implying?"

"I don't imply. I state. You spied on us 'night one' when I had Michele make the grilled cheese sandwiches."

Tonia blustered. "That's ridiculous. It wasn't me."

"Another lie. The cameras caught you on tape. I wanted to give you the benefit of the doubt for I, of all people, know how that feels, but it sure seemed like you were spying on us. Whatever the case, you did see Michele use those pep-pers and you'd know that I'd remember, too. It was easy to frame her that way."

Michele stood beside Jeff, facing Tonia. "You did it? Why?"

Tonia's dark eyes flared with anger. "Why do you think, Sex Kitten? You clouded his vision, made it so that no one else had a chance to win."

Jeff faced Michele. "She's right. You do cloud my vi-sion so that I can't see anyone but you. You're my choice, Michele. Please, stay."

* * *

Angel and Cristina were on their way to the building site when RW texted.

Come to the great hall.

Okay. We'll be right there.

"I guess the party was moved inside," Angel said to Cristina. They were just about to enter the hall when Cristina grabbed her arm and pulled her back into the corridor.

"Oh, my God. Antonia is here," Cristina whispered.

"What? No, that's impossible." Poor Cristina was so frightened that she was seeing gang members everywhere she looked.

"Look over there. The woman with the dark hair in the corner talking to that tall redheaded guy. That's her. I can see the *cuchillo* mark on her from here."

Angel leaned over carefully and peeked. It was the same young woman Angel had seen snooping around in RW's wing. She'd thought she recognized her voice. And sure enough, the woman had a knife tattoo behind her ear. She gripped Cristina's shoulder as if her ex-boyfriend's blade had stopped her own heart.

"What do we do?" Cristina asked.

There was no question, Angel had to protect the ones she loved. Where was RW? Taking out her cell phone with trembling hands, she texted him.

The woman talking to Jeff is Cuchillo's sister!

Jeff was furious. How dare Tonia sabotage Michele.

"We're done here. Tonia, pack your things and—" Jeff began.

"Don't move!" a guard said, his gun drawn and pointed

at Tonia. Two more guards joined him. Several people in the crowd cried out in fear and everyone scattered behind him.

"What are you doing? This is unnecessary," Jeff said. "Put your guns away."

Seeing guards and guns, Tonia lunged and grabbed Michele. Before Jeff had blinked, Tonia had a knife to Michele's throat.

"Get back," Tonia yelled. "All of you."

Michele's eyes were wide and pinned to him. The fear in them slashed him.

"Everyone, calm down!" Jeff lifted his hands and willed Tonia to look at him. "Let Michele go and you can walk out of here. No one will stop you."

"Sorry, son, but she can't leave." Suddenly, Dad was beside him, whispering so that only Jeff could hear, "She's one of Cuchillo's gang members. She'll kill Angel."

Jeff stopped breathing. His Michele was in the arms of a killer.

"I walk out of here now. Understand me?" Tonia snarled. Her blade looked deadly.

Jeff's heart hit the floor. "Don't hurt her!"

To Tonia, RW said in an incredibly controlled voice, "We don't even know why you're here. Why pull this elaborate charade in my home?"

"I told you in my application video. Family is everything. Something was stolen from my brother a long time ago. He wants it back."

"I know you're looking for Angel. She's not here," RW said.

Tonia's gaze swung from Jeffrey's to RW's and back again. "Liar. Your PI said you're hiding her."

Jeff swallowed hard. RW's private investigator had been killed by the gang. Had they made him talk?

"Angel's here. I can feel it. Since she liked horses, we thought she might be working in your stables. The chef interview was the opportunity to snoop around. Plus, I wanted to win."

"Get the hell out of my home!" RW roared. "Tell your brother to leave my family alone or I will come for *him*. Got that, Antonia? Cuchillo has never met a man like me. I'll send that bastard straight to hell."

Tonia's eyes widened at the threat. She released Michele and ran out the door. Michele slumped to her knees.

"I've got you, sweetheart." Jeff scooped her up and carried her to the couch. She'd been nicked. "Get me a clean cloth!" he yelled to the crowd. "Someone call the doctor."

RW sent one of the guards to follow Tonia and find the rock Cuchillo was living under. Cuchillo's gang had a knack for slipping off the grid and RW had lost the trail when they murdered his private investigator.

"Where's Angel?" one of the sisters said.

"Oh, Jeff. Did I ruin your night?" Michele's voice was so soft.

"No, sweetheart. You did everything right." Jeff held the cloth to Michele's cut and applied pressure. His heart was pounding so hard he thought it might explode. After a few minutes he checked the cut and was relieved to see it wasn't bleeding badly. "You're going to be okay, sweetheart." He wanted to carry her out of there and straight to his bed. He'd been so afraid for her and now he just wanted to touch her everywhere. Taste her. Feel her heart beating strongly against his bare chest.

"I was so scared," Michele said softly. She reached up and put her hand on his cheek.

"I know. Me, too." He ran the pad of his thumb along her cheek. He kissed her then, deeply, filling up all the dark wounds in his thundering heart, and let the world fall away.

Fifteen

Jeff had canceled his date for last night. No great loss. He hadn't been too excited about it anyway.

Right now, he was concerned about keeping Michele safe. He could have lost her and that thought alone terrified him.

After the doctor had checked her out and determined the flesh wound didn't need stitches, Michele said good-night and Jeff walked her to her room. He wanted her in his bed but didn't say so because she seemed exhausted. He bunked down in the room next to hers in case she had nightmares or needed anything. He didn't sleep a wink because he was replaying the whole evening, trying to figure out what he would have done differently. He wasn't impressed with his performance but Michele had been strong, courageous and thoughtful from the start of the catered event to the dramatic end. Her food, other than the sabotaged dipping sauce, was artistic and delicious.

Chloe had been right—the best chef had risen to the top. There was no doubt in his mind that Michele Cox was the chef for him. She'd proved that she was ready for the job and had bravely conquered her insecurities.

Jeff, on the other hand, was even more worried because the closer he got to Michele, the more he realized he was the wrong man for her. Hell, he and his screwed-up family had almost gotten her killed! He wouldn't have forgiven himself if Tonia had hurt her badly. He cared about Michele, wanted her, needed her more than he dared admit, but she couldn't fall in love with him. He wouldn't let her. It would kill him to hurt her like his father and mother had hurt one another. He wouldn't allow that to happen. He would have to get married to someone else.

When he heard her rustling around in her room, he knocked on the door.

Her expression was a mixture of happiness and surprise. "Jeff! Good morning."

He leaned against the door frame and breathed in her freshly showered scent. "Are you feeling okay?"

She touched the small Band-Aid on her neck. "Yes. I'm fine. It was just a scratch."

He breathed a sigh of relief. "Good. I've got plans for you. Thought we'd better get an early start."

Her brow creased. "Am I cooking or are we going on another outing?"

"Neither. You deserve a break. Plus, it has come to my attention that you've never been on a yacht before. And, as far as I can tell, you have not spent the day on the Harpers' private beach up the coast."

Her smile was so damned beautiful. "I can't say I have done either of those things, no."

He shook his head. "We'll have to rectify the situation immediately. Wear something warm for the morning and pack your bathing suit and a towel. I'll provide the picnic lunch. We need to celebrate your new job, Chef Cox."

Her mouth opened. "You really meant it last night?"

"Of course. I mean it this morning, too. I choose you, Michele. You're my chef."

She squealed and threw her arms around his neck. He stumbled backward, emotion warring inside him. Finally, he wrapped his arms around her and hung on. He kissed her right there in the hallway with her feet off the ground.

It seemed as if he couldn't stop kissing Michele Cox.

His new chef. The woman he wanted but couldn't marry. What in the hell was he going to do?

His yacht was amazing. So much rich, dark wood and shiny metal. It looked like it was brand-new. It was the biggest boat she'd ever seen and she was surprised when he called it "the small one." Apparently, RW had several yachts all over the world. She couldn't fathom it. But she did love being on the gorgeous vessel and was lulled by the movement and the peaceful sea.

They'd been cruising up the coastline for twenty minutes already, close enough to shore so she could see the jagged edge of the bluffs and the coves. She wished they could keep going to San Francisco, or Hawaii, until she remembered she had a job to do in Plunder Cove. She didn't have to dream of running away anymore. She'd be living in paradise and working in the career she loved again.

She'd figure out a way to bring Cari to Plunder Cove, too. Surely, there was a group home nearby who could take her. It would take Cari a while to readjust to the new place but Michele was sure her sister would love digging her toes into the sand and meeting the horses the Harpers owned.

And getting to sail on the blue Pacific with Mr. Sexy was a nice perk. She understood why he had pushed her away for a week. He was busy with the restaurant, and the competition had been difficult. Plus, he was distancing himself because they were two people who wanted different things. She agreed it was best they didn't spend too much time together because her silly heart always wanted more. She kept reminding herself that Jeff didn't want to, or was unable to, give her more of himself. She needed to be realistic. This connection they had wasn't going to last.

"Want to drive?" he asked.

"Can I?" She felt like a kid being handed the car keys for the first time.

"Come on over." He stepped back and made room for her. Tentatively, she put her hands on the wheel.

"Relax. It's easy." His deep voice rumbled in her ear, sending delicious shivers up into her scalp. And then he put his hands on her shoulders.

Relax? Her body heated up and her thoughts zeroed in on the way his large hands felt on her. Why had she worn a sweatshirt? She wanted his hands on her skin. He pressed into her and she could feel his hard stomach muscles against her back. How she wanted him. She closed her eyes and breathed in his scent. Her eyes flew open again when she remembered she was driving his expensive boat.

Besides, she had no business enjoying his hands on her body or daydreaming about his lips. She was going to be working for him and didn't have any idea what impact their new working relationship would have on their...situation. She didn't really know what to call their relationship.

They had smoking hot chemistry but that was the *easy* part. The dangerous part. When she was close to him she wanted to climb into his lap, let herself go, and take him with her to ecstasy. It was going to be hard enough working for him and wanting to kiss him every day, but she couldn't *relax* and let down her guard or she'd fall hard for him. She was already tilting heavily in that direction with her feet slipping. One more of his sizzling, mind-melting kisses might topple her defenses.

Giving in to her desire for him again could only end badly for her. He'd made it clear that he wouldn't fall for her. She'd be a fool not to believe his warning. No matter how many times she fantasized about Jeff Harper, he wasn't her dream man. He'd eventually marry someone else and she...she'd have to let him go. Which was going to be incredibly difficult now that she would be working for him.

Jeff directed her to pull into an alcove. He dropped anchor and turned off the engine.

He stripped off his sweatshirt and for the first time she

got to gaze at his lean, hard chest, arms and stomach in person. The pictures in magazines didn't do justice to his amazing physique. Her fingers itched to touch the red curls on his chest and trace each muscle all the way down the dark V into his shorts.

"Ready?" he asked.

Nope. Her defenses were crumbling. She was in serious trouble here.

He rowed the dinghy to the shore and she helped him pull it up on the sand. It was a pretty little beach with white sand and clumps of rocks at the water's edge.

He tossed his bangs out of his eyes and grinned like a kid. "I haven't been here in years. The old firepit is still there. And the inner tube Matt and I used to float around on. This is like a blast from the past. Let's see if we can catch a crab in the tide pools."

"Okay. Let me just put this blanket down and I'll catch up."

He gave her a thumbs-up and jogged to an outcropping of rocks. She smiled as she stretched the blanket on the warm sand. She liked seeing him like this. Boyish, not so intense.

She needed to watch herself.

She had no business playing with fire.

But she really, really wanted to. Once again, she had the desire to show him what love looked like. If only he could see how easy it was to let himself go, to allow himself to feel, then maybe he could open his heart to her. She believed a loveless man could learn to love. She wanted to give that gift to him.

And today—with the chef job lined up and her sister taken care of—she felt brave.

So when he jogged back and sat beside her she said, "Is this a real date?"

He ran a finger down her shoulder. "As real as it gets."

He hadn't seen anything yet. "I seem to recall our last

date was rudely interrupted. Can we pick up where we left off?"

He grinned. "You want to sit on my lap?"

"Yes. But, no. I have another idea." The last time she climbed on his lap things flew out of her control too quickly. If she was going to show him how to feel loved she would need to slow things down a bit.

"Lie back on the blanket."

His gaze was intense—curious and cautious—but he did as she asked.

"Now put the towel under your head. I want you to watch me touching you."

She didn't know what she was doing, and it was probably a really bad mistake, still every inch of her begged to get close to him.

He tucked a towel under his head and watched her.

Starting at his fingertips, she made slow, sensual circles around the nail beds and gently petted his knuckles. She traced each bone and vein she could see under the skin.

He had a fine sprinkle of freckles across the back of his hand. She rubbed his skin softly, slowly, feeling the hairs on his hand lift with her touch.

He had large, strong hands. Turning them palm up, she traced every line. She looked at him, silently asking permission to keep going.

"It feels good." His voice was rough.

She was feeling things, too. Lots of heat. Tons of want. She'd never touched anyone like this before, never wanted to. She couldn't seem to get enough.

She massaged his fingers, pressing deep into the pads of his thumbs. He curled his fingers around hers, giving her hand a squeeze, like a hug.

"Your arms now." Why was she whispering? They were alone on a private beach.

She circled his wrist bones, dragged her nails up his forearm and then softly rubbed her way back down toward his wrists. Goose bumps rose on his arms. She pressed harder and smoothed them back down. Squeezing his biceps, she marveled at the muscles beneath her hands. Turning his arm over, she used her nails and soft touch along the length of the underside of his arm. His skin was smooth, not freckled on this side, silky. The bend of his arm was a kissable spot and she put her mouth there, pausing.

"Don't stop. Keep going." The growl in his voice made her look up. His gaze was intense.

She felt an answering zing in her core.

"Shoulders." Her voice was huskier than normal. She squeezed, massaged and ran a feather touch over his shoulder muscles.

God, he was so beautiful.

She ran her palm over his collarbone and dipped her fingertip into the hollow of his neck. She could feel his pulse beating fast there. He was breathing faster now, too, as was she. This slow, burning touch was working her up quickly.

Honestly, she'd been burning since that incomplete night on the coast. Maybe longer.

She caressed his neck. She ran the back of her fingers over his strong square jaw and chin.

She didn't want to miss one inch of him.

His eyes watched her every move. That sexy look was giving her goose bumps of her own. She wanted him. Inside her. She'd never felt such a desperate heat before her.

His lips twitched as if he knew what this was doing to her. If he gave her his signature cocky grin it was game over.

She cleared her throat and pressed her legs together against the ache building there and placed both her palms on his pecs. She made circles over the muscles and played with the nipple.

"Michele." Her name came out as a sexy growl that turned the heat to full melt-level. "Don't stop."

She rubbed the nipple again and twisted his chest curls. "I love your red hair."

"There's more to play with."

She lifted her eyebrow and looked down. *Oh.* He was fully aroused.

She was losing control of herself.

Very slowly, she caressed each stomach muscle of his gorgeous six-pack, working her way down. His breathing was fast now, almost as fast as hers. She circled his belly button with her middle finger and gently tugged on the hairs below it. Those were fun to play with, too, but she wanted more. Lifting her head, she saw heat and desire in his expression.

Good, she wasn't alone.

She ran her hand over his shorts, pressing against his erection.

He sucked in a sharp breath.

"Jeff?" she said quietly. "I want to kiss you."

The groan he made was music to her ears. He reached for her. Running his hand through her hair, he made a loose ponytail and gave it a gentle tug so that her chin tipped up.

She was looking into his eyes when he said, "Oh, babe. I want you."

It was as if she'd waited her whole life to hear those words. She pulled his shorts down and took him in her mouth.

This she needed.

Michele was touching him in a way he'd never experienced before.

With reverence.

With smoking heat.

Like she adored each millimeter of his skin and couldn't get enough of him. It was driving him wild. He was hard and wouldn't be able to hold on much longer. All this from her touch? Hell, what would it be like if he was deep inside all that heat? He needed to make love to this woman right now.

When she put her lips around his erection and sucked, a light show went off behind his eyeballs.

"Michele, stop," he somehow managed to say.

She pulled back, quickly.

"I'm too close. And I want to be inside you."

"Oh," she said softly.

He sat up and slid the bathing suit straps off her shoulders. He nuzzled the hollow of her neck and her moan almost made him lose it. "Sorry, sweetheart. This is going to be faster than I'd like but I want you too badly to wait. Take your suit off and I'll get the condom."

Thank God he'd decided to bring one.

She nodded. Her eyes were hooded with desire.

They were both ready. She was on her knees on the towel and beautifully naked.

"Hell, you are so damned gorgeous," he said and pulled her on top of him.

Skin-to-skin, her breasts to his chest, thighs pressed together, hearts beating hard, and he had one thought—*she's perfect*.

When she eased him inside and all that slick heat encased him, he closed his eyes to memorize her touch, everywhere.

And then she started moving and all thoughts left his brain.

She gripped his shoulders and her pace was fast. Apparently, she was close, too. He eagerly joined in the race to glory.

Cupping one of her beautiful breasts, he had the fleeting thought that he wished he could have spent time sucking and kissing her warm body.

Next time.

He sucked her nipple. She arched her back and cried out, coming quickly. He smiled and flipped her over so that he was on top. She wrapped her legs around him. Holding on to her thighs he went deep.

"Oh, yes, Jeff."

He kept going, loving the sexy smile on her face.

A few more thrusts and she cried out again, sending him over the edge. The light show going off behind his eyelids was better than Independence Day.

Michele and her gentle touch—her sparkle—was exactly what he'd needed. For the first time in a long time, he was free.

Sixteen

She didn't know how much time had passed, but she was hungry. Apparently, Jeff was, too.

"What do we have here?" she asked, rolling over to examine the picnic basket. "Did you make us lunch?"

He nodded. "Ham and cheese. My specialty."

"Can't wait to try it."

They sat side by side, legs touching, chewing in silence. Something had shifted between them, more than just giving in to sex. She could almost hear him thinking. But she didn't pry. Didn't ask the questions burning on her tongue.

He took his last bite, rolled the plastic wrap into a ball in his hand, and that's when the words poured out. "When I was six years old, I only ate mac and cheese."

"My sister was the same way! We had to trick her to try other foods."

"No tricks in my family, just demands. 'Eat your food, Jeffrey.'" He raised his voice to sound like a woman's. His mother's? "'Clean your plate or you won't get any food tomorrow.' That sort of thing."

"That's harsh."

"Sometimes I preferred to *not* eat. Like seafood night. Hell, I really hated squid."

She pressed her other hand to her heart. "I knew it. You didn't like my first dish! I wish I had made chicken."

He swallowed hard. "You didn't know. What happened

to me when I was a kid wasn't reported in the gossip rags. Families don't talk about crap like this. They cover it in dirt and pretend it's dead."

She didn't dare interrupt.

"So yeah, back to the story. I was a picky kid and one night when I refused to eat, my mother said she'd had enough of my whining. Seafood pasta was her favorite dish and by God, her son was going to eat it without a peep. Dad wasn't there, but she made everyone else pretend that I wasn't there, either. After several minutes of being ignored, I threw my plate. Shrimp and noodles slid down the wall. I'd never seen my mother that angry before. She grabbed my arm and dragged me outside. I whimpered, but she said, 'Don't be a baby!' and pushed me inside the toolshed. 'Cry and I'm never letting you out.' And then she locked the door.

"Matt had told me to stay away from the shed because snakes crawled under the crack in the door. It was dark. The cold seeped in. I screamed until my voice was hoarse and my throat was raw. I tried to find a tool to dig out, but they were too high for me to reach. I dug in the dirt with my hands, but the ground was hard. It was freezing cold and I believed I was going to die in that shed all alone."

"Oh, Jeff!" Michele covered her mouth. She'd been psychologically beaten down by Alfieri, but she had been an adult at the time, one who could walk away from her abusive boss. Jeff had been a small child. She couldn't imagine what his mother had done to him deep down inside. She quivered with the need to touch him.

"When did she finally let you out?" Her voice cracked and her eyes burned with tears.

"Mother?" The chuckle he produced was sandpaper rough, humorless. "She didn't. She wanted to teach me not to be a crybaby. Emotions were a sign of weakness in her world. I understand now that something was broken in her genetic makeup that made it impossible for her to love anyone. She passed that broken gene to me."

A person incapable of loving? Michele still didn't believe it.

"I'm sorry, Jeff. No one should ever treat a child like that."

"You're crying." He gently wiped her cheek with the back of his hand.

Softly she said, "Emotions are human, normal. Especially for a little boy. Your mother should've known better. What did your father do when he found out?"

"Mother told him she'd ordered the staff to bring me in and they refused. It was a lie. Donna, the cook, heard me crying the next morning and found me curled up on the dirt floor of the shed. I'd wet myself from fear. When she opened that door, I ran to Donna and held on like I'd never held anyone. The staff banded together and told my mother that if she came into the kitchen, they'd all quit. Since my mother had no idea how to cook for herself, she agreed. I was safe from her in the kitchen." He tossed his hair off his forehead. "To this day, I don't like to eat alone or be in small dark places. That's why I don't usually take elevators."

She frowned. "But the GIF. You were in an elevator with a maid."

"Right. I was getting to that. The GIF was orchestrated by the hotel owner to ruin me." Absentmindedly, he stroked her hand. She hoped touching her calmed him as much as it did her. "Finn had threatened physical harm if we filmed his hotel. It was the first time a hotelier had been so aggressive. It made me wonder—what was the guy hiding? I took my own camera inside. Michele, I could bury Finn with the negative press on the kitchen alone. You would've been horrified."

"So, you got it all on film?" She watched his finger make lazy circles on the top of her hand and felt the touch all the way to her bones.

"And then some. Employees told me about bad workplace conditions. Safety violations. Codes ignored. Cover-

ups and payouts. It was going to be the best episode ever."
He let out a deep breath. "It'll never see the light of day
because Finn stationed guards near the stairs, forcing me
to take the elevator. I didn't have a choice. I had to get the
tape to my producer. Stupid, rookie move. I should've expected Finn would pull some sort of devious stunt but this
was…" He shook his head.

She was starting to understand. "Because you are uncomfortable in small places."

He laced his fingers with hers. "Yeah. I was already
shaking when I got into the thing but there was a maid
inside, so I tried to act cool. But when the elevator got
stuck…" He shook his head. "It was one of my nightmares
coming true."

She could feel his palm sweating and gave his hand a
gentle squeeze.

"Then the maid removed her blouse."

"She *what*?"

"Yeah, that seemed strange, but women do weird things
for celebrities. I was still pressing buttons to get the elevator going when the woman grabbed me and kissed me."

Michele's mouth dropped. "No! She was a total stranger!"

"It happened so fast. Nothing seemed real. When she
started grinding against me, I woke the hell up. I tried to ex-
tricate myself. Gently. And then the lights went out. Blackness inside a box with only a slight crack of light under the
door… It was like the shed. I was disoriented, terrified.
When something grabbed my ass and pinched… I fought.
The elevator lights came back on. The maid was on her butt,
cussing up a storm. Her bra was torn. Her hair a mess. She
had a red mark on her cheek."

The torment tangled in his starburst irises made her want
to hug him, but she didn't move for fear he'd stop talking.
She sensed he needed to get this out.

"Finn had tampered with the elevator, turned off the
lights and paid the maid to come on to me while recording

the whole thing. Releasing the first part, the sex scandal bit, ruined my career. He's holding the second part—the section that looks like I attacked the maid—as blackmail," he growled.

"She kissed and grabbed you! How can he use that against you?"

"Blackmail works best when the victim is caught on tape. People believe what they see, even a lie."

Shame heated her cheeks. Even she had believed Jeff was having sex in that elevator.

"This isn't fair! If a man had grabbed me in an elevator, I would've fought back, too, Jeff. Don't be ashamed. You did nothing wrong."

"Sweetheart, I'm six foot three and over two hundred pounds. Lots of muscle. She was tiny. You are tiny."

Something in his tone worried her. She cocked her head, trying to read his expression. Why did he mention her?

"I'd never hurt a woman, Michele, I swear." He looked at his hands as if he had weapons attached to his fingertips. "I have bad genes. I'm not good at relationships or connecting with people the right way. What if I am exactly like my mother?'"

Now she understood. "Oh, Jeff." She touched his face tenderly. "Have you talked to anyone about this? A doctor or therapist?"

"This is the first time I've told anyone this stuff. You don't understand. I'm trying to improve my reputation. If any of this gets out—my childhood, what really happened in that elevator—the Plunder Cove hotel will be done. I need to see this dream to the end. I need it to be the best it can be."

"It will be."

It had to be.

For both of them.

They didn't talk any more about his past—or his fears of what his future held—instead they had a nice day on the beach, exploring the tide pools, bodysurfing in the waves, walking on the sand. They held hands, kissed and talked. It had to be the best day she'd had in years.

They were making out like teenagers on the blanket when a speedboat pulled into the cove. Jeff started to sit up and Michele turned to look, too.

And saw a telephoto lens pointed at them.

"Get down," Jeff told Michele as he covered her head with his arms.

But it was too late.

The camera had caught him and a woman in a compromising position. Again.

Seventeen

They scrambled to grab their stuff and hop in the dinghy to make it to the yacht and catch up with the photographer. Jeff didn't care as much about his reputation as he did Michele's. Everyone already thought he was a playboy. Michele didn't deserve to have her name and personal details dragged through the dirt. If he could catch the guy, he'd talk some sense into him and pay whatever it took to kill the shot. "Hold on," he told Michele, glancing over his shoulder to make sure she was safe before he floored the yacht across the waves. He drove the boat like a madman for a few minutes before he acknowledged the truth.

It was too late. The cameraman had a speedboat and knew how to use it. Jeff slowed the vessel. Running he hand through his hair he faced her. "Sorry. There's no chance."

Her chin was high but he could see the worry in her eyes. "What will he do with the photos?"

"It'll be okay. Come here, sweetheart." He took her in his arms.

She lifted her head and the usual sparkle in her eyes had turned to flashing fear. "Those private pictures of us were…intimate."

Dammit. He saw all too clearly how he was messing up her life. "He'll sell them to the highest bidder. I'll get the PR team on it, see if we can buy them before someone else does."

"And if they can't buy them? What if Finn did this as another way to destroy you? He'll post them everywhere."

Yeah, he would. A firestorm raged inside his gut. How could he protect Michele?

"We have to stop Finn," she said with fierce determination.

He ran his finger down her cheek. "This is my fight, not yours. I shouldn't have dragged you into it. You shouldn't be with a guy like me."

She wrapped her arms around him and pressed her cheek to his bare chest. "What if I want to be with a guy like you?"

He sucked in a breath. Her words were a soft rain on the fire in his chest.

"Even with all my past?"

She rose up on her toes and pulled his lips toward hers. "Yes."

That night, Jeff slept alone. He'd kissed Michele goodnight and told her he had work to do. He'd worked with the PR team until dawn to no avail. They couldn't find any information on the photographer in the speedboat.

He'd never really worried about the women in his paparazzi shots before. This time he did care and would do anything he could to keep her out of his press.

What was he going to do about Michele?

Being with her had changed him.

Despite the paparazzi interrupting his and Michele's last kiss on the sand, he felt like he'd become a new man overnight.

He'd never found a woman he could talk to like her. Hell, he'd told her things he'd been afraid to admit to himself. Yet she hadn't run, hadn't judged. And she'd touched him like no one ever had—with reverence, kindness, and heat that had rocked him to the core.

Damn, they had sizzling chemistry. Even though he hadn't slept the entire night and had to get his head into the job at the restaurant site, he was still aroused thinking about their time on the beach. He wanted her now.

He slipped a note under her door.

"Please join me for dinner tonight. Yes, it's another date. Say yes."

He couldn't wait to see her naked again and drive deep inside her—maybe in his shower and then in his bed. Maybe twice in his bed.

At dinnertime, he called it a day at the building site and headed back to the house to find Michele. Since the chef competition was over, Donna and the rest of the cooking staff had come back to work. He was happy to see them, but a little disappointed that Michele wasn't in the kitchen. He'd grown accustomed to seeing her sweet face screwed up in concentration as she cooked. Not to mention her cute ass bending over the oven.

He was getting hard just thinking about her.

Only one thing to do…bound down the hall, take her in his arms and show her how much he'd missed her. When he got to her room, she was talking on her phone and sitting on a lounge chair on the balcony. The setting sun framed her in golden light and the ocean breeze lifted her long hair. He watched her stare out over the gardens.

God, she was stunning. His heartbeat sped up and there was a strange warmth filling him. He'd never felt anything like that before. It both scared and awed him.

"Yes, I see why you were in total lust with Jeffrey Harper," she laughed. "I get it. Boy, do I get it."

He grinned. She was talking about him, huh? He liked that more than he dared admit. Would she talk about his blue eyes, his red hair or his six-pack? Those were the three things most articles mentioned about him.

"He's a good man," she said.

Her words stunned him like a flash of sunlight on a black day. No one had ever called him a good man before and hearing it from her lips melted something hard that had been lodged in his chest. It also worried the hell out of him.

He wanted to be the man Michele thought he was. But there wasn't anything good about him. That wasn't going to change. He'd sleep with her for a while, make sure she had a good time, but then he'd have to follow through with his promise to his dad and find a wife.

The idea didn't sit well with him anymore.

"It happened fast, but yes," she went on softly. "I'm falling for him."

Warning bells rang in every part of his psyche.

She can't be in love with me.

Michele went on, "Please, don't let Cari see the picture of us at the dinner party. She'll think I'm marrying him and that's not going to happen. We want different things."

That knocked him back.

Michele didn't believe they had a future together, either. It was the truth. He needed to marry someone he couldn't hurt.

So why did her words sting so damned much? He turned around and walked away.

Michele was disappointed when Jeff hadn't come to collect her for dinner last night. One of the staff had dropped off a note that said Jeff had work to do and she should eat without him. He seemed to be extremely busy working on the restaurant.

The next morning, still dreaming about that beach encounter, she went into the kitchen and found the regular staff in place. She smiled and introduced herself to them. When an older woman with white hair named Donna stepped forward to shake her hand, Michele hugged her instead.

"Thank you for taking care of Jeff," she whispered in Donna's ear. "He told me about the shed."

Donna pulled back with wide eyes. "He told you?"

Michele nodded. "The secret is safe with me."

"Oh, sweet girl. Jeff has needed someone like you his entire life." Donna pulled Michele into a huge bear hug.

They nodded at each other, insta-friends.

"What can I make you?" Donna asked.

"Actually, I was hoping I could jump in here with you and make a lunch for Jeff." Her brain was overflowing with recipes. Her cooking muse was back.

"Of course! He'd love that."

"I won't get in your way. I'm leaving in a few days anyway."

"What? No, you can't go."

"I've got to go back to New York to collect my things, pay rent and figure out how to bring my sister to California. But I want to do something nice for Jeff before I go."

"Sure, hon. My kitchen is your kitchen."

Later, Michele went down to the job site. The framing was finished. The restaurant seemed to be coming along faster than Jeff had said it would. It made her realize that she had a lot to do to be ready for opening night. She'd ask Donna if she could use Casa Larga's kitchen to create new recipes for the restaurant. Her brain was bubbling over with ideas.

Jeff came out of the building. He wasn't smiling and he didn't come close enough to touch.

Why the distance?

"Michele, what are you doing here?"

"I brought you lunch."

"That wasn't necessary."

She frowned. His vibe was all wrong. Was he mad at her?

"I know. I wanted to…" *See you. Touch you. Kiss you.* "…feed you. That's all."

He took the bundle from her hands. "Thanks."

She stood there, wondering what was going on with him. "So…"

He waited.

Okay, then.

He was busy or in a bad mood. She rushed on. "I won't take up any more of your time. I just wanted to know if I could go home for a couple of weeks to check on my sister. I miss her terribly. You know, if there was one thing I could change it would be to have her live with me. She needs round-the-clock care but I am sure there must be group homes in California, even if I have to drive a ways to get there."

She saw a subtle shift in his demeanor, a softening. But it passed quickly. He crossed his arms over his chest, closing himself off. "Fine. Distance between us is probably a good thing right now."

She blinked. "Jeff, what's the matter?"

He stepped closer and she could feel the intensity rising off his body in waves. "You can't love me, Michele. I won't allow it."

Her mouth opened. "Excuse me?"

"I told you. I'm broken, just like my mother. I sure as hell don't want to hurt you, of all people. God, Michele, you're special. Sweet. The gentlest person I've ever met. It'll kill me to cause you any pain. That's why we should stop seeing one another, except professionally."

You can't love me. She didn't know how he'd known, but it was the truth. She was starting to fall for him.

She couldn't help it.

"Jeff…" She reached for him but stopped, not wanting to see him recoil from her touch. "Maybe if we give it a little time—"

"I'm almost out of time."

"What do you mean?"

Instead of answering her question, he said, "Go home and see your sister. I'll give you three weeks to decide if you still want to work for me, knowing that I have to marry someone else."

Her heart broke. "You have to? Or want to?"

"It's not my choice. My father has made it part of my

work contract. I have to marry someone when the restaurant is finished."

If her jaw could have hit the dirt, she would be tripping over it. "That's...months away."

The muscles in his jaw flexed. "I keep hoping I can change his mind, but he's a stubborn bastard."

None of this seemed real. He'd slept with her knowing he would be marrying someone else? "Who...?"

He lifted his hands. "I haven't found a bride yet."

"This is crazy! Your father can't make you do this."

"He can. I promised I would abide by the contract. I signed it." He exhaled through his nose. "Listen, I'm sorry. Not for what we had, that was amazing, but I can't get you messed up in my family drama, because you are too important to me."

"As your chef," she clarified.

"And I hope as a friend. But I leave the decision up to you. Think about it while you are in New York. If you don't want the job, I'll call Freja. I never wanted to hurt you."

He turned and walked away.

The kitchen stoves and appliances arrived that same day.

Jeff was busy directing the installations and didn't think about Michele, much. But when the sun went down and he had to eat dinner alone, their discussion weighed on him. The hurt look when he told her he was still marrying someone else tore him up, especially knowing that he'd put that sadness on her beautiful face. He cared about her, more than he should. Letting her go was for her own good. Once she was in New York she'd see he was lousy boyfriend material. She deserved so much more.

God, he should've chosen Freja for his chef. At least then he wouldn't torture himself every time he stepped into the kitchen. He wasn't good about abstaining from treats he couldn't have. Not being able to kiss Michele would be hard. That is *if* she decided to return. For her own good she should never return. But for *his* good? He still wanted her beside him. What a selfish bastard he was.

Even now he wanted to see her, touch her, inhale her sweet perfume. He went to find her to apologize for being so harsh earlier and beg her to stay. But he found her room empty. She'd already left.

What if she didn't come back? Had he lost his best chef? The only woman he'd ever cared about?

This was RW's fault. Dad was the one making Jeff get married. If he didn't have that stupid cloud over his head, he could date Michele and not worry about the future. They could simply enjoy one another for a while. Be together for as long as it lasted.

He didn't want to think about his own role in creating this heartache.

He stomped into RW's wing determined to make his father change his demands. He passed the guard and stepped into a dark hallway.

"Dad?" he called. "You in here?"

No answer. Frowning, Jeff turned on the hallway lights and knocked on RW's door. Music was playing inside. A strange foreboding came over him. Something wasn't right. He opened the door and stepped into total blackness. He fumbled around to find the light switch and was startled to see his father sitting at his desk drinking bourbon while a Mexican song blasted.

His father didn't drink. As far as Jeff knew, he didn't speak Spanish.

What the hell was going on?

"Dad? What's wrong?"

"Angel left. She took Cristina and the boy and drove away. How can I stay here and…breathe? I can't do this, any of it, without her. She was the only person who saw past this…" RW slapped his own chest "…this stupid man."

Jeff had never heard so much pain in his father's voice, in anyone's voice. "Where did she go? Is she all right?"

The look in his father's eyes was heart wrenching. It reminded him of the pain he'd been pushing past since he'd ended things with Michele.

"I don't know. How can I protect her when she won't let me? She said she couldn't put me at risk. Me! As if I wasn't dead before she started treating me."

Jeff ran his hand through his hair. "Let's go after her."

"No, dammit! Cuchillo will expect me to follow her. It's too risky." He grabbed Jeff's collar. "Swear you won't go after her."

Jeff gripped his father's wrist. "Fine. We'll wait for her to contact you."

"I'm not a patient man."

Jeff snorted. "Yeah, I know. But unless you have a better plan…"

RW shook his head and lifted the bottle to his lips.

Jeff pulled it away. "That's not helping. You stopped drinking, remember?"

"For Angel. She told me I couldn't see what was right in front of me from the bottom of a bottle. But without her… I lost my family and now my…angel. I'm alone." RW slumped over his desk.

"You're not alone. I won't leave you." Jeff hoisted RW up from under his arms. "Come on, Dad. Let's walk it off."

The next morning, Jeff woke up and cracked his back. He'd had a lousy night's sleep in the chair beside his father's bed. But at least his father's problems had kept Jeff's mind from lingering on Michele.

RW opened his eyes and cursed, gripping his head. Jeff handed him two aspirin and a bottle of water.

"Glad Angel isn't here to see me like this," RW said, his voice gravelly.

Jeff shrugged. "One bad night. Put it behind you and do better."

RW lifted his lips in a half grin, half grimace. "You

sound like her. Of you three kids, she worried about you the most."

"Angel worried about me? Why?"

"Chloe told us about what your mother did to you in the shed and Matt told us that you worry you can never fall in love."

Jeff bolted up. "What the hell? You all sat around talking about me behind my back?"

"To help you, son. That's what families do." RW rose, too, swayed a little and put his hands on Jeff's shoulders. "I swear, I didn't know your mother left you out in the shed."

When RW grimaced that time, Jeff wondered if it was hangover pain or from imagining what his little boy had gone through. Part of him wanted his father to feel real pain. A white-hot poker of justice.

Something to block out his own pain over mistakes made.

"Bullshit. How could you not know how she was? Why didn't you stop her, Dad?"

RW nodded. "You're right. I should've been there to save you. It was my fault, Jeffrey. That's another thing on me that I need to make amends for, a bad one. Give me the blame and let your shame go."

Weakness seeped into Jeff's legs. "I need to sit down." He'd never heard his father accept the blame so quickly, and then apologize. It knocked him back, and he crumpled into the chair.

"Listen to me, son. You're nothing like your mother. You are ambitious, thick-skinned and strong. That's why your mother took her anger out on you. Not because you're like her, but because you are like me. She probably didn't even know that's why she picked on you so much."

Jeff blinked. RW had never been this open with him before.

"Another thing, I know you think your mother was incapable of loving. That's bull. Your mother loved me until I got sick. Something broke inside me and I couldn't love her anymore. I got mean and hurt her, too. Together, we raged World War Three on one another and destroyed…everything. I was too deep in my own hole to understand at the time, but I see now. Angel showed me the light."

Jeff hung his head between his knees. His limbs were heavy. "I don't know what to say."

"Say you're done hiding from your own damned feelings. Your mother and I hurt you badly and you don't want to hurt like that again. I get it. Trust me, I do, because you are like your old man. But if you don't let yourself feel, you'll never truly live. I want you to live, son."

And then, without any warning, RW wrapped his arms around Jeff.

For the first time in his life, Jeff buried his head in his father's shoulder and held on.

Eighteen

Michele flew to New York like a regular person—no chartered jet, yacht or limo. It was strange to be in New York again. Nothing had changed, except her. Days passed and she still felt out of place in her own home.

During the day, she stayed with her sister and answered the hundreds of questions that Cari's caregivers asked about the Harpers. They all wanted to know what Jeff was like in real life. The more Michele talked about him, the more she missed him. It was a sweet ache that wouldn't go away.

Did he think about her?

When she was back in her tiny apartment, she whipped up recipes one after the other. She kept a pad of paper on the countertop and by her bed so she could write down the rainbow of flavors that fired inside her brain.

Joy. That's what it felt like. Her cooking anxiety was gone.

So, apparently, was Alfieri's voice. Cooking for Jeff had silenced the negativity inside her.

She was free.

Man, she couldn't wait to create some of these dishes for Jeff. He'd love her mildly spicy chicken parmigiana. She smiled, thinking about how much he'd loved the grilled cheese sandwich she'd made for him. That was the first time she'd kissed his spicy lips and he'd asked her to eat with him.

Who was eating dinner with him now?

A horrible thought stopped her pen—what if he was married by the time she returned? Could she work for him then? She honestly didn't know if she could. It would hurt too badly. Her pain would be bad enough but watching him self-destruct with a person who didn't care about him, who maybe only wanted his money or fame? She couldn't bear the thought.

A friend. That's what he said he wanted her to be. Would a friend let him do something that would end up harming him?

No, she had to stop him from marrying a woman who would not love him. Because, heaven help her, *she* loved him. Desperately. Without question. She'd never loved a man before but she understood that love was about risks and she was willing to risk it all for Jeffrey Harper. She wanted him to be happy. She wanted to make the rest of his life sweeter than he could ever imagine. To do that…she would have to be brave and go for what she wanted—him.

Biting her lip, she knew what she had to do.

She called him and was disappointed when his voice mail picked up. How she'd wanted to hear his deep voice.

"It's Michele. If you still must get married…" Screwing up all the courage she could muster, she said, "Marry me. We're good together. Really good. Friends with benefits. I want you to be happy and I can make you happy. I know what I'm getting into. Please, call me back and we can…" she laughed "…plan a wedding. Call me."

She hung up and stared at her phone. Did she just ask a man to marry her?

Falling back on her bed she laughed out loud. Yes, she did.

Jeff was busier than he'd ever been but he couldn't stop thinking about Michele.

Would she come back?

And if she did, would he be able to keep his hands off

her? He didn't think so. All he'd thought about, dreamed of, imagined since she left was Michele. He was glad he didn't have his cell phone with him at the site. He couldn't stop checking social media or searching the web for pictures of her. When he found nothing, the hole in his heart widened. He turned his phone off and buried it in his sock drawer.

RW showed up at the building site, looking ragged and drawn. Like a strong California sundowner wind would blow him off his feet.

"Hey, Dad. Have you heard from Angel yet?"

RW shook his head. The muscles in his jaw flexed. "I'm working another angle so she feels safe to come back once and for all."

Alarms went off in Jeff's head. "What sort of angle?"

"Taking the fight straight to the bastard himself. Cuchillo invaded my home. Now he'll see what that feels like."

Jeff didn't like the sound of this plan. "Ah, that sounds dangerous. I'm not sure you're up to that sort of fight, Dad."

The flash of fury in his father's eyes startled him. "I'm exactly the one for this fight. He hurt Angel and will pay for that. Don't worry, I'll make sure our family is protected."

Now Jeff was thoroughly worried. He would talk to Matt and figure out what the old man was planning.

"Dad…"

"I'm done discussing this." RW ended the conversation by walking around the building to check out the progress. Typical Dad move—walk away when he didn't want to hear any more.

Matt and I will figure it out.

Jeff continued working. It was all he could do with so much on his mind.

When RW reappeared ten minutes later, he said, "It's coming along."

"Yep. The kitchen will be fully functioning by the end of the week. Just have the rest of the dining area to finish up."

It was the first time he'd seen RW smile since Angel

left. "I'm proud of you, son. This project is just what we both needed."

Warmth spread inside Jeff's chest. "Thanks, Dad."

"I haven't seen anything online from Finn lately." RW frowned. "I wonder what he's up to."

"Maybe our lawyers scared him off."

"Doubtful. I'll check into that, too. Okay, son. I'll leave you to your work."

Jeff watched his father walk away and wondered what *he* was up to.

Almost two weeks had passed since Michele left. It felt like a thousand. When was she coming back? Would she? The questions haunted him night and day. Jeff and Matt were insulting each other and playing an extremely aggressive game of pool when RW stomped into the pool house waving a newspaper. "What in the hell is this!"

Chloe rushed in behind him. "Dad, some of those go back to the start of the year before Jeff came home."

Jeff walked around the pool table to see what they were looking at. The headline read, "Jeffrey Harper's Harem." Below that were two pages filled with pictures of him on dates.

"No way. Are those women you've dated *this* year?"

Chloe bit her lip. "I have our image guys on it. But I'm not sure what they can do to help you, Jeff. These appear to be real pictures."

Matt cocked his head. "Oh, look, there's Michele Cox. And there she is again at the beach."

Jeff pressed his fingertips to his temple. "Finn did this."

Chloe nodded. "Sounds like something he'd do."

"I don't care who took the pictures. I've already gotten angry calls from shareholders. You're supposed to be building a respectable image, Jeffrey. Not—" RW slapped the page "—a harem."

"You told me to find a bride!" Jeff yelled.

"I didn't tell you to date every female in the northern hemisphere. You're sabotaging your career and hurting the family in the process. It's time to choose. Marry one," RW ordered.

Jeff wasn't ready to discuss it. He didn't know when he'd ever be ready to marry.

The only woman he'd made love to recently was Michele. She saw through the television celebrity image, the rich Harper prince, the cocky hotel critic, and saw the real him. Messed up childhood and all.

No one else got him like she did.

He didn't want to think about what that meant.

"What are we going to do about Finn?" Jeff asked instead.

"Leave him to me. I'll settle the score but we need him to come here. I can't go to New York, in case Angel needs me here. Plus, I'm working on something."

Jeff and Matt exchanged looks. So far, they hadn't figured out what RW was planning to do to Cuchillo.

Chloe studied RW's face. "How will you get Finn here?"

"I'll invite him to come see how the restaurant is coming along. Jeff, make sure your chef is ready to make him a meal he will never forget."

"When? Michele is not due back for another ten days." Jeff's gaze went to her picture. The one on the beach was his favorite. He traced her jaw with his finger.

"Michele Cox is not coming back. She tendered her letter of resignation this morning. To me," RW said.

Jeff turned around so quickly that the room spun. A low hum of despair started at the base of his tailbone. "She quit?"

"That's what happens when you let people down. She called you several times and you refused to call her back. Don't you understand what I am trying to teach you with this project?" RW's voice was raised but there was a thick undercurrent of sadness in it. "The townspeople. Our employees. People we care about. Harpers don't get to crap on anyone anymore. You lose good people that way...for good. I expect better of you."

Jeff slammed his hand on the pool table. "I didn't get her calls, Dad."

"Jeff, I bought you a new phone. Is it not working?"

"It's fine. It's just...my phone is... I turned it off. Social media was destroying me." He didn't explain that it was more the lack of seeing Michele anywhere than seeing his negative posts that were killing him.

Chloe said. "Did you bury it in your sock drawer like you used to?"

"Hey. How did you know I hid things there?"

Chloe smiled. "You're still the same. You know that? You always hid the good stuff there. Candy bars, comic books... I'll go get the phone."

Matt patted his shoulder. "Explain it to Michele. It's just a misunderstanding."

"Is it?" RW's nostrils flared. "Did you treat her badly, son? Could she have seen this two-page spread this morning and decided she didn't want to be another notch on your bedpost?"

Jeff opened his mouth. No words came out.

"If you want to be respected, you have to treat people with respect. Why can't you learn from my mistakes instead of making the same ones? This is yours to fix. Figure it out." RW stomped out the same way he came in.

Matt shook his head. "We really need to find Angel. Are you okay?"

No.

His mind was spinning, searching for answers. Jeff scrubbed his face.

She quit?

He'd really thought she'd come back, even if they couldn't be together anymore.

"I'm fine." His voice was full of gravel.

Matt rubbed his shoulder. "Of course, you are. Hey, you know what's different in these pictures? I just figured it out."

"You're still looking at those? Give it a rest."

Was Dad right? Had Michele seen this, too? Did she feel like just another woman in his bed? Hell, he could see her sparkle even in the grainy black-and-white shots. Could feel her touch way down deep.

She was nothing like the others.

"No way. Look. This is too good to pass up." Matt sounded amused.

Jeff didn't want to look. He'd forgotten many of their names already.

"It's a bunch of women I dated, so what?" Jeff snarled.

"No, jackass. Look at *you* in the pictures. Here's your ugly mug with all these women. Serious, glum, bored, practicing your multiplication tables in your head..." He pointed across two rows. "Now look at you with Michele. Both pictures. See the difference?"

Jeff leaned in closer. "I'm smiling at her."

"Bingo. A real smile, man. Like you feel it down to your toes. You are into her, totally and completely. At least, that's what I see in those two photos and not in the others. Hell, if I didn't know better, I'd say that guy in those two pictures with Michele—" Matt grinned. "That dude is in love."

Jeff looked closer and saw what Matt recognized. He seemed like a different person in the photos with Michele. A person he'd never seen before.

He *was* different with Michele.

A surge of heat flooded his gut. It wasn't love, it was... hell, he didn't know what to call it. But it was...something.

Chloe raced in, out of breath, and shoved the shiny new phone toward him. "Here. Play the voicemails and call her right now. Tell her...tell her anything, something. She's good for you. Get her back, Jeff."

He stepped away from them and listened to the messages. All ten of them.

The air was sledgehammered out of his body. He slumped onto a bar stool and listened. A lump was in his throat when he closed the cell phone and faced his brother and sister.

"Matt, can you fly me to New York tonight?" he asked.

Matt raised his fist to the air. "Hell, yeah! Let's go get her."

"No. I have a score to settle with an asshole named Alfieri. That's all."

Chloe's eyes were full of concern. "What did Michele say?"

He swallowed but the damned lump wouldn't move. "She asked me to marry her. A few times. Eight, I think. Then waited for my answer. When I didn't call, she told me she never wanted to see me again. Another man had stolen her joy once, and she wasn't going to go through that again."

Matt sucked in a hiss of breath. "Go talk to her, bro. You can fix this."

The heat in Jeff's gut begged him to race after her, grab her, kiss her until she changed her mind and came home with him.

But his mind knew otherwise.

"She's right. I'd only break her beautiful sparkle. Crush her joy. I don't deserve her."

Matt made a half grunt and used one of his little boy's catchphrases. "No, duh."

"Matt!" Chloe slapped Matt's arm.

"What? He *doesn't* deserve her. That's a given. We Harper men are totally screwed up. But here's the thing…" Matt wrapped his arm over Jeff's shoulder. "The right woman can make you a better man. I'm proof. I wake up every damned day amazed that Julia sees anything in me and go to bed praying, begging, that she never stops. Without her, I'm nothing. With her, I'm Matt on steroids, a flipping superhero." His grin was full of awe. "With all the powers."

"Go to her," Chloe said. "Love her, Jeff."

He couldn't. He didn't know how.

Nineteen

Michele was moving on. That's what she told herself.

What choice did she have, since there was no going back?

She'd laid it all on the line for him, and he hadn't even called her back to blow her off.

She owed Jeff a lot for helping her to see clearly and get her cooking mojo back. He'd taught her that she didn't need any man to tell her who she was. Michele Cox was still a kick-ass chef. The voice in her head was her own. She was small, but she was also mighty, and she had the power to take care of herself and her sister now.

She was alone, yes, but she didn't have time to dwell on it because she had three good job offers already. She would decide which one to take by the end of the week. Her goal now was to save enough money to start a restaurant of her own. A small one. Nothing like the posh restaurant Jeff was going to have, but it would be great. It would be hers. Stickerino's, she might call it—after the horse who carried the heroine to the pirate's treasure.

How she wished she could have kept the pirate as her treasure.

But he didn't want her, or at least, not enough.

So, she was moving on and she would stop thinking about *him*.

Eventually.

That was her plan anyway, until that two-page newspaper article hit all the stands with two pictures of her kissing Jeffrey Harper and her short-lived romance became the topic of conversation everywhere she went.

And the paparazzi found out where Cari lived.

Jeff had intended to come to New York for Alfieri, and Alfieri alone. He hadn't planned on seeing Michele, but now he had to. Because he had her money in his pocket and had a question to ask her.

Or that's what he told himself.

About seventeen times.

But his insides were thrumming with heat and excitement at the thought of seeing her again. *Just to give her the money and ask her the question*, he reminded himself for time number eighteen.

He didn't dare get too carried away. She probably hated him for not calling back after her emotional, heartfelt messages. And he knew he'd done the right thing by letting her go.

And yet, he still wanted to kiss her.

When he pulled up in front of her flat he couldn't help but notice the photographers. They were like a committee of hungry buzzards waiting outside. She didn't appear to be home. Good. He pulled up directions to the group home where he'd paid her sister's rent and sped off.

Dammit, reporters were parked outside the group home, too. Why in the hell were they bothering Michele's sister? Putting on a baseball cap, he walked inside.

The attendant at the front desk looked up warily. "Can I help you?"

"Hope so. I'm looking for Michele Cox."

When she saw who he was she squealed and then told him he'd just missed her. Michele had taken her sister to horseback riding lessons. The woman gave him the directions.

The vultures had beaten him to the stables, too. Police

had been called and they and the stable owner were pushing the photographers off the private property. When an officer asked him what business he had at the stable, he said he was there to pick up one of the riders—a woman with special needs and her sister.

"I'm the owner," a woman said. "I'll let you pass if you tell me the name of the rider you are here to pick up."

"Cari Cox," he replied. "Her sister is Michele."

The woman grimaced. "Oh, good. Michele must've texted you, too. I was just getting ready to call one of my stable boys to come back to work and go rescue them."

"Rescue them?"

"One of the photographers opened the gate and went into the ring to get a picture of Cari, which, as you probably can guess, didn't go over well. She doesn't like strangers. She started screaming, the horse spooked and ran out of the gate with Cari on its back. Michele ran after them and then she got injured—"

"Michele is injured?" His heart just about exploded in his chest. "Where is she?"

"She texted that she twisted her ankle and can't walk. She can't make it to where Cari's horse is because the terrain is steep."

"Where? Can I drive there?"

"No. Can you ride?"

"Yes."

"Then take my horse. She's saddled up and ready to go. I'd do it myself but I have to make sure these nutballs don't sneak back onto my property—"

"Text Michele. Tell her to sit tight. I'm coming." He would fly if he had to. He stopped telling himself lies about why he'd come to New York because he needed to hold her and kiss her pain away.

"That was fun! Really fast. I was like Rosie," Cari squealed and giggled in delight.

"Sure, laugh. It's all fun and games until your sister nearly breaks a leg running after you."

"You dance funny."

That's because Michele had stepped in a hole and twisted her ankle. "I wasn't dancing."

Out of nowhere came the memory of Jeff's hands on her hips at the dinner party. Now those were real moves. She shook it off. She didn't have the time or the stamina to be heartsick. What did it matter that she missed him like crazy? He'd made his feelings clear by not returning her calls.

"Can you give your horse a little kick and steer him toward me? I can't hop on one foot that far. And this other one is…" She looked at her leg. It was terribly swollen already. Oh, God, was it broken? "It's not good."

"My horse likes the grass here. He's hungry."

"He gets plenty of food in the stables. Let's take him back there where he can have a proper dinner and I can get some ice for my leg, okay? Come over here so I can ride with you."

"No. You are too heavy. Only one cowgirl on each horse."

Michele cursed under her breath and tried hopping on one foot. It was no good. The path was rocky and steep. Cari's horse had found a grass-covered mesa at the top of the hill. How was she going to make it up there? Crawl?

"Ahoy, there. Need a lift?" A voice called behind her.

She couldn't see the man, but she was overjoyed that the owner had sent someone to rescue her and Cari.

"Yes! But please, don't spook my sister's horse."

It took a small feat of balance to be able to turn her body on one foot without slipping down the steep embankment. By the time she did, the horse and rider were already beside her.

"Did someone order a cowboy from California?" he asked.

She blinked. No. It couldn't be.

"You're not real."

He laughed then and her heart did funny things in her

chest. "Tell that to my horse." He slid down and stood beside her. His starburst baby blues seemed to take her all in. "Are you hurt?"

She pressed a hand to her heart.

Oops, did he mean her ankle? "It might be broken."

He bent over and checked it out. When he touched her leg, she bit her lip to keep it from quivering, not entirely from the twisted ankle pain either.

Jeff is here.

Why? What does it mean?

"I don't think it's broken, but you twisted it good. Let me help you up on the horse so we can have a doctor look at it. Do you want the front or rear seat?"

She realized there wasn't much room for him to sit behind the saddle. "Rear."

Once he got her situated on the horse, he swung his leg over and sat in front of her. She had a sudden dilemma. Should she touch him? For the moment, she kept her hands to herself.

"My sister is over there." Michele pointed. "She's pretending to not see you."

"I can see that. What am I supposed to do?"

"Cari, this is a friend of mine named Jeff. He's very nice," Michele called out.

"The pirate!" Cari clapped her hands.

Oh, dear. "Um. Yes." Michele leaned over and whispered. "Sorry. Someone must have mentioned your family history. Cari's favorite book has pirates in it."

He grinned. "So, Cari, how would you like to go with me and your sister on an airplane back to a pirate's castle?"

"Yay!" Cari cheered. "Right now?"

"What?" Michele said. "You can't just tell her things like that."

"Listen, sweetheart. It's not safe for you two to be here by yourselves right now. I saw the paparazzi. They're everywhere because of me. Let me fix it. If you aren't around here, they'll leave after a while."

"But, I have a life here. A job to accept."

"It will all still be here if you want it, but I was hoping you'd change your mind about the resignation and come back to Plunder Cove. For good. If…you'll accept my proposition. But first, let's go get your sister, okay?"

She stared at his back. *Proposition?*

"Okay?" he asked again.

"I…don't know what I'm agreeing to."

"Fair enough. Tiny bites. First, we rescue your sister and that fat horse."

"I agree."

"Great. But I'm not moving until you wrap your arms around me. Safety first."

Tentatively, slowly, she wrapped her arms around his waist. He took her hand and pressed it against his chest. Capturing it next to his heart. She could feel the strong beat beneath her palm. He felt so good in her arms, even when she knew he didn't feel the same way about her. Her heart was cracking from the bitter sweetness of it all. She wanted to stay like this forever, touching him, breathing in his manly cologne, listening to his deep voice. Holding out hope that he wouldn't say he didn't love her. Again.

"That's better." His voice was hoarse. "Hell, I missed you so hard. Please, say you'll come back with me."

Her inhale caught in her throat. The only word she could muster was, "Why?"

"I'm miserable without you. I still need a chef, and that job is still yours, but you deserve more. Which reminds me…" He reached into his pocket and pulled out a thick envelope that seemed to be full of…money? "This is yours. I had a little chat with Alfieri. He was overcome with the desire to pay you what he owed you. With interest, of course."

"That's…no. Now I know you're not real. I must have hit my head when I twisted my ankle."

"Does this feel real?" He lifted her hand and kissed her knuckle. Then he turned her hand over and kissed her palm. "Or this?"

"Yes," she said softly. She felt those kisses all the way down to her throbbing ankle. It was all she could do to not beg for more. "I'm so ashamed. I should never have let Alfieri treat me like that."

"Sorry, sweetheart, but that's pure bull." He swiveled around and pinned her with his gaze. "He assaulted you with his words and actions and robbed you. You have nothing to be ashamed of. I'm glad you got away from him and I told him so…in something like words."

"You didn't hurt him, did you?"

"Hell, I wanted to. But I think my old camera crew will hurt him far more than I could unless he agrees to change his ways. They'll pop in on him and interview the staff on a regular basis just to make sure he's a kinder, gentler Alfieri. So that he doesn't do to others what he did to you."

"Thank you."

"There's more. I found out he'd promised you a partnership in the restaurant and that's when the coincidence hit me. I need a partner in *my* restaurant while I build and run the hotel. Someone I trust. That's my proposition. Will you be my partner?"

She cleared her throat. "In the restaurant?"

"What do you think? We can get the finest care for your sister and you two can live together again. It's perfect."

Almost.

"What about your wedding plans?"

His shoulders stiffened. "RW may not like it, but if you agree to come back as my partner, I'll break my agreement with him."

"You won't get married?"

"No." He swiveled so she could see his face. He went on, "And you and I can focus on our careers. I can take care of you and your sister and together you and I can create the best restaurant the world has ever seen. Say yes."

"And we, the two of us, will be real partners? Nothing more?"

He stiffened again. "You are much more. You are important to me, Michele. I hope you see that. I don't want to jeopardize our...relationship, or our restaurant, in any way. I need you."

She sighed. He would never love her. "I see."

It wasn't the partnership she'd been hoping for—it wasn't the one she'd bet her heart on when she'd left him those voice messages—but she'd get to be with him and she'd be doing what she loved.

She'd spent too long without what she wanted and even if he never loved her back, she would take everything he'd give.

"I say yes."

She put her head on his back, breathed in his most excellent manly smell and took a second to notice all the places they were touching.

Just then Cari's horse decided to come down and join theirs.

"Weeeee!" Cari said. "Let's go to the pirate castle."

Twenty

The day arrived. Finn had been invited to Casa Larga to see the restaurant and taste some of Michele's new creations. RW knew the bastard would come. Finn owed him.

RW met him in the circle of the driveway. When Finn got out of the limo with a swagger, RW's blood boiled.

"Hello, old friend." Finn held out his hand.

RW took it and shook, but then he squeezed, dug his nails in and refused to let go until he had Finn's full attention. "You were only supposed to threaten him. Convince him to leave the television show and come to work for me. That was the deal."

Finn squinted and yanked his hand back. "It worked, didn't it?"

"I didn't tell you to attack my son," RW snarled.

Finn shrugged. "Attack him? I sent my best girl in there. Jeffrey was the one who went ballistic. What in the hell is the matter with him?"

"Nothing," RW said.

The problem is mine.

All RW wanted was what was best for his son. Creating hotels was in Jeffrey's blood, in his heart. RW had done everything he could to convince Jeff to design the hotel at Plunder Cove, but that damned show, *Secrets and Sheets*, got in the way. RW had taken drastic measures to put an end to it by asking Finn to nudge Jeffrey in the right direction.

That had been a mistake.

RW was heartbroken to see that he'd been responsible for Jeffrey's internal struggles. It all stopped now.

"I want the videos and the photos to end. Hear me? You are done," RW said through gritted teeth.

"I hear nothing but hot air whistling in my ears, Harper. I'll stop when I have the episode he filmed of my hotel. That's my deal."

RW's hands clenched into fists. Rage pounded behind his eyeballs.

Chloe came out the front door, effectively ending the clandestine meeting. "Mr. Finn! Welcome. Please follow me to the restaurant. It is not finished yet, but the kitchen is fully functional and we have seating in the courtyard." She guided him to a comfortable table next to the firepit. "Enjoy!"

Jeff walked outside to the patio. "Finn, I can't say I am happy to see you."

There was a loud crash inside the unfinished restaurant. A drill, somewhere around the back of the site, made a horrible grinding sound followed by cussing.

The commotion made Finn grin. "Your restaurant is just as I imagined it."

"We're still getting the kinks out."

"I can only imagine that your hotel will be just as kinky." Finn picked up his cell. "I'm going to film this meal and Tweet it."

"Great." Jeff hoped Michele was ready. "Red or white wine?"

"A glass of each."

"Of course." It was a struggle not to grab the man by his collar and throw him out, but Dad had a plan—something he hadn't completely shared with his sons.

Imagine that.

Finn was working on both of his wine glasses when Michele softly called, "Order up."

Jeff picked up the plate. Michele had made her signature chicken cacciatore but the sauce was better than Alfieri's. Michele had fed him an early spoonful and he thought it was the best thing he'd ever tasted—next to Michele's lips. He missed her mouth and running his hands over her body.

Finn took a bite and rolled his eyes. Overwhelmed, he mumbled, "Holy crap. It's better than sex."

Jeff lifted his eyebrow and Michele nodded. They'd heard Finn all the way in the kitchen, since RW had bugged the table.

"Round two," Jeff said before he left the kitchen.

"Give him a knockout punch for me." Michele winked.

Damn, she was amazing.

Having her as his partner in the restaurant should've been a dream come true. She was the perfect, hardworking professional who created the best meals he'd ever eaten. If anything, she was too perfect, too dedicated. He was the one who had trouble focusing with her so near. He longed to sweep her away and find quiet moments for just the two of them. But he didn't, because they'd made a deal and he was determined to hold up his end of it. No matter how much he hated it.

A professional relationship with Michele wasn't enough. For the first time in his life, he wanted more. Something big was pounding inside him, burning to get out, struggling to have a voice to tell her what he probably knew all along—he wanted Michele. Forever.

He doubted she'd ever want him. Not after he'd let her walk away. He should have fought for her, begged her to stay in his life, instead of offering her a simple partnership. It wasn't enough. He'd blown it.

To Finn, Jeff said, "How's it going? More water? Another bottle?"

"More food. This is the best damned meal I've ever had."

Finn shook his head, his eyes already having trouble focusing. "You did something right. Your chef is brilliant."

"I agree. But she is more than a chef. She's my partner. The best part of me." He hoped she heard that.

"Bully for you. What's for dessert?"

"Get ready, because Michele's tiramisu is the best, sweetest thing you will ever taste. She has her own secret spices from Italy plus a rare organic cocoa from a small farm in Ghana. You will swear you have died and gone to heaven."

"Enough jaw-flapping, Harper. Bring it on!"

Absolutely, you arrogant prick.

He went back into the kitchen. He'd done his job sparring with the man; it was time to let his dad deliver the final blow.

RW sat at the table across from Finn. "Enjoying your meal?"

"I have never tasted anything like it. Such a pleasurable surprise. Where did you find your chef?"

"Jeffrey found her, not me. But I'm going to tell her not to serve you anything else unless you stop releasing clips from Jeffrey's sex tape."

Finn snorted. "You call *that* a sex tape?"

"What would you call it?"

"I don't know. A Photoshop masterpiece? It's flawless. I dare you to find anyone who can tell where I sliced the sections together."

"What about the woman? Is she really a maid?"

"No. She's one of my best hookers. Gorgeous tits. Sweet ass. She really brings in the dough, so I only charge her a small referral fee."

"Pimp commission, you mean."

Finn sipped his wine. "Tomato, tomato."

Listening in the kitchen, Michele sucked in a breath. "Did you know Finn ran a brothel in his hotel? "

"Some of the employees I interviewed hinted at something going on behind the scenes," Jeff said. "He's a real creep."

"And he made it look like you had the sex issues! I can think of stronger words than 'creep.'"

They continued to eavesdrop on the conversation outside.

"Interesting discussion," RW said. "So now that I've fed you a great meal by Chef Michele Cox and let you be the first to experience this amazing up-and-coming Plunder Cove restaurant and hotel, I want to ask you nicely to stop blackmailing my son."

Finn shrugged. "No can do. I haven't gotten what I want yet. Wait until you see what I do with the next segment of video. With a little cut and splice wizardry, the world is going to think your son is one twisted sucker."

"Why are you doing this?" RW growled.

"You know why. He still hasn't televised how fantastic my hotel is. I need people to believe it's perfect. There's a lawsuit breathing down my neck."

"You want Jeffrey to lie to the public."

"Well, damn, RW, I can't have Jeffrey telling the truth! I watched what he filmed on my own security cameras. That episode would bury my hotel. I'd be run out of New York. That's why I had to create the fake sex tape. Your son has too damned much integrity to be pressured into turning over that episode. He wouldn't listen to reason."

RW crossed his arms. "And that's where he and I differ. Integrity? Not so much. Fierce determination to protect what's mine? You haven't seen anything like me. Guards! Take this scumbag off my property."

Finn laughed. "Right. Good one. Where's my tiramisu?"

RW picked up the tiny camera stuck to the flowerpot. And pointed to the recording device on the bottle of wine. There was another one under the table and a third one under his chair. "Seems like you are the one caught on tape, Xander. It's going to be a great commercial for the restaurant."

"You wouldn't dare."

"I'm releasing the part where you talk up the food. That's good stuff. If I see even one more shot, video, GIF—*any-thing*—on the internet about Jeffrey, I don't care who posts it, I'll release the entire video shot tonight to the press. All of it. Understand me?"

"But…" Finn sputtered. "I thought we had a deal."

"We do now. Good luck, Xander. Do not cross me."

Michele stood in the kitchen beside Jeff, listening to every word. When Finn started demanding his dessert, she fed it to Jeff bite by bite. She had absolutely no intention of giving anything more to that vile Finn.

He'd blackmailed the man she loved to try to force him into lying. How preposterous was that? Jeff didn't lie.

"Holy sweetness, Batman. This is amazing," Jeff said with his mouth full.

"Catwoman. I had the costume and everything."

He cocked his eyebrow. "Babe, I'd love to see you in that costume." He waggled his finger for her to feed him more. With each spoonful, his eyes rolled back in pure delight. The look did wicked things to her. How she wished they were still dating.

When they heard the guards throwing Finn off the property, Jeff said, "I don't need to have my producer give me the Finn hotel episode now. Finn just sealed his own fate."

Michele cheered, "We did it!" And jumped into his arms.

The kisses on his cheeks, jaw, neck and lips? Well, she couldn't stop them if she tried.

And she hadn't tried.

Somewhere in the back of her mind, she sensed that it was a mistake. They had a deal to be partners only and she'd kept her side of it until tonight. But his lips were an intoxicating mix of dark chocolate, cinnamon and rum. Everything began to spiral out of control. His hands dove into her hair and held her head as they devoured each other's lips.

God, he tasted and felt so good.

She barely registered that he'd sat her down on the counter. All her thoughts were centered on this man. His tongue plunged inside her mouth. His hands roughly grabbed her butt.

She wanted more, needed more. Wrapping her legs around him, she pulled him closer until she could feel his thick erection pressing against her panties.

"Michele." The way he growled her name melted her.

If this was a mistake, she was going to make it big-time.

He was hard and she was desperate. She ground herself against his zipper. "Please," she begged. "I need you."

His groan of desire made her wet.

He cupped her through her panties, pressing his thumb against her nub, and nearly short-circuited her brain. She tossed her head back and arched as he rubbed in circles. Panting, she was in a frenzy to get him inside her.

She wanted to come with him. Biting her lip, she unzipped his pants.

His eyes were blue pools of hot desire. "Condom." He yanked his wallet out of his back pocket and took out a silver packet. When he was ready, he lowered her until he filled her.

This. Was. Perfect.

He started thrusting and she held on to his shoulders, rolling with him. Taking him in as deep as she could. "Michele." That growl again.

With each thrust, he said her name, never breaking eye contact. "My Michele."

He took her higher and higher until her body screamed for release and yet she tried to hang on so they could come together because she'd wanted him for what felt like forever. She needed this one moment to last for as long as she could stretch it out and save each second of it in her memory. She'd keep it locked away in her cracked heart, safe, perfect for the times when she was lonely. Alone. Love with Jeff was beautiful and so hard. It broke her even now as she knew he'd pull away again, needing to push her out of his arms because he couldn't feel what she did. He didn't know how to let himself fall for her.

"Sweet Michele," he said with a contented sigh against her neck. He was spent. She let herself sail away with him.

A few minutes later he said, "Don't move."

Move? How could she? Her body was a puddle of happy pudding.

He disposed of the condom and came back to wrap his arms around her. Against her neck he said, "One of these days, I want to take my time with you. Go slow."

Tears pricked her eyes. He was thinking of a future with her. "Slow, fast, I'll take you any way I can get you." She still meant it. She'd risked it all over and over for him, and she'd do it again. There was only one thing she craved in return—his whole heart.

Her body pulsed with her need for Jeffrey Harper and because she couldn't contain her emotions any longer, she let them out. "I want to be with you, Jeff." She loved him. Pure and simple.

"I'm right here, babe." He nuzzled her neck. She sensed that he was distracting her, trying to steer her away from the discussion to come. He knew what she was going to say.

Her insides crumbled because she thought she knew what he was going to say, too, still she pressed on because she had to hear the words. "Are you? Or will you push me away again and tell yourself you can't have a real relationship?"

That's when she saw it—something sharp and raw twisted his beautiful face. He stepped back. "What do you want me to say?"

"The truth."

He swallowed hard, as if his throat was coated with sand. "I've always told you the truth."

"Not about your feelings. Those you shield, protect and bury deep. Say what you think about me, about us. Not what you worry we'll become but what we really are."

He shook his head, his blue eyes clouded. "I don't want to hurt you, Michele. I never did."

"The only way you'll hurt me is if you don't let yourself hang on to what is real and special, standing right here in front of you."

"Michele, this isn't easy for me." A thread of warning rumbled in his voice. He didn't want to talk about his feelings.

She couldn't stop now. "Remember when you said you wished you could feel something real? Feel this." She pressed his hand to her chest. Her heart was pounding hard. "Please, Jeff, I need you to see the man I see—an amazingly gorgeous guy who is worthy of love. Don't you see that, too?"

He didn't answer for a long moment. Tipping his head toward the ceiling lights, he let out a deep exhale. She could tell he was struggling. "When I look at myself, I see a guy who has a restaurant that needs attention and a hotel to finish." He rubbed her arm, slowly, sensually. "Standing next to a beautiful and amazing chef who is going to put our restaurant on the map. I don't want to screw this up."

Damn. He just did.

She'd wanted to believe he cared for her so badly that she'd ripped her heart out of her own chest and handed it to a man who'd warned her he couldn't love her. She couldn't do this anymore.

A tear dripped down her cheek. "Being the head chef of a five-star restaurant isn't enough. I want more for you and need more for me. I wish you could see us like I do."

Until Jeff was brave enough to trust himself and her, she had to step away. She wouldn't give up the job she loved, but she needed to let the man she loved slip through her fingers. She had to let him go.

Everything hurt. It was almost as bad as the day Mom died. She couldn't breathe, but her legs, they could move. She fast-walked outside.

"Michele, wait!" he called after her.

She kept going because she didn't want to see him or hear any of his pretty words. Especially not the way he said her name. None of it was as real for him as it was for her. It never would be.

"Stop!" he called. "Please don't leave. I don't want to lose you."

She turned around and was surprised by the sadness she saw in his eyes and the tenseness of his jaw. "I'm not leaving. I love what we're creating together in the restaurant. I just… I can't date you anymore if you don't care about a real future with me. It's too painful."

He kneaded his neck, as if trying to release the tension she could see in his body. "I'm not any good at this, Michele. I've never been in a relationship before and I don't want to fail you. Hell, I wanted to protect you. From the press, my family, from me."

"From you?"

He stepped closer, his gaze boring into hers. "Yeah. I don't deserve you. I never did. But the truth is that I want you, Michele, more than I can say, more than I ever thought possible. I started crushing on you the first time I saw you on television cooking with such finesse and poetry in action. I've fallen hard every second after that." He wrapped his hands around her waist. "I'm not me—the real me— without you. Please, give me a chance to show you what I feel."

He pulled her to him and kissed her then and the whole world started spinning around her like she was flying. After several minutes he finally pulled back, pressed his forehead to hers and gazed into her eyes. "Did you feel that?" he asked. "I love you, Michele."

She blinked and tears sprang off her eyelashes. "You love me?"

"Hell, yes, with everything in me." His voice choked with emotion. "I'm a mess, sweetheart. I've never felt like this before." His words flowed out like the breaking of a dam. "This—you and me—it's intense. Consuming heat, burning need, but good, too. Warm and sweet. Your touch heals me. When you left, every part of me ached. I was ill with the need of you. Starved for your touch. The wanting of you tore me up inside. I love you so damned much that I can't think straight. I was afraid to admit it, afraid of who I'd become if I let you love me. I don't want to hurt you like my parents hurt each other."

Her heart was so full it hurt. "That won't happen because you are not them. You, Jeffrey Harper—" she held him as tightly as she could, their hearts pounding together "—are mine. We'll figure this all out together." She wrapped her hand around his neck and pulled his lips to hers.

When they finally came up for air she said, "I love you, too."

He exhaled. "Hell, that makes this next part easier." He linked his fingers with hers and kissed her wrist, sending shivers up her arm. "I had a whole thing planned out for tonight. Been working on it for days, but you sort of messed up my timing. Not that I'm complaining about how you preempted it."

"What thing?"

"Sunset yacht cruise up the coast to our beach. Bonfire. Champagne. This." He pulled a box out of his pocket.

She gasped.

He cupped her cheek with his big, warm hands. His gaze bored into her soul. "If you'll let me, I'll be the guy by your side, your partner in life. The one who encourages you and touches you as deeply as you touch me. I want to fall asleep to the rhythm of your breathing and wake up wrapped around you. You inspire me and make me laugh. You heal me and warm all the coldness inside. I want to do all those things for you and more. Much more. Let me be the man who makes *you* happy. Please let me love you for the rest of our lives. I promise I'll get better at it. I'll talk to a therapist, do whatever it takes to get brave for you."

He dropped to his knee in the grass. "Michele Cox, will you marry me?"

She squealed, "Yes! Oh, Jeff, yes!" And then she dropped to her knees and kissed his spicy lips.

Epilogue

The small crowd filed in, taking their seats in chairs by the wedding pagoda at Seal Point—the place where Jeff and Michele had their first date under the canopy of stars. The waves crashed below and a mocking bird sang an artistic medley while Jeff snuck around the back of the restaurant to steal a peek at the bride.

Cari was in the doorway shifting her feet side-to-side, watching her dress swish with her movements.

"Hey, pretty lady. Where's your sister?"

"In there." Cari pointed to the dressing room. "Michele said you aren't supposed to look."

He grinned. "Aw, come on. Just a quick peek. Maybe a big old kiss."

Michele's voice came from somewhere inside. "Tell that sexy man out there to save his kisses until he says, 'I do.' And no peeking!"

Cari screwed up her face in confusion, trying to remember all the words. "She says, um…"

He pulled Cari into his arms. "I heard the bossy woman. I can give you a kiss on the cheek, though, right?"

"Yep. You're gonna be my big brother."

"Can't wait." When he kissed her cheek, Cari giggled. "Okay, tell my love to hurry up. I'm dying out here. She needs to come out and be my bride right now."

Chloe rounded the corner. "Get out of here! It's bad luck.

And you don't want to smudge her lipstick. We just got it right." Then she kissed him on the cheek. "Love you. Now get up front."

"Fine. So many bossy women in here. I'm going."

"Jeff!" Michele called out.

He didn't stop to wonder why she'd called his name. She needed him and that was all that mattered. Screw bad luck. He ran past his sister and Cari and into the bridal room.

Gorgeous didn't begin to describe Michele. She was so beautiful that he couldn't breathe right and his lips felt wonky and his eyes were too full. His legs were full of sand.

"Do you still want to marry me?" Michele asked. "Now's your chance to call it off."

He forced his sand-filled legs to wobble toward her. Her eyes scoured his face, stopping on his lips. Did she see them trembling?

"Sweetheart, I have never wanted anything more. I love you, Michele. With all my heart. Please don't doubt that, but…"

Her lip started to tremble, too. "But?"

"You are so much better than me." He swallowed. "Do you really want to marry *me*?"

She let out a long breath. "Hell, yes."

He kissed her then and smudged her lipstick all over the place.

The wedding was running late, but he didn't care. He'd kissed his bride. All was well with the world.

When he was standing by the pagoda, butterflies of anticipation filled him. Michele was finally going to be his.

Matt bumped his elbow. "You've got this, bro. Just keep your eyes on her. She'll pull you through. I knew she was the one for you. Knew it all along."

RW nodded at him. "We all knew it."

Sure you did, old man.

Jeff took an extra moment to assess his father's demeanor. His eyes were clear, but there was still tightness around his mouth and eyes because Angel hadn't come home. No one knew where she was. Dad was dealing with it by "working the angles." Jeff was only starting to understand what that meant.

Matt had friends in the Bureau who'd slipped him intel that RW was working with the FBI to go after Cuchillo. That scared Matt but Jeff understood that a man would do what he had to do to protect his woman and bring her home safely. Besides, RW knew what he was doing. Jeff had a strong sense that the thing with Finn had started out as RW's devious plan to bring him home. The man was a scheming genius.

If Jeff hadn't met Michele, he'd be furious instead of grinning his fool head off right now.

The music started up and Jeff squinted to see the love of his life. If this wedding didn't happen soon he was going to combust. He was desperate to start his life as a married man with his sparkly bride. He was going to love her with everything he had and then learn how to love her even more.

Just then, a car roared up to the parking lot and the back door flew open. Jeff couldn't see who it was but he sensed the sudden tension in the air. Red heat covered RW's face and his eyes fired up with an intense, unnamed emotion. Matt's face was pale and his body rigid.

Who was it? Jeff still couldn't see.

A figure stepped out of the car, walking toward them with clipped, deliberate movements.

And then he knew.

"Oh, hell." Jeff turned to Matt. "Who invited Mom?"

* * * * *

SIN CITY SEDUCTION

MARGOT RADCLIFFE

To Nicole

CHAPTER ONE

PARKER JONES LOVED her job. Didn't just tolerate it like some of her friends whose chosen careers made the Sunday scaries look like a slasher film, but really loved it and couldn't imagine doing anything else. Except possibly swimming-pool-raft model; those people always seemed super happy, and lounging in water with beverages was a skill she'd be happy to cultivate on a professional level. In reality, however, she was a food writer for the online magazine *Gastronomic*, so her days out of the pool were spent traveling and eating delicious food across the country, her current city being Las Vegas.

And as she watched Hugh Matteson, ex-NFL quarterback and owner of the restaurant she was currently reviewing, saunter across the floor of his extremely successful barbecue joint, Blue Smoke, she couldn't help but add another bullet point to her gratitude list.

Decked out in a deep violet suit with a white

shirt, lavender pocket square and no tie, he looked like he had the world on a string, a confident smile curving his firm lips as if he'd never not had a reason to be happy. Medium brown hair, clipped short, was pushed back and sideways away from his forehead and was just basic-bro enough to ground him in the realm of the living. His jaw was square and strong, the likes of which would compel Gaston to take up facial exercises. Sharp hazel eyes (she'd googled him, obviously, because research) were lit with an enterprising spirit she recognized in her own.

One of his big paws was casually shoved into a pants pocket, sure and easy as if everyone he spoke to was a friend and not a complete stranger. Straight white teeth completed the picture, but she knew that one of his incisors was crooked. A pale white scar, nearly two inches long, was etched across his left cheek and another jagged one separated his right eyebrow into two parts. In some of the photos she'd seen of him he'd worn a steel bar with a screwdriver piercing in the space between the sections, but it was absent today. Apparently, that's what his former teammates called him, the Screwdriver, because he never stopped driving. She didn't quite get it, but apparently, football or whatever.

He wasn't handsome; that was a silly, pale word to describe the sheer mass of man and the obvious contradictions that made up Hugh Matteson, ex-athlete, successful businessman and, lest she forget, tabloid fodder. Even before her research, she'd recognized his name from the constant press coverage his breakup had received. Several years ago, his fiancée dumped him. Not such an extraordinary story, but the timing was unforgettable. The breakup came shortly after his career-ending injury and mere weeks before their wedding day, and then was brutally followed by said fiancée's elopement to this very town with the guy who replaced Hugh as the New York Comets quarterback. It would have broken lesser men, but no one looking at Hugh now would ever guess that he'd once been the most pitied man in sports.

He exuded sheer magnetism and Parker felt an electric pull in the pit of her stomach that she rarely, if ever, felt. Part of why she loved her job was because it freed her from her responsibilities home in Chicago, also known as her father, who was still recovering from the fact that his wife (and Parker's mother) walked out on them nearly fifteen years ago. Her life on the road was hers and hers alone. The fact that Hugh wasn't relationship material wouldn't stop her from having fun with him. Because he looked like he could be a veritable Disneyland in bed.

As a rule, all her relationships ended the next morning anyway, because she was on the road most weekends and rarely home, but also because attachments weren't really her thing. When your own mom walks out on you, it tends to shake your faith in the reality of commitment.

Returning her attention to her plate of barbecue, she had to admit that she was tragically underwhelmed by the food. So having fun with the owner, who, considering his lackluster food, was the only smoking-hot thing in this particular barbecue joint, was probably a bad idea. There was an air of the generic everywhere, in fact. The floor-to-ceiling wood paneling and sunbaked longhorn skulls perched high on the walls screamed typical roadhouse decor, but it was something she could forgive because it was Vegas, the city that had invented camp, forgotten it, and then invented it again. It was better than the sports theme she'd expected at any rate, so points for that.

Pulling out her tablet, Parker began typing her initial thoughts for the review she'd write later. She'd ordered nearly everything on the menu, including two sampler platters consisting of sausage, brisket, ribs, pulled pork, salmon and chicken along with corn bread, collards, baked beans, and mac and cheese. The different barbecue sauces themselves were bland, which was downright heresy for a barbecue place. The smoke on the meat was just enough, but it was obvious that they used the same kind of wood to smoke all their varieties of meat, which was such a cop-out.

She managed to type out a few notes, but kept getting distracted. Hugh was working his way around the perimeter of tables that ran along the outside wall and eventually she abandoned even the pretense of working to watch him. Smiling at a blue-haired woman in an I Heart Las Vegas sweat-shirt who had reached out and taken his hand, the corners of his eyes crinkled and lit up his whole face, which without the smile tended toward men-acing. Her breath stopped at the sight, not quite a catch because she was a grown woman, but edg-ing in that direction. His free hand abandoned his pocket and covered the woman's hand in his, a warm two-handed grip, before he crouched to get down to her level so he could hear her better. Parker had no idea what the woman was saying, and her expression was serious, but by the end of the con-versation they were both laughing.

Then as if in slow motion, Hugh rose from his crouch, turned and caught Parker right in the act of blatantly staring at him. Turning back to her food would have been the best thing to do, but in-stead she held his gaze, because, hell, she wanted to. After a moment she looked away because star-ing was rude, but that look had communicated what she'd wanted. That, yes, she agreed with America that he was aesthetically advantaged, and also yes, she'd like to explore that advantage in a behind-closed-doors type of situation. Because that was what her work life was about. When she was on the road, she could be herself instead of her father's caretaker or the girl her friends still coddled because her mom ran out on them for a flashier life.

Then he was coming her way, making a bee-line through other hopeful diners whose yearning eyes followed him as he passed them by. Her throat tight, she inconspicuously slid her tablet off the table and back into her bag so he wouldn't have another reason to be suspicious. Except upon further thought she should have acted like she was reading a book. No one ate alone without a buffer of some kind and here she was with half the food in the restaurant in front of her. Nervous and hating it, she took a drink of beer, one thing she couldn't complain about. From a local brewery in town, the light hoppy effervescence was the perfect fit to wash down rich, smoky barbecue.

Wiping the foam away from her mouth, she looked up to see him standing there and her entire body froze, with the exception of her wet hand sliding over the paper napkin spread across her lap.

"Enjoying your meal, ma'am?" he asked, an amused eyebrow raised, the one with the scar. His voice was grumbly and rough as he eyed the pile of food eclipsing the surface of the scarred oak table.

"Indeed," she got out, having second thoughts about engaging with him. Either he'd clock her as a reviewer right off the bat or he'd assume that she was the lone competitor in a food-eating contest.

Either way, she'd feel guilty for the unflattering review she'd ultimately be writing.

He held out his hand, but then thought better of it when he saw that her fingers were caked in barbecue sauce. "I'm Hugh Matteson, the owner. Just wanted to make sure we were taking care of you tonight."

Looking up into his eyes was an epically bad idea, because she'd love to be taken care of by this guy. He was even better up close, dark scruff shadowing that movie-star jaw; hazy green eyes ringed with brown were clear and amused, hands so large she bet he could hold a toddler in his palm. He was also imposing, well over six foot five, and smelled like a man who took care of himself—musky cologne hung on the air like a summer's breeze over a marsh, intriguing and mysterious. She fantasized about forgetting the article altogether and taking him back to her hotel room for the night.

"I'm Parker Jones," she finally said, starting and stopping again around the bubbly catch in her throat from the beer.

"Were you expecting someone else?" he asked pointedly, his gaze cataloging her many entrées. "Or a group of people?"

"No, it's just me," she admitted, giving him what she hoped was a cheeky smile. *Like "I'm just a girl who couldn't decide," not "I'm writing an article about your mediocre food."*

Part of her wanted to admit who she was, because she'd never been shy about writing unfavorable reviews before, but she wanted to flirt back with him even if it wouldn't amount to anything. He was, after all, a famous athlete, and she was a woman with barbecue sauce already crusting around her fingernails.

"I just really like barbecue," she added when he still hadn't responded.

That caught him up and he laughed, eyes crinkling, dimples in all their glory, that lickable crooked incisor up close and personal. His voice was lush and deep, plunging like an ocean wave pulling away from shore. An answering pull in her middle had her shifting in her seat. This was probably the reaction he received from every woman he met, which was just the reminder she needed to stop her X-rated thoughts right in their tracks. He was the kind of guy who could ruin her life, and it still wasn't quite put back together after the first time.

"I can see that," he finally managed, that amused grin still firmly in place. "But I've always been partial to a woman who could eat."

She laughed. "Oh, don't worry, I can eat."

"Apparently," he said, leaning back just slightly on his wing tip's heels.

They smiled at each other then in a moment of shared amusement and she felt the bubble of anticipation in her stomach grow.

"Parker Jones," he repeated, the words rolling off his tongue experimentally. "That name sounds familiar for some reason. Like Lois Lane or Jessica Rabbit."

Shrugging, she met his eyes again. "Sorry, don't know. To my knowledge I've never been a comic book character, and we've definitely never met."

"No, I would have remembered you," he agreed.

"Are you sure? I'm not always surrounded by tables of food."

He smiled again, their eyes still locked as if glued to each other. Breaking contact, she shoved a forkful of brisket in her mouth, nearly choking at the amount and the fact that it was far too dry.

Seeing her distress, he took a seat in the round wooden booth, his arm poised to make contact with her back, but she shook her head vehemently as she swallowed. "I'm fine," she choked out, reaching for her mug of beer.

Guzzling it down, she felt his eyes on her, saw him gesturing to a nearby waiter who wasn't hers. "Can we get two more of whatever she's drinking? Quickly, please."

"Oh, that's too much," she rasped, waving the request away.

"One's for me," he stated simply, as if she'd invited him to sit at her table.

In fact, once she'd fully caught her breath again, he decided to help himself to one of her ribs as if they were old friends having dinner together. Watching him chew was like a porno, that tight jaw, gnashing and grinding. She really needed to reevaluate her choices if this was the kind of thing she'd been brought to, getting turned on by a man eating. Honestly, it was too much, and yet admittedly, also very on-brand.

"Are you from Vegas or just visiting?" he asked, throwing the clean rib into the basket already half-full of them.

"Just visiting," she informed, taking another sip of beer. She wasn't eating any solid foods until he went away and it was safe to chew again.

"Where are you from then, Parker Jones?"

The waiter set down two frosty mugs of beer, the foamy white heads just barely not running down the sides, and she wondered exactly what she should say. Revealing too much about herself would be a problem. It wasn't outside of the realm of possibility that as a restaurant owner, he'd read her stuff. "Chicago."

"And you're in Vegas by yourself, or just this dinner?"

"Vegas."

He seemed to consider that for a second. "Business or pleasure?"

Shit. She didn't want to lie, but he was going to ask her what she did and she wouldn't have a good answer. Unfortunately, she was a terrible liar, so it would have to be the truth. "Business."

"Let me guess," he said, looking over the wealth of food again. "Soup kitchen director?"

She laughed, not expecting a joke. At least not a funny one. "Nope. Though I have volunteered at plenty of them."

"Good for you," he said, his eyes sliding over her face and down her chest. She wasn't wearing anything revealing, just a pair of jeans and a black V-neck T-shirt with a fitted burgundy blazer. All choices designed to hide any sauce or grease stains she might incur during the sampling process.

Nonetheless, his gaze stopped on her cleavage, and those tingles of anticipation rolled over her skin like a long-lost friend knocking at her front door after an extended absence. It'd been a long time, but she remembered them like it was yesterday. He quickly collected himself, straightening in his seat and meeting her eyes again, vaguely apologetic. If he hadn't just tried to save her life when she was choking, she might have given him a hard time about it, but she also didn't want to draw out the conversation considering what she was hiding.

"And you own the Blue Smoke Restaurants," she filled in. "And used to play some kind of sports game?"

That got him smiling that shy, humble smile again, his eyes drifting downward and his tongue sticking in his cheek. "Football," he supplied, eyes dancing with amusement. "The sport, that is."

"Gotcha," she said. "The one with the ball."

"Yeah, that one," he replied, shaking his head at her playful obtuseness. "So what do you do?"

She took a deep breath, having spent their entire conversation trying to figure out the answer to this very question. "I write for a lifestyle magazine." Not technically a lie, so: points.

"That's pretty cool," he said, his thoughtful gaze catching hers again.

Those hazel eyes were intelligent and sharp, at turns making her feel as if she were the only person in the room, but she knew at the same time they were evaluating his waitstaff and his diners' satisfaction.

"Yeah, it's my dream job."

"A lifestyle magazine," he repeated. "So, like, laundry tips and stuff?"

She shrugged, the anxiety crawling up her back. "I'm not too into laundry," she hedged. "It's more like menu planning and leisure activities." *Like where to eat*, she thought guiltily. Where was that waiter with her check and please don't let him ask the name of the magazine.

"Ah," he said, grabbing the platter with the chicken and sausage. "You mind?"

She shook her head.

"Thanks," he said, unrolling the extra setting of silverware the waiter had left, probably anticipating another person after all that she'd ordered. "I haven't had dinner yet and I don't know that we have enough take-out boxes for all this anyway."

Her eyes shut. Dear God. She knew he was just joking but still struggled against the embarrassment climbing up her neck. Oh, it was so, so bad.

"I just wanted to try a little of everything," she explained lamely, not ready to give her cover away regardless of how it might look. She didn't care what he thought of the amount of food she'd gotten. "It all sounded so good and I'm only in Vegas for a couple of weeks."

"Your first time?"

"No, I've been several times."

"I've never been a huge fan of it," he admitted, "but it's home for now. My real one is a ranch in San Antonio where I grew up."

"San Antonio is great, though the tiny Alamo was a bit of disappointment."

He laughed again. "Yeah, well, I think that's the point. The little guys lost the battle, but Texas came back to win the war. Think about how small the actual building is, and they defended it to the death against a larger and more powerful Mexican army. They knew they would die and did it anyway."

"Fair enough. Disappointment retracted," she said, holding up her hands in supplication. "I should know better than to disparage Texas in the first place."

"Texas forever." He grinned, repeating the popular catchphrase and holding up the longhorn steer sign on his hand, pointer and pinkie stretching up proudly.

She rolled her eyes, watching as he chewed on a piece of sausage, his expression turning thoughtful.

"Parker Jones, lifestyle writer in Vegas on business alone. You got any other plans besides eating the best barbecue in town tonight or would you wanna get out of here?"

And then Parker thought she might choke on just actual air this time.

She didn't choke again, but came damn close. Holy shit. Was this really happening? A one-night stand with a famous football player? One-night stands never gave her this much agita and she knew it was because this one was different. She was already enjoying herself and could actually fall for him. Her heart beat a chaotic jangle in her chest and sweat coated her palms. Rubbing them discreetly on her jeans, she met his eyes and her shock must have shown.

"I don't mean for that," he said quickly, holding up a hand. "I mean, not that I wouldn't. Hell, of course, but I just meant I could show you around. You know, as a local. I'd hate to think of you doing this whole trip alone. Besides, I don't meet many women who can eat this much, so I feel like this is my opportunity to get to know the kind of girl who at least gives it a shot. There are a lot of points on the board for making the effort."

It was a joke she couldn't *quite* laugh at, but she appreciated it and she wanted to stay with him. Didn't want the warmth of his body heating her left side to suddenly vanish without her really memorizing it to take out at a later date when she was back home, a place she was always slightly miserable if she were being honest.

"Sure, I just have to pay the check and we can go. Since apparently I can't box this stuff up."

Chuckling at the throwback to his previous joke, he stood, holding out his hand to help her from the booth. "How about I have the leftovers sent to where you're staying."

"But the check," she pointed out.

"It's on me, sweetheart. Keep your per diem for the next place you visit."

She bristled at the patronizing endearment and the per diem crack, as if she couldn't afford to go out to dinner on her own. Like she was just some girl who couldn't make it in the world and had to depend on her job's petty cash to buy her enough food to eat for an entire month.

Suddenly, it felt like she had rocks in her mouth, dry and crackling, and she wanted to grind them between her teeth until they were dust.

He must have read her displeasure because he held up a hand. "We can have the bill sent to your hotel, okay? I was just trying to be nice. If I can't buy a girl dinner at my own restaurant, I don't know when I can, you know?" His tone was overly conciliatory, which only served to irritate her more.

"Maybe I'll just wait here for the check. I have an early day tomorrow and I'm very tired," she backtracked, yawning to make it more believable.

Hugh crossed his big arms in front of his gorilla-wide chest, the tailored fabric of his suit pulling over the bulging muscles outlined underneath. Although it looked like it, he wasn't trying to be intimidating; she thought it was just his way of digging into his stance, which was obviously going to be to try to get her to go out with him. "Ms. Jones, I'm sorry if I offended you, but we've been looking at each other tonight the same way I hope people look at my food when it comes to their table. I don't pick women up in my restaurants ever and I'm interested, so I'd be grateful if you'd give me another chance and come grab a drink with me."

As far as apologies went, it was pretty good, but she'd already made up her mind not to do it since it was a bad idea for a lot of reasons. If things had been different and she hadn't been intending to write a review of his restaurant, she would one-night-stand the shit out of this guy, but alas, life was only that simple for the pool-raft models.

"Listen," he began just as she opened her mouth to tell him the aforementioned resolution. "I haven't been on a real date in years, not one with a woman who minds if I pay a check or not anyway, and I know we literally just met, but you seem pretty cool. I have it on good authority that I'm not great at this shit, so if you could cut me some slack I would really appreciate it."

She smiled; she couldn't help it. He didn't have to be vulnerable with her but he'd gone there, and it took guts to do that with a complete stranger.

"Whose authority?" she asked idly, still deciding what to do. "Who doesn't think you're good at picking up women in your restaurants? Seems like that would be pretty easy."

His lips thinned at the playful jab and his look was bland. "Well, my ex-fiancée for one."

"Did you call her 'baby' and try to put her in a corner?"

His thick eyebrows came together at the old movie reference. "No, that doesn't even make any sense."

"Well, you called me sweetheart and I hated it, just like I would hate to be called baby. And your offer to pay for my meal put me in a corner, metaphorically, if you know what I mean. So if you think about it, it really works on a lot of levels."

Hugh stared at her, a corner of his mouth twitching.

"You know what we call this entire conversation in football?" he asked, arms still crossed and that meaty thumb drumming impatiently on the upper bicep of his opposite arm.

"A touchdown?" she tried.

"Nope, intentional grounding. Where you try to kill the play before it even begins."

"It sounds like your words are saying you didn't like my joke, but your face is saying that you did."

He laughed for real then, the sound rich and deep, warming her belly more than his food had. "Yeah, I fucking liked it. I like you, too, so will you forgive me for trying to get what I have to assume is one of the largest meals ever ordered in my restaurant taken care of?"

She met his eyes, shaking her head at his food crack. "One drink and then I really do need to get home."

"Fair enough." He waved over a waiter to explain the situation about her leftovers and check.

"What hotel?" he asked.

"Halcyon."

"That's a good one," he approved.

"It's pretty for a casino in Vegas," she admitted, finally rising from the booth.

He offered her his arm and she slipped her hand through, trepidation filtering through her body along with just plain anticipation.

"And your fiancée might be right that you're bad at the pickup, but your follow-through is exemplary."

"You have no idea just how accurate that statement is," he told her, his tone edged with a delicious dash of danger and irony.

CHAPTER TWO

HUGH DIDN'T GET nervous as a rule. He'd faced down the largest men in the country running at him at speeds only athletes conditioned over the course of their entire lives could achieve, so a girl in his restaurant shouldn't have made him as edgy as he was, but Parker Jones was doing it. And not just because she had a chest not even his famously large hands could get around, though that was a huge plus.

He hadn't been interested in a woman beyond sleeping with her in a long damned time. If that was a commentary on him as a person, so be it, but after the hell he'd been through with his ex he hadn't trusted his own judgment to pick women. The scandal was long gone, but he'd never really gotten over being the nation's poster child for cuckolding. Nor the fact that Amanda was happily married with the family they'd dreamed about. He'd thought he'd have three kids by now, but the thought of finding someone who wanted him for him and not who he'd been as a player was too much work.

So the fact that Ms. Jones gave him some butterflies didn't mean much. She didn't even live in
the city, and a little what-happens-in-Vegas action
was just fine with him. It didn't matter that when
he'd caught her staring at him earlier, something
inside him had flickered on. She was beautiful with
cool blond hair and warm brown eyes, curves that
lasted for days, and expressive lips that he'd wanted
to lick his own barbecue sauce off of. And now he
also knew she was sarcastic and fun as hell.

He held her hand, small and soft nestled in his
long-fingered grasp, wondering when was the last
time he'd done something simple like that for a
woman and coming up short. Maybe he really had
taken himself out of the game for too long, like the
guys said, but every time he thought about really
giving a woman a chance he remembered all that
bullshit with his ex. If girls didn't want to be with
him for the money and notoriety, then they really
wanted to be with him because they felt sorry for
him. He honestly didn't know which was worse.
But already Parker didn't seem to care about either
his money or his past, which felt good. The sympa-
thetic head tilt was usually the first thing women
gave him, whereas she'd just lit him up and thrown
his money back in his face. Already, a small piece
of him felt liberated.

"When did you retire?" Parker asked when they
got outside, a gentle breeze blowing a lock of pale

hair across her face. His yellow McLaren was sitting in the first spot near the door.

"Six years ago."

He guided her toward the car, but she resisted, pulling her arm and breaking their forward momentum. "I assumed we were walking somewhere."

"We can if you want, but all the bars around here on the Strip are pretty much tourist traps."

At her raised eyebrow, he gestured to his car. "I'm not going to kidnap you and take you back to my place against your will. This is not that, I promise. Just a drink, like we agreed."

She didn't look completely convinced, white teeth chewing nervously at her dark pink lip. If she'd been wearing lipstick it had worn off, probably during her meal.

"But if it did end up being more, would that be the worst thing?" he threw out because fuck it, they were adults. "I mean, like, as long as we both want to."

She shook her head and he shoved his hands into his pockets. Hooking up usually wasn't this hard for him. Most girls would have asked to drive his car by now, and he couldn't even get Parker to have a drink with him.

"We can have a drink on the Strip if you want. Totally innocent and you'll be close to Halcyon. The problem is that I'll be bothered by fans at those kinds of places and we won't actually get to talk."

She considered him and he waited as patiently as he could. "Okay," she finally said, her tone still dubious.

"The place I have in mind would be private but it's too far to walk, so if I don't drive we'll have to use an app and ride in some guy's car."

"I had a lovely minivan experience on the way here," she claimed primly. "He even had a candy bowl, so I bet you feel foolish for being so snobby about ride-sharing now."

She pulled her phone from her bag and started tapping away. He accepted what was happening because after a moment of surprise that she'd easily wrested control from a situation he thought he'd been manipulating masterfully, he realized he actually kind of enjoyed not being in charge. It was a theme that ran through his entire life. He made his own decisions, the decisions for his parents, he'd managed his team on and off the field, he was always in charge of what he did on dates, he managed an entire chain of restaurants, but now here he was in the parking lot of his own restaurant waiting for someone else to decide his fate tonight. He hadn't known it was a thing that he'd enjoy, but he didn't hate it.

"I got the luxury option for you," she told him. "Whatever that means for a person who drives a car for a living. The app says a black Acura sedan."

"I'm sure it'll be fine."

"You're suddenly amenable to the car?"

He shrugged. "No, but I'm not going to argue with you."

Their eyes met in a benign challenge that he found oddly exhilarating, like when he was on the sidelines watching the other team play just waiting for his turn to go back out on the field. Only instead of the playing field being full of elite athletes, it was a single woman with a body designed to make men crumble before they could even attempt a play.

"Good," she told him, a corner of that full mouth raising in a playful smirk. "I hate difficult people."

He snorted because they hadn't been together for more than a half hour and he knew she wasn't exactly easygoing. And neither was he, for that matter. His own baggage was so heavy only a man of his imposing stature could carry it. He didn't fault her for knowing what she wanted and doing what she needed to do to get it.

"What?" she asked, reproach in her tone when he didn't follow up his snort with an actual response.

"Both of us are difficult, sweetheart. It's why we're standing here on the street together waiting for a car we don't need instead of me finishing the night talking to my guests and you eating your weight in barbecue. We like it."

Just then the black Acura pulled up, the familiar emblem of the car service on the windshield.

"Not bad," he told her, and she just rolled her eyes.

Taking one last look at his own car that he loved

and cherished, he helped Parker into the back seat of their ride, his fingers itching to cup the ass he could barely take his eyes off of as she bent to get inside.

"So where are we going?" she asked, oblivious to the fact that he was seconds away from completely mauling her.

"Oh, did you not want to choose?" he asked, meeting her eyes in the relative darkness of the back seat. The blue lights of the restaurant's sign shone onto her face, highlighting her pursed lips, which only made him want to kiss that know-it-all expression off of it.

"It's your town," she argued.

"Structure," he instructed the driver, a young man in his twenties who was more or less indifferent to their presence. He had a dirty-blond manbun and beard that looked like it was taking its time filling in.

The kid pulled away from the curb, and because Hugh had become intensely private about what he shared with the public, he stayed silent for the short five-minute drive to Structure. The bar was on the top floor of the Crown Royale casino and had breathtaking 360-degree views of the city, but mostly he'd chosen it for the privacy. Because he wanted privacy with Parker. Every single dirty thing he wanted to do to her demanded it.

They rode the elevator to the club's entrance,

where they were enthusiastically greeted by Jesse. He requested one of the semiprivate spaces.

"Nothing but the best for you, Hugh," Jesse breathed, her eyes going dewy and sentimental. "And thank you again for that little loan. It really helped me out."

"Loan implies I want it back, sweetheart," he told her, giving her a wink. "I don't. Consider that car a gift from me to you."

She leaned up to give him a kiss on the cheek, her long blond ponytail swaying back and forth behind her. "You're the best, Hugh."

Jesse was a young girl in her twenties, but had a broken-down car and a small child she needed to provide for, so he'd provided the money to replace it. Structure was one of his favorite places in the city and he'd gotten to know the employees very well over the years, and when she'd needed help, he helped. He would have done it for anybody really, and often did. It was part of the reason he didn't have relationships. Everyone wanted a piece of him and the only pieces he was willing to give any woman nowadays had dollar signs on them.

He felt Parker's eyes on him and knew she could be thinking any number of incorrect scenarios. But he'd never slept with Jesse. Not that he wouldn't, but he hadn't. That said, he'd given cash gifts to a lot of women he'd slept with, not because he'd felt strongly about them, but precisely because he didn't. Relationships weren't gonna happen again as far he was concerned. He'd loved Amanda and she'd made him the literal laughingstock of America, which meant that now, if he had to pay women to leave him alone, he'd do it.

Following Jesse, Hugh led Parker through the club, which was comprised of small rooms and nooks furnished with couches and easy chairs. The decor was Vegas-style Roman, weathered columns reached from the floor to the ceiling and created an intimate space. Dim lighting threw shadows on the paintings of nude women and men on the walls enjoying life's baser pleasures. Gold-leaf ceilings and bloodred furniture gave the place a lurid feel, like just being there was the first step in finding Eve's apple and getting to sin for all eternity.

Jesse led them to a small corner room, cordoned off in case people like him showed up, with two red velvet couches and a single gold lamp with a deep red shade that cast the whole space in a muted, sensual glow. A gold coffee table sat in between the couches and he held open the red velvet drape for Parker to enter.

He sat next to her on one of the couches and fought the urge to take her hand again, wanting to feel her skin, to learn it, feel it warm up in his until they were sharing heat.

"I've never even heard of this place," she said, taking in the decadent room.

"It was the only bar we could go and actually hear each other," he explained. They were far enough away and enclosed so that the music from the bar was a dull rumble in the background instead of a roar. But that wasn't the only reason he'd chosen this particular place. He only did what he wanted now and he didn't want to take selfies or answer questions about his glory days—he wanted to flirt with a girl.

"It looks expensive," she observed, playing with the gold tassel on the lamp.

He shrugged. "I don't know what expensive is anymore," he told her honestly. He was also done pretending he was some "aw shucks good ol' boy" so people liked him. He was a multimillionaire, closing in on nine digits, and he wasn't going to apologize for it.

Her eyebrow raised and that corner curved up in her signature smirk again. "Look at you," she purred. "Mister big football man."

"That's right," he said, inching just the slightest bit closer to her as the waitress arrived to take their drink order. He rattled off his favorite red wine, feeling Parker's eyes on him.

"Maybe I didn't want wine," she said when the waitress had left them alone again.

"You should have spoken up then. It's not like you've had a problem with that so far."

She laughed, shaking her head at the truth of his statement. "Were you sad to retire from football?"

Getting comfortable, he stretched his arm across the back of the couch until he could almost touch her long blond hair with his fingers. "Yeah, the first couple of months were fucking devastating. It was the thing I'd done my entire life. I literally didn't know anything else outside football, but I had a business degree from UT so I thought I might as well use it."

"What did you injure?" Her eyes involuntarily scanned his body for what might be out of place.

Damn, he did not want to talk about this shit. Not right now. It was not at all sexy, but Parker was the long game. He already recognized that even if *long* in this case meant however long she was in town.

"It was late in the fourth quarter against the Steelers, a really physical defense, and I got tackled head-on. I had a compound fracture in my leg, which isn't too big a deal when you're a regular person, but the NFL was over for me. The recovery alone was nearly a year, then the conditioning to get back into shape would have been another. I would have been over thirty by the time I could even think about returning to the game, and no one ever has after that kind of injury."

"So you like running the restaurants?" she asked, changing the subject, which he was really thankful for.

"Hell yeah, I love eating and building something of my own. And I'm in charge, just how I like it."

She rolled her eyes at his pomp, but then gave the hand resting on the back of the couch a quick squeeze. "I'm sorry about the injury," she said, her voice steady and earnest. "Do you live with pain?"

He shook his head, but it wasn't the entire truth. No one left the NFL without some measure of pain management. It was the nature of the job.

The waitress brought them their wine and two glasses, and Hugh poured them halfway full.

"Pinot noir is my favorite," she told him before taking a small sip, those fuck-me lips closing over the delicate rim of the wineglass. His cock twitched with the X-rated visual of what they'd look like closed around him, her guarded eyes looking at him with want and need and completely lost to lust.

"After the accident, I toyed with buying a vineyard and bottling my own wine, but decided I was more of a smoked meats kind of guy."

"Definitely seems more on-brand," she agreed, a corner of her mouth lifting.

"You like making fun of me?" he asked, calling her out on the smug smile.

She shrugged. "Was I?"

Their eyes met, heat darting between them until finally he took a drink of his wine.

"What? A football player can't be into something highbrow like wine?"

"I didn't say a word," she claimed, even though she'd said enough without any words at all. "I think you're very sophisticated. Your car probably costs more than my house, so I wouldn't presume to make those kinds of judgments. Plus, this was a deep-cut wine choice. I'm impressed."

"Do you cover wine in your lifestyle magazine?" he asked, hoping to find out something of substance about her.

"Sometimes, but I'm actually a trained sommelier," she revealed, and he raised an eyebrow in surprise.

"What? A girl who eats unlawful amounts of barbecue can't be into something highbrow like wine?" she asked, throwing his own words back in his face.

Damn, he liked her. Liked getting as good as he gave. His ex had wanted him to tiptoe around her feelings like they were Tiffany glass, whereas Parker could dish it out and take it with a smile. It was sexy as hell and his cock throbbed again, coming to life by slow but unstoppable degrees.

"Which leg?" she asked when he didn't have a response right away. He'd been too busy fantasizing about fucking her on the gold coffee table beside them. Hell, probably the Persian rug would be good enough for the filth he had in mind.

He stretched out his left leg, the one on the outside of the couch, far enough to nudge her foot with his own. It was an innocent touch, just his wingtip nudging her black canvas sneaker, but he felt it in his dick and the back of his head which was clouding over from lust.

"Sorry," he got out, kneading his leg the slightest bit. "It's a little stiff."

She looked suspicious at first, and rightly so, because it was a major line of bullshit. It'd been the other leg in the first place, and in the second place that leg didn't hurt at all.

"Do you need a hot compress or something?" she said, raising an eyebrow.

"Might be nice if you could massage it for a minute, just to warm it up."

She laughed, the sound high and incredulous. "You've got to be kidding me."

"You're not going to just let me sit here in pain, are you?"

"Don't you have something you could take?"

He shook his head. "I don't like pills."

He jerked at his leg without even an ounce of shame. He wanted her and knew she wanted him, too, from the lingering looks, the jumping pulse at her throat when he touched her, the way she worried that lip. They were two strangers who liked each other; it wouldn't be a big deal if they saw it through. It was the very tagline of Vegas, for fuck's sake. He would be doing her a disservice not to offer her that kind of opportunity on her visit.

"Maybe I should go," she suddenly said, standing up. "Seems like you need to tend to that leg anyway."

He shot up then, too. "Please don't. I was just kidding about the massage."

"What are we really doing here, Hugh?" she asked. "It's not like we came out together to form a lasting friendship. I'm only here for a month."

"I just want to get to know you." And a month was a long damn time.

"Or you want to fuck me," she said baldly, the words shooting straight to his groin.

He didn't bother to deny it. "Of course I do. Look at you, and you've been riding my ass all night. We've been fucking each other with words since the moment I sat down at your table. But I get it, it's too soon and you want to go, but can I please have your number? Because I'm serious about wanting to know you."

Her mouth opened, ready to stick him with whatever accusation might render the truth of his statement null and void. But instead, she just murmured, "Fuck it," and pulled all two hundred and fifty pounds of him to her.

His lips met hers in surprise, but it didn't take him long to shift to straightforward lust. Once he got his bearings he took control from her, crowding her into the dark corner of the room where they blended in with the black around them. Hidden from all the dirty shit he wanted to do to her.

She pulled her mouth from his and glared at him. "And if you pay me for this, I swear to God I will claw your eyes out. I don't need to be taken care of."

The words were clear and a corner of his mouth lifted. No, he didn't suppose she was. "Noted."

So he yanked up her T-shirt, running his hands across the smooth skin of her sides and back, diving into the kiss again, coaxing her mouth open wider this time. Her little whimpers of pleasure drove him beyond madness, and he slipped one hand from under her shirt to tunnel back up into that silky halo of hair, adjusting her head so he could go even deeper, their tongues feasting on each other, excavating their secrets with desperate curiosity.

Sticking his knee between hers as an invitation, she didn't leave him hanging, riding hesitantly at first, but then moving her hips in earnest. It was the sexiest thing he'd ever seen, ever been a part of. "You're sexy as hell, Parker," he breathed hotly against her lips, swallowing another one of her greedy moans. "Ride me, sweetheart. I want to see you come."

So saying, he flicked open the placket of her jeans as his other hand drifted from her back to her breast, testing the heavy weight in his big hands. He wouldn't have cared if she had small breasts or large breasts—frankly he was more of a big-picture person—but fuck if that flesh didn't overflow in his meaty hands, making his cock throb a bass beat under the metal zipper of his pants. His hips started moving in time to hers as she rubbed over his leg, her hands grasping the lapels of his coat, tugging him against her but in turns pushing him away as she arched into him.

Sliding his hand in her pants, he found her slick and hot. He'd give a lot to be able to see her, to lick and suck until she was screaming louder than the music on the dance floor, but this was what they were doing right now. And then later he'd ask her to come home with him, so they could do this right and he could make her breakfast in the morning and then whatever the hell else she wanted. Hell, maybe even an actual date at some point.

She threw her head back, pale neck arched in pleasure as he ran his thumb over that sweet, lust-soaked nub. Changing the tempo and the pressure, he learned what she liked, what sent her closer to the edge, could feel the muscles in her abdomen tense against his arm. "Come on, baby," he whispered in her ear, his thumb pressing on the verge of pain just to torture her. "You know you want to come. No one can hear you, no can see you, but you know they're all there, just down the hall, don't you?"

She whimpered against him, bucking hard against his leg, and he let his hand move farther down, pumping two fingers inside her, agonizing over his own arousal as her moans got lower, more guttural, as if the sensation was coming from deep inside her.

"Fucking touch me," he commanded, unbuckling his belt and dealing with the zipper. He couldn't handle it anymore. He wanted to slide his cock into that dripping pussy and fuck her in front of every single person in this bar, wanted them to see him give her pleasure. The music was quieter in their private corner room, but it pounded through his veins like the downbeat to his own racing pulse.

Her cool hand weaved inside his boxer briefs, pulling his thick cock out, the tip already leaking. Their eyes met as she lifted her hand and licked her palm before running her thumb down the underside, teasing, testing, gauging his reactions. He pumped harder inside her, using three fingers now, stretching and exploring, loving her gasp and her involuntary squeeze on his cock in answer. She regained herself, straightening her back and taking his mouth again as her hand flew over him. He grunted against her mouth as they got each other off with the entire world down the hall. It was indecent, erotic, lewd, and it was only a hand job. He'd had his first in middle school, and yet nothing he'd done since compared to the heat in his stomach, the pooling of energy in his back, electric tentacles grabbing his insides up in a rough, greedy fist of passion so tight he could barely breathe.

Frantically, he pulled her shirt up under her bra

because he was going on her stomach—that was the only option at this point.

They were in a rhythm now. He was back on her clit rubbing in time to her quick, staccato strokes, designed to drive him insane with the featherlight abrasion of her hand. "Harder," he instructed, his thumb on her clit following suit.

"You're bossy," she breathed, taking his order, her hand clasping around the base of him and dragging up slowly and firmly. He couldn't get enough of that measured climb.

"Don't know why you'd think otherwise," he growled as her hand ran over the tip of him, lubing her up again to better handle him, to deliver even more mind-bending pleasure.

"I didn't say I didn't like it," she gasped, giving one last good tug before her head fell back and she cried out her orgasm. He swallowed the sound with a kiss, knowing that while they were unlikely to be discovered, the possibility existed.

Coming down, her eyes glazed in the dim light, she squeezed him again, pumping like mad until all his muscled contracted at once and he let go, spurting onto her stomach in thick bursts as his knees grew limp and worthless.

He met her eyes, working for his next breaths, and was stunned by what had just happened. The hottest moment of his life with a woman he barely knew in a club he knew too well begat a feeling of

serenity he hadn't felt in years. Maybe the sense-
lessness of it was what he needed, a fling with
someone who normally wouldn't give him the time
of day. Parker wasn't a football groupie or someone who just wanted his lifestyle; she was someone
who'd nearly fucked him in a public place just because she liked him. He really hadn't known how
powerful that would be.

He reached into his jacket pocket, pulling out
the two-hundred-dollar silk pocket square, and
cleaned her stomach off, going against his cave-
man instincts to rub it into her skin so he was part
of her. He'd save that for another time, because
after discovering this kind of chemistry, there was
no doubt that there'd be another time.

Gently pulling her shirt back down and dealing
with her jeans, he dropped a light kiss on her forehead, brushing his thumb across the apple of her
cheek. "That was fucking crazy," he told her, helping her down from his leg, making sure she had her
balance before taking her hand.

She just nodded, still dazed by what had happened.

Looking up at him, her mouth opened and then
closed again. Before finally she said, "I need to go
to the restroom. Sorry."

And then she was rushing up the hallway.

CHAPTER THREE

PARKER CHANGED HOTELS the second she got back to Halcyon so that Hugh wouldn't find her, which she regretted. Not for giving Hugh Matteson a hand job in a bar, because that had been pretty epic. And running out on him at Structure was equally crappy of her, but in light of her article it would have been a major mistake to sleep with him and she definitely would not have been able to resist doing that if she'd stayed. The night had been world-shaking and they hadn't even had sex, so yeah, she'd needed to get the hell out of there.

Because she wasn't *not* going to write a truthful review of his restaurant. Hugh was a nice guy and she'd already lied to him. It sucked, but it would have been way worse if they'd actually had sex. Especially because her boss had published the review on their website as a teaser for the ten-page Las Vegas spread that would be in next month's physical issue. Because his name was attached, the story was already quoted all over social media, which meant the chances of her getting another opportunity to sow her wild oats with the Greek god of restaurant investors were pretty dismal.

She had a very real fear that Hugh was out there, even now, looking for her. When she'd called Halcyon to see if she'd left her toothbrush in the room, they'd sent over a message from him. An envelope with his phone number. Nothing else. So yeah, she knew enough about him to know that he wouldn't have taken being walked out on very well. She'd be livid if he'd done it to her, so she could only imagine how someone with that much pride would feel.

She flipped through program she was holding, vowing to stop thinking about Hugh. Which was difficult because she was getting ready to judge a barbecue competition for the Las Vegas Food & Wine Festival. For over a year she'd been scheduled to be a judge and it was generally one of her favorite things to do. She loved encouraging amateur chefs and often found a lot of amazing talent who ended up going on to really successful careers in the industry. Now it was just a reminder that she wanted to have sex with a local barbecue restaurateur.

Another plus to judging, she'd get to be inside an air-conditioned tent soon, because the heat was killing her. She'd spent the morning walking around the festival, chatting with vendors and chefs, trying not to feel miserable in the intense desert heat.

Her phone rang just as she was about to make her way to said air-conditioning. When she saw it was her dad she held back a sigh, but knew she had to take it. Leaning against a bushy green golden rain tree, she answered.

"Hey, Dad," she greeted, idly watching crowds of festivalgoers wander from one vendor to the next.

"Parker, honey," he responded, "I miss you."

"I miss you, too."

Parker loved her dad. But she spent most of her time at home making sure he went to work, making him dinner, generally being kind of a mother to him. All because her own mom had run out on them.

"How's Vegas?" her dad rasped, his voice sounding like he'd just woken up. It was a bad sign that he was sleeping so late in the morning. She knew from experience that it was usually when the depression crept in. "You put my money on twenty-seven?"

She forced a laugh she didn't quite feel. "No, not yet," she told him. "I haven't really had a chance to gamble yet." *Because on my only free night I gave a former NFL quarterback turned restaurateur a hand job in public* was what she didn't say. Her dad was a football fan, sure, but obviously not that much of one.

"I will before I come home, though," she promised. "How's everything up there?"

She thought she heard a sound in the background and then her dad was clearing his throat. "Everything's good up here," he assured.

"Is someone there?" she asked, putting a hand on her other ear to block out the music being pumped in from the overhead speakers.

Her dad coughed. "Nope, just me here. Probably hearing the television or something."

"Okay," she said slowly. "Well, just remember to get to work soon and call me if you need anything, okay?"

"Will do," her dad said. "Miss you, sweetheart. Hope you come back soon."

"Miss you, too, Dad," Parker returned, holding back a sigh. Her dad never outright asked for her help, but he had a way of making her feel like she needed to be home. It was why she loved her job so much. Sometimes she just needed space from her dad to be herself instead of the good daughter who took care of her father and didn't make questionable decisions. Her life on the road involved a lot of decisions the Parker at home wouldn't make, but ones that kept her sane. Her mom had run out on her, too, something her dad often forgot. Parker wasn't going to be like her and leave her dad alone, but sometimes she had to admit that she thought about it. Fantasized about being free to do what she wanted.

Parker ended the call to her dad and shoved the phone into her purse, glad that everything was okay at home.

Leaving her spot on the tree, she went in search of Karen, the fiercely competent organizer who'd contacted her about the festival in the first place. When she found her, juggling a tablet and two clipboards, she checked Parker in and led her to the judging tent. Set up with five chairs at a long table covered in white linen, the tent was dark and cool, and Parker couldn't have been more thankful if someone had also handed her a cold beer.

"Thank you again, Karen," she said when the woman showed her to her seat, which happened to be next to one of her personal heroes, Michael Barton. He'd been at the forefront of the farm-to-table food scene that was now exploding on a national scale and they'd become close acquaintances over the years. "I really love being a part of these festivals."

Karen smiled, her brown eyes warm as more judges entered the tent. "No problem, honey. I love the magazine. And Michael recommended you himself, in fact."

"I appreciate that," she told Karen. "I'm looking forward to the food. I feel like I should be paying someone for the opportunity instead of the other way around."

Karen laughed, her eyes drifting over Parker's shoulder to where Michael was making his way toward them, his pace speeding up when he saw her. But it wasn't Michael who caught Parker's attention; it was the man who appeared in the open doorway that had effectively shoved her heart in her throat.

"Fuck," she whispered under her breath. Of course Hugh would be a judge for this kind of event. He was a local celebrity. Fuckity fuck fuck fuck. She should fake an illness and bow out. That was the only option.

Michael's brow furrowed. "Here I thought you'd be happy to see me, darling," he pouted, kissing the top of Parker's hand. It was shocking how little chemistry or attraction there was in the gesture, considering the man who was now checking in with a festival employee could inflame her with a single brush of his finger.

"I am so glad to see you, Michael," she apologized, the words coming out on top of each other as she gave him an air kiss on the cheek as was their custom. "But I need to use the little girls' room before we get started. Please excuse me."

Then she booked it out of the tent, giving Hugh her back before he could have possibly seen her. She kept moving, past Michael's seat to the other end of the table, nearly tripping in her haste to escape.

She pretended to go to the restroom she didn't need and then wound her way back to the judge's tent, peeking inside to see if everyone had been seated yet. Her plan, if it could be called that, was to wait until everyone was in place and then surreptitiously take her seat. With any luck, his chair would be far away and she could completely avoid him. Then she could sneak off afterward and never talk to him again.

She watched as everyone took their seats, Karen standing in the middle of the tent scanning the area for Parker. Her time was nearly up.

Spotting her name card on the table, she bit back an audible curse. The whole bathroom charade had been for naught because on the other side of her empty chair sat Hugh Matteson, looking like an Adonis in his matching baby-blue pants and vest with white shirt and navy tie. There'd be no stroke of luck for her this time. She'd be sitting next to not only the very guy she'd walked out on after a public sexual indiscretion, but the guy who owned the restaurant she'd reviewed only days earlier.

Basically, it was going to be a really bad afternoon. Because while she'd sat beside plenty of people she'd given bad reviews to and not batted an eyelash, she hadn't almost slept with any of those people. Nor had she lied to them about what she did for a living.

With exaggerated slowness, as if she were going to face her execution squad, she slithered to her seat like the serpent-ish creature she was, nodding to Karen on her way.

She pulled out the folding metal chair beside him, but Hugh didn't even glance her way. He'd obviously figured out who was sitting beside him, considering the big white placard with her name printed on the front and back sitting on the table. Which meant the anger she could feel pouring off him as tangible as the chair in her hand was not imagined.

Luckily, Michael hopped up to help her get seated before she could even acknowledge Hugh. Small blessings and whatnot.

"Darling," Michael began, the warmth in his voice reminding her that she wasn't a completely horrible person. "Where are you staying? Let's go out after this. It's been too long since we caught up."

Crap. If she told him, she was going to have to switch hotels *again*. A fact that was driven home by the fact that Hugh cleared his throat ever so slightly beside her. The heat of him was radiating outward in waves and she was disturbingly aware of every single bit of him, from his putty-colored suede shoes to the way he'd rolled back the sleeves of his dress shirt to show off the finest forearm to ever grace certainly a food and wine festival, if not the universe itself.

"Let's definitely catch up," she told Michael, trying to focus but feeling like she was failing. "And I still need to review Toast and Jam. You know I live for a good lunch spot," she said, changing the subject from her hotel for obvious reasons.

Michael waved his hand as if dismissing the idea. "I would love it, of course, but it's very casual and probably not worth the travel time. But my new place will be opening in Chicago by the end of the year, so you will be the first on that, I hope."

"Oh." She involuntarily clapped her hands together, her voice a little too squeaky from the shredded nerves of sitting by Hugh with so much unsaid. "That's so exciting! Chicago has an amazing food scene, but it's light on that magic you make with vegetables. I didn't even like artichokes before I had your soufflé and now I sometimes find myself daydreaming about them."

She could have sworn she heard a snort coming from Hugh's direction, but Karen took to the microphone to announce that judging would begin and the conversation with Michael was cut short. Karen went down the table introducing each judge, one of whom was a local food critic and another a local famous chef. She and Michael were the outsiders of the group.

When she was finished and Michael was distracted by the judge on the other side of him, Hugh finally spoke.

"You're a good writer," he said, his voice deep and only loud enough for her to hear. She could feel his eyes on her but refused to look at him. Could not look at him, in fact, due to crippling mortification the likes of which no mortal person should ever have to experience. "Maybe you should try your hand at fiction, too, since you're so good at lying."

"I didn't lie," she gritted out of the corner of her mouth so that Michael couldn't hear.

"You have got to be shitting me. You told me you wrote for a lifestyle magazine. *Gastronomic* is a food magazine. Food is right there in the damn title, darling." He bit off the word like an insult, clearly mocking Michael's earlier familiar endearment.

"Food is part of life," she threw back, but knew it was lame. Knew all of it was futile. She deserved whatever he gave her, which taking in his tense shoulders and locked jaw was going to be even more unpleasant than she'd anticipated.

He was fully glaring at her now, but she ignored him and kept her gaze straight ahead.

"For all I knew, you could have been dead," he growled as Karen finished up and the first contestant plates were passed out. "I almost called the police until the hotel told me you'd checked out."

"I'm sorry for scaring you," she admitted, her tone low and earnest. "But surely you realize now why I had to leave. It was a conflict of interest."

His snort was 100 percent real this time. "Yeah, so you could write your shitty review about my restaurant?"

"If anything, my review was more complimentary because of what happened between us," she said, knowing how idiotic the words were as soon as they left her mouth. What had been her purpose? To curry his favor by insulting his livelihood but giving a backhanded compliment to his sexual prowess? Had the situations been reversed, she would have punched him in the face. "I don't mean that," she backpedaled, finally turning to see his face.

It was a mistake. A big one. The revulsion in his eyes was so naked that her breath caught. Running out on him had really hit a nerve with him, she realized, then understood, duh, it was pretty much what his fiancée had done to him. Unfortunately, it was pointless to try to explain to him that she actually resented how loyal a person she was, so instead she would stop being such a whiny baby and simply atone for her behavior.

"Hugh, I really am sorry. I know what I did was shitty," she entreated, still whispering so that Michael wouldn't hear. "But I had no idea you would be at the restaurant that night, had no idea you'd talk to me or that we'd have a connection. I tried to end it before we left your restaurant, but you were persuasive and I liked you so I went along with it and by then it was too late to tell you about the article without looking like an asshole. I don't think either of us expected it to go longer than one night, so I went for it."

A little anger did clear out of his hazel eyes, but they were still wary and not at all happy. Instead of feeling like an unwanted rodent in a sewer, she'd at least graduated to a well-regarded lab studies rat. She'd take it. Anything to get through the rest of this day. They had over fifty barbecue entries to sample and she'd never had less of an appetite.

Michael must have heard them talking because he craned his neck over the table so he could see both of them.

"Hi there, Hugh," Michael said. "Congratulations on your restaurant. I'm hearing great things, which isn't always the case for celebrity places."

"Thank you," Hugh said, his voice subdued as he watched Michael with hooded eyes. "I appreciate that."

"You know, Parker here knows barbecue inside and out," Michael informed Hugh, unable to read a room, or tent, apparently. "She quite literally wrote the book on it. You should have her check out Blue Smoke."

For fuck's sake.

"Oh, she came," Hugh said, leaning into the double entendre with a pointed look in her direction. "But apparently wasn't impressed."

"My review for Blue Smoke came out a couple of days ago," she informed Michael, whose kind green eyes widened with understanding.

"Ooh," he finally said, leaning back to mouth the words *I'm sorry* to her.

She shook her head. It wasn't his fault the tension between her and Hugh was a living, breathing monster, slobbering its displeasure all over the judging panel.

Suddenly Michael stood up, hastily tucking his scorecard under his arm. "I'm going to go speak to Karen about…" he started. Paused. Then, "Something. See you two in a jiff."

She watched as Michael took his plate to a seat farther down the table and away from the two of them. She didn't blame him and would have done the exact same thing.

Instead of sparring with Hugh, she took a bite of the rib Karen had put in front of her. After another bite, she started scoring.

"Your review was wrong," Hugh grumbled, finally breaking the tense silence. She pushed her rib to the front of the table, where there was an industrial-size garbage can waiting for it.

"Hugh, maybe it was, but I'm entitled to my opinion. It's my job. And Michael is right—barbecue is my specialty."

"I'm from Texas. I think I have the upper hand in barbecue," he challenged, voice snide.

"If you'd bothered to read my bio or book, you'd know that I grew up working in barbecue restaurants. Then I spent an entire year traveling across the country learning barbecue from the most renowned and decorated pit masters. I got my first job as a writer calling out other magazines for not giving barbecue its due, so if I know anything about food, it's what goes on a grill."

Hugh's hazel eyes narrowed, and she looked away again because he was too intense and she was too on edge. She had angered a beast and had no idea what to do. She was from a family who didn't talk about their feelings, just bottled them up and pretended they didn't exist. So being on the receiving end of Hugh's out loud and proud ones was like trying to navigate a map in a foreign language.

"If you know so much then why don't you open your own restaurant instead of crapping all over everyone else's hard work?"

"First of all, I did not crap on your hard work. And I like this job because of the travel and the writing. I get to try the best food in the nation. It's an amazing opportunity. I have no desire to run a restaurant where I'd be burned out and miserable within a year."

Hugh wasn't impressed with the answer, but she didn't care.

One of the contest employees set another plate in front of them and she tasted and rated.

"No one else has given me a bad review," Hugh finally responded. "I can't help but think it was retribution for what happened between us. Maybe you were embarrassed or something."

That got her back up. "What would I have to be embarrassed about? We got each other off in a club.

It was probably one of my poorer decisions in terms of possibly getting arrested for public indecency, but I'm not embarrassed by it. We were hot as hell for each other. It happens."

He laid a hand on the back of her chair, that long arm and tan hair-dusted forearm catching her attention as he leaned in so no one else could possibly hear what he said. "It doesn't always happen and you know it. We went at each other like animals, you ghosted me, and then stabbed me in the fucking back. If we weren't already over, I would drop you so fast your head would spin."

She could feel his breath on her bare neck, goose bumps lighting up her skin as she sucked in a breath at the insult.

"I didn't stab you in the back," she whispered, but it was faint and sounded lame even to her own ears.

"Why did you run?"

"I told you. It was a conflict of interest."

"It was already a conflict of interest before you ran off. Try again."

He eased up when someone came by with the fourth sample, but when they left again he leaned in close enough that her ear grew damp under his breath.

"Try again, Parker Jones. I knew your name was familiar. I've even read your book, you know? Granted, I revisited it again this week just to make sure it was the same person, but there was your picture right on the jacket."

"I didn't lie," she insisted weakly.

"No, you're right, I should have put it together just by the amount of food you ordered, but I liked you so I ignored it. Why did you run?"

She desperately tried to think of an answer.

But then he decided to continue. "I'll tell you why I think you did. It's because you're a coward who hides behind her little computer and judges everybody else before anyone judges her. When have you ever had anything you've made judged?"

She rolled her eyes. "Every day for two years in culinary school and then every day for three more years in Manhattan working for some of the best chefs in the country. I've been judged, Hugh, and I know how to critique food fairly and honestly. If you have a problem with my article, take it up with my boss."

Turning, she met his eyes, soul-deep irritation replacing her embarrassment. "You know what really bothers me? In fact, it pisses me off. That I had to go through years of grueling training, both physically and mentally, and still have my expertise constantly questioned by restaurateurs who don't know a damn thing about food. You're just some ex-jock who thinks he can throw anything together and call it barbecue just because he's from Texas and has grilled out for Sunday dinner. The rate of failure for celebrity-owned restaurants is incredibly high for one reason: people come initially for the novelty and then they don't come back because the food is shitty. Maybe people have told you your barbecue is good because they want to kiss your ass, but that's not really my thing. So maybe you need to check yourself before calling out real professionals."

With that, she shoved a huge bite of rib into her mouth and ignored him. She was so livid she could barely breathe.

She filled out the scorecard, making a real effort not to let her foul mood skew her ratings. Then she shoved the plate of food into the trash.

"I usually played ball on Sundays, so there wasn't really time to grill."

She glared at him, sucking in air, her eyelids fluttering in irritation. "You know what I mean."

He studied her, not looking upset by her pointed outrage, but almost thoughtful. "So you ran away because my barbecue was bad?"

"Hugh, your barbecue is not bad. That is not what my review said. I just thought it wasn't remarkable. For a lot of restaurants that's exactly what they want, but I'm picky about barbecue and my readers want food they can't get anywhere else. I don't know that Blue Smoke qualifies, and that's the whole story."

His tongue pressed into the side of his cheek as he sat fully back in his seat, his hand finally, *finally*, falling from the back of her chair.

Relieved, she chewed on a palate-cleansing cracker and sat back as another plate was put in front of her.

"Why don't we put our skills to the test then?" Hugh said, regarding her thoughtfully. "We could make this interesting."

"This cooking competition?"

He shook his head. "We could have one of our own. You and me."

Her brow furrowed. "What do you mean?"

"I mean we'll each make a plate of barbecue, have it judged impartially and see who wins. If you win, it'll be a great story for your magazine, and if I win, you'll know I'm better."

"No way," she said immediately. She was not spending any more time with Hugh Matteson. He would devour her whole. One hand job and she'd been ready to give him five stars and the gold medal for barbecue; no way was she sticking around for some bootleg competition with him that he'd probably rig.

"You scared you'll lose?" he taunted.

She took a bite of the pork, shaking her head. "I just don't want to spend more time with you."

He laughed at that, that wolfish grin with the crooked incisor giving her the shakes. He leaned in again and that deep rumbling voice taunted her. "You are such a chickenshit. What's the matter? Know you can't keep your hands off me? Even though I want to, I know I can't keep mine off you.

I've relived what we did in that club every hour of every day since it happened. Truthfully, sometimes more than that."

Parker swallowed, her breath stuck in her throat and her eyes closed against the wave of prickling anticipation that swept over her body. She shook her head, wanting it all to stop, yet knowing she wanted it to continue more.

At his low, knowing chuckle, she snapped back to reality.

"Fine," she bit off. "I'll do it, but if I win you have to sell *my* barbecue sauce in your restaurant and online store."

"Done," he declared, his grin triumphant. "And if I win, I get one night with you."

She snorted. "I'm not cattle, Hugh. I won't barter away my body for a barbecue competition. If you want me, you'll have to win me on your own wits. Unfortunately for you, I'm a lot more complicated than barbecue."

She shoved another plate in the trash.

But he wasn't finished, apparently, because he moved his chair closer to her, leaning in all the way so it looked like he was going to kiss her neck, but it was really just a distraction because in the same moment he put a hand high on her thigh, where a rush of heat surged.

"Better watch out, Parker," he murmured. "You just accepted a challenge with the only man in

Vegas who has always been the odds-on favorite to win."

She closed her eyes and nodded. She hadn't needed the warning; she was already well aware that she was in very deep trouble.

CHAPTER FOUR

"HAVE YOU DECIDED what you want if you win?" Parker asked Hugh, standing in the middle of the deserted kitchen of Blue Smoke.

It was late and Hugh was tired after the long day of judging at the festival, but he'd convinced Parker to come and see his kitchen under the guise of fair play for their competition. A competition he didn't exactly want to participate in, but it had been a good way to prove that she was wrong about his barbecue. It didn't mean he was quite ready to forgive her lie, because he was still pissed about that, but he believed her reasoning. That said, lying wasn't something he ever tolerated.

Ordinarily, he would have walked away and never given her a second chance, but the reality was that he hadn't been able to forget her. He'd been with a lot of women and nothing compared to what they'd had at Structure. He still felt her touch on his skin, smelled her citrus scent on the air, and he knew he wasn't going to let go that easily. He at least wanted her in his bed before he moved on to the next.

She was wearing some kind of flowy peach skirt that ruffled out above her knee and a white T-shirt that emphasized a chest he'd been remembering on a loop since that first night, too. Her long blond hair was pulled up into some messy knot on top of her head, with more and more strands falling onto her face and neck as the day had gone on. Despite the relative coolness the tent had afforded, they'd been sitting in one-hundred-degree heat eating barbecue and he'd spent most of it imagining himself licking up the single droplet of sweat he'd seen rolling down the back of her neck. He'd almost just done it, too, until she'd wiped it away with a napkin.

So, yeah, he was going to pursue this as a physical relationship, but that's where it would end. Parker Jones could not be trusted.

Of course, right at this moment she was the one who looked low-level pissed that he'd dragged her to a restaurant kitchen after hours when no one was around. He'd been maneuvering her all day, simply because she deserved it. He could give a shit about the review, but that she'd been operating on a lie of omission dug deep into him in a way he couldn't shake. Seeing her order that night, his first thought had been that she was a reviewer anyway; he didn't see what the big deal would've been if she'd just told him the truth. It wasn't as if she was held to some kind of food journalist code of ethics where his knowing she was a critic would somehow corrupt her review. It was just scared bullshit because whatever this was between them was combustible and she knew it, just as he did.

"I'll tell you if you admit that you writing that review wasn't the only reason you left," he said, baiting her.

"First of all, you're going to tell me anyway because I'm not agreeing to a competition unless I know what you're getting if I lose," she challenged, like the boss she was. "But since you want to be cute and hassle me first, I will admit that had I planned to write a positive review, I would have admitted what I did for a living."

That unintentional tell had him smiling. "I get it," he drawled, rocking back on his heels. "You didn't want to hurt your chances of a one-night stand with me by telling me the truth. It had nothing to do with journalistic integrity."

Parker shrugged. "So what? You hit on me first."

"No problem," he clarified, "just making sure I understand. And then you felt so guilty for using me for my body even though you were writing a crappy review, you cut out on me."

"I wouldn't say guilty," she said. "I don't feel guilty about writing the review."

"Of course not," he snarked. "Why would you feel guilty about that?"

"Because your food is fine, but it's not upscale," she told him, standing right in the middle of his own restaurant's kitchen. She might be a liar, but she also didn't pull her punches.

"I never said it was upscale," he told her. "Those were the words of another food writer, so hate to burst your bubble there. Furthermore, the people who come to a restaurant associated with me aren't coming for upscale barbecue. I know exactly who my customers are and sales just keep going up."

"Your price point is not at the family-friendly restaurant level," she argued, arms crossing under that magnificent chest.

He stretched his neck, trying to keep from reaching for her. Regardless if Hugh the person was still pissed at her, his dick had already forgiven her, bought her flowers, and was ready to move in together. "Are you going to keep droning on about business or are you just going to admit you were wrong and take your clothes off?"

"Excuse me?" she choked, and the satisfaction of catching her so off guard was very deep.

"I mean just what I said. We both know that regardless of the content of your review, which for the record I'm fine with, you owe me an apology for lying. So let's have it."

Her brown eyes narrowed. "I already apologized at the festival."

"Did you?"

She nodded her head and he smiled. "Well, I don't think I heard you, so maybe you should try it again. Maybe it'll stick this time."

"I'm out of here," she said, glaring at the command and grabbing her canvas bag from where she'd tossed it earlier on one of the stainless steel worktables.

"I thought something really bad had happened to you, Parker," Hugh reminded her. And this was a true fact, because he had honestly been concerned for her welfare, especially when he'd thought she'd passed out in the bathroom or something. The thoughts that had spun in his mind, like if he'd actually been taking advantage of a sick or drunk person, for instance, had been monumentally shitty. She'd appeared to be in possession of all her faculties, but when someone disappears like that anything seems possible. "You could at least acknowledge that. I mean, I called your damn hotel to make sure you were okay. And then you didn't even text me at the number I left the concierge to let me know. Do you know how much of a risk it was to leave my phone number with someone? The last time I gave it to a woman in a bar, she sold it. One thousand times. Made nearly a hundred grand. Yet I gave it to a random hotel employee just so I could know you were okay."

She regarded him, those warm brown eyes
shrewd and assessing, as if he were lying. He didn't
know what it said about him, but he was getting off
on her skepticism of him. Being who he was, most
girls just gave him what he wanted either because
he was rich or they felt sorry for him. While he
wasn't complaining, he was also very aware that
his most distinguishable trait was that he was a
workhorse. Fed off the drive, the goal, the raw, un-
fettered grinding toward what he wanted. If she
thought that her back-off attitude was pushing him
away, she couldn't be further from the mark. It only
made him want to work harder.

Then she blew out a breath, a piece of blond
hair alighting from her face and then plopping back
over her eye. "I meant I was sorry when I said it
earlier, Hugh," she repeated. "I have felt guilty for
days about it and I don't know how else to get you
to believe that, but it's true. I was afraid because
we'd already made out and I hate lying, but that's
no excuse for being a coward, which is what I was.
It is, in fact, the only reason I've agreed to this ridiculous, and pointless I might add, contest."

He leaned back onto one of the big industrial
ovens. "That was a lovely apology, thank you," he
grinned. "I accept your prostration."

She rolled her eyes, still holding on to her bag.

"So you think it's going to be that easy to beat
me, do you?"

Shrugging, she met his eyes. Not saying anything, but her meaning was clear. She wasn't worried about it at all.

"You know, I won't be using the recipes I use for the restaurant."

Still, she didn't look bothered. Fuck, not for the first time, he wanted to kiss that smug smile off her face. But he'd settle for needling her instead.

"Where are you staying now? Just in case you decide to wimp out of this competition, as well?"

"Do you want my blood type and Social Security number, too?" she asked, hands poised testily on her hips. "I'm not telling you where I'm staying so you can have access to me whenever you feel like it."

"Hotel staff isn't allowed to just give anyone your room number, Parker."

"Yes, but you're—" she waved her hand up and down in his direction "—you, so they'll do anything to please you."

That was probably true and why he'd asked for her hotel, but it wasn't as if he was going to stalk her there.

"You have a pretty low opinion of me if you think I'm just going around Vegas browbeating innocent hotel employees into letting me into women's rooms. If you want to know the truth, I could be single-handedly causing the plastic garbage heaps in the ocean for all the room keys I've had slipped in my pocket over the years."

It was the wrong move. He saw it as soon as the words left his mouth, but fuck it, he wasn't going to hide the truth of who or what he was.

"I'm sure lots of women do give you their room keys, but I'm not going to be one of them."

"But if you hadn't written that review, we both know we were headed back to one of our places."

"You don't know anything like that," she insisted, glaring at him openly.

He ran his tongue across the back of his teeth, watching her. She was bald-faced lying to him.

"We both know that night was off the charts. I don't know why you're trying to deny it now. I was fucking there and I remember every second of it," he said, his voice low as he took a few steps toward her. He wasn't going to get in her space. He didn't need to. He was big enough that getting closer drove his argument home. Case in point, she took a couple of steps back. "I have relived it too many fucking times to count. Even after I knew you'd written that review where you called my food, what was it? Ah, yes, 'lacking substance.' Even after that, I couldn't stop thinking about that night. Couldn't stop finishing it in my head. So don't fucking tell me you haven't. You've already lied to me once. Don't do it again, Parker."

He'd really done it now. Her eyes were shooting fireballs right at his face and her hands were clenched at her side, the knuckles stark white against her tanned skin.

But then after a moment she blew an audible breath through her nose, closed her eyes, then opened them again, her fists falling open at her sides. When she met his eyes again, she was calm.

"Are you going to show me where I'm cooking for the competition or are you just planning on hitting on me this whole time?"

"Ideally, hitting on you," he admitted, unashamed. "But I can show you around, too. Just to make sure you don't call foul play when I blow your shit away."

A corner of that cute bow mouth quirked, but she didn't take the bait. The confidence in her belief that her barbecue could beat his was sexy as fuck, and honestly, he didn't care if she beat him. He was a businessman and football player before he was a master of barbecue. He'd never fashioned himself otherwise. The food in the restaurant was good and designed for mass production, because his goal had always been a national chain. If he'd wanted a single restaurant of critical acclaim, he would have built one, but being adored by a few was never his thing. He went big. Always.

"Not gonna crack, are you?" he taunted with a good-natured smile. "Admit you want to punch me a little."

She rolled her eyes again and pulled out her

tablet from her gray canvas bag. Tapping it, she brought up a notes app and starting typing something. "Walk me through the kitchen?"

He shoved his hands in his pockets because apparently playtime was over.

Pointing to the oven, he said, "This is the oven."

Her lips pursed. "Just show me the smoker, please. And do I need to buy all my own ingredients or will we be working from the same basic ones?"

"You can use whatever's here, but I imagine we'll both want to use specific brands or types of stuff that aren't in the kitchen, as well. We'll check out the pantry after I show you the smoker."

"Great," she said, her smile more of lips being pressed together instead of genuine pleasure.

He laughed, shaking his head as he led her out to the back where six stainless steel smokers, each the size of a large refrigerator, sat on the cement floor of the outdoor kitchen extension. The area was covered, but also ventilated, because the smoke had to go somewhere. In the corner was a mobile smoking unit for when they went on the road to different area festivals or food truck rallies.

Parker went to work, taking pictures of the smokers, noting how many racks each one held. He explained how they worked and had to admit that she asked intelligent questions. Not that he'd thought she wouldn't. Her article had been thoughtful and thorough, after all.

"So mesquite is the traditional Texas wood used in barbecue, but it tasted like you chose hickory to smoke yours. Why is that?"

He raised an eyebrow, impressed that she'd noticed. "I use hickory for pork, mesquite for beef, maple for poultry."

Small white teeth appeared, worrying that puffy bottom lip. He felt a jolt in his dick, remembering those teeth on his tongue.

"I don't think whoever was smoking that day did that. I tasted hickory on everything," she told him, meeting his eyes.

He shrugged. "I do random checks every so often to make sure food is being made the right way. Other than that, there's not much I can do. Sometimes people forget, maybe the wood was out of stock, any number of things could happen on any given day. I'm more concerned with the quality of the cooking and the consistency of the service. No typical customer will ever know if something should have been smoked with mesquite instead of hickory."

The unspoken part was that she had. But Parker was no typical customer. The reality of a restaurant on or near the Las Vegas Strip was that it didn't really matter what your food tasted like as long as it got to the table fast, it was reasonably priced, and there was a lot of it. His place was better than most as far as quality so he wasn't going to sweat a few mis-smoked meats every now and again.

Parker seemed to accept this and went ahead with her perusal of his smokers, turning knobs, sniffing inside for some reason, asking about the speed at which the trays inside rotated. Seemingly satisfied with his answers, she scooted past him to look at the wood piles and he got a whiff of sweet citrus, like how lemonade tasted on a hot summer day.

"Are you finished?" he asked, crossing his arms over his chest, hoping the stance would hurry her along. While he was amused by her copious note-taking, he had a real agenda here, which was to get her into bed, and he wasn't sure helping her beat him in a competition was going to make that a reality.

"Getting scared already?" she quipped, the first real smile he'd seen from her all night. She must really have a true affinity for barbecue because for the first time today she seemed completely comfortable.

He smiled back, meeting her crinkled eyes. "Sweetheart, I couldn't care less if you beat me. I'm not a chef, I'm a businessman. And if your sauce is good, I'll be happy to sell it for you."

"You still haven't told me what you get if you win," she reminded, brow furrowed.

He thought about it, not really sure there was

anything he wanted that he couldn't just get on his own. "If I win, you work for me."

A light eyebrow rose. "I'm not a waitress or a chef, pal, and I don't need a job."

"I know, but I have a lot of chefs on my payroll to add input to the menu, make tweaks, offer suggestions, and I'm opening new restaurants all the time. It'd be a good business move to bring another on board for free, especially since you're so knowledgeable about barbecue."

In the back of his mind, he also knew it was a reason to stay in contact with her after she left Vegas, and he mentally reined himself in. He'd more than learned his lesson in ignoring the warning signs in women. Amanda's treachery had started with little white lies. Then the big stuff had crept in, no sex for months, going out with the girls every weekend and having no time for him, only wanting to be seen with him at team events where her lover also was, generally being annoyed with every single thing he did. He should have known, but he'd been so busy and had thought it was just a phase or stress about the wedding. Then the injury happened and he finally had the time to figure out what the hell was going on.

The news made it seem like Amanda had left him, but that wasn't the truth, though if he weren't a true gentleman, he'd have told them the real story. That first time he'd found the text messages between them and believed her lies that she and Todd were just friends. It wasn't until he saw it with his own two eyes, the two of them fucking in his own god-damn bed, that he kicked her out. She'd apologized and even wanted to go forward with the wedding, claiming that she loved him and had made a mistake, but he wasn't an idiot.

As if the situation couldn't get more fucked, in the middle of all of it, she'd found out she was pregnant with Todd's baby and he decided to marry her. Hugh didn't know what the lovebirds were up to now and didn't care. But he wasn't going to ignore that kind of shit in the future. Parker had lied once. He'd give her a pass for sex, but he needed to be firm on not letting things with them go any further. Sex with her was already too close to the fire for his comfort.

"Sure, I can be in your consultant pool, but you only get a year of free service."

She clapped her hands together. "Now can you show me the pantry?" she asked, nodding at the back door of the restaurant. "I need to get back to my room. I have an early breakfast tomorrow."

He opened the restaurant door for her and let her pass through back into the kitchen. "So if you're not going to tell me where you're staying, at least give me your number so I can reach you."

"Why? Now that you know my last name, you can DM me on social media."

He rolled his eyes. "I'm not going to slide into your DMs, Parker. Do me a solid, make me a contact. I deserve at least that much for all my worrying."

Lips pursing, she motioned toward his pants pocket. "Well, hurry up and put it in before I change my mind."

He couldn't help it; he snorted. "I feel like I'm getting a preview of what would have happened the other night if you'd stuck around."

Her eyes rounded in surprise and then immediately narrowed in disgust. "Oh my God, you're awful."

And then she was leaving him in the doorway and heading back to the main kitchen area.

"Pantry's this way," he called, still laughing at himself.

He heard her huff, but then she appeared in front of him again.

"Rule number one of this contest," she announced, spearing him with a glare, "no inappropriate comments. The physical part of our relationship was an anomaly and we will not be repeating it."

He crossed his arms over his chest and gave her a glare of his own. "I'll agree to the inappropriate comments, but there's no putting the physical part of us in a box. It is what it is."

"That's nonsense," she clipped. "Rule two is that Michael will be one of the judges."

"It isn't nonsense. You know what's between us.

I'm hotter for you than my fucking smoker right now."

This seemed to irritate her extremely.

"I'm fine with Michael being a judge," he told her, throwing her a bone. He was just trying to remind her how good that night had been, not drive her away. That said, he wanted her clear on what it meant to him and that he thought they should do it again as soon as possible. "But let's also get someone local."

"And probably a third person, too. Someone completely impartial."

He shrugged. "To be honest with you, you'd really have to look under a rock to find someone who wouldn't want me to win a contest. I'm pretty famous in case you didn't know."

Parker snorted. "I guess we'll just have to find someone who you've already slept with. I'm sure they're vaguely disappointed."

He smiled slowly. "That's a population who unquestionably knows I'm a winner."

"You're an idiot," she muttered, pulling open the door to the pantry.

She stepped into the room, which was just as large as the kitchen itself, filled with enough food for an entire week of operation as was custom. Scanning the contents, she looked no-nonsense again as she wrote down what was on each shelf for her own esoteric purposes.

"Meat locker?" she asked.

He led her out of the pantry and down another hallway to the double doors of the meat freezer. He was running a barbecue place, so he'd spared no expense on where he kept his meat. It was a big enough place to store the huge monthly shipments of meat from Texas.

Opening the door, she peered in. "Holy shit," she breathed. "That's a lot of meat."

He couldn't help it, he chuckled again, but she didn't seem to mind this time. Stepping farther into the space, she looked around at the hanging sides of beef in awe. "This is awesome," she breathed, and he cocked his head.

He'd never shown a woman his meat locker before, but maybe that had been a mistake, because Parker was mesmerized by it, her eyes darting around in wonder. Hell, he was kind of jealous she wasn't looking at him that way. It really brought a whole new angle to feeling like a piece of meat.

But then she was shooing him out of the room. "It's freezing," she claimed. "Let's go. Should I get my own meat then or should we use the same?"

He led her back to the kitchen, turning when they'd reached her bag. "You're welcome to my meat anytime, Parker."

"Honest to God," he heard her mutter, her arms crossed over her chest and her head down.

He was smiling, but then her arms dropped and

he saw her nipples through her thin cotton shirt, hardened from the freezer. Damn it, that comment had backfired on him, because now his own figurative meat was as hard as those frozen sides of beef.

"When do you want to do this thing?" she asked, her eyes on his, ready to get back to business. His mind was anywhere but.

"On a Monday when the restaurant is closed makes the most sense."

"Great, let's plan for Monday," she said, clapping her hands together. "That's two days for you to pretend you can beat me. I can hardly wait."

He ignored her trash talk and pulled out his phone. "Your number, Parker," he reminded.

She rattled off some numbers with a Chicago area code he recognized and he went ahead and called her right then to make sure she wasn't lying. Her phone echoed in the empty space and she looked annoyed. Then she stuffed her tablet back in her bag and headed for the door out to the dining area.

"Parker," he called when she'd reached the door. "I may lose the cooking competition, but that other part we discussed, where I need to win a night with you on my own wits? Just be warned, that's one I won't lose."

He watched with satisfaction as she absorbed the words and left him alone in his kitchen, more determined than ever to live up to his own words.

CHAPTER FIVE

PARKER HAD NO doubt that she would win the competition with Hugh. She'd been perfecting her barbecue sauces for over ten years, making friends and renowned chefs taste countless iterations until finally calling them perfection. However, the industrial smokers in Hugh's restaurant were the wild cards. In the past two days she'd been researching like mad to figure out the ratios of wood to meat in one of those suckers. She'd even talked Hugh into letting her have two practice runs with them before the competition.

Thankfully, he hadn't been there when she'd done so, but he was here in the flesh now. Standing mere feet away from her at his designated oven, he was stirring a pot of sauce on a burner. In a pair of cotton black shorts and a light blue T-shirt with the Blue Smoke logo on it, all those muscles swelled out, their remarkable peaks and valleys on full and proud display. So distracted by thick calves that could crush a metal barrel, she could almost forget they were competing against each other.

"Are you ready for this?" she asked Hugh, checking her stopwatch to see how much time her ribs had left in the smoker.

"Yeah, I'm more than ready to be done with this, if that's what you mean. It's fucking nine hundred degrees and we could be making out in my pool, but instead we're doing this cooking bullshit."

After a grueling day in said heat, Parker's hands flew straight up in the air. "You're the one who ordered the competition! I was fine without it. But your pride was hurt by my review and here we both are, sweaty and hot, and not in a fun way."

His shoulders shook with laughter. "I don't give a fuck about my pride. But you deserved it for lying to me and making me worry."

"We both know that's not true. Quit yammering and cook. I have stuff to do," she ordered, pointing her spoon at the pots on his stove top. "And that gas is too high. You're probably burning your sauce."

He rolled his eyes. "Mind your own sauce, lady," he complained. But then, avoiding her gaze, he turned down the gas on his burner.

The timer on her phone went off and she went out to the smoker patio to get her ribs. Opening the double doors, she took the internal temperature of the pork and, satisfied, transferred them to the grill for a couple of minutes until they got a light char, and then returned inside.

Hugh spared her ribs a glance, but didn't say anything. Parker scooped some of her sauce into three spouted dishes and arranged everything on a platter. The sauce needed a second to cool down anyway before it could be served. She was ready for the first judging.

After a few minutes, one of Hugh's waitresses, a petite redhead, popped in to collect the ribs for the judges. Another Hugh admirer that Parker ignored. If anything happened between them, it would just be sex, and it didn't matter if she was the only one or if he had someone else the next day. Which he probably would.

Shaking the unpleasant thought from her head, Parker got back to work on her other sauce for the brisket.

She noticed that Hugh was leaning against his oven, watching her again.

"Are you not cooking?" she asked, putting her hands on her hips. Only ten minutes left until she needed to get the brisket out of the smoker.

"Yeah," he said, gesturing to his stove top. He ran a white towel over his forehead, collecting the moisture there. A bead of sweat slithered down his golden neck and into the open vee that revealed the start of an impressively defined collarbone, and she thought she might faint from the pure indecency of it, but he wiped that away with a towel, too, grinning knowingly at her.

"I don't have time to flirt with you," she barked, turning away from him to splash a bit more hot sauce into her pot.

"That's a damn shame," he said, his eyes on her chest. She knew there was a ring of sweat around the collar of her shirt. Felt it like a warm, wet hand around her neck, but there was nothing she could do about it. It was Las Vegas in summer, and even though the kitchen was air-conditioned to high heaven, she was still standing directly in front of three open flames and going outside every twenty minutes to check on the smokers that were baking in the sun. There was no getting away from the heat, literally or figuratively.

"Give it a rest, will you?" she begged. "I'm not going to sleep with you."

He stopped stirring and watched her add a bit of salt to a sauce. "I'm confused about why that is again?"

"Because I don't want to," she told him. Of course, she wanted nothing more than to sleep with him, but perversely, she also didn't want to give him what he wanted more.

"Liar," he laughed, brushing his big body past her on his way outside to the patio.

She blew out a relieved breath. Being in the same room with him all day was hell. All she wanted to do was rip his shirt off and jump him, contest be damned. He could put her on his payroll all day if he wanted as long as she got to finish what they'd started that first night.

Her phone dinged. She rolled her eyes at Hugh's text message.

Get out here! Your chicken is on fire!

Laughing, she texted him back a thumbs-down for his lame attempt to get her out to the patio again. He'd been doing it all day. Earlier he'd texted her that he saw a puppy, which had been a struggle not to verify.

When it was time, she did go out to collect her brisket. She'd made three and put them on completely separate racks just to account for any uneven cooking that might occur in the smokers. Basically, nothing was being left to chance. That just wasn't who she was. Not in the kitchen and not in life.

However, one thing she had not planned on was Hugh lounging in a plastic chair, naked from the waist up and fanning himself with his shirt. He was such an ass and totally doing it on purpose to drive her bonkers—and it was so working. Between the heat, the pressure of the competition and resisting him, it was just too much. She was only one freaking woman.

"You are shameless," she accused, pointing a finger at him.

He peered at her, still waving his shirt as he regarded her with slit, lazy eyes. "Pardon?"

"If you were that hot, you could have gone back inside," she pointed out, yanking open the doors to her brisket. She would not look at his bare chest; he didn't deserve it. If he wanted to sit over there looking like a sweaty Adonis, good for him. She wasn't having it. She was here to win a contest and then...well, and then maybe she'd let herself ogle his bare chest. Because it was really something to behold. Out of the corner of her eye, she saw the eight-pack carved elegantly into his tanned flesh, corrugated like tough steel and covered with rough velvet. Dark hair covered his chest, thinning out to a perfect line that disappeared under his shorts.

"I could have gone in," he admitted. "But I need to be out here to make sure you're not turning up the heat on my meat. My ribs got too hot and you were the only person who could have changed the temperature."

She rolled her eyes. "I did not turn up the heat on your meat," she gritted, turning to him. But then she saw his eyes glittering and that he was once again teasing her, goading her into saying the ridiculous sentence about his meat.

"You're a child," she complained, sitting the last brisket on her tray before closing the smoker doors.

Glaring at him, she left him on the patio to glory in his own juvenile antics.

Within a minute, Hugh was back in the kitchen as well, with his shirt intact, just in time for the red-headed waitress to collect their new plates. Parker started cleaning up her space.

The waitress came back in to let them know they had ten more minutes until the chicken tasting, so Parker and Hugh returned to the patio to get their chickens. Once back inside, Parker immediately started shredding hers with two wooden devices that looked like large combs. Trying the meat, she was satisfied that it was tender and flavorful. She could taste the sweet smoke from hardwood coals permeating the meat and it was going to be delicious with the tangy mustard sauce.

Taking a deep, relieved breath that it was all over, she put the last of the sauce onto the judging tray, confident that she had it all in the bag.

As the waitress left the kitchen, Hugh threw his towel on the counter.

"Hell, yeah!" he hooted, shoving his fist in the air. "We did it!"

His deep voice echoed in the empty cement room and she laughed at him. "You tired?" she teased. "I was barely getting started."

"You're so full of shit, Parker."

He tossed a juicy slice of brisket into his mouth and stared at her as he chewed, that strong jaw gnashing and grinding. It was hot as hell, nearly as hot as she was. "That's damn good," he said, drenching another piece of his beef with sauce and stuffing it into his mouth. "I don't think you're gonna be able to beat that dry rub."

She shrugged. "We'll see."

Flipping off all the burners, she started washing the utensils she'd used.

"Fuck that," he barked. "Cleaning crew will get the washing."

"It's not a big deal," she told him. His employees had volunteered to work today for time and a half, but that didn't mean they wanted to. Plus, it gave her something to do besides watch Hugh eat in the sexiest way possible. This whole day had her strung out, and she was ready to go back to the hotel and jump in the cool hotel pool with an ice-cold margarita.

But then Hugh was beside her at the sink, helping her wash dishes, and the very thing she'd been avoiding all day was right up against her. She knew he was doing it on purpose, getting in her space, making her all too aware of how she'd been wrapped around him in the dark room, riding his leg until she came.

Taking a few steps away from him, she started drying what she'd washed, creating enough distance between them that she could no longer be taunted by the lingering fresh scent of his deodorant still alluringly present underneath the overwhelming smell of woodsmoke.

"Whoever wins," Hugh eventually said when he'd washed nearly all of the remaining dishes, "we'll go out for a celebratory meal."

Parker looked at him speculatively. "You'll keep your shirt on?"

"No promises," he grinned, that crooked incisor melting her.

"Then my answer is no."

He laughed. "I've never met a woman so scared of my bare chest. You must be two seconds away from clobbering me."

"In the face," she muttered.

He was still laughing when Michael entered the room. "Guys, a decision has been made."

Parker met Michael's eyes and he smiled, so she knew she had it in the bag. Pulling out the front of her shirt and fanning herself with it, she realized she probably wasn't presentable for the judges. Her back was soaked in sweat; her hair was a limp mess on top of her head, damp strands falling down her neck. Making a quick stop in the bathroom, she ran cold water over a bunch of paper towels and freshened up. Redoing her hair and reapplying a bit of makeup was all she had time for, but it at least made her fit for the public eye.

She and Hugh made their way into the dining area where the judges were stationed, him accidentally bumping her as they tried to go through the doorway at the same time.

"Ladies first," she scolded him.

"You were going too slow," he accused, a corner of that wide mouth lifting as he looked down at her from his significant height.

"My legs are short," she informed. "I'm not a giant like you."

"Those legs are just right," he said, and she rolled her eyes at his incessant flirting. It was almost too much to even be true now.

In front of the judges, Hugh was even worse, chatting to all of them like they were the best of friends. Parker wondered if it was all an act, the gregarious football star shtick. Was the confidence so innate in him just covering up something soft and fragile? She wouldn't be the one to find out anyway, so she should probably put the curiosity away. Being curious about Hugh would lead nowhere good.

Fortunately, none of his schmoozing mattered in the end.

Michael stepped forward with the scores. "The rib round went to Parker, brisket went to Hugh, and chicken went to Parker, with Parker's averaged score being nine-point-five out of ten and Hugh's being eight-point-five. It was a great afternoon of barbecue, but that makes Parker our winner!"

Parker grinned at Hugh, whose thick arms were

crossed over his chest as he read the anonymous score sheets the judges had displayed on the table.

"This is hogwash!" he bellowed, pushing the sheets aside and giving the panel his best glare. But she knew he wasn't really upset, just playing it up. He pointed to the man-bun reporter for the newspaper, whose face froze in fear. "You better make it clear how close of a contest it was, pal."

"It wasn't a close contest, though," Parker pointed out, enjoying putting her hand directly over an open flame. "I wiped the floor with you and your weak barbecue."

His tongue shot to the inside of his cheek as he regarded her. "A lightning round. You and me, no smoking, no studying or working ahead, just us at the grill."

She rolled her eyes. "Fine. Far be it from me not to hand you your ass again if that's where you want it."

A thick eyebrow shot up, but she ignored him and his rude behavior. "You guys mind trying a burger?" she asked.

Everyone nodded their heads and she slapped Hugh on the shoulder. "Let's go, big guy, so I can beat you again. Triumph suits me."

He just grinned at her and it was trouble.

To Hugh's credit, he fired up both grills without a problem and they were able to get to work. He'd chosen to use already ground beef while she located the equipment to grind up sirloin and a little bit of pork butt. It would make for a more tender and flavorful burger. She made sure he didn't see what she was doing, though. And to top it off, she also added a crapload of butter to the mix because fat was what made burgers great. Then she hand-whipped some homemade aioli with tons of garlic and hot sauce, and caramelized some Vidalia onions until they were crispy and sweet. There was no way he was winning this, either.

However, as she stood in front of the grill in stifling heat that was over one hundred degrees, sweat pouring down her body, she had to wonder if it was worth it. She'd already beaten him at the main competition; this was all just to soothe his wounded ego. Again.

Flipping the hamburgers over, she placed a slice of smoked gouda cheese on top.

"Gouda?" he scoffed, his crooked nose wrinkling. "Miz Fancy-Pants over there."

"What are you using," she threw right back, "American? Just remember to take the plastic wrapping off."

"Smoked cheddar," he clarified, looking smug. "And there's nothing wrong with American cheese."

"Except that there's no food in it," she pointed out.

"What do you call all that cheese flavoring then?" he asked, grinning stupidly at her, clearly enjoying their non-argument argument. And that's when she realized that she actually liked Hugh Matteson. Not as some dumb hot jock who would be good in bed, but as a live human person who could make, and more importantly, take a joke. It wasn't good news for the no-strings-attached kind of affair she'd planned on.

She took her patties off the grill, along with the buttered and toasted sourdough buns, and went off to construct the burgers. Slathering either side of the buns with the aioli and same thick sweet barbecue sauce she'd used on the brisket, she added the onions, a couple of pieces of crunchy bacon and a juicy slice of tomato.

Hugh, on the other hand, just breezed into the kitchen, slapped the standard toppings on his burger, including squeeze bottle mayo, lettuce and tomato, and seemed to call it a day.

"You don't actually want to win, do you?" she accused.

"I just don't need my burgers to be precious is all," was his gruff retort. "Not every damn thing needs a fancy-ass mayo. You got truffle oil in there, too?"

"Nooo," she drawled. "I don't mind food trends, though. Bringing new foods and ideas to the forefront is exciting."

"That's all well and good, but a burger is a burger. It doesn't need to be gussied up."

"I know you're purposely trying to irritate me."

"Well, if you'd had to watch sweat dripping down your cleavage all damn day, you'd be fucking testy, too," he bit off, staring at her T-shirt pointedly. "Now let's get this finished so I can get myself into a cold shower."

That got her blood boiling. "You're the one who suggested this burger insanity!" she shouted at him, her nerves and patience shot. "We could already be in cold showers!"

His tongue slid to his cheek again as he met her eyes. "Yeah, but then I couldn't see you all sweaty." Then he winked at her and she swore if he were just a little bit closer she would have punched him right in the face.

He sauntered out into the dining area again and she nearly stomped after him, fuming all the way.

That is, until she won that contest, too.

She didn't bother to gloat, though, just smiled sweetly at Hugh as she bid Michael and the other judges goodbye.

Finally, it was just the two of them left in the restaurant and she returned to the kitchen to collect all the gear she'd brought, bearing the heat again when she went outside to get her utensils and the rest of the wood she'd brought for the smokers. She knew she was soaked, but it was over and she could finally hop in the hotel pool.

"Listen," she told Hugh when she got back to the

kitchen, "you don't have to bottle my sauce. This was fun, but I think I proved my point. I'm more than qualified to make a judgment about barbecue."

He faced her straight-on, hands on his hips. "I never thought you weren't, Parker. But lying pisses me off and you lied straight to my face even as you were coming apart on my leg. I didn't deserve it and I didn't like it." He said it all without his normal bluster and dramatics. Just a simple statement of how he felt, which she took in.

However, as she stared at his mulish expression, she realized that it had all been just punishment to him. He'd found her guilty and had handed down his sentence. She wasn't sure she liked it. It meant that they were involved in something together when she needed this to be physical attraction only.

"Come on," he said, waving her toward the other end of the kitchen. "I have an idea to cool us down."

She followed, a little trepidatiously, because now she didn't really trust him.

When he stopped in front of the meat locker, her gaze flew to his and all her conflicting feelings took a back seat. "You're a genius," she breathed.

He nodded, hoisting open the thick door and ushering her through.

"Oh my God," she breathed as the cold air hit her flaming skin like aloe on a sunburn. "This… is paradise."

Hugh flipped up his shirt and groaned. "I've been waiting all day to do this."

Parker swallowed hard because despite being inside an actual freezer, Hugh's abdomen got her heated.

"And, Parker, we're doing the sauce. All of them were goddamn delicious."

CHAPTER SIX

HUGH FELT ALMOST ashamed of how easy it had been to get Parker into the freezer with him. It wasn't entirely selfish, because his internal body temperature was at boiling from standing by the grill for that final burger and he imagined she was no different. He'd suggested the last burger challenge with every intention of getting her in the freezer afterward.

And it had been a good idea on his part, too, because she was looking at him as if he were Santa Claus and the Easter Bunny rolled into one.

"Good, huh?" he asked.

She nodded her head vigorously, holding her arms out from her body and fanning her shirt, the same way she'd been doing all damned day, driving him insane as the thin cotton caught at her chest and allowed him tantalizing peeks at creamy bare skin that were everything and not at all enough.

"Why haven't we been doing this all day?" she asked, her voice breathy with pleasure.

A good question, but mostly because his whole plan had been to seduce her with cold air, which he was rethinking now as goose bumps popped up over the bare skin of her arms and legs. She'd be ready to leave anytime now and he'd be right back where he started. His seduction game apparently needed some work, because he'd been doing a lot without much success. Or maybe what he was pursuing was different. He'd never had much interest in complicated women before, but Parker was bringing it out in him. He hadn't realized how much he liked to work for a woman in his bed, so it was a novel experience.

"I didn't want to interrupt the contest," he said instead. "You looked very intense."

"I was chill," she argued with a goofy smile that had him fighting his own.

Instead he snorted. "Yeah, chill," he mocked. "You barely knew anyone else was in the room. And you weighed your spices, for Christ's sake. I've never seen anyone do that in the history of my life."

She shrugged unapologetically. "My recipe is very exact."

"Well, now it's mine." The words were out of his mouth and he realized by her startled glance that she hadn't thought about that yet.

Her eyes narrowed dangerously and he felt it in his dick. What the hell was happening to him that he liked her anger? "Did you throw the contest just to get my recipe?"

"No, I certainly did not. But after tasting your sauce, I have to admit that it's better than mine and since you're a known entity in the food world, it doesn't hurt to have you featured in my restaurants."

"Oh my God," she drawled, pointing an accusing finger at him. "You did lose on purpose!"

"I did no such thing." And he hadn't, but it had occurred to him that bottling her sauce and adding another one to his restaurant could never be a bad idea. He liked to rotate them out anyway, and having a food critic create a sauce did give a kind of respectability to the operation that as a former sports figure he lacked.

She met his eyes, fire sparking in the ice-cold air. "I don't believe you. I retract my terms. I don't want to give you my recipe."

"I know, sweetheart, but a deal is a deal. It's in the newspaper and everyone is going to want to try the new sauce. Which one do you want to do, the Carolina mustard sauce? That would be a brand-new addition to my lineup, so it's what I'd prefer. And it's fucking legit dynamite."

The compliment seemed to take the wind out of her sails.

"You're much smarter than you look," she grumbled.

"I hear that a lot," he said, chuckling. "What's got your panties in a bunch, anyway? You'll get all the money without any of the investment, just like you planned in the first place when you made that your prize."

She pulled out her mass of hair from the elastic band, combing her fingers through it and grabbing the loose strands back up before anchoring it on the top of her head again. All that was well and good, but what it did mostly was draw his attention back to her chest arching out, stretching that Cubs logo to new proportions, hard nipples at full attention. He was in major trouble if he didn't get his hands on her soon.

"Yeah, but this whole thing is your doing," she pointed out with a deep frown. "You goaded me into a competition. Possibly just to get my sauce."

"Wait a second," he said, raising his hands up as if to ward off her inaccuracies. "I may have suggested the contest to show you a thing or two, but you dictated the terms of your victory. Don't blame me for turning a potentially bad situation into something profitable."

She stared at him, brows still drawn together in frustration, but her eyes met his and he knew she'd accepted that he was right. For what it was worth, he understood her irritation. She was giving up something incredibly valuable in her sauce recipe. But if anyone wasn't going to screw her over, at least not figuratively, it was him.

"I'll have a lawyer draw up my terms," she told him finally. Then she ran her hands up and down her arms. "Man, this feels so good."

"I know," he agreed, wondering how he had a full hard-on in a deep freezer with no less than twenty sides of beef and pork hanging from the ceiling on thick meat hooks. It wasn't a romantic setting but he had it bad for her. The cutoff shorts that barely covered her round ass were sending jagged bolts of lust straight to his dick. He wasn't much of a baseball fan, either, but from now on the Cubs were his number one team. She did miraculous things for T-shirts.

"I had fun today," she said, meeting his eyes again. Hers were warm and melty, not that she meant them to be in the context of their current conversation, but just in general. Parker was a bad-ass, but her eyes gave away the fact that she was also sensitive and he felt that now as he watched her. Felt closer to her because he had shields up, too. "You're a pretty good trash-talker."

He laughed. "Yeah, I typically tone it down for the ladies, but we got pretty creative on the field."

"What was your favorite insult?" she asked, eyes sparking with curiosity.

"It's not for public consumption," he said, not going to say any of that shit out loud. No damn way.

"Oh, come on," she taunted. "I'm not a child, Hugh. I can take a little trash talk."

He thought about what he could possibly say that wouldn't have her thinking he was a cretin. "Guys would call each other's moms all kinds of stuff that was not nice, so those had to be the worst. And I'm not going to repeat them because I have a mother and she deserves better."

Parker crossed her arms over her chest, staring him down.

"You can glare at me all you want, but I'm not sharing," he dug in. "Let's just leave it at, I'm good at trash talk."

She looked like she might not let it go, but then her eye caught on a slab of beef. "You really have this shipped in from Texas?"

He nodded. "I own a ranch, remember? I supply my restaurants."

"So you have, like, actual cowboys on your ranch?" she said, eyebrows raised in interest as she moved in between the rows of meat.

His lips thinned. "Yes, there are cowboys there."

"But you don't do that?"

"I've been known to rope a bull or two," he admitted. "Why? You got a thing for cowboys?"

She shrugged. "I don't know, I've never really thought about before, but I probably could have one."

That made him smile. "Oh, yeah? What else could you probably have a thing for?"

Their eyes met and she shook her head, coming out from behind a side of beef to stand in front of him again. "Nope."

"What?" he drawled innocently, knowing exactly what she meant, but wanting her to say it out loud.

"I've never had a thing for football players."

"Good thing I'm not a football player."

"You know what I mean."

"Sure do," he agreed. "You don't want to admit you have a thing for me."

She raised an eyebrow. "I have a thing for you? You're the one panting after me all day like a starving dog."

He laughed. "I mean, characterizing me as a dog is a little harsh, but I concede your point. But then, I don't have any problem letting you know I have a thing for you. As I've mentioned, that seems to be your problem."

She didn't look impressed, so he continued, taking a step toward her. She took a step back, straight into the beef, and let out a high-pitched scream. The sound was muted in the soundproof space. Nevertheless, it was funny as hell.

"Don't worry, it's already dead," he informed her, laughing his ass off as she wiped at her arm where it had touched the raw meat. Any parasites had been killed off in the initial freeze or else he would have suggested a joint shower for her to get properly sanitized.

"Okay, I think I've cooled down enough," she declared in a huff, marching toward the door.

He stopped laughing and everything in his being wanted to just block her path, but he was a big guy and his size was intimidating so he was very cautious of using it like a weapon. He stepped aside, allowing her to pass, but before she got to the door, he said, "So when are we going for that celebratory dinner?"

Turning on her heel, she speared him with a serious gaze. "You know it's not a good idea."

"Is it because you kind of work for me now?" he asked, just to send her off again. He wasn't ready for her to go yet, enjoying their game.

"I do not work for you at all," she growled, her head tilting forward in irritation.

"Sure feels that way to me," he continued. "I'm making your product. I'm selling it and giving you money. Is that not how business works?"

"You're the worst," she muttered, her hand on the doorknob. "And FYI, that actually makes it sound like you're working for me."

"And I'm glad to do it," he told her. "I'll stop teasing if you agree to dinner with me."

"It's not even worth it," she grumbled to herself, head down.

Then facing him head-on, she pulled off the T-shirt of his personal mental torment, treating him to a strip show he would have paid good money for. "You want me, Hugh? Come and get me. I honestly don't know why I'm resisting anymore other than the fact that you're an impossible human being."

He got caught up staring at the two glorious mounds of flesh pressing out of her sheer, pale yellow bra. He was definitely going to lose his mind if he didn't touch her as soon as possible.

But then he saw her shiver and jolted into action.

"Come on," he growled, grabbing her hand and her shirt from the floor, "you're going to get hypothermia."

He led them next door to the pantry and snatched his own shirt off as well, tossing it carelessly to the floor.

Her eyes locked on his chest, she fanned herself. "Maybe we left the freezer too soon."

"This up to your standard?" He was messing with her because he knew exactly what he looked like. And worked out nearly every day to get there.

"On closer inspection, your abs could use a little work," she told him, meeting his eyes again.

"Get over here, Parker," he ordered. "I've been waiting too long to get my hands on you again."

She slowly made her way toward him and he braced himself for what was to come. He could easily take charge of this whole thing, but he had a girl who'd just stripped in a meat locker so despite the fact that he couldn't trust her, he quickly decided that he was going to do every damn thing to make this a regular event until she left.

"You are sexy as hell," he said, finding it hard not to watch as her breasts jiggled the slightest bit with every step she took.

The pantry was dark, just a hanging trio of shaded lights over a steel table in the middle of the room, but he could see everything he needed to. He hoped to hell the table was sturdy because as soon as Parker got close enough, he scooped her straight up in his arms and sat her down on it.

Maybe it was wishful thinking to imagine he could let her be in complete control. Next time. And he would make damn sure there were some next times.

She leaned in and dropped a kiss on his collarbone, making him shiver against his will. "You're sexy, too," she said, her voice soft. "An ass, but also sexy."

"Aw, sweetheart," he purred, "you're too nice to me."

And then he finally took her mouth, those sweet bowed lips softening under his own. He tangled his hands in her hair, the strands on her neck slightly damp, which really got his dick pulsing with need. He hauled her closer, her legs wrapped around his back, and he pressed into the waiting warmth between her thighs. Heaven was in his pantry, he swore to God.

Her tongue breached his mouth and he grunted, grinding his hips against her. Their fire was rising fast and furious, her nails biting into his back as she explored his mouth. He let her, loved feeling her small tongue against his, the sensuality of it, the intimacy. He'd missed that a lot since his breakup, being part of someone. She tasted like sweet diet soda and smoky barbecue, the perfect summer combination, and he pulled on her, egging her on and bringing her deeper into him so they didn't know where one ended and the other began.

"These fucking shorts have been driving me nuts all damned day," he growled against her mouth when he finally came up for air. He gripped her sides and lifted her so she could slide off the cutoff jean shorts that should be outlawed on her, they were so absurdly fitted. "Take them off. Take it all off."

He could feel her heart beating against her ribs and her eyes locked with his as she slid the jeans off onto the floor, along with her yellow bra and panties. "That's right, sweetheart," he murmured, not quite ready to look down at what she'd uncovered. "You like doing what I tell you?"

Her eyes flared, but he just raised an eyebrow because they both knew the truth. "You can tell me what to do, too," he taunted her, biting down on her tender earlobe. "I promise I'm very obedient."

She snorted and he sat her back on the table, taking her mouth again. He allowed her no room to think, took her over, inhaled her, ate at her mouth until she was limp in his arms, yet still pulling at the hair at the base of his skull.

Reaching into his pocket, he took out his wallet and dropped the condom on the table, meeting her eyes. If she wanted to stop this, now was the time.

Instead she rocked against him and he fucking loved it.

"How do you like it, Parker?" he murmured, gaze sliding down the sickest fucking body he'd ever seen. Her waist was pinched and it flared out into hips that were made for his big hands to grip. He pulled her closer into his waiting cock, grinding against her until her wetness darkened the front of his shorts.

He cupped her perfect globes in his hand, leaning down to take an unimaginably soft nipple into his mouth, sliding his tongue in circles around it until gently sucking the tip, the quiet sound erotic in the silent pantry where nothing else existed besides them.

"Gentle?" he suggested when she didn't respond to his question, running a thumb whisper-soft over her nipple.

"Or not?" he posed, giving the nipple a good twist, her whimper of pleasure making his cock throb spastically against his pants.

Switching nipples, he took the beaded tip into his mouth, sucking ever so slightly on it, barely running his tongue over it, her hips grinding into him to get closer.

And then he pulled it hard into his mouth, feeding off her groan.

"Hard it is," he murmured, applying the same treatment to the other nipple.

She reached down and unbuttoned his shorts, pulling him out of his underwear.

Parker watched as he got larger with each stroke, the flesh hardening in her hand. The feel of her around him was so damned good, he wasn't sure how long he could make this last. Taking her nipple again, his tongue explored every ridge of her, the smooth skin of her breast, tugging and shaping the elongated point, gently nibbling at it until she'd abandoned his cock and was digging her nails into his back.

Wrapping his hands in her hair, tugging just the slightest bit, he tilted her head down as his other hand ran down the middle of her stomach and into the silky folds he'd been sense-remembering on his fingers since their night at Structure. He held her there, wanting her to see every bit of it.

Their eyes were both focused on his finger as he slowly slid it inside her, watching it disappear into her soft channel. He crooked it and she shivered as he found that rough patch there, rubbing tenderly over it because his control was ready to snap. Two fingers were next and he pumped them inside, loving when her hips began to move and her breathing grew audible in the room.

Spearing three fingers inside her, he leaned down to take her mouth, swallowing her little moans of pleasure. She tasted like smoke and sugar and he was near bursting. "Tell me what you want now," he ordered, running a thumb over her budding clit. She was close to the edge, he knew that much. Her legs were locked tight around him and her breathing was tense and short.

Watching her, but still tilting her head down, he ran his hand up and down her slit, bathing it in her arousal. Then he gripped his cock, coating himself in her as he stroked himself.

Her intake of breath was satisfying and she grabbed back at the condom, but he shook his head. "Tell me what you want."

Eyes clear, she matched his gaze. "I want you inside me right now."

Smiling, he grabbed a kiss and then stepped back from her.

"Too bad," he told her, raising an eyebrow. "Because I want you to suck me."

If he thought she'd be irritated with his purposeful about-face, he was wrong, because she immediately slid off the table to her knees in an effortless move.

Cupping his sack, which alone had him locking his knees for support, she licked up the underside of him from root to tip, the vision of that pink tongue driving him to the brink. When she pulled his tip into her mouth his hand shot out to grip the table, his knuckles going white as she took the rest of him into her mouth. She was so fucking good at it, tugging and sucking with alternating pressure and contact, sometimes sliding him all the way out so just her tongue was tracing the slit, lapping up his pre-come.

"I want to do filthy, unspeakable things to you, Parker," he growled, pulling her up before he came. He was going to be inside her when that happened.

Her smile was feline and satisfied. "Good."

He picked her up, loving her yelp of surprise, and laid her out flat on the table with her legs dangling over the edge, all of her bared to his gaze at once.

"Arms up," he commanded, watching as she obeyed, her fingers curling over the edge of the steel.

He ripped open the condom and rolled it on, not sure if he could wait any longer to be inside her even though the need to torture her mindless was also powerful. In the end, though, he couldn't wait.

"You ready?" he asked, placing himself at her entrance, his hips moving of their own volition as he pushed just the merest fraction of an inch into her.

"Do it, Matteson," she demanded, hips lifting.

A smile on his face, he slammed into her, praying she could take it, waiting for and reveling in her grin as she did. She was liquid heat around him, living, breathing sex made for him. Every move she made, every sound that left her mouth, enveloped him like a lasso of dirty lust and desire, pulling and tugging on his insides as he pumped into her.

With every stroke, his sack tightened up, that knot in the small of his back gathering pull as he slid in and out, her satin muscles clinging and clamping over him, expressly designed to drive him to the pinnacle of pleasure.

"Fucking hell," he gritted, running a thumb over her clit, the resulting jerk of her hips a counterpoint to his thrusts. "You're so damned tight."

They went at each other then like animals, bucking and grinding, but he held her hands down the whole time, needing the anchor, wanting her to feel the full force of what they were together, which was a conflagration unlike any he'd ever experienced. She let go, her back arching and her insides gripping him until he exploded, darkness shuttering his eyes as all his muscles tensed up and then relaxed, a wave of relief and bliss washing the urgency away, leaving only gratitude and intimacy in its place.

Their breathing was the only sound in the quiet room as Hugh slowly returned to earth.

Eventually, he leaned down to drop a soft kiss on her lips. "I think that makes us both winners today."

CHAPTER SEVEN

"YOU WANT ME to do what?" Parker barked into her phone at Hugh.

"Two of my head chefs are sick and the other two are out of town," he repeated. "I need your help."

"You want me to cook at your restaurant to-night?" she asked again, because he could not be serious.

"Yeah, I'll pay you whatever you want for the night. I just need someone and I know you can cook."

"You seriously don't know anyone else in this town who could cook for you? There are tons of other barbecue places."

"Listen, Parker," he said, sounding stressed and agitated, "if you don't want to do it, that's fine. But just tell me because I really need to find someone for tonight before dinner begins and I'm totally fucking screwed."

"Why can't you do it?" she asked, pressing her luck.

"Because I'm a goddamn restaurant owner, not

a chef!" he bellowed, which should have made her scared but instead had her grinning. She liked it when he went all quarterback on her.

She just couldn't cave too easily, not after last night in the pantry where he'd completely blown her mind. If she wasn't careful, he could have her doing literally anything for another taste of him. And it wasn't even because his body put those of all other men to shame; it was because he was thoughtful, creative and just Hugh. Maddeningly bossy, fun as hell and too clever by half.

"I'll do it, Hugh," she finally relented. "But you have to be there with me. I'm not going in blind or alone."

"You got it, Parker," he said, breathing a sigh of relief. "Don't take this the wrong way, but right at this moment, I've never loved a human being more."

She laughed. "No problem. I'll head over there now to get a handle on what to do. I assume the meat has at least been in the smoker for the day?"

"Yep, it's all ready to go for a regular opening time," he confirmed.

When she got to the restaurant, it was true that the meat had been smoked, which was a load off her mind.

Hugh made his appearance in the kitchen wearing another mouthwatering suit. This one beige with peach threading, paired with a white shirt and peach tie. As usually, he looked cool and confident in a suit that on another man would have looked like he was trying too hard.

His gaze raked over her with so much heat she literally thought she might catch fire. The dude did not hide how he felt about her physically. All bets were off since last night, too. His texts were outright pornography and this morning he'd tried to initiate videophone sex, which she'd turned down because she'd had a brunch and also, what person looked their best first thing in the morning? That said, she felt the same way he did. Her thoughts were only about him. Much to her dismay, because she could not get involved with a man like Hugh who would break her heart faster than one of his quick grins. Just remembering the way he'd completely ignored that Jesse at Structure was in love with him. That's how she'd look one day if they kept sleeping together, like a lost puppy lapping up his measliest of affections and still begging him to love her. Jesse seemed like a nice enough girl, but Parker had no interest in being one of his castoffs or charity cases. That was for her regularly scheduled life, thank you very much.

"Why no phone sex?" he demanded, stopping in front of her, eyes still hooded. "Do you know the kind of painful morning wood I woke up with after reliving last night probably a thousand times over in my dreams?"

"Well, we could be repeating that right now, but

apparently I have to cook for however many people want a taste of your food tonight."

He ran a hand through his hair, clearly frustrated by it, too. "Usually the manager handles this kind of shit, but apparently one of the chef's parents died, which is why two of them are out of town at the same time."

"You don't have to keep apologizing, Hugh, but my payment will be high."

He crowded her against the long stainless steel table, identical to the one he'd had her on last night. "Tell me last night is what you're thinking about right now," he murmured, setting his lips against hers.

"It's one of the things," she admitted when he let up.

"Are you against phone sex in general or just today?" he asked. "Because it's very important to me."

She shook her head. "You're cracked."

His lips went fully in then, taking hers in a searing kiss that had her leaning against him on tiptoes. He picked her up and sat her on the table again, but she immediately slid off and gave him a speaking glance.

"Your employees will be here any second," she reminded him, and even though she wasn't an actual employee she wasn't going to just make out with him where anyone could see.

"I'm the boss," he continued without a shred of embarrassment, "and I like access." He nudged his mouth against hers again, waiting for her to grant him said access. Then he nuzzled her cheek until his lips reached her ear. "And by that I mean, I want video access when I call."

"I'm not your sex dummy, just available to fornicate whenever you please," she informed him, her head bending back to glare at his eyes. He was very large and sometimes she forgot, but crowded against the table she couldn't even see beyond his wide shoulders, which was grounding.

He ignored her, leaning down to nuzzle her neck again, and she couldn't help bending to the side to give him just want he wanted, better access. Lazy tingles of pleasure rose up on her skin like happy reminders of what he could do to her body.

"I don't want a sex dummy anyway," he murmured against her ear, his breath warm. "I thought one night would do it, but I was wrong." He drew small kisses back down the side of her neck.

"Come over tonight," he coaxed, his hand running up her rib cage.

She was definitely in danger of getting addicted to him, alarm settling in her belly at the thought. His big hand spanned her back as he gathered her into him and she would have given him whatever he'd asked. Luckily, what he wanted was something she wanted, as well.

"Yeah, I'll come over," she told him. "But it'll be nearly midnight before I get out of here. Are you sure you're up for it?"

"Are you insinuating I'm too old to be up that late?"

She shrugged. "I would never."

"You better be ready, sweetheart, because you'll be tired, but I'll still be demanding."

"So will I," she said, pushing at his chest as an employee entered the kitchen, but he didn't let go of her. It was as if he was already staking his claim and it sent shivers but also more trepidation sliding through her. The kid waved and then made his way to the employee lounge to clock in.

"That's my girl," Hugh murmured, the hand on her back drifting down to give her ass a powerful grip before letting her go completely.

"Excuse me," she choked, staring threateningly at him.

He just stuck his tongue in the side of his cheek and lifted one Hercules-esque shoulder in an unconcerned shrug. "Couldn't help it." He grinned. "I like that ass."

"Just go get the stuff I need for prep," she ordered, pointing an authoritative finger to the pantry.

He waggled his thick eyebrows, the one with a slash in it drawing her eye as he obeyed and disappeared from the kitchen. She'd seen a lot of scars on his body last night but hadn't wanted to ask about them. And honestly, had more important business to attend to besides dredging up old memories that might be unpleasant for him, but that didn't mean she wasn't curious.

Pulling on an apron from the rack on the wall, she mentally prepared herself for a rough night. She'd worked her fair share of years as a line cook in restaurants in Chicago and New York, as sous chef and eventually head chef for a famous Manhattan restaurateur, so she knew the toll it took on the body. It wasn't the only reason she'd left the kitchen, but a big one along with needing to be at home for her dad more. She enjoyed not having traditional hours and backbreaking work, but she was excited to cook for people again.

She went back to the prep room where Hugh and the other employee, whose name tag read Doug, were chopping up a mountain of onions.

"You located the prep sheet then?" she asked pointedly.

"No," Hugh drawled, his voice muffled under the red handkerchief covering the bottom half of his face. A pair of oversize goggles covering his eyes, he looked so ridiculous and yet she'd never been attracted to him more. "I just decided to kill myself cutting a million onions for the fun of it."

Her lips thinned in irritation, which made him grin. Turning on her heel, she went to the pantry and he followed.

"Fuck, this is harder than I thought," he said, stopping with her at the door. "I can't believe we have to do this tonight and I wasted all day not being naked with you."

She playfully shoved him out of the way and they entered the pantry. "If you give me sex eyes all night, I'm going to pour hot barbecue sauce on your head. I have work to do. Don't make it any harder than it's already going to be."

Picking through the various ingredients, she piled a few items in her arms.

"That just gives me more ideas. I'd love to lick barbecue sauce off of you and would be more than pleased if you'd do it to me."

She threw the orange she'd been holding at his chest, but he caught it in midair before it made contact.

At her surprised look, he deadpanned, "I was an elite athlete."

Shaking her head, she asked, "So do you have a preference on what specials are served?"

"No, but you don't have to do all that anyway. I just need somebody to run the kitchen tonight. All I've got are a bunch of line cooks who wouldn't know management or fine dining if it bit them on the ass."

"Oh, no, I want to cook the specials. I want to show your customers good food for a change," she joked, to which he responded with a playful scowl.

She shooed him back to the prep room while she checked out the refrigerators, where she found that some fresh fish had come in with the current day's date on it. By the time she'd planned and gathered ingredients for her dishes, it was nearly time to open.

"You ready?" Hugh barked, entering the kitchen with buckets of prepped vegetables. She shook her head, ears virtually throbbing in pain.

"Do you know how to speak at a normal volume?"

"Was that not normal?" he asked with mock innocence. "I'm trying to get you pumped up, Jones. Gonna be a long night, gotta stay alert."

"There's only one quarterback in this kitchen tonight and that's me, Matteson," she reminded him, pointing her thumb at her own chest.

That got him, a wide smile cracking his tanned face as he saluted her. "Yes, ma'am."

"Just go do something useful," she directed, not in the mood to banter with him. She had a kitchen to run.

After introducing herself to the kitchen staff, she started on the waitstaff. She explained her two specials in detail and then got to work running orders for the line cooks, which basically meant making sure the dishes for each table got ready at similar times so that some weren't waiting under the heat lamp and drying out.

When a special order came in, she got to work cooking, and as the night progressed she found herself cooking more and more specials and leaving Hugh to expedite on his own. He was an absolute natural at it since it was basically a management position where he could make sure the dishes were being prepared correctly and sent out on time. Directing and barking instructions all night in that near-deafening voice was driving her insane, but she'd bet money that dishes had never made it to customers so quickly.

He was charming, too, following every direction with a compliment and every instruction with encouragement. By the end of the night, she allowed that she had a healthy dose of respect for him. They'd made a good team in a pinch, but she hoped like hell it was her last night in a kitchen for a long time.

Lights out and everyone gone, she pulled a stool from under the stainless steel island and slipped off her sneakers with a sigh of relief.

Hugh came back into the kitchen and smiled when he saw her. "There she is, MVP of the night."

Leaning back against the table, she looked up at him, too tired to even smile. "How are you still this energetic?"

"I got a lot of breaks in and being back here was pretty cool. I do my walk-throughs and stuff, but

I was pretty ignorant about how a kitchen really works. I had fun bossing people around again."

"You were a good expediter. You have a real future in kitchen management."

He laughed. "Let me take you to my house, Parker. You look hot and sweaty, which we both know I'm into, but also exhausted. My hot tub will get you fixed up."

She didn't have the strength to deny what she wanted so she nodded.

"What are you doing?" she yelped when he scooped her up into his arms as if she were a child and not a grown woman.

"You're dead on your feet. I'm carrying you to the car."

Instead of arguing, her head fell against his wide chest. Her eyes threatened to shut but she came to again when he gently placed her in the passenger seat of his Maserati SUV.

"No McLaren tonight?" she asked when his hand was on the door to close it.

"Had hauling to do."

He shut the door and she smiled. There was no way on earth he was hauling stuff in the back of the leather showpiece that was this car. Compared to her late-model Nissan, it was next-level luxury and he knew it. Up to this point, she'd only been vaguely aware of just how rich he was, but now it was in her face for real. Another reason she was glad this was a two-night stand. Okay, maybe she'd push it to a three-night stand, but that was it. They lived in two completely different worlds. Hers was taking care of her dad and writing a simple magazine column, and his was being king of the world.

Their disparate lives only became more apparent when they pulled into a gated community and then through another gate that guarded his actual home. She'd been around this area of Vegas before—Summerlin was a growing food enclave for Las Vegas locals—but she'd never actually been inside one of the gated developments. Not that she could see much now, either. Once inside, she could only make out driveways and the tops of houses in the distance.

His own house was surprisingly modern. Two spare rectangles, one of smooth gray plaster and the other long, stacked layers of natural stone, were flanked by a higher level behind them that seemed to curve toward the sky. The two sides were separated by a cut-out entryway, but he didn't stop the car in the driveway to enter in the front door, instead following the paved road downhill into an underground garage.

"Oh, so I guess you're rich or something," she joked when they were riding the elevator from the basement garage, which had been filled with cars with names and fancy emblems she'd never heard of or seen.

He shrugged. "You could say that."

She wasn't strapped for cash in any way. In fact, made a great living for an expensive city. More than that, she was proud of what she'd accomplished, but Hugh was clearly beyond wealthy.

She wasn't intimidated, but her respect for Hugh was deepening in a way she didn't necessarily want. Falling for him for real would be an awful idea, not only because she couldn't live in Vegas and take care of her dad at the same time. But because she'd never actually fallen for someone before. She was a love virgin, and letting a playboy football player break the seal would be too stupid for words.

Besides, she was never leaving Chicago. That much had always been clear. Her dad needed her and she wasn't going to be the second female in his life to walk out on him. He was the only family she had in the world and she protected what was hers. So she needed to keep her head on straight and remember that Hugh was just for now, despite how much he made her smile or how light he made her feel. As if he was someone who could carry an equal share of the load for once. She was so used to doing everything on her own that just the idea weakened her knees, unraveling a knotted ball of tension in her chest.

To think that her real life could be as easy as her life on the road. That was the dream she hadn't dared.

"I hope you don't mind, but I had one of my assistants grab you some clothes so you can stay overnight," he informed her as if a discussion about it wasn't needed.

Which it wasn't. She was allowing herself another night with him. If not, she wouldn't be in the elevator at all.

"Thanks," she said, oddly touched. "That's very thoughtful of you."

He nodded just as the elevator doors opened directly into what, given the masculine decor and the enormous bed, was clearly his bedroom.

"Well," she snorted, folding her arms across her chest as she stared out the elevator doors, "that's presumptuous."

His shoulders shook with laughter. "Yeah, I guess if you didn't look like you might tip over any second, it would be."

"You promised me a hot tub," she reminded him, peering up at him from under her lashes.

"The clothes, including a bathing suit, are up here, but we can just sleep, Parker."

"You have some soda? I'll get a second wind." Just sleeping was a no-no. That was way too much like a relationship, and this was sex only.

"Clothes are in the bathroom. Go change into whatever you decide. And I don't drink soda but I'm sure my assistant has some stashed somewhere for parties."

She watched him exit the bedroom. Across from the elevator was a wall of windows that opened to a private terrace. Lights from a pool broke up the black night, the emptiness beyond reminding her that they were in the middle of the desert. The bedroom itself was furnished with dark wood furniture, the walls a deep navy, the bed covered with a puffy white duvet, and the carpet charcoal and plush. A massive television anchored nearly one entire wall opposite the bed and a large blue color-block painting akin to Rothko graced the wall across from the terrace doors. It wasn't overly fussy but it was comfortable and masculine. Also, lacking Hugh's big personality, but she guessed he hadn't really put much effort into decorating his second home.

The bathroom, too, was modern like the architecture of the house would suggest. Clean lines and angles gave order to the space with not a curve or furniture placement out of line. Muted white-and-gray Carrara marble blanketed every surface and made it look expensive but not flashy. Sitting on one of the two vanity counters on either side of the room were two large shopping bags along with a smaller bag from a beauty store, which she assumed were the clothes and toiletries Hugh had been referring to.

Peeking inside the small bag she saw every toiletry she might need, and luxury items at that. There were several pairs of pajamas, a couple of swimsuits that were clearly too small but she imagined that was probably by design, and what looked like jeans, a pair of shorts and some T-shirts for tomorrow. A package of underwear and two bras were also included. It was extremely thorough and she'd pay him for it, but she didn't even know that she could fit all of it in her suitcases to go home. She hadn't left any space for Vegas souvenirs since casino chic wasn't really her style.

Parker stripped down and pulled on the black swimsuit, a two-piece tankini number that basically shoved her boobs up to her eyeballs it was so small, but it didn't matter. With any luck, she'd be out of it soon. Just the thought of getting into that hot tub with Hugh was making her neck tingle in anticipation. Being in his car had been like being inside a Hugh cloud, darkly sensual and smelling like his cologne, and that feeling was only deepening now that she was in his home.

Returning to the bedroom, she noticed that a panel of the window wall was retracted and she stepped out onto the terrace to see Hugh already in the tub with five different bottles of soda and a glass of ice sitting on the ledge.

"I didn't know what you'd want," he explained.

The hot tub wasn't a standalone piece; it was sunken in the ground like a small circular pool, the jets streaming out and the water bubbling around Hugh's massive shoulders.

"Nice suit," he remarked, his eyes sliding lazily over her. He was sitting on the seat that lined the circumference of the tub, his arms propped up on the ledge. She took the two steps down into the sparkling teal water until she was fully ensconced in the rehabilitating warmth with an open bottle of diet soda in her hand.

Sitting across from him, she lay her head back on the ledge, letting the jets pulse on her muscles, and sighed. "This was an inspired idea. Thank you."

Hugh didn't say anything for a second, then she felt him pick up her foot from the bottom. Massaging it, he met her eyes. "I should be thanking you. You helped me out tonight and it really meant a lot to me. I hope you know how much I appreciate it."

Their eyes meeting, she got the sense that not many people did things for him. He was all about giving favors, yet rarely asking for them. The car he'd bought for Jesse as if he'd given her something as insignificant as a piece of gum instead of an expensive vehicle. That's the kind of man he was, and she'd been able to do something for him. It felt good to give him that and she hated it because she shouldn't feel that way.

She wanted to tell him not to worry about thanking her, either, but only a moan of pleasure came out of her mouth because at the same moment he dug his thumb into the sensitive and sore ball of her foot. "Oh my God," she breathed. "You're good at this."

He shrugged, the movement causing his abdomen to literally ripple, and she shivered in response. "The team had a fleet of world-class massage therapists. I learned what I could from them."

He moved to her toes, pulling each one just the slightest bit. By the time he was finished and moving on to the other foot, she thought she might be in a contentment coma, she felt so relaxed.

"Is that soda working or do I need to carry you to bed?" he finally asked, his voice deep and soft in the still night air.

It was hot outside even though it was dark, but the sting was out of it and the air was cool on her bare wet skin. "Working, I think," she admitted, knowing that she might be tired, but she wanted him more than she wanted sleep.

"Your specials sold more than any other dish tonight," he informed her, still holding her foot, though the massage had petered off into a light caress. "People loved them. Especially the barbecued fish tacos."

"Fish never gets enough play in the barbecue world, but it's such a mistake because it picks up whatever flavor you stick on it."

"Have you ever thought of starting your own restaurant?" he asked. "You're a really good chef."

"Thanks," she told him, opening her eyes to meet

his. "I've thought about it, but tonight reminded me of what it was like. I'm not ready to revisit that life again. It's why I left the business in the first place. I'm a much better eater than I am a cook."

He smiled. "That makes two of us." Then he paused, regarding her again. "You know, I wasn't kidding about having chefs who work on menus for the restaurants. I know I lost the competition, but I'd be in your debt if you'd contract as a consultant for me. It wouldn't interfere with the job you already have unless you wanted to help me open new locations, and I'd really like your opinions. Obviously, my sauces could use some work."

Parker grinned at him because he could be so incredibly nice and not a huge bossy-pants at all when he wanted to be. "I promise to give it full consideration. Either way, I appreciate the offer."

"Good," he said with a firm nod of his head. "Now get over here so I can touch something better than your damn foot."

She laughed but didn't move, so he reached out and hoisted her into his lap until her legs were straddling his waist and her arms were propped on his shoulders.

"Why did you even bother wearing those shorts?" she asked, annoyed that they'd have to readjust, which was awkward in a hot tub. She was eager to get this show on the road and didn't want the barrier between them.

He shrugged. "Seemed polite. And it gave me somewhere to put the condoms." Her gaze went behind him to where he was pointing. Several condoms lay just under a couple of towels. She appreciated the forethought.

Instead of moving her, he gently lifted up and slid the green board shorts off. His cock was already at full mast and she caught his eyes.

"I've been nursing a semi ever since I saw you bending over to get something out of the oven." His hands ran over her ass again, gripping the backs of her thighs as he readjusted her over his length.

Laughing, she leaned into him until their lips met and it was as if she'd never been tired. Her body was immediately energized and ready to go and got even more so when she felt him pulling at the bottom of her suit. Balancing her on his legs, he held her back as he tugged the stretchy fabric off. Satisfied, he returned her to her previous position and instead of removing her swimsuit top, he just pulled the cups to side so that her breasts were framed right in his face for his pleasure.

Greedily taking a nipple into his mouth, he reached behind him and handed her the condom. Bolts of desire lashed at her core, wanting to take him now and tired of waiting. She was needy and hot and far too eager to feel him inside her, already addicted to the rush of that huge, strong body pumping into hers. Ripping open the condom, she rolled it on him as he sucked a little too hard on her nipple, that massive, swarthy hand all but engulfing the white skin of her breasts.

When she had the condom on, she felt his fingers trail down her abdomen and into her folds. He was checking to make sure she was ready and she knew without a doubt she was. When he was satisfied, he placed himself at her entrance and eased her down onto him.

She sighed and let her head fall onto his shoulder. "We'll just take it easy, baby," he murmured, rocking her hips gently against him. "I got you."

The rise and fall was just that, slow and easy, and when it was over he picked her up and carried her into the house, snuggling against her in bed.

CHAPTER EIGHT

THE ROOM WAS dark when Parker woke up. Stretching out her legs against Hugh's soft sheets, she felt languid but refreshed. Grabbing her phone from the nightstand, she squinted against the bright blue light as she read the time. It was already nine o'clock, which was when she realized that the entire wall of windows had been flanked by blackout shades, so not even the barest hint of sunlight peeked through. A clever idea and just another thoughtful thing Hugh had done for her that was making it harder to keep things casual with him.

Thinking about him, she reached out to the other side of the bed hoping to initiate a lengthier redo of the night before, but instead of a warm Hugh she got a handful of cold sheets. It was a real shame, but the thought that she'd overstayed her welcome propelled her out of bed. She flipped on a lamp and headed to the bathroom, where she brushed her teeth and washed her face before returning to the bedroom just as Hugh was coming in.

He was shirtless again and a pair of gray athletic shorts hung loosely on his hips, highlighting the severe vee cutout at his waist that disappeared beneath the elastic band. Sweat dripped down his chest and his brown hair was damp, pushed straight back from his forehead. He'd clearly been working out already, which made her feel definitely like she should have been out of his house already.

His eyes darkened when he saw her in the pajamas he'd procured, a revealing peach set of silk shorts that barely covered her ass and a camisole that was loose around the waist but choked her breasts. She vaguely remembered putting on the first thing that she grabbed after coming in from the hot tub last night. And she was thankful for the choice because he was looking at her like he wanted to devour her.

"You worked out?" she asked, awkward now and not knowing if she should go back to bed or go change clothes in the bathroom. She should have already changed, but she hadn't wanted to spend a lot of time in there if he needed to use it. Her knowledge of what a restaurant chain owner did on a daily basis was lacking. For all she knew, he needed to go in to an office somewhere this morning.

He nodded, still staring at her, which was incredibly unnerving. "I wanted to let you sleep," he added. "You were really beat last night."

"Thanks," she said. "I was just coming to find you. I guess I'll get out of your hair now."

He didn't respond, just shook his head back and forth, his eyes locked with hers. "You want to leave now?"

"Um, I guess?" she asked. "I thought maybe you had work to do."

"The only work I want to do right now is on you."

She looked from left to right, wondering exactly what that meant, but also kind of knowing.

Hugh pulled off his shorts to reveal an already impressive erection; even in the dim light of the lamp there was no mistaking it. Her eyes closed, remembering how he felt inside her, letting the ripples of anticipation wake up her sleepy body.

In response, she pulled off her pajamas so they were standing ten feet apart, completely naked, staring at each other as if they'd never seen anyone naked before. And honestly, she couldn't remember anyone at this point. Her sex life was already going to be measured by before and after Hugh Matteson.

He nodded to the bed. "Lie down. On top of the covers."

Assuming he was going to join her there, she followed his directive. Admittedly, she would have done anything he said when he talked in that no-nonsense voice, which sent waves of need clamoring for space all over her skin. However, he didn't join her, but stayed rooted to the floor, his eyes taking in every inch of her, from toes to head. Maybe in another life she would have felt self-conscious about being on such blatant display, but the way he was looking at her, his eyes dark and his big hand stroking that ruddy, thick erection, was too erotic for those kinds of thoughts to even enter her mind. She was proud of her body anyway, but being watched was different, more intimate, which he knew and was obviously why he was doing this. It was easy to fuck someone; it was something else to share a moment of need with them.

He was drawing it out for both of them, to strengthen the connection they had. She was kidding herself that this was about just sex because from the moment he'd given that hotel room employee his phone number knowing the possible consequences to himself, she was on her way to being under his spell. After her mom left, she'd gone from being a teenager with a normal, protected life to an adult who had to take care of herself and her dad. After just a few days with Hugh, that protected feeling kept creeping in again, an invitation to lighten her load for a little while. From checking on her at the hotel, to cooling her down in the meat locker, to providing her with a hot tub, to massaging her feet last night. It was the most a man had ever done for her and they'd only known each other for a week.

Her eyes met his, a light of intensity in his, drowning out the good-natured playfulness she'd grown so used to with him.

"Touch yourself," he commanded, still stroking himself.

Her shoulders twitched with the order, but she knew she was going to do it. If this is how he wanted to start the morning, far be it from her to stand in his way, especially since she was dying to have him.

"I was disappointed you weren't here when I woke up," she told him, parting herself with a finger, finding the folds already wet.

"Is that right?" he asked, his voice deeper as his cock grew darker, stiffer in his hand as he stroked lazily, gripping harder every so often.

When she nodded, a corner of his mouth quirked. "So did you already get off?"

"No," she said, her voice catching as a jolt of pleasure kicked through her. Watching him watch her was short-circuiting her brain.

"Too bad." He took a step closer to the bed until he was standing right in front of her, and from that angle he could see exactly what she was doing, her entire core on display to him. Her knees were drawn up, and his gaze narrowed on her finger.

Their eyes met again, but she was distracted by the tip of his cock, glistening now with drops of liquid.

"You're really hot," she blurted, wanting it to be

sexier, but not in any condition to be eloquent. She was so close to the edge, but more than that she wanted him, needed to feel his touch.

"Faster," he demanded, even as his own hand went slower, became more measured. "You're really hot, too, Parker. Look at yourself right now, spread out on my bed for me like my own personal feast. You're the first woman I've had here, and it was worth the wait."

Her eyes flew to his in question but he didn't elaborate, just pointedly looked to the hand at her core that had stopped moving at his admission. "Faster," he reminded.

She obeyed, flying over her clit, her back arching as her whole body ached for release. Her skin was on fire, too tight on a body that was struggling to break free, bracing against a tidal wave of desire so acute she could barely breathe. Air entered and exited her lungs on noisy gasps until with a final arch, she let go, falling into a warm pool of euphoria.

When she came to, Hugh was no longer at the foot of the bed but beside her opening the bedside drawer and pulling out an unopened box of condoms. Tearing into them, he had himself sheathed in record time, meeting her eyes as his finger made a crooking motion. He held out a hand and helped her off the bed, only to bend her over it, his hand sliding up the back of her thigh and squeezing one of her ass cheeks.

He kissed a line down her spine, both hands now kneading her behind. "I've been waiting to have you like this since we met."

Then he was pushing into her from behind as her hands curled into the duvet, her insides stretching at his invasion. He was slow this time, too, just like last night when he'd been so gentle with her in the hot tub, but the urgency was there, just contained. Squeezing her ass, he drew a finger down the seam, and her muscles jumped uneasily. Then before she knew what was happening, he laid a firm smack on her right cheek.

She yelped, her body jolting in surprise, seating him deeper inside her. Her skin smarted but he rubbed it gently away until the throb turned into pleasure, all the disparate sensations he was perpetrating on her body coalescing into a divine madness. Nothing he did was enough. She wanted more of him. She couldn't see him, didn't know what he was thinking, only knew the thick slide of him in and out of her, the softness of the cotton she was clenching in between her fingers like a lifeline. None of it was *him*.

"That's payment for lying to me the first night," he growled, still rubbing the spot he'd slapped.

He pushed in, hitting that magic spot inside her.

"Or rather your reward, since I know you liked it."

She whimpered as he left her almost completely, the big broad tip of him poised at her entrance.

"You want it again?" he prodded, that big hand kneading the other ass cheek.

Her eyes closed, she didn't respond, just arched against him, wanting him to move, to smack her behind, to do anything just so he was closer to her. That's all she wanted, was the connection to the only man she'd ever felt this good with.

"Is that a yes, sir, I'd like to be punished?" he prodded, and she could hear the smile in his voice as he pushed back into her with enough force to make her sigh with pleasure.

"Words, Parker," he reminded, pulling her hips up to adjust his angle of entry as if she were weightless.

"Yes," she finally choked out, her orgasm building by rapid degrees. Her muscles were tensed, eyes squeezed shut, and her hips were moving without any rhyme or reason in an effort to find release.

Just as she was nearing the top, her inner muscles clenching around his invading cock, his hand found her other cheek, this time a little harder, and the sting was bliss. He laid a featherlight kiss over the abraded area and she went over the edge, grasping at the duvet like she might literally fall into an abyss without something to hold on to.

Spent and delirious, she felt him grip her hips, his broad fingers digging into her sides as he let loose, fighting for his own release when he reached around to her clit to fire her back up again. In what seemed like an instant she was careering over the cliff again, only this time he was there with her, bowed over her back, his hot breath on her shoulder as he growled his own explosion.

A final kiss on the middle of her back, then he pulled out of her, running a hand over what she had to imagine were red marks on her ass, and then disappeared into the bathroom. When he returned, she still hadn't moved and his weight compressed the bed as he lay against the headboard and pulled her up into his arms.

"That was next-level," he murmured, placing a soft kiss on her forehead.

She nodded against him, gliding a hand down his chest. "I liked it."

That made him laugh and they fell into an easy silence.

Lying on top of the duvet, an industrial steel ceiling fan moving the air slowly across their bodies, Parker felt completely mindless except that she couldn't stop thinking about how she was the first woman he'd had in his bed. That had to be just a throwaway comment to make her hot because she knew his track record with women; he'd done nothing to hide the fact that he was in demand and had taken what was on offer. Statistically, he would have needed to bring at least one or two back to his house. It just didn't make any sense.

The room was dark and quiet and she was draped across Hugh's chest as he played with her hair, twirling it around his finger as if they had all the time in the world instead of a few short weeks until she went back to Chicago. She could spend all day here in his room without a moment of regret. She was in that deep already. It wasn't good news.

Her phone went off and she grabbed it from the dark wood nightstand. A text from her boss that read, READ YOUR EMAIL.

Parker sighed. Her days might be spent eating and writing, but she still very much had people to answer to. Propping back up on Hugh again, she opened her email and read the one from her boss. Apparently, the barbecue contest with Hugh was a hit with readers and she wanted Parker to write her own story about it coupled with a profile on Hugh.

Frowning, she tapped out a response, hoping that Hugh wouldn't have a problem with it. It felt like taking advantage of him now that they were sleeping together. Most concerning, though, was that if he agreed, it meant she'd have to spend more time with him, which wasn't good for her already-in-jeopardy quest to keep things casual between them.

"What was that sigh about?" Hugh asked, his hand drifting from her hair to trace a line down her back.

"My boss wants an article about the contest and for me to do a profile on you for the magazine."

Hugh's eyes grew ornery. "An entire article just about me? Written by you?" When she just rolled her eyes, his arm tightened around her. "That'll be fun. Maybe too X-rated for *Gastronomic*, but I'm up for it."

She playfully bit his pec. "You don't mind?" she asked. "I don't want it to look like I'm using our relationship for access. I can say you aren't interested, it's not a big deal. I mean, you did lose the contest, so that will already be in the magazine."

"You're asking me if I'd like free press on one of the most-read food sites in the country? Consider yourself in possession of a Hugh Matteson all-access pass," he teased, waggling his eyebrows like the goofball he was.

She face-planted on his chest and she felt it rumble underneath her with laughter. "I'm all nervous now. I've been reading your articles and you've already ripped a couple of my favorite places to eat. I can only imagine what you'll write about me as a person."

She laughed and kissed his shoulder, noting how tense it had gotten. Could he actually be nervous? It seemed impossible that he could have any insecurities at all. "You've been reading my stuff?"

"Of course," he told her. "I read basically your entire archive the day I found out about your review. By the way, what's your deal with pickling anyway?"

She propped herself up on an elbow, peering down into his face. His hair was a mess and he smelled like a man who'd worked out, rich and musky.

"Pickling is great, easy, and adds a completely different dimension to sandwiches. Imagine a hamburger without a pickle. Imagine pulled pork without a tangy coleslaw. You can't—it just doesn't work."

"You wrote an entire article on pickled garlic, Parker. That's messed up."

She laughed, playfully smacking him on the shoulder. "Don't knock it 'til you try it." She tried to climb off him, but he pulled her back into him. Instead of resisting, she fell into his arms.

"You can pickle all of my garlic," he said, grinning. "What do you have going on for the rest of the day? Can you stay here? We can shower together, I'll make you breakfast, we can go swimming, watch a movie, anything you want."

Staying with him all day was a mistake, but as she looked down at his face and the little piece of insecurity visible behind his eyes, it was one she couldn't help but make.

"Race you to the shower?" she asked, hopping up from the bed and running full-on to the shower.

She didn't make it far at all before he caught her, hauling her up against his chest and kissing the back of her neck. "I win," he murmured against her skin as he walked them both toward the shower. "Fucking finally I win something."

Much later, she watched from his kitchen island as he cooked her breakfast. Some kind of omelet that she barely paid attention to because he was wearing just a pair of shorts again, and so not just the immense size of his kitchen was distracting her.

Like his bathroom, it was a large space with even more white Carrara marble.

"Your house is really nice," she told him.

"Thanks," he said, cracking another egg into the skillet.

"Do you like it?" she asked, pulling out the tablet she always kept in her bag. Now was a good a time as any to start the profile.

He glanced at her, a slight frown on his face. "Why do you ask?"

She shrugged. "I don't know, it just doesn't scream Hugh to me."

That made him grin. "You think you know me already?"

"A little," she told him, grinning back.

"Yeah, well, this is just a place to be, and I got it mainly for the big garage. My real home is in Texas at the ranch, but I get to spend less and less time there as business expands."

"You miss it," she guessed.

"Yeah, and I miss my family. I've spent most of my adult life on the road and I bought the ranch hoping to spend more time with them, but it kind of hasn't turned out that way because of the restaurant growing as quickly as it has."

He threw some chopped-up peppers, onions and manchego cheese into the omelet.

"Why Vegas?" she asked, genuinely curious. "I know it's your flagship restaurant, but you couldn't make Texas your home base?"

"The ranch is in the middle of nowhere outside of San Antonio," he explained. "So it's not a place for a restaurant and Vegas is the closest restaurant to home. I can catch a flight and be there in two hours if I need to."

"Why not just open a place in San Antonio then?"

He raised an eyebrow at her. "You want me to enter the ultracompetitive Texas barbecue market? Really? I mean, I might as well set my money on fire."

She laughed. "Am I hearing doubts about barbecue ability from the great Hugh Matteson?"

"Listen," he said, pointing a black plastic spatula at her, "I never claimed to be a chef and if you're going to succeed in Texas, you better be the best. I'm already competing with the Big Top here in Vegas and they're killing it even against the strength of my name."

"So what I'm hearing is that you're scared," she teased, tapping away at her computer.

A hunk of cheese landed on her keyboard and she laughed harder at him. "What the hell?"

"You know, maybe if I had trust in an actual chef who could create a competitive menu, I could move home and tend to my sickly parents," he said, giving her a meaningful glare.

"Wait a second, are your parents really sickly?" she pressed, concern settling her. "Why didn't you say that before?"

He flipped half an omelet over the top of the other side. "No, they're fine," he grumbled. "But opening a place in San Antonio would have to be something new and outside the box."

Looking pointedly at her, he slid the omelet onto a plate and placed it in front of her along with a side of salsa, sour cream and crushed-up tortilla chips for makeshift huevos rancheros. Then he got to work on his own omelet.

"You don't really want me to create a menu for a restaurant you open," she told him. "I'm not even Texan."

He shrugged. "Opening yet another Texas barbecue joint in Texas isn't a smart idea. Like I said, whatever I did would have to be different, something no one there has ever seen before."

Their eyes met and excitement, plain and simple, climbed through her like carbonation from a shaken-up soda bottle. It was stupid and she wasn't going to go into business with him, but just imagining all the awesome dishes she could come up with given carte blanche to make a menu was making her itch to get into the kitchen.

"We barely know each other, Hugh," she pointed

out. "Just because I beat you in a barbecue competition doesn't mean I'm cut out to create a menu for you."

"Do you know how much barbecue I tasted from the country's renowned barbecue cooks when I opened Blue Smoke? Hundreds. Literally hundreds, Parker. None of them compared to your stuff. Hell, I even liked that pickled carrot salad whatever the fuck you put on the side of the brisket and I don't even really like carrots in the first damn place."

"Even if I wanted to, I can't move," she informed him, cutting into her eggs. "Chicago is my home base and I can't leave."

As he dropped more toppings into his omelet, she regarded his back. The lines of his muscles formed wings out to his arms and she let her mind focus on how hard he worked on his body instead of building imaginary dreams of creating a menu for a restaurant that didn't exist.

"Family's there?" he asked.

She nodded, then realized he couldn't see her. "Yeah, my dad. Mom left a long time ago."

That had him turning around. "Sorry about that, sweetheart."

"It's okay, but my dad still isn't really over it. He lives with me, so I kind of have to stick around."

"Gotcha," he said, not pressing her further on the issue, which she appreciated. "But you're able to travel."

"Yeah, of course, it's my job," she said. "He's not sick or anything, just depressed most days."

"Because of your mom leaving?"

"He has always been a little depressed," Parker acknowledged, "but it got worse after Mom left. He couldn't hold down jobs for very long and stopped seeing his friends. It's gotten better in recent years, but I can't leave him all alone in a city without me. Family sticks around."

"Yeah, they do," he said. "Except a lot don't. I didn't, obviously."

She met his eyes in warning. Horning in on her personal life was a no-go area for her.

"Look, I'm not judging your choices," he back-pedaled. "I just think it's a shame you're tied to a town when you could be doing whatever you want."

"I am doing what I want," she told him. And it was true. She wouldn't rather be doing any other job. Creating a menu for Hugh would be great, but she'd never give up her magazine job. And if she got a little lonely because life on the road kept real relationships away, well, that's what this thing with Hugh was for. It generally didn't take more than a week with a guy for her to know that she was better off alone.

Hugh turned to her, accepting her answer with a small smile. "You're a good daughter," he said, then pointed to her plate. "Now eat. It's going to be a busy day for both of us."

"I thought we were just going to hang out and swim," she reminded.

He raised an eyebrow and she realized what he meant. She shook her head because he was insatiable, but it also meant more to her than she was willing to admit.

"Am I really the first girl you've had here?"

His fork paused in the air on the way to his plate. Glancing up, he looked the slightest bit hesitant, but then said, "Yeah."

"How can that be?"

His tongue slid into his cheek like it so often did when he was thinking. "Because I didn't think I'd have to kick you out in the morning."

"Wow," she said, leaning back to stare at him.

"It just means you're the first girl I wanted to stay, Parker," he said, oblivious to her heart falling to his feet. "So it sucks to hear that you're in Chicago for life."

She opened her mouth to say something, but he just shook his head. "Eat."

She did as she was told because sex or no sex, she liked Hugh Matteson. Which meant she needed to cut this Vegas trip short because the truth was that somewhere between ordering her first meal at Blue Smoke and eating an omelet in his kitchen, her heart had been put in danger.

CHAPTER NINE

HUGH WAS HAVING a pretty shitty day, which was a rough kick considering how great yesterday with Parker had been. Having her in his house all day as they'd eaten insanely good food, fucked hard and talked their way through the hours had made the day go by in the blink of an eye. For a fun fling, it was the best he'd ever had.

However, yesterday seemed like a thousand years away as he pulled out of the parking lot of the sports bar where he'd met up with an old football buddy.

His friend had delivered the news that Amanda and Todd's third child had been born. They'd sold the first pictures to some gossip rag, a little girl with Amanda and Todd's blond hair and blue eyes. While Hugh didn't want his ex in his life, it was yet another reminder that he was no closer to the family he'd imagined he'd already have by now. Todd was living the life he'd planned for himself, still playing ball, big family. Today it was fucking him up more than usual. Thirty-five wasn't old, but most of his close friends had a couple of kids and happy families, and he was still alone as always.

He'd stopped playing the field in any real way years ago, too. Building the business and fucking around with whoever was available had gotten in the way of him putting any real effort into finding someone. But he wanted a certain kind of life, hated that his house was so quiet and empty when he came home at the end of the day. Having Parker around brought out the stark truth of how lonely he was. He'd buried himself so deep out of fear of getting hurt again, he'd blocked everything out.

For years, he'd avoided looking at pictures of Amanda, Todd or their family. Today, he'd finally admitted why. Seeing the picture of that little baby made him acknowledge that her betrayal still hurt. He'd given Amanda everything. He'd met her in college and they'd grown up together, gone from young adulthood to adulthood side by side. He'd trusted her like his own family, and she'd screwed him over in the worst possible way.

As he navigated the Summerlin streets in the fading late-afternoon sun, he thought of Parker, wondering what she wanted for her future. Was she content having casual relationships on her travel gigs or did she want to settle down, too? After what she'd told him about her family last night, he wondered if she even knew herself what she wanted.

He took the elevator to his kitchen and when the doors opened the smell of food immediately hit him. He remembered that he had an appointment with Parker for his profile tonight and that he'd given her his code. It was a measure of trust he didn't lend to anyone, not even his assistant, but he wanted her to be here whenever she wanted. He'd just change it when she went back to Chicago anyway.

He saw her at the stove, cooking in only an apron, and his heart pretty much stopped in its tracks, his pensive mood evaporating as if it had never existed.

"You're a miracle, Parker," he growled, stalking toward her.

At his advance, she backed away, waving a wooden spoon between them to fend him off, which was a good move because that apron was exactly one nanosecond away from being a floor rag. "Nope, not yet, everything will burn if you distract me."

"You've got to be fucking kidding me with this," he bellowed, throwing his hands up in the air in exasperation. "You can't dress up in a child-size apron and expect me to be hands-off."

He reached for her again, but she slapped his hand with the spoon.

"Come on, baby, I'll let you smack my ass with

that if that's what you're into," he cajoled, crowding her into the corner of the counter, reminding her of what they'd done yesterday. "You can put me in handcuffs, whatever you want. I'm flexible."

She snorted. "Yeah, right."

Looking over her shoulder, he saw that she was frying up some sausage in a large stainless steel skillet.

"From scratch?" he asked, noticing the meat grinder on his counter.

"Yeah," she confirmed.

"Oh, it's gonna be a good night!" he hooted, rubbing his hands together in anticipation.

She leaned up and planted a kiss on his cheek and he gave her a smack on the ass in return. It was well-deserved after taunting him this way. He was only a man. Who could resist a naked woman in only an apron?

Yelping, she backed away from him. "Go over there," she ordered, pointing to the island where a cold bottle of beer was already waiting for him.

"What's all this about anyway? You actively trying to make men fall in love with you?" he asked, settling into the barstool to watch the naked cooking show apparently. "Because I'm as close to proposing as I've ever been." The words were light and joking, but after his lunch he'd be lying if it hadn't crossed his mind that Parker could be the one, which frankly chilled him to the core. Not only could she not be trusted, she was leaving in a couple of weeks. Two extremely good reasons to keep things casual.

Parker looked back at him. "I've been doing research for your profile, so I saw the news about your ex today. Figured you could use a pick-me-up."

Their eyes met and his gut took another massive hit on the day. No one had ever done something like that for him before. He had tons of people whose job it was to cater to him, but no one was doing it just because they cared if he had a shitty day. Hell, for his birthdays, Amanda usually just bought lingerie for him or booked them both a trip to somewhere she wanted to go. At the time, it'd seemed thoughtful enough, but now he knew better. Maybe he needed to let the lying in the beginning go. Because between caring for her dad, who frankly mostly sounded like a deadbeat, and cooking him dinner in the nude after a rough day, it was time to accept that she was a good person.

"That's really sweet, Parker," he finally said, holding her eyes a little too long probably, but craving the connection. "I appreciate it."

"You're welcome," she said, turning to flip over a sausage link. She tossed a salad with a wooden set of tools he hadn't known he had and stirred some sweet potatoes in a skillet.

He was vaguely interested in the food, but mostly he watched her ass shake as she moved, which was intentional and downright obscene. He was counting down the seconds until she'd let him go at her. It was the sweetest kind of torture to sit so close to her and not touch her. The gold light of the setting sun streamed through the large plate glass windows that overlooked his backyard, giving her blond hair a halo and gilding her pale skin in a dusky glow.

Turning from the stove, she regarded him, but he was mostly looking at her exposed side boob. "Do you want to talk about it?" she asked, her voice hesitant.

"About my ex?" he asked, not following the conversation due to all the naked.

At her nod, his head fell back and he looked at the ceiling wondering how to navigate this minefield. He hated talking about this kind of shit, especially having had to deal with it all in the public eye at the same time his entire life went down the toilet.

"I don't miss Amanda," he finally offered, figuring he owed something to her since she was cooking him dinner. But hell, he was so tired of the pity. "She was someone I chose when I didn't know any better. Young and dumb, you know how it goes. But I do want a family, and that they're expanding theirs does remind me that I'm not close to that place yet, when I thought I'd be well into fatherhood at this point in my life."

Parker regarded him, turning down the burners on the food to really give him her attention. "I think we all think life will look different at certain stages than it does, I guess. My parents had that kind of life. I was already five years old by the time my parents were my age. I can barely imagine having a cat right now, let alone a child."

"I can, though," he admitted. "Imagine having a family, I mean. I've been financially stable since I graduated from college. The hours I work are flexible and designed for a family. I've been ready, just not able, I guess."

"Maybe you're not as ready as you think?" she suggested. "Because you're obviously a man of action, and like you said, you've been in a good position financially to have a family. Obviously something's been stopping you these last six years from having a serious relationship with someone who could be the mother of your children."

She'd hit the nail on the head. He hadn't found or wanted to find a possible mate whom he could truly build a life with. "You're probably right."

"Have you dated anyone since your ex?"

"Not seriously," he told her.

She looked at him like that was the answer.

"Yeah, well, I've got some trust issues."

Parker smiled. "Naturally."

"I might not mind dating you," he said, the words coming out of his mouth without thinking. It was too much truth for the both of them, but he found he didn't regret it.

"You're under the spell of pork," she laughed, her nose crinkling adorably.

He shrugged. "Maybe, maybe not," he told her. "But you're the first woman I've ever even considered dating. And you've already lied to me once, so either I really like sausage or even I'm willing to accept that there's something good between us."

Her eyes widened at his admission, and he thought he'd scared her, but then she collected herself. Difficult to do in a mini apron, all things considered. "The news about your ex is just scaring you into a rash decision."

"Right," he told her, meeting her eyes, trying to figure her out. They had something here; she had to know that. "Except she's had a child before and I didn't run after the first woman available to date."

"I have to go back to Chicago in two weeks anyway."

"You know, I have my own plane," he reminded her. "I can come to Chicago whenever I want."

"You want to be in a long-distance relationship with me?" she asked, a dark brow winging up skeptically.

"I don't fucking know," he growled, irritated that he was getting nothing back from her. It wasn't every day he asked women to date him. In fact, it was never. "I don't do this shit, but I know we're having a lot of damn fun, so maybe, yeah."

Her brown eyes looked startled again, mouth

opening and closing before a popping sound from the skillet distracted her. She turned to give the food a look, and he was pissed that he'd blown the conversation. Hell, it wasn't as if he wanted to get married or some shit.

"Are you not over your ex?" Parker asked, setting the spoon down on the counter and facing him again. "I mean, is that why you haven't dated anyone?"

Hugh nearly choked. "Hell yeah, I'm over her. Her betrayal, well, I don't know if I'll ever get over that shit to be honest. You don't forget it when the person you trust most makes a fool out of you in front of the entire world."

"No one who knows your story thinks you were humiliated," Parker said. "People look up to you even more because it means that kind of stuff can happen to anyone, and yet you got the last laugh. You're a successful businessperson and he's warming the bench."

"That shit doesn't matter to me, Parker," Hugh told her. "When you get to my level of fame, you realize pretty quickly that people don't give a shit who you really are. Story or no story, humiliation or no humiliation, I'm just a walking stereotype or meal ticket to most people. And that's fine, I roll with it, but when it comes to letting people into my life for real, I've been picky as hell."

"That's sad, Hugh."

He shrugged. "It's just my life."

Parker met his eyes and he had no clue what she was thinking about. It also didn't escape him that she'd completely derailed their original conversation about dating, which had him wondering just how damaged she was, too.

Another pop in the skillet broke the silence and her attention was back on the stove top.

"It's ready," she eventually announced, grabbing the white ceramic plates she'd set out on the counter.

"The food looks great, Parker," he told her when she turned around again, "but you have to know that it isn't what I want to eat right now."

She rolled her eyes, but turned the burners on low before hopping up on the counter and spreading her legs. With a raised eyebrow, she leaned back and met his eyes. "Your choice, Hugh."

Grinning, he stalked toward her once again, wondering when the last time was that he'd felt so light, so carefree. So happy. That was the word he was looking for.

Eyes still locked on hers, he sank to his knees in front of her, which put him at the perfect height to see her sleek mound, glistening just the slightest bit with arousal. He loved that he turned her on so much. Her hands went around her back and started untying the apron, but he stopped her.

"Leave it on," he said.

He didn't waste any time finding her. Gently

pulling apart her folds and touching his tongue to the finest thing he'd ever tasted. Her sighs echoed in the empty kitchen and he found her nub, licking and sucking until it came to life under his tongue. Ways to take her flipped through his mind like his own personal sex catalog, but it didn't matter in the end because any way they did it would be the best way. She barely had to look at him and he got hard, and she'd gone to the trouble of making him a meal just on the off chance he might be upset.

Pushing one finger and then two into her as he sucked, he wanted her to know how much that simple gesture meant to him. For a person who spent most of his time working and knowing that when people gave him stuff it was because they wanted something in return, what she'd done was special.

And shit, he didn't have a condom in the damned kitchen. All that time flirting with her as she cooked and he could have been getting a condom. She was literally making him dumb.

"I don't have a condom," he cursed, rising from his knees with the intention of carrying her aproned ass into his bedroom.

Parker pulled a foil square out of the tiny front pocket on the breast panel, meeting his eyes with a smug grin.

He caught her lips in a thankful kiss that quickly turned X-rated, her legs locked around his waist and his hands grabbing up her mass of hair.

He kissed her neck, her exposed collarbone, her shoulder, her elbow, anything he could get his hands on. He wanted to know every part of her so he could find her in the dark if he had to, which was obviously madness, but if it was he didn't want to be sane. In this moment, where old wounds were gaping open, exposed to the light of day, he wanted to be in Parker in all ways.

He noticed that her hand had found one of the wooden spoons in his utensil crock. Their eyes met, hers twinkling with mischief, and he regretted pursuing this in his kitchen. He should have known there'd be revenge for last night. She was going to punish him for liking it so much, and it'd been hot as hell to smack that perfect, ripe ass. The way her flesh wiggled on contact and the soft pink handprint afterward reminded both of them that they were skirting the edge of appropriate.

"Strip me then," he ordered, stepping away so she could maneuver his clothes off.

She bit her lip, unsure if he was being for real. He'd let her do any damn thing she wanted to him— he was that kind of gone, but letting her think she couldn't was just fine, too.

After unfastening the button of his jeans and pulling on the zipper, she pushed them down his thighs until he kicked them the rest of the way off. She lifted up his shirt at the hem, her gaze catching on his chest again, which nearly had him grinning.

Then he was naked and bared before her, waiting for any retribution she might want to enact.

In fact, he turned around for her, looking back and meeting her eyes. What he found there got him in the gut, the curiosity, the hunger, the empowerment. He was a big guy, could bench press her with little to no effort, but sometimes it got old, being that person, the guy always in charge. For once, he wanted to feel what other people, who could let their guard down for a moment, felt. Be who he was for a moment and not who the world needed him to be. To not feel like a beast among men, but vulnerable and not pushed aside as somehow superhuman.

He also liked the pain, almost missed being tackled on the field, letting those bottled-up and suppressed emotions out in a physical way. There wasn't much like it outside of sports, but he was open. But he'd never trusted anyone enough before now to even consider it.

She leaned forward, running a hand down his back, over his ass and down his thigh over where one of his scars stood out in white relief against his tanned skin. "I don't like to imagine you hurt," she murmured, dropping kisses along his shoulders as her hands explored the hard, ridged tissue.

"Those days are over," he told her, voice low because the moment was stretching and he was aching for her and something else he couldn't name.

He'd been so isolated that Parker's caring for him cracked open something inside him.

"But you still hurt," she pressed, and he could barely feel her touch, only registering it when she traced around the edge of the scar that traveled up nearly the entire length of his thigh.

"Not so much, I just wanted in your pants that first night," he admitted, watching as, eyes hooded, she picked up the wooden spoon again.

His cock jerked and she noticed, an eyebrow arching up. He took himself in hand, stroking as she decided what she wanted to do.

White teeth tugged at her bottom lip and he dared her with his eyes to do it, to give him what he'd given her. To cross a line they hadn't with others. He could almost taste the pain, yearning for it almost as much as he wanted to be inside her.

"You deserve it," she told him, her grip shifting on the handle, as if trying to muster up the courage to surrender to the moment, to take them over the edge together.

"I do," he agreed, his hand moving faster over his dick, the rocketing sensations from his toes to his balls making his knees weak.

And then she did it, pulled the spoon back and gave him just a single whack on the meatiest part of his ass cheek. It stung, but barely, but the sly look on her face had his cock jolting against his grip.

Turning back to her, he grabbed the condom

from the counter, their eyes locked as he rolled it over himself, shock and desire on her face as the spoon clattered loudly onto the marble. For his own part, he'd never felt so powerful; that he trusted her with something so raw of himself had him shaken, but also steadied him. He was making the leap to trust her, letting go of the fear he'd been clinging to, and it was exhilarating.

He latched his hands on her waist and lifted her straight up off the counter and slid her slowly down his body and onto his waiting cock, the angle of her body leaving her virtually helpless, their eyes locking as her legs finally caught purchase around his thighs. Carrying her to the wide white living room couch, he laid her down and their mouths crashed against each other as he pushed forward into her. Her cries muffled as she bit his shoulder, clawed at his back, it was all madness, the battle for more, and the race toward release.

"Parker," he growled when she pulled at his hair, urging him to go harder.

"More," was all she said, bucking against him as they rode their way messily and loudly toward pleasure that had him reassessing everything he'd ever known about sex.

When he came, the pleasure hazing his vision, the only thing he knew for sure was that he had to have her in his life.

CHAPTER TEN

PARKER WAS ON her second day of observing Hugh at work, which was taking place in a rented office space in Summerlin. She was crossing the parking lot of his building when she got a text from her dad again asking when she was coming home. A medicine ball of guilt weighted her stomach because she'd been having so much fun and didn't even want to go home. The thought of going back to Chicago, being tied down again for however long until her next trip, had her chafing.

More importantly, she didn't want to leave Hugh yet. It wasn't even worth denying that she had feelings for him anymore. It wasn't casual, it wasn't safe, and she didn't care. Not after the look on his face when the elevator doors had opened on the day he'd found out about his ex's new baby. He'd looked so sad and lost and completely unlike the in-charge badass he usually was. And when he'd talked about wanting a family, she'd felt his longing in every word and knew she'd wanted to be the one who made it better for him. At least for that day. She'd still have to go back to Chicago soon, but not today.

Putting her phone and thoughts about home away, she regarded Hugh's office. It was a nondescript blush brick building on a busy street only a fifteen-minute drive away from her hotel. His front door was glass with white block lettering on it that said Matteson Corporation. The name made her smile. No one could fault Hugh for not being straightforward.

She knocked on the glass office door and Hugh appeared in the doorway behind the small reception area, a broad smile on his face as he waved her inside.

Her heart caught on the fact that he was genuinely happy to see her. Hugh wasn't shy with his emotions. It was crazy to her that he'd been without someone in his life this long. She couldn't help the dark thrill of swatting him with the spoon. All of their sex was intense, but she'd understood then that he'd wanted the pain. Maybe thought he deserved it, maybe it was just an unexplored kink. She didn't know the whole answer, but there was more to Hugh than the confident, wisecracking bro he showed the world. He had rivers of complications beneath the surface and part of her ached for him, wanted to take even a little of his pain away, though she couldn't stick around for the long haul.

"You made it." He smiled, gesturing for her to enter the back office.

"I did." She smiled back, feeling shy because she wanted to be able to hug him, but they weren't that so she couldn't. And it sucked.

He led her into his office, which was pretty standard issue. White walls and a drop ceiling, plain brown commercial carpeting, a sleek glass desk with a silver laptop open on top. Two plastic coffee cups were sitting next to a stack of files.

"You don't keep all your football stuff in here?" she teased, but would actually like to see some of it. There was nothing of Hugh in his Las Vegas house and she yearned to know the real him. The one who got depressed about a picture of a baby and massaged her feet without asking.

"Nope, all that shit is in San Antonio. Got a big ol' man cave for it."

"I'm sure it's quite something."

He held out one of the coffees to her. "Caramel latte, coconut milk, half caff, no whip," he informed her as she took it.

His words caught her up because she'd never actually told him that was her preferred drink; he must have just remembered her ordering it once while they were out. Hugh paid attention and cared for her and it was so lovely that she couldn't speak for a second.

"Thank you." She beamed at him. "I'm impressed that you remembered."

Hugh shrugged. "I remembered because it's the goofiest damn order I've ever heard. What the hell is wrong with plain coffee?"

"Are you an old man?" she joked, sitting at one of the two black armchairs in front of his desk. "That's not plain coffee in your cup," she pointed out. "You even added whipped cream."

"I felt so sorry for the baristas I just ordered two of your drink to make it easier for them."

That got her smiling. "And because you knew it sounded delicious."

"Get out of here," he grumbled as he took an extra-long sip, his eyes laughing. "What kind of person doesn't get whipped cream anyway?"

He scooped up some of his topping with a spoon and ate it, purposely twirling the spoon around in his fingers first. She could feel liquid pool at her core, remembering being in that moment. He'd given her the power over him, reciprocating what she'd felt the night before, and allowed himself to be vulnerable in a way not many men would ever do. It was precious to her that he trusted her enough to be completely open with what he wanted.

It didn't help her state of mind that he was dressed casually today, which should have been less sexy than his normal suits, but wasn't. Instead it revealed more of his bare flesh, which took her from a low buzz of sexual awareness to a "heated skin and crossing her legs" kind of need. A white polo shirt tightened across his massive chest and hugged his biceps, and the small vee at his neck exposed his strong throat and the top of his golden chest.

"Whipped cream is only for special occasions," she scolded, giving him a speaking glance. They had actual work to do today, and while sure, she'd already imagined having sex on his desk and licking whipped cream off his bare chest, it didn't mean they were going to do either of those things. They probably were going to later, she hoped, but not right at this moment. Because, again, work.

"Damn right." He grinned, leaning back in his own chair.

"So just go about your day," she told him, "and I'll ask questions as I have them and take notes."

She'd just leaned over to pull out her tablet when his phone rang. He answered it, watching her as she set herself up on other side of his desk so she could write while he talked.

When he got off the phone, he tossed it onto the desk and met her eyes. "Looks like the buildings in Los Angeles and Charlotte are good to go," he informed her, obviously pleased with the development.

"Los Angeles is a great food town," she agreed. "And Charlotte is getting good, too."

"I hate LA," Hugh admitted with a grimace he'd

be mortified to know she found adorable. "Too much bullshit."

"Is that not where you shot your sneaker commercials?"

He grinned his shit-eating grin that both terrorized and aroused her. Crossing his hands over that sinfully rigid abdomen, he goaded, "You searching my back catalog of commercials?" he asked.

"No," she all but sputtered because she was totally busted. "I just remember it from television. There were palm trees and stuff."

"Mmm-hmm," he drew out, waggling his eyebrows.

"You're the worst."

"You know, you can see this," he said, moving his hand to indicate his body, "anytime you want, sweetheart. Just say the word."

She rolled her eyes.

"So you're opening two new restaurants," she said, changing the subject with another pointed glare. "Will they be the same as the others or a different menu?"

"Similar," he said. "Blue Smoke is Blue Smoke, but we do try to improve and update with each location."

She tapped away, taking notes. "So do you see an end in sight to opening new locations? You now have eleven with these two new ones."

"They say if your business isn't growing, it's

failing, so I'll keep doing whatever that means, but I don't want to grow so big that I lose all control over quality and management. Obviously, I'm very hands-on at this location because it's the first and the biggest, but I visit every restaurant at least four times a year. So I don't want to get big enough where I can't do that anymore."

"Do you like traveling?"

"Yeah, and honestly, I can't imagine my life without it at this point," he answered. "I grew up on the road because of football and I like seeing new places. As we've talked about, I'd ultimately like to settle in San Antonio, but if I had to be there all the time I'd lose my mind."

"Same." Parker smiled. It was how she felt about being at home for too long, as well.

Then he met her eyes, his very serious, almost tentative, which was novel because his confidence was big enough to circle the earth on a loop. "Parker, maybe this isn't my business. Fuck, I know it's not my business. But what happened with your mom?"

Parker shifted in her chair. The trick to being a successful adult was to not think about her mom too much, so these kinds of questions were like picking at a Band-Aid covering an open wound.

"You don't have to answer," he followed up at her silence, "but I feel like all my shit is just out there and I don't know anything about you. Except your coffee order."

He paused again, then held her gaze. "And I want to know more."

She would have made a joke and kept it light if he hadn't said the last, but she wanted to go deeper with Hugh.

"She didn't leave until I was fourteen. And I've actually talked to her several times over the years," Parker admitted, though she'd never told her father as much. It would have only hurt him more. "She lives in Florida working as an assistant for a real estate developer. She's remarried to said real estate developer. I think she's living her best life, to be honest with you. I forgive her for leaving, but I don't know that I need to have a close relationship with her at this point in my life."

Talking about it made her feel unworthy all over again, same as the day her mom had left. People who mattered still had moms. If Parker had been at all important to her, she could have visited over the years, but she'd chosen not to. Not that Parker would have seen her anyway, but still. Some token trying would have been the least a mother could do.

Hugh's face was a careful blank mask. "She ever tell you why she left?"

Parker blew out a breath, the old insecurities from that time seeping out from under the door she'd closed them behind all those years ago.

"Yeah, it was a lot of excuses, but mostly that she hadn't loved my dad in a long time and wanted a new life. My grandmother lived in Florida then, so she had family there. In her defense, she waited until I was in high school and could take care of myself. I don't hate her, but I missed her when she left and that kind of pain doesn't just go away. I can be glad that she's happy, but mourn that she was a shitty mom to me."

Hugh reached over the desk and grabbed her hand, pulling her up until she was walking to his chair. Arranging her so she was in his lap, he met her eyes. "So you're afraid to leave your dad like she did," he guessed.

Parker nodded, squirming on his lap because she wasn't a child. She didn't need to be in his arms to talk about her mom, but hated that she liked it. He settled a big paw on her knee, stilling her.

She sighed and answered him. "I know how it feels, so I know it has to be ten times worse for him." Also, it wasn't was if her mom had even asked her to go with her to Florida, which only re-inforced the fact that she must have been a pretty unremarkable child. Certainly not special enough to catch the heart of a football star millionaire en-trepreneur. Her dad was the only person who gave a shit if she was gone or in Chicago and that meant everything to her, so she'd enjoy the time she had with Hugh, but knew how it all would end.

Hugh's mouth softened as well as his gaze and she had to remind herself of that fact once again. He was not for her.

"She's an idiot," he declared loudly, as if that was the whole story.

"You don't have to do that," Parker told him. "I'm over it. Honestly."

"Yeah, I do, because it's the truth. Any person who doesn't want to know you, your mom or a random person on the street, is an idiot. Even though your coffee choice is shit and you made me the laughingstock of the barbecue world, you're pretty awesome."

Parker shook her head. "Thanks, Hugh. But I worry more about Dad. He's fine, but I know his heart is still broken."

She saw pieces of her dad in Hugh. Not that Hugh was pining for his ex the way her dad was, but that he hadn't moved on with his life since the breakup. It was as if they'd both had a plan and when it hadn't gone their way, they'd just shut down that part of their lives.

"I like you, Parker Jones," Hugh said, giving her a gentle kiss on the forehead. "You're a good egg."

She raised an eyebrow, needing to lighten the mood. "Are you sure you're not a seventy-year-old man? Maybe recite me a parable next?"

"Not yet," he said, waggling his own eyebrows, the slit one making her knees sweat as usual.

"Just do your work," she ordered, pointing to the desk at large and trying to get off his lap.

He let her go, but slowly until their entwined fingers were their last contact, and she returned to her seat.

Then he proceeded to pull out a couple of over-size manila files and placed them in front of her on the desk. "This is what's on my agenda today."

She flipped open a couple of the files and saw a bunch of typed-out sample menus, art boards and summary descriptions for, not Blue Smoke, but several different kinds of restaurants.

"You're going to open another chain?" she asked.

He shrugged. "I don't know yet. I was thinking about it. These are some of the concepts I've been pitched by either fellow investors or sought out from renowned chefs who don't necessarily have the capital to start restaurants on their own. What do you think of them?"

Leaning back into her seat, Parker leafed through the packets as Hugh did his own typing on the computer. By the time she'd reached the end of the stack, she wasn't sure how much time had gone by.

Hugh quirked an eyebrow when she finally looked up.

"Nothing I haven't seen before," she told him honestly. Some of the food would be good for a small to medium city, but nothing was going to make a splash in the food world. She wouldn't make a special trip to a city to go to any of those places for *Gastronomic*, at any rate.

Instead of being irritated, Hugh looked amused. "What would you do if given carte blanche to create your own restaurant?"

She shook her head at him. "Nooope," she drawled, "you're not gonna get me that way."

"Can't blame a guy for trying," he said, those laugh lines around his eyes already so endearing. "But that's what those people in that folder were told to do, dream big and go for what they wanted. I don't know what the difference is if it's your idea in that folder, too."

It sounded good, she had to admit. She'd love to think of a concept from start to finish and then see it all come together. But she was sleeping with Hugh, which meant that anything less than being an equal partner in a venture like that wouldn't feel right.

But then the idea took hold, her mind unable to let it go. If she got a loan maybe she could invest as a full partner, which was different from being on Hugh's payroll. But then what if it failed and she still had to support her dad? It was too risky.

"The difference is that I don't want to be your employee," she told him. "We're involved."

Hugh opened his mouth to speak, but then changed his mind.

"I hear you," he eventually said. "The way I see it, though, is that you've already told me you don't want to date long-distance so once you leave, what's the problem with throwing some ideas around with me? Apparently we won't be involved at that point."

Parker wasn't an idiot. She heard the underlying frustration in his words, but she also didn't like being backed into a corner. She'd given him reasonable explanations for not wanting to do either thing. No matter how great Hugh was, and he was extremely special to her, there was no way it was going to happen. His life and her life might as well be on two separate planets. Her parents had been together forever and her mom had still cut out for a simpler life. Was Hugh, a millionaire football star and entrepreneur who didn't know what expensive was, really going to stick around for her complicated one? Odds were extremely doubtful.

One of the reasons they got along so well was because they had fun together. But that was only her part-time life. While she was on the road, she got to be the free and easy Parker who only had her great job and awesome food to worry about, but in Chicago it was different. Real life was there. And honestly, not to be trite, she kind of needed everything in Vegas to stay in Vegas.

"The problem is that I don't want to and I actually don't need a reason," she told him, giving him a speaking glance, which had a corner of his mouth lifting in wry amusement.

"You're killing me, Jones, but damned if I don't like the way I'm going out."

Parker gave the folder once last glance before meeting his eyes. "And just think, I still have over a week to go."

CHAPTER ELEVEN

"So you got into restaurants because of your dad?" Parker asked, her pink lips forming words that Hugh was not paying any attention to. They'd been doing this profile thing all week and while he liked having her around most days, he was getting antsy. Only a couple more days and she was gone from his life forever. He didn't know what he was going to do about that when the time came, but the eventuality was driving him nuts.

"Why don't you stay at my place until you leave?" he asked, ignoring her question. "You're barely at the hotel anyway and it'll be easier to finish the profile. Plus, I'll even let you use one of my cars so you can check out restaurants during the day for work."

Parker stared at him. "How is that an answer to my question?"

"I've answered the question before," he complained, irritation rising that she was avoiding the

question he posed that it had been damned difficult for him to ask. He didn't even bring women
to his house period, let alone ask them to basically
live there. "A friend from the league invested in a
bunch of restaurants and he was living easy. But
my dad mentioned that I could capitalize on my
Texas upbringing and start a barbecue place and
so here I am."

He pinned her with his gaze again, gnawing on
the inside of his cheek because he was nervous.
The last time he'd lived with someone it had ended
in him walking in on her screwing somebody else.

"Answer *my* question," he demanded, raising
his eyebrow in a way that used to scare the shit
out of rookies.

Parker hesitated and he braced himself for her
refusal, but instead she nodded.

His head dropped forward in surprise, the breath
he was holding rushing out. "Really?" he asked, his
voice nearly squeaking like a teenager's.

"Yeah," she said, shrugging. "I need to do my
own laundry. The hotel dyed my favorite white shirt
pink. Also, I'm sick of wearing flip-flops in the
shower."

"Someone does my laundry, too," he admitted.
"But go to town on your own if it makes you feel
better, and no flip-flops needed."

He stood up from his desk, the chair making a
clatter as it fell backward in his haste. "Let's go

get your stuff now, then. It's almost eleven and you don't want to pay for another whole day in the hotel."

Looking at him from under her eyelashes, she shook her head as he hastily righted his chair. "Are you okay?"

"I'm just sick of being in the office," he told her, which was true. Usually he went out for more meetings, but he'd pushed everything back so he could spend time with her, and he was getting really damn sick of these four generic white walls. "We can stop at Blue Smoke on the way home. Which place were you going to review tonight?"

"I'm reviewing a place for lunch," she reminded him. "That's why I'm here earlier than usual."

"Good," he said, clapping his hands together. "I'll go, too."

He'd tried to bully her into letting him come on more of her review trips, but she'd argued that she didn't want the service to be influenced by his celebrity presence, blah blah, excuses excuses. But they only had a few days left and he was man enough to admit that he wanted to be with her.

"Let's just get my stuff first, okay?" she suggested, probably sensing his agitation.

He nodded, ushering her out of his office with a hand on the ass he was coming to think of as his.

When he squeezed it, she turned on a dime, her hands on her hips. Just as she was about to lay him out, he took her mouth. And shit, it felt good to kiss her. Within seconds her lips were pliant against his and her arms were around his neck. He let her go, sighing as he touched his forehead to hers.

"We have to stop," he grunted, the words more to stop himself from going any further than to explain it to her, "gotta check you out."

He could feel her nod against him and then he pushed her out the office door, following closely behind her so he could smell the citrus scent that had a Pavlovian effect on his dick.

"Did I get you a little too hard?" he asked her once they were in his car and on their way to the Strip.

Shaking her head, she started typing something on her phone.

"What are you doing?" he prodded.

"Emailing my boss to tell her I'm checking out and to cut you a check for the amount we would have paid the hotel since you probably can't take my work credit card."

He swiped the phone straight from her hands and put it in his pocket where she couldn't reach it. "No fucking way are you paying to stay at my house."

"There's no way I'm not turning in a bill for an entire week of lodging and explaining to my boss that I instead decided to shack up with a restaurant owner I met while technically on the clock," she shot back, glaring at him.

"She'll know that's what you were doing anyway if you ask them to send the check to me!"

"I was planning on giving her your business address and saying that you offered me one of your empty rental units," she explained.

He took in a deep breath through his nose to calm his shit down. Paying for her stay at his house made their time together transactional, as if it was just business, and it pissed him the fuck off. Every single other interaction he had with women since Amanda had been just that. But from the article, to the competition, to the profile, all of it had been personal with Parker.

But they didn't have much time left and he wasn't going to argue with her. He handed her phone back. "Fine," he bit off, "have it your way."

Within seconds she was typing away and his fists closed around the steering wheel, his knuckles whitening.

Pulling up to the hotel, he was pretty much back together. She was staying at his house; that was enough. With any luck, he could get her to spend entire days in bed with him that ended with neither of them able to walk.

Hugh helped her pack up her belongings, which didn't take long, and then they were off to lunch at Marrakech, a Moroccan restaurant, for Parker's review. He'd never actually been there before so he was looking forward to it. It ended up being an exercise in torture because it was basically watching Parker eat, which always made him hard as a rock. He picked at his meatball tagine even though it was delicious and watched as she took two to three bites of five different dishes.

"I think it's good," he eventually said.

She nodded. "Decent."

They finished up lunch and returned to the car. "Do you want to go back to my office to write your review or back to my house?"

"I thought you wanted to swing by Blue Smoke," she reminded him.

"Right," he muttered, for some reason now annoyed with the prospect. It was already four o'clock so the dinner crowd would be on its way. A good time to check in to make sure everything was running smoothly. Not that it usually didn't run smoothly, but it was his job and he normally enjoyed it. But now it just seemed like something to take away from his time with Parker. Which she, on the other hand, seemed to have no problem with.

He didn't like this feeling at all. The unfamiliar desperation that was settling in even as he tried to bat it back. Pulling into the parking lot of his restaurant, he turned to her. "I've got a small office in the back you can use to write your review while I circulate," he told her.

"Thanks," she said, smiling at him in that way that suggested she was grateful to him for being thoughtful. It damn near ripped him apart every time. The fact that no one had done shit for either of them was the problem, and every little nugget of caring was lapped up like they were starving. He knew the feeling all too well, hated that she did, too, but liked that he made her happy. It made him feel less on an island.

He spent the next hour traveling from table to table chitchatting to people like he normally did, except he wasn't into it as usual, his mind on getting back to Parker. When he finally made a full circuit through the whole dining room and checked in with his chef, back from sick leave and ready to go, he went to collect her.

"Finished?" she asked, smiling up at him. Today her hair was in a ponytail and she wore a pair of jean capris with holes in the knees and a black T-shirt with embroidered silver stars. The outfit was not at all suggestive, but the shirt was fitted in all the right places and the jeans embraced her ass like a hug, drawing attention to that tight waist. He stretched his fingers out in an effort not to grab hold of her.

He was struggling overall because this manic feeling just wouldn't go away, pressing down firmly on his chest and not easing up. That he was letting something of extreme importance slip away every minute he didn't tie her to his bed and make her stay with him. He needed to get his shit together and stop being such a wimp. They both knew this was a fling and that's where it needed to stay. He needed a family and a woman who would stick. Parker, who couldn't even mention the word *feelings*, wasn't going to fit the bill. But that knowledge didn't stop him from wanting it all the same.

When they got back to his house, he grabbed a couple of bottles of beer and suggested that they swim. Parker hadn't wanted to change into her swimsuit, but sat on the edge of the pool with her legs dangling in the water and drinking a glass of red wine while he waded in the shallow end. He often swam laps in the pool, but this was one of the only times he'd just hung out there with someone.

"I've been thinking," she told him, "I don't need to be a partner, but I could take another look at those restaurant proposals and tweak the menus a bit."

"Is that right?" he asked. Maybe things weren't as hopeless as he'd thought. She was interested in what he'd proposed, but for whatever reason, she was afraid to take the chance or didn't trust him enough. "I have the proposals in my home office, so we can check them out again tonight."

"I like the one centering on local ingredients in Maine. I think it has promise."

"It didn't even have any lobster on the menu," he scoffed, flopping onto his back to float. "What's the point?"

He didn't need to see the look on her face to know that her lips were thin and she was gazing upward. It was what he'd wanted to happen when he'd made the statement.

"That's the whole point," she told him, as if speaking to a recalcitrant child. He loved it. "Learning what Maine has to offer outside of a lobster roll. I just think the menu needs to be broadened a little so it's less like a hippie commune and more accessible to everyone."

"I could get behind it," he said, still floating. "But is there really anything there to take it outside of Maine, you know? Local is local. We're not taking local Maine ingredients to Montana or something. So we're limited on growth."

"You could make it regional," she suggested. "All of New England. Or that could be your whole new chain concept. Every restaurant focusing on the local fare, but with your fill-in-the-blank."

His head shot up then and he stood up, water sluicing down his chest and back. He met her eyes, swiping wet hair from his face, interest pricking at the back of his neck. "So each restaurant has different food but an overarching concept that connects them all?"

"Yeah," she answered, and he felt the excitement in her eyes in his own veins.

"I like it," he boomed, pointing emphatically at

her as his other hand clapped the water. "I like it a lot, Parker."

She grinned. "It's good, right? And you could start with that Maine menu and go from there."

"It's so good," he agreed, grinning.

Swimming over to stand right in between her legs, he brought her down for a kiss and his legs went liquid at her sigh. Fuck, he was going to miss this. He was going to miss her, period. But he really needed to stop acting like a lovesick teenager because they still had a couple of days and she was living at his house. That was good enough, and then he could concentrate on finding a wife. Because if nothing else, this time with Parker had shown him just how great a real relationship could be. And he was ready to find that again.

"So this is a subject change, but I have another question for the profile."

"Shoot," he allowed, "but then we need to think of an overarching concept."

"Do you ever miss football?"

He shrugged. "I miss hanging out with the guys on the regular, but I see them often enough. Playing ball? Every once in a while, but I always figured I'd teach my kids, and I look forward to that."

"You'd let your kids play football even though you got dangerously injured?" she asked, surprised.

"I'm more talking about just tossing the ball in the backyard, not turning pro necessarily." He'd loved playing ball and even still thought about coaching sometimes when he got bored of just doing business as usual, but he volunteered with enough youth football camps and had his own coming up next month that it was just all the fun without the pressure of winning like coaching would be.

"Do you want kids?" he asked, cursing because it was too soon. And it didn't matter anyway.

She flicked at the water and he kicked himself for asking. It wasn't his damned business; they weren't even in a relationship.

"I've never given it much thought, to be honest," she told him. "My dad is around and I've never had a serious relationship, so it wasn't something I honestly considered would ever happen."

"But you're not against them," he clarified, his heart pounding hard in his chest, as if he had a stake in this game.

Parker shrugged, finally meeting his eyes. "No, I wouldn't say that."

And then when the silence stretched for a moment, he found himself asking, "Do you not want to find someone at all, Parker?"

That shrug again, the one he was coming to realize might be her avoiding talking about a real issue. "I do, I just haven't, and the whole happily-ever-after thing never really seemed like a possibility. I just have to look at my dad to know that sometimes it's not worth the trouble. Plus, my lifestyle has never been conducive to it so it hasn't felt like I've been missing out."

Hugh was no therapist, but the look on Parker's face, the one trying to hide the fact that she wanted to believe she could find happiness but wouldn't take the chance, was telegraphed as clear as day. He didn't know her parents, but they'd really done a number on their daughter. Her dad by convincing her that love was conditional on her staying by his side and her mom by making her think she wasn't worthy enough to accept or demand more.

He understood more than he wanted to admit. The whole world loved him, but the only woman who had really known him had found him highly replaceable.

"You're gone a lot, is that it?" he finally managed, giving her an out from admitting that she didn't think anyone could love her if her own mom didn't.

"Yeah, I had a boyfriend back in college for about two years or so, but nothing serious since then. I'm gone at least two but often four weekends out of a month, and sometimes weeks or months at a time if it's an assignment like this, where we really want to explore the food culture. It's just challenging to get something going."

So she hadn't even tried, is what Hugh was hearing. Parker was too scarred from her mom's leaving to even try. That made him really sad and he dunked his head under the water to avoid the pity-ing look that was probably all over his face. He had a caring woman who was still carrying around a lot of pain and he was pretty clueless about how to help her heal. Despair crept over him because he hadn't wanted to admit it, but he knew that the feel-ing taking hold of his insides was love. And there wasn't a damn thing to do about it.

He felt a disturbance in the water and resurfaced to find that Parker had stripped down to her bra and panties and joined him in the pool.

"It looked too fun to miss out." She smiled, send-ing a huge smack of water into his face.

Yeah, it was getting damn near impossible not to admit.

"You're going to regret that," he warned as he stalked toward her, but knew once he got his hands on her, regret would be the last thing they felt.

CHAPTER TWELVE

PARKER LOVED BEING at Hugh's house. Not only was it way better than her hotel, which had been constantly crawling with tourists hell-bent on drinking so much they forgot their entire vacation, but it had Hugh in it. Hugh, who had graduated from her favorite indulgence to a basic necessity.

With only two days left, she was having a mild freak-out because it was the end of their time together and she knew it was probably the last time she'd ever see him in her life. It wasn't as if they lived in the same town where they might run into each other or something. This was it. The melancholia was creeping into her cells slowly but poised to take over her whole being once she stepped on that plane to Chicago without him.

She'd played it all wrong. All the lessons she'd learned over the years with guys about how not to get attached, swerving around any possible feelings, leaving them before they left her. Moving in with Hugh had been the ultimate in foolish decisions, because she never wanted to leave. Waking up alongside his too-warm and yet perfect body every morning was better than the thousand fantasy relationship scenarios she'd constructed in her head over the years when the monotony of living with her dad became too much. In her wildest dreams, she couldn't have come up with a person who seemed so unsuited to her and yet fit her more perfectly than Hugh.

He made her breakfast every morning, handed out massages like candy, left her alone when she needed to work or go review a restaurant, patiently answered the most inane questions about his business, and it went without saying that the sex continued to climb in intensity because they both felt the weight of their imminent ending.

But most of all, he made her laugh, and she hadn't realized how much she hadn't been laughing until Hugh.

The years between now and her mom leaving felt like long, empty years in comparison and part of her felt like going back to Chicago was a return to that. Year after year of only existing and never living. But imagining a future with Hugh, she didn't even have the tools. Couldn't imagine staying with anyone and watching them eventually walk away, or her doing it. A month with Hugh and leaving felt like her heart was being ripped out. Being in an actual committed relationship and having him walk away? Hell no.

Which was why she was finishing up her last review and leaving tomorrow. She'd lied and told Hugh she was leaving the day after because saying goodbye was impossible, and if she told him she was leaving, he'd try to get her to stay and/or go into business with him. Which would break her resolve.

The fact was that she couldn't ever leave her dad alone.

For Hugh or for anybody.

She parked Hugh's silver Audi convertible in his garage and took the elevator to the main floor. Hugh was in the kitchen with his shirt off, blaring hip-hop, a baseball game on mute on the television, and tapping away on his laptop. The man could not tolerate silence.

When he noticed her, he smiled, waving her over to the island where he had a cold beer waiting for her. The same kind she'd said she'd liked at his restaurant that first night. The fridge was stocked with that and tons of other random stuff she'd mentioned liking over the course of their month together. Just like she'd taken to finding out and making his favorite meals on the nights they stayed in and doing yoga with him in the morning even though she hated it. She just wanted to show him how much he meant to her. How much all of this time had meant.

"Last work meal of the trip," he boomed, holding up his hand for a high five. "How was it?"

She slapped his big paw, but instead of letting her go, he caught her fingers in his and pulled her in between his legs as he swung the chair around to face her.

"It was good," she told him. She hadn't tasted any of it even though she'd saved the best restaurant for last. Worrying about leaving tomorrow had made it difficult to do anything but cry right into her eighty-dollar steak. For the past two days, tears were very close to the surface, which was stupid because she literally couldn't remember the last time she'd cried. Maybe that animated movie about the toys? It was hard to say.

"What are you doing?" she asked, breathing in the familiar, brightly musky scent of him.

His smile was huge, the corners of his eyes crinkling with excitement. "I just got off the phone with my lawyer," he informed her, grabbing a small stack of papers sitting on the island beside him. "And he drew up an agreement of what it would look like if we did a restaurant together. So just take this with you, look it over, give it to your own lawyer, no pressure. But I want you to know that there's an offer on the table if you want it. A real one, not just one you think I made because we're sleeping together."

Parker had never hyperventilated before, but she feared she was on the verge of it. Her heart was beating so fast she could barely count the beats in her head like she normally did to calm down, and it felt like she couldn't draw a full breath into her lungs.

She nodded numbly at him and took the papers, pretending to look even though the words were just a blurry mess as she continued to stare blindly at them.

"Hey," he asked, standing up and pressing a thumb under her chin so he could see her, concern etched on his handsome, scarred face. "You okay? This isn't to scare you, Parker. I know you've said no before, but I wanted you to at least have all the details so you could make an informed decision. There are two agreements there. One where you could own part of the business with me and the other to only be a menu consultant, which means helping with the menu and concept like we talked about in the beginning. There wouldn't be as much traveling or financial risk involved."

The pay was ridiculous, she saw that, for the consultant. The investment option wouldn't pay out for a while until the restaurant made a profit, but he was really tempting her with the consultant option and he knew it. This is what she'd wanted to avoid by lying about leaving. So much of her wanted to say yes, but the fact was that when she left Vegas tomorrow she was going to be in pieces. It wasn't a matter of if, but just how awful she was going to feel leaving Hugh. The idea of then turning around and seeing him on a merely professional level was impossible. She couldn't do it, she knew it. Nor could she ever do a long-distance relationship. Saying goodbye on a regular basis? She might as well be tearing off her own arm on the regular. That's what it would feel like if today was any indication.

So instead of answering, she did the only thing left to do and kissed him with everything she had. To somehow burn how she felt into his skin so he would know just how much she cared for him.

Their lips met in a bawdy, openmouthed, angst-fueled storm.

Hugh picked her up and carried her to his room, where the wall of windows was retracted. The sun was setting in the desert, the gradated shades of neon red and purple and gold still lighting the sky just enough for them to see each other. He laid her down on the bed and a light breeze floated into the room as he climbed on top of her, returning to her mouth.

"Stay with me a few extra days?" he murmured against her lips, their foreheads together, their warm breath hovering in the air between them like their own intimate world.

"Maybe," she said, because she was leaving tomorrow anyway. What was one more white lie?

"Say yes instead," he whispered, the words

sounding more like a plea than as the suggestion he'd meant. "Stay."

The words were on her tongue—she wanted to say yes, to just let go and let him be part of her life and actually take a chance on the first person who'd made any effort to be there—but they wouldn't leave her mouth. Maybe she was just that broken. She didn't know, but her heart hurt and that was something she hadn't felt since her mom left all those years ago.

"You deserve to be happy, Parker," he continued when she remained mute. "Choose it."

If her heart was stone, which sometimes she'd thought it was, it was nothing but a soft, doughy mass of love after his words. And yet she couldn't take the chance. So she did the only thing she could, her lips finding his mouth again in a fury of unacknowledged emotions and pipe dreams.

His hands found the hem of her shirt, pulling it up and off along with her pants. The warm desert air hit her skin and she felt exposed physically and emotionally. Hugh's lips were on hers as she tugged off his shorts, impatient and desperate to have all of him. His body was large, blocking out the entire rest of the world from her view, and it didn't matter. She didn't feel claustrophobic or caged in; as always, Hugh just made her feel protected and safe. She did not know how she was going to leave him at all, dreaded it with every contrary fiber of her being. Even now, solidly in his arms, she didn't want to be anywhere else ever. She could live inside the cocoon of his brick house body.

He reached over, grabbing a condom out of the bedside table, and her thighs clenched in wanton anticipation, just pushing the reality that she was leaving away long enough for her to enjoy one last night with the best man she'd ever known and the best sex she'd ever had.

"You make me happy," he whispered against her lips, dropping down to her neck, kissing everywhere he could reach. It was lovely and tender and downright heart-wrenching when he got on his knees, kissing up her thighs, worshipping her skin as if she were the first woman he'd ever known.

Fighting back tears, she pulled him up until he was over her again and wrapped her legs around his back, pulling him into her. He positioned himself at her entrance, his head bent and broken eyebrow just visible, and a wave of longing hit her so hard that she had to score her fingernails into her palms to keep from crying. Raising his head again, their eyes met as he inched slowly into her, letting her feel every bit of him. The playfulness that had become a hallmark of their sex life was gone. They were without the jokes or quips because everything she wanted to say couldn't be said.

"You make me happy, too," she finally breathed as he began to move.

He swallowed then, the lump in his throat bobbing as he accepted the words. Dropping his forehead to hers, their lips barely touching, he moved in her, slowly at first, the slide purposeful and measured, designed to draw out their pleasure and let her know how he felt inside her, as if she could forget. As if she'd ever forget anything about him.

Their mingled breaths sounded in the quiet room, passing through the inside, and eventually moved outside, swept away with the breeze, just like she would leave tomorrow. As if she'd never been there.

She wrapped her arms around him, pressing him closer, as close as he could possibly get as they moved together as one, their bodies grinding and grasping against each other for release. His thick shaft slid in and out of her, drawing over her sensitized flesh. Hot bolts of sensation zipped up and down her skin as he gripped her ass, adjusting her angle so he could go deeper, hitting that spot inside her that had her gasping into his mouth in mindless bliss.

"Parker," he choked out, the corded lines of his neck bulging with the effort of holding back. Reaching between them, he thumbed her clit and she flew into the abyss, arms still clutching around him as if she'd never let him go.

"Just go," she whispered, floating down from space, giving him permission to let loose.

And he did, pumping savagely into her, his fingers gripping hard into the flesh of her ass. She came again, the climb violent and the explosion fierce, eventually giving way to mellow contentment as he groaned his release, his whole body suddenly going slack underneath her touch.

He murmured something against her lips that sounded like *thank you* before he rearranged them on the bed so that she was in the crook of his arm.

She almost promised him that she wouldn't leave, wanted to say the words so badly, but couldn't.

"I really like you, Hugh," she finally murmured, knowing they were a pale substitute for what she really felt.

"I really like you, too, Parker," he returned, squeezing her closer into his warm body.

Snuggling against him, she placed a single kiss over his heart to make up for the words that were too dangerous to say and eventually fell asleep.

Hugh woke up to an empty bedroom, knew it as soon as he opened his eyes. Maybe even before his head hit the pillow last night, he'd known Parker was gone.

The look in her eyes when he'd asked her to stay had given her intention away; the fear he'd seen there hadn't been normal. But it also meant that she felt the same way he did and was scared as fuck. It was a fear he could get behind and relate to, if the pain knocking his chest inside out was any indication.

Bolting out of bed, he checked her drawers for confirmation that she was gone before pulling on some of his own clothes. Then he shot down the elevator into his car.

He went to the airport, which was usually a half-hour drive, but he made it there in twenty minutes in part because it wasn't even seven in the morning yet but also thanks to his outrageous speeding.

Parking his car illegally at the drop-off, he handed the keys to a kid taking luggage whose eyes got huge when he recognized him. "Move it if you need to, pal, I'll pay."

Not even caring that the possibility of never seeing his beloved McLaren again was extremely real, he ran into the airport with no idea what airline Parker might be on. So instead he just bought a ticket to Chicago and ran to gate after gate with flights to Chicago searching for any sight of her.

And then finally, when he'd just about given up hope, she stood up from one of the vinyl beige seats intending to board.

Racing once again, he caught her arm just as she was about to take her place in the boarding line.

Her eyes were huge and she looked as if she was already about to cry, which he had to ignore because there was no time and there were things that needed to be said.

"I love you, Parker," he said, not even playing around. "And I don't want you to go."

She stared at him, her eyes impossibly large and unreadable. There was fear, yes, but something else he couldn't quite put his finger on.

Opening her mouth, she tried to speak, but then just shook her head as if whatever she said wouldn't matter anyway.

They announced for passengers to board again and she took a step back from him. His heart sped up and he felt just like he had that day he'd walked in on his ex and his best friend, betrayed, certainly, but most of all, he just felt alone. Again. And he fucking hated it. Loathed the idea of going back to his empty house without her in it.

"Stay with me, Parker," he told her, giving her an out. She didn't have to lay it all out on the table today; he'd be satisfied with more time. "You know you want to."

"It'll just be harder to leave," she finally said, shaking her head. "I'm sorry, Hugh."

His hands fisted. "I can't believe you're doing this," he gritted, his presence already drawing attention from the other passengers in the seating area. "This is something good. Don't fuck it up."

"We said it was just the month," she reminded him. Her words, a callback to their beginning, were lame to his ears. They'd agreed on a month when they'd known nothing about how great they could be together. It was complete and utter bullshit.

"Yeah, we made those rules, which means we can change them," he tried.

She was the last person left to board in her group, the attendant looking expectantly at her. So he did the only thing he could think of and pulled her hard into his arms, catching her mouth up in a kiss. He gave her everything, the love, the affection, the regard, fear, anger, wasted hope, just let it all go because there was too much inside him to hang on to all of it, praying that she'd accept and believe it.

"I need it to be just the month, Hugh," she choked out when the kiss was over.

And so he wiped away her tears and let her go. The old him would have gone after her, demanded that she listen and they give it a shot, but he knew it was Parker's ball now.

He watched her board the plane and though his heart was shattered, it was no small epiphany that he'd still had one to be broken in the first place.

CHAPTER THIRTEEN

As SOON AS Parker had left Hugh's house for the airport, she regretted it. Knew in her bones that she might have just irrevocably screwed up the best thing that had ever happened to her. She'd managed to hold off tears that even she was surprised hadn't shown up when he'd found her in the airport until the car ride back to her place in Chicago. But as soon as she'd gotten inside the same model Acura from the car service that she'd taken that first night with him, they'd flowed in earnest. The driver had wordlessly handed her a box of tissues, and also, inexplicably, a lollipop, which she now held on to for dear life as if it were the one tangible thing separating her from a complete emotional meltdown.

Finally trudging up the cement stairs into her house, sleep was the only thing on her mind. She had no mental or physical energy for anything else.

Except that when she opened the door, dropping her purse straight onto the ground in exhaustion, the first thing she saw was her dad holding hands with a woman on the living room couch.

Jaw in the dropped position, she stared as the two jumped apart as if they'd been caught doing something far more serious than hand-holding, her father sputtering Parker's name in shock.

"I didn't know you'd be home so soon," he croaked, standing up and wiping his palms on his pressed khakis. She hadn't seen her dad wear anything other than sweatpants and jeans for years now. Didn't even know he owned a pair of khakis, in fact.

But she didn't concentrate on that so much before her gaze fell on the woman beside him, who was also now standing. Wearing a pastel-flowered skirt and a denim button-down top, she looked like a kindly aunt who carried wicker baskets full of flowers home every Friday after work and baked cookies every Sunday.

"Dad, are you dating?" Parker asked, finally meeting her father's eyes.

As he shoved his hands into his pockets, Parker felt the tiniest bit of hope open up in her chest.

"I wanted to tell you about Sally, sweetheart, but I thought you'd be upset."

Parker laughed. "Upset? Why?"

Sally and her father looked at each other hesitantly before her father nodded in reassurance.

Then Sally held out her left hand for Parker to see, and on it was a small but lovely diamond ring.

"We're getting married," Parker's dad said, pride in his voice, but with an edge of fear.

Parker blinked in surprise, not quite believing it, but the shock was quickly followed by joy.

"That's wonderful, Dad!" Parker beamed, happiness bubbling up in her chest like a shaken soda. "Why would I be upset about that?"

Her dad's feet shuffled around on the ground, clearly uneasy about his next words. "Well, Sally's got a house in Avondale and all."

Parker laughed. "Dad, I assumed you'd be moving out. And it's okay. I've only ever wanted you to be happy." She crossed the room and pulled him into a hug, motioning for Sally to join. Relief coursed through her veins, the melancholy over leaving Hugh still there, but stronger was the feeling of determination that she could set things to rights. That she could finally leave her past behind and concentrate on her future.

"I want you to find love, too, P," her dad said, squeezing. "You are the best daughter a man could ever have and I owe you everything. Your mom will never know the kind of woman you are in spite of her and that's her loss. Go be happy, sweetheart. Wherever that is. You don't have to worry about me anymore."

"You were never a burden, Dad," she assured him, her eyes wet because for all the complaining over the years, she wouldn't have changed having that time with her dad for anything.

"That's a lie and we both know it, sweetheart," her dad said. "You changed your entire life for me—don't think I don't know it."

Parker shook her head, knowing the real truth. The one she'd been denying since her mom walked out on them. The one that had become blindingly clear when Hugh had begged her to stay with him.

"I was using you as excuse, Dad. I was just too afraid to find someone and move on because of what Mom did to you. So I always had to be the one to leave." Just like she'd left Hugh and every other guy who'd ever tried to get close.

And now just like his ex, she'd left him alone again and heartbroken. Because her fear went so deep, she didn't even think about hurting other people, only worrying about her own protection.

"Parker," Dad said, "that's on me, too. I should have set you straight when you never brought anyone serious home. Don't ever let your mom take away your happiness. She's not an evil person like I've been saying all these years, but don't let someone who has chosen not to be a part of your life have such a negative influence over it. Trust me, I had to learn that lesson the hard way."

Parker blinked back more tears and allowed herself a moment to let it all settle. To accept that her mom had left, yes, but it said more about the kind of person she was than Parker. Her Dad had shown her love in a million ways over the years. Words and deeds that she simply hadn't let be real or penetrate because she'd have to admit she was affected by them in the first place.

"I love you, Dad," she finally managed as his hand gave hers a squeeze.

"I love you, too," her dad said. "But you'll still come by sometimes, okay, maybe cook for us? Sally is a grand woman, but she's no chef."

"Of course, Dad," she told him, giving Sally a watery smile.

Sally left them to go into the kitchen, but Parker's dad kept hold of her hand.

"So I met a guy," she started, because she knew what she had to do now, but was also more scared of what would happen if she did. "But he's wary of relationships, too, and I don't want to hurt him by running away again. I already chickened out and left him once. What if I do it again like Mom did to us? Just cut out if things get too difficult?" And they would, she knew, because Hugh was the biggest pain in the ass in America. Followed closely in line by her.

Her dad gave her hand a shake, giving her a fierce expression, his dear brown eyes like hers, familiar but serious. "You took care of me for the past ten years, Parker, at the expense of your own wants and desires. I don't want you to have to do that for someone else again, but if that doesn't prove you've got staying power, I don't know what does. And any man who lets you go isn't worth it anyway."

"Thanks, Dad," she told him as he pulled her in for another long hug. Maybe she did need to have a little more faith in herself. At the very least, she needed to give herself her own shot at being with Hugh.

"I'm still serious about those meals, though, so you better visit your dad here in Chicago."

Parker smiled, giving her dad another squeeze. "You could always come to Vegas, too, you know."

"You couldn't keep me away," he whispered back, and she knew he was teary, too.

CHAPTER FOURTEEN

PARKER TOOK A deep breath as Hugh made his entrance from the back kitchen into Blue Smoke's dining area. It was so much like the first time she'd seen him, and yet completely different. Then he'd looked confident and warm, without a care in the world, and now he looked drawn and removed, his eyes drained of their signature humor. She'd been the one to do that to him, take away a bit of his shine. And that felt supremely crappy, but she was here to make it better for both of them. She only hoped he'd let her.

Her table, the same one they'd first sat at, was once again loaded up with baskets and dishes as it had been the night they'd met. She'd also included the first iteration of her barbecue sauce, which she'd managed to get straight from the distributor since it wasn't actually available yet. That joint venture between them felt important to emphasize at the moment.

Watching as he made his way through the diners, she got the sense that he was actually actively avoiding looking at her table, maybe because like her, he thought of it as theirs. He was always so aware of his surroundings, but tonight he only paid attention to each table he greeted, never glancing around the restaurant, focused on the immediate task and that alone. He was dressed in a charcoal suit, no tie this time, a couple of buttons undone at his collar. His hair was pushed forward over his forehead instead of back and she saw the glint of a silver earring in his broken eyebrow. She was too far away to see what it was, but was dying to know.

Finally, as if in slow motion, he turned, his gaze floating past her table, clearly avoiding it like she'd thought, before her presence registered and his eyes slammed back to her.

That eyebrow quirked and he simply nodded as if he'd been expecting her, his long legs eating up the distance between them in seconds.

She had an entire speech prepared, of course, but before she could even say hello, he pulled her out of the booth and into his arms, his mouth finding hers as if they'd been apart for years instead of days. Her arms wound around his neck, tightening until she might as well be trying to choke him; his did the same around her waist, drawing her in so tightly to him as if they could meld into each other. And it was fine with her because she never wanted to be separated from him again.

"You good?" he asked, finally letting her up for air, his gaze fierce as he stared down at her.

She met his eyes, seeing that the new earring was a silver ball on the bottom and an orange-and-black flame on top. Made sense. He was no longer a football player, he was in the grilled meats business, so an open flame was much more accurate.

"Yeah," she said, breathing in the familiar, deeply fresh smell of him.

Because she knew she had a lot of miles still to climb, her hands started sweating and her stomach lodged in her throat. All she wanted to do was beg for his forgiveness. Also, just multitudinous floods of tears were burning behind her eyes because she missed and loved him so much her body couldn't even handle all of it. Considering how short a time it had been since she'd seen him, trying to even imagine breaking things off completely had been ludicrous on her part.

"So, hi," she finally said in response to the expectant look on his face.

Hugh peered down at her from his significant height. He shook his head and then repeated the inspection before that scarred eyebrow shot up again, waiting.

"Hi, Parker," he said, some of the humor back in his voice, steadying her nerves. She had not completely screwed this up, so there was hope. The actual hard part, though, committing to Hugh for real, was the treacherous mountain she still needed to climb.

She nodded, words sticking in her throat for just a moment, before she gestured for him to sit down at the table.

Pulling out her leather portfolio, she opened it and put it in his lap for him to look at. Over the years she'd collected all kinds of ideas and recipes and snapshots of interiors she admired because in truth helping him open restaurants was the perfect job for her. Creating something from scratch. Hugh had given her that and it was one of a thousand things she'd never have allowed herself to dream about without him.

"I know we tossed a lot of ideas around and I'd build a menu for whatever kind of place you wanted, but I wanted to start with the ideas I have for a restaurant in San Antonio."

His gaze shot to hers, locking there, the green of his hazel eyes softening to sea green.

She nearly caved then and leaped over the table and dragged him out of the restaurant, but she had something to prove first and she would not be deterred.

Pointing to the menu, and also the food in front of them that she'd spent the day cooking in his kitchen before service started, she informed him, "This isn't traditional barbecue. The only way it even makes sense as barbecue is that fact that it's smoked. But nothing on the table has been smoked with wood and the sauces are also smoked. The proteins aren't necessarily traditionally associated with barbecue, but instead use a lot of local to San Antonio ingredients. For example, I used autumn sage, an edible plant specific to the area that you can either eat as is, or smoke and infuse a sage flavor. I did it here to all the meat and also the vegetables, which isn't something any restaurant is doing as far as I know. At least not in San Antonio. I just happened to be able to find the sage here at the specialty market, but you get the general idea."

When Hugh didn't say anything, instead reaching out to try a piece of lightly smoked and grilled trout, she went on. "I don't claim to know a lot about decor, but the concept is fresh so I think that's how we should keep the decor. And it would separate us from the rustic and dark traditional barbecue places."

After he went through a couple of baskets and plates, trying the food, but giving no indication of how he felt about it, he pulled out the sample board for the interior. Deep chocolate fabric swatches, buttery birch wood samples, and deep blue and green tiles made up the decor, and he touched everything before placing that on top of the menu at his side.

His silence was driving her crazy, but she was happy to endure it if only to be in his presence. "I'm not wedded to the decor at all, I just wanted to give you an idea of what it could be. I also had a logo made," she added, pulling another mock-up from her file that she'd had a friend do on the fly. She'd thought it turned out pretty well, though.

"Ember," he finally said, nodding approvingly at the name of the restaurant. "I like that."

Finally meeting her eyes, he looked expectantly for her to continue. So she took out the contract he'd given her before she'd left.

"I signed it," she told him as she handed it over.

Instead of looking at the papers straightaway, he let the moment stretch, and once again, she thought she might vomit.

"Consultant or partners?" he asked, his gaze intent on her face.

"Partners." Nothing less. Ever.

That broken eyebrow again, the one she saw when she closed her eyes at night willing herself forget him.

"Does that mean we can't be involved romantically?" he pressed, those bodybuilder arms crossing over his chest. The white fabric of his button-down stretched with the movement.

"Um, if that's what you want," she hedged, confused about that kiss if what he wanted was just to be business partners. "My dad is getting remarried so I'm putting my house in Chicago on the market. I don't have liquid funds yet to invest as a full partner, but I will."

The look he gave her was loaded, as if to say he was disappointed in her for not actually saying the words that needed to be said. Which was fair. This whole experience was testing her limits, but if being with Hugh had taught her nothing else it was to go balls-out, as he would say.

"I love you, Hugh," she grumbled. "Is that what you want me to say?"

That all-or-nothing smile again, the larger-than-life football player who'd made her feel like she was the most important person in his life and in the world. She would never get tired of seeing it on his face and hoped she could make him as happy as he made her. She'd waited nearly thirty years to tell someone she loved them and it had been worth the wait.

"I'm sorry," he said, putting a massive hand behind his ear, "I didn't hear you."

"I love you!" she shouted, her hands lifting above her head in frustration and complete elation. Just saying the words felt like starting a new and better life. One she shared with Hugh.

"Get over here," he ordered, sticking out his hand. "Now."

She clambered over the bench seat, not wasting any time getting into his arms again. He pulled her down into his lap so she was straddling him, the rest of the diners be damned, their eyes joined, and she could stare at the crooked nose, scars and broken eyebrow forever.

"I like the new earring," she told him, drawing a thumb over the flame.

He grinned. "Yeah, well, the old earring didn't quite make sense anymore and I thought I didn't need one, but then I realized I just hadn't known how to fill the empty space. But turns out I found exactly what I wanted there."

She shook her head at what he was really saying, but also absurdly happy because that's how she felt, too, that he filled the empty spaces.

"And I wish you would have given me more of a heads-up that you were coming back because I already bought a place in Chicago."

Her head dropped in surprise. "What?"

He ran a hand through her hair, dropping a kiss on her temple. That freshly clean Hugh scent invaded her brain like a drug, sending pleasure waves through her entire body.

"Yeah, I'd planned to move my home base to Chicago so we could at least still date if you didn't want to be in a serious relationship."

She pulled back, meeting his eyes, her heart growing into one of those gigantic cartoon hearts. Happiness flowed through her, jubilant and fizzy. Hugh Matteson was the last person she ever thought she'd fall for, but he was also the best person she'd ever met. "But you want to move back home to San Antonio."

"Not as much as I want to be with you," he told her as if she were a child. "I love you, Parker. My home is wherever you are."

She almost had the thought that she didn't deserve him, but that was old thinking because she finally believed that she did.

"I'm sorry I didn't say goodbye. I was in a terror state," she joked. "I honestly don't even know how I left. I didn't want to at all."

His lips met hers in a gentle kiss that settled all the guilt her speech had dredged up. They were together for real and it was awesome. All that time spent thinking she wasn't fit for a relationship, and she'd found the perfect one without even really looking.

"I forgive you, Parker," he said, his eyes serious. "I understand being scared, but you can't shut me out again."

"I won't," she promised, and she meant it. Their future was too precious to screw up. She'd found a partner in life who could keep up with her, propel her even further, and make her laugh along the way.

"Good," he said, "because we have a lot of work to do, including buying a house in Chicago and restaurant space in San Antonio."

Parker smiled and gave him a huge kiss. "I can't wait."

He squeezed her against him and her arms wrapped around him and she never wanted to let go. And if she had her way, she never would.

"Neither can I."

* * * * *

COMING SOON!

We really hope you enjoyed reading this book.
If you're looking for more romance
be sure to head to the shops when
new books are available on

Thursday 26th September

To see which titles are coming soon, please visit
millsandboon.co.uk/nextmonth

MILLS & BOON